THE
ROCKET MAN'S
DAUGHTER

moving elements of her complex character, making her a compelling and relatable heroine with plenty of room to grow and be shaped by the challenges she faces in the plot. This is a powerful work of wartime fiction that I would highly recommend for its attention to detail in both period and characterization.

—USA TODAY Bestselling Author K.C. FINN,
Readers' Favorite Reviewer, Author of *The Mind's Eye*

"There are numerous twists and turns and lots of high tension in The Rocket Man's Daughter and I found it almost impossible to put the book down. An exciting book that moves very quickly, with characters you care about and many nail-biting, emotional, and horrific scenes that bring these times in history vividly to life."

—LUCINDA E. CLARK, Readers' Favorite Reviewer,
Author of *Truth, Lies, & Propaganda: in Africa*

"A bracing story of a young woman's rebellious spirit against Nazi indoctrination and her response to totalitarianism. Klara Neumann's family has personality galore, and I loved the mixed bag of characters. The writing is descriptive and the suspense is thick, making this a book that was nearly impossible for me to put down."

—JAMIE MICHELE, Readers' Favorite Reviewer,
Author of *Little House of Mercy: Love and the Great War*

"An epic and gripping story that celebrates the resiliant nature of the human spirit, demonstrating its ability to find hope amid adversity. With a large cast of characters and an immersive narrative, there is plenty to enjoy in this fascinating portrayal of World War II that does not shy away from the horrors and atrocities committed by the Nazis, and later, the Russians. The stakes are always felt to be high because of the realistic and gritty tone of the narrative, and you're never sure if your favorite characters will make it out alive. This book is an absolute treat for historical fiction readers."

—PIKASHO DEKA, Readers' Favorite Reviewer

Bruce Gardner

THE ROCKET MAN'S DAUGHTER

A Novel of Family, Faith & Resistance in Nazi Germany

Zino Publishing
Petaluma, CA
brucegardnerbooks.com

Editing: Natalie Griffin
Cover Design & Interior Formatting: Melinda Martin, melindamartin.me

Publisher's Cataloging-in-Publication Data
provided by Five Rainbows Cataloging Services

Names: Gardner, Bruce E., author.
Title: The rocket man's daughter : a novel of family, faith, and resistance in Nazi Germany / Bruce Gardner.
Description: Petaluma, CA : Zino Publishing, 2025. | Includes bibliographical references.
Identifiers: LCCN 2024923556 (print) | ISBN 978-0-9998811-7-0 (paperback) | ISBN 978-0-9998811-8-7 (hardcover) | ISBN 978-0-9998811-6-3 (ebook)
Subjects: LCSH: Berlin (Germany)--Fiction. | World War, 1939-1945--Fiction. | Anti-Nazi movement--Germany--Fiction. | Bonhoeffer, Dietrich, 1906-1945--Fiction. | Bonhoeffer, Dietrich, 1906-1945--Fiction. | Suspense fiction. | BISAC: FICTION / Historical / 20th Century / World War II & Holocaust. | FICTION / Thrillers / Historical. | FICTION / Thrillers / Military. | GSAFD: Historical fiction. | Suspense fiction.
Classification: LCC PS3607.A73 R63 2025 (print) | LCC PS3607.A73 (ebook) | DDC 813/.6--dc23.

To Nancy, Tina, Jeff, and Maddie

CAST OF MAIN FICTIONAL CHARACTERS

(In Order of First Mention or Appearance in Initial Role)

Klara Neumann

- 1934–1937: Member, BDM (League of German Girls/Hitler Youth)
- 1938–1945: Psychiatric nursing research assistant and (after 1942) secret supporter of German anti-Nazi resistance efforts

Erich Neumann

- 1934–1937: Professor of Physics, Technical College of Berlin
- 1938–1945: German Army Rocket Scientist (Guidance and Control Specialist)
- Father of Walther (eldest), Elke (middle), and Klara (youngest)

Elke Neumann

- 1934–1937: Section Leader, League of German Girls (Hitler Youth/BDM)
- 1938–1945: Trainer, BDM and National Socialist Women's League

Gerhard Bremmer

- 1934: SS Major, Liebstandarte Adolf Hitler (Hitler's Personal Bodyguard Unit)
- 1935–1943: SS Lt. Colonel and Chief, Berlin Criminal Investigative Police
- 1944–1945: SS Colonel and Assistant Commissioner, A4/V-2 Rocket Program

Joshua Peters

- 1934–1938: Son of US Deputy Ambassador to Germany
- 1944–1945: First Lieutenant, US Office of Strategic Services (USOSS)

NOTABLE HISTORICAL FIGURES

(Those with Speaking Roles, in Order of First Mention or Appearance)

Adolf Hitler
- Führer (Dictator) of Nazi Germany

Heinrich Himmler
- Reichsführer (Leader) of the Nazi SS Paramilitary Organization

Wernher von Braun
- Chief Scientist and Technical Director for Nazi A5 and A4/V-2 Rocket Programs

Walter Dornberger
- Colonel, Overseer of German Army Rocket Development Projects

Arthur Nebe
- SS Senior Colonel, Head of Nazi National Criminal Police ("Kripo")

Dietrich Bonhoeffer
- Pastor, Co-founder of German "Confessing Church" Movement

Arvid and Mildred Harnack
- Dietrich's cousin and his American wife, co-leaders of Berlin resistance cell

Herbert Pfannmüller
- Director, Eglfing-Haar Mental Asylum

Hans Kammler
- SS Major General, Special Commissioner of Nazi A4/V-2 Rocket Program

Arthur Rudolph
- Civilian, Technical Overseer of V-2 Rocket Production, Nordhausen Facility

Robert Staver
- Major, US Army Ordnance Department (Special Missions V-2)

CONTENTS

*"People look at the outward appearance,
but the LORD looks at the heart."*

—1 Samuel 16:7

HISTORICAL PREFACE

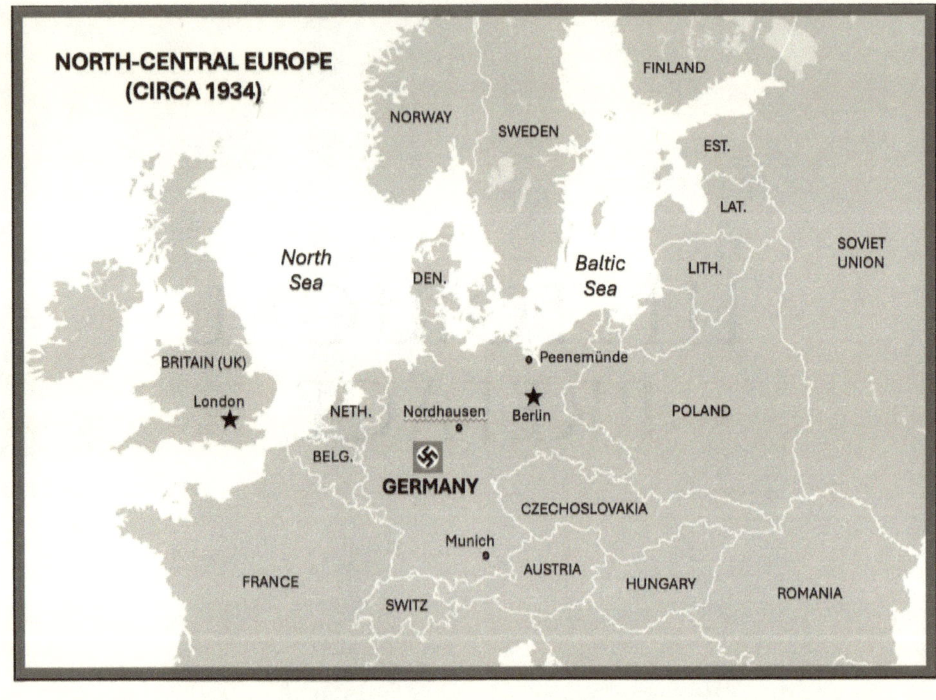

NORTH-CENTRAL EUROPE
(CIRCA 1934)
FINLAND
NORWAY
SWEDEN
EST.
LAT.
North
Sea
DEN.
Baltic
Sea
LITH.
SOVIET
UNION
BRITAIN (UK)
Peenemünde
London
NETH.
Nordhausen
Berlin
POLAND
BELG.
GERMANY
CZECHOSLOVAKIA
Munich
FRANCE
AUSTRIA
HUNGARY
ROMANIA
SWITZ.

By late June 1934, Adolf Hitler's incredible rise to the position of supreme power over the German nation was nearly complete. Appointed a year and a half earlier as the Chancellor of Germany by the democratically elected central government, Hitler was now on the verge of attaining the goal for which he and his Nazi Party had long been striving: a unified national dictatorship under *the Führer's* sole command.

Sieg Heil! To the vast majority of Germans, the prospects looked bright indeed. Germany's defeat in World War I had led to fifteen years of national disgrace and economic misery under the ineffective elected government. But now, Hitler's promised "Thousand-Year Third Reich" would undoubtedly restore and preserve forever the nation's honor, power, and prosperity.

Only one obstacle remained in Hitler's path to unchallenged supremacy.

That obstacle was a rumored national coup orchestrated by Ernst Röhm, the decorated WWI hero, co-founder and Chief of Staff of the dreaded *Sturmabteilung* (SA). The SA was the Nazi Party's original paramilitary enforcement wing, which now comprised over three million brown-shirted stormtroopers.

Röhm and his SA Brownshirts, who reported directly to Hitler, were the enabling force behind the Nazis' surprising victories in recent national elections. They had helped to fix the outcomes through their vicious beatings and murders of Nazi political opponents, especially Communists, Social Democrats, and wealthy Jewish businessmen. The Führer himself had recently expressed his deep gratitude for Röhm's personal loyalty over the years.

Unfortunately, Ernst Röhm had allowed his powerful position to swell his ego to the point where Hitler's closest advisors now feared that Röhm and his SA were plotting a takeover of Germany's national army. It was a scenario that the advisors knew would be unacceptable to the proud army generals, who had always despised the SA and its thuggish tactics. Any takeover attempt by the SA would inevitably lead to violent army resistance, disrupting the country and imperiling the entire Nazi movement.

Hitler's advisors proposed an audacious solution. First, they suggested, assassinate Röhm and all other high-ranking SA leaders in a swift, coordinated effort. Second, place the SA under the overall command of Heinrich Himmler, whose rival paramilitary organization—the black-uniformed *Schutzstaffel* (SS)—included Hitler's personal bodyguards.

By doing this, the SS would eliminate any SA threat to take over the national army, thus relieving Hitler's concerns about provoking an uprising of aggrieved army generals and political leaders. Hitler agreed to the idea, and Himmler ordered units of his elite SS Blackshirts to prepare for action.

The night of June 30, SS hit squads made their rounds in Berlin and other major German cities. They barged in on leading SA officials who were still in bed with their wives or mistresses, gunning them all into bloody pulps. In one case, they employed pickaxes to hack one of the men to pieces. Ernst Röhm himself was executed by the SS the following day.

Röhm's demise marked the effective conclusion of the Nazis' infamous "Night of the Long Knives." At least eighty-five SA leaders and other Nazi political opponents were brutally executed. A week later, the official word would reach the lower ranks of the SA and the general public. Hitler's grip on the pinnacle of national power was now unshakeable. The deadly competition between the SS and the SA was over.

The Blackshirts had triumphed...

PART I

BLACKSHIRTS RISING

CHAPTER 1

Berlin, Germany
July 8, 1934
(One week after Ernst Röhm's assassination)

Klara Neumann was ready to explode.

Really! How could *any* young teenaged girl be expected to sit this long in the second-row church pew between her parents, politely listening to the gloomy Reichsbishop's endless sermon?

To Klara, it all seemed like torture. *Especially* when a long-anticipated afternoon of lunch, fun, and a secret meeting with two special friends awaited her at Tiergarten Park as soon as this dreary service ended.

Halfway through the Reichsbishop's hour-long tirade laden with accolades to Hitler and exhortations for all faithful Lutherans to fully embrace the new, enlightened version of Christianity offered by the Nazi-endorsed "German Christians" movement, Klara could no longer contain her boredom. She crossed her arms impatiently and stared up at the Berlin Cathedral's ornately decorated dome ceiling. Closing her eyes, she let out a long sigh. It was loud enough to draw an annoyed stare from her sixteen-year-old sister Elke, who sat in front of Klara in the first row along with seven of her smug, pig-tailed girlfriends. All of them were members of the BDM[*].

Unfazed, Klara made a sour face and briefly stuck her tongue out at her sister, prompting Elke to respond in kind before huffily turning back around in her seat.

"Klara!" whispered her mother, Gertrude, as she grabbed her daughter's knee to stop it from bouncing. "Would you *please* stop fidgeting? You are fourteen years old, not seven!"

Klara glared at her devoutly Lutheran mother, knowing she had no more desire to be subjected to all this bombastic glorification of the Führer than Klara did. And in Gertrude's case, Klara knew the reason was not simply boredom. Last week, she'd heard her mother complain to her father: "I just can't believe that little man with the silly-looking mustache—who worships no one but himself—is going to lead us all to anything but catastrophe." Her father had tried to placate her. He'd argued that while Hitler might have some aggressive, self-idolizing tendencies, "the man has done some very good things for the German people, and we should all just give him a chance and wait and see."

Wait and see, wait and see, Klara thought crossly. *How long do I have to "wait and see" if this stupid, boring excuse for a sermon will ever come to an end?*

Resigned to her fate, Klara gritted her teeth, settled back against the pew and folded her hands demurely in her lap. She glanced across the aisle to the second row where her eighteen-year-old brother, Walther, sat next to Heinz Schröder, his best friend and fellow freshman economics student at Berlin University. The two young men, quite unlike the grim-faced, brown-uniformed Hitler Youth boys in the front row, appeared to be less interested in the sermon than in frequently craning their necks to obtain a better view of the row of pretty BDM girls. That came as no surprise; Klara knew for a fact that Heinz had long had a major crush on Elke, and lately, Walther seemed interested in just about anything wearing a skirt.

---

[*] BDM: *Bund Deutscher Mädel* ("League of German Girls"); the Hitler Youth female wing open to girls aged 14–18.

She lifted her hand and touched the small garnet pendant of the necklace that Walther had gifted her on her birthday last year. It was sweet of him to do so, but part of her couldn't help wishing it had come instead from Willi Schulz, the cute, towheaded boy who sat behind her in secondary school math class. Klara had heard from a friend that Willi was attracted to her. The problem was, he was shy and awkward when it came to casual, one-on-one conversations with Klara or other girls. Her attempts to engage him always seemed to be met with a polite grin and embarrassed excuse that he needed to go catch up with his friends.

Oh, if Willi only knew how crazy I am about him, he'd—"

An elbow nudged Klara's upper arm. She looked up to see her father, Erich, staring at her rather severely. Suddenly, his thin, handsome face relaxed into an affectionate smile, his chestnut brown eyes twinkling. He winked and gave her a light pat on the knee before folding his arms and turning his face back toward the pulpit.

Just like Vati, she thought gratefully. Always ready with a gentle word or touch to help her relax and focus when she was upset or distracted by something. Always happy to patiently explain things to her when she didn't understand. Quite unlike the dictatorial, overly stern fathers that almost all her friends seemed to be plagued with.

One reason for the difference, as she'd once overheard her mother explain to a friend, was her father's penchant for calm reflection and meditative thought on just about everything he considered important in life. It all went along, Mama had said, with his scientific mindset and burgeoning career as a noted teacher of physics and rocketry at the Technical College of Berlin. Klara suspected another reason for Vati's tender ways with her was that—perhaps because she was his youngest—she was clearly his favorite. Neither Walther nor Elke seemed to elicit the same degree of genuine warmth and empathy that he habitually displayed toward Klara. This had, no doubt, contributed to their stiffer, more formal relationships with him.

Snuggling a bit closer to her father, Klara tried to concentrate on the sermon. It was a lost cause; within seconds, she closed her eyes and allowed her mind to drift back to that pleasant memory of her first lesson from Professor Erich Neumann on the "Basic Principles of Rocketry."

∼✦∼

She was only seven when she'd wandered into Vati's study on the second floor of their well-appointed home in the wealthy Charlottenburg district of Berlin. She still remembered her delight as he took her into his lap and gave her a demonstration using a top he'd made of wood as a Christmas present for Walther. He'd said the top, when it was spinning, acted a lot like the bigger and much more complicated "gyroscope" that he was working on for the army.

After setting the toy twirling on the smooth surface of his desk, he showed her how it would always restore itself to an upright position—even after he poked it fairly hard with his finger.

"One day, Liebchen," he said proudly, "something like this little spinning top will help keep a big, tall, powerful rocket that's on its way to the Moon perfectly straight while it's travelling up through the windy, bumpy air. That way, it won't wobble all over the place and then tip over and come crashing back to Earth!"

"Oh, can I twirl it? Can I please, Vati?"

"Of course, dear. Here, give it a try."

When she did so, she twirled the little device so hard and awkwardly that it fell off the desk and crashed on the floor, breaking in half. Terrified that her father would be angry with her, she burst out crying.

Vati would have none of it. He'd hugged her closely and kissed her on top of the head. "There, there, Klara. It's all right. It's only a small toy, and Walther doesn't play with it anymore. Now don't you fret. I know you didn't mean to break it. You know I love you, Liebchen, and I always will, even when you make mistakes."

∼✦∼

"*We Lutherans who support the new 'German Christians' movement stand on the ground of Positive Christianity,*" bellowed Reichsbishop Müller, startling Klara out of her recollection. "*We profess an affirmative faith in Christ, one that befits our race and is in accordance with the German Lutheran mind and heroic piety. Mere compassion, we* say, is nothing but charity. It leads to presumption paired with a bad conscience, which ends up effeminizing a nation . . ."

Klara could practically feel her mother's body tense beside her as the Reichsbishop rambled on.

"Yes, it's true that we know something about Christian obligation and charity toward the helpless. *But we also demand the protection of our nation from the unfit and inferior. And therefore, marriages between Jews and Aryans must be prohibited!*"

The entire front row of Hitler Youth, including Klara's sister Elke, exploded in raucous applause, prompting many others in the congregation to do the same. Klara glanced at her father and noticed his closed eyes and tightened jaw. Though she was unsure of all the reasons for Vati's apparent lack of enthusiasm, it reminded her of his comment to Mama last week. He'd said he was "sick and tired" of being pressured by his university's president to join the Nazi Party in order to maintain his research grant with the German Army's experimental rocketry program. "Politics and rocket science are like politics and religion; they don't mix well," he'd complained, an observation with which Mama agreed wholeheartedly.

Reverend Müller had just resumed his diatribe when a sudden commotion from the church's entrance caused him to stop mid-sentence. A man in black uniform with a kepi cap and swastika armband stood in the middle of the open doorway. Sounds of shouting, drums, and blaring horns poured in from outside.

"*Heil Hitler!*" the man yelled, shooting his right arm straight out and up in the now ubiquitous Nazi salute. "Forgive me, Herr Reichsbishop, but the Führer's motorcade is approaching, on its way to the Reich Chancellery. We thought it imperative to let you know."

Reverend Müller returned the salute and broke into a wide grin. "Well, my brothers and sisters, it appears we will have to conclude my message next week. Right now, we have other priorities to attend to." With that, the Reichsbishop exited the massive pulpit and hurried down the aisle toward the entrance. A group of excited congregants, led by the Hitler Youth boys, fell in behind.

All the BDM girls gathered around Elke. They seemed to be seeking her guidance on whether to join the exodus given that Vati, Mama, and many other congregants didn't appear eager to hurry out themselves.

Those girls truly look up to my big sister, Klara thought enviously. It made sense, of course. Selected at the age of thirteen to be the "national poster girl" for Hitler's newly formed *Jungmädel* organization for females ten to fourteen, Elke had recently been elected as the Charlottenburg BDM section leader. Now sixteen, she seemed to represent the Nazis' epitome of Aryan feminine health and beauty. Nearly five and a half feet tall with light blonde hair, piercing sea-blue eyes and a gorgeous, photogenic smile, Elke possessed the trim, well-formed build of a natural athlete. She excelled in competitive gymnastics—exactly the kind of physical activity that the Nazis encouraged all German girls to take up to "prepare their bodies for birthing and motherhood responsibilities."

"We girls need to get out there," Elke said firmly. "The Führer expects it." She eyed both her parents in turn to see if there was any sign of resistance. Hearing no objection, she stepped toward the aisle. "Let's go! Klara, are you coming with us?"

Klara hesitated. She had not yet joined the BDM and had no desire to kowtow to her sister's commands. Her only wish now was for her family to get a move on to Tiergarten Park, where after a nice picnic she could sneak away for a private rendezvous with her friends. "No, I'll go with Vati and Mama when they're ready."

Elke shrugged. "Suit yourself." The BDM girls walked on down the aisle chattering excitedly as Klara's brother Walther and his friend Heinz followed discreetly behind. No doubt, the two were appreciating the opportunity for closer observation of some of the more mature, well-endowed members of the group.

As the sanctuary emptied, Erich Neumann looked at Klara and his wife with a resigned smile. "I suppose there's no point in us hanging around here any longer. May as well join the crowd."

Gertrude scowled and shook her head. "Indeed," she muttered. "We may as well, since even Jesus appears to have left this building to see our wonderful Führer."

Once outside, Klara and her parents hurried to join the rapidly growing crowd that stretched along both sides of the street for at least a block in either direction. The excitement was palpable. Everyone seemed to be smiling and jabbering as if at a carnival. Small swastika flags were everywhere, waved by children and adults alike. Young boys scrambled up the trees lining the walkway, hoping to obtain a better view. Brown-uniformed SA stormtroopers spaced themselves along the curb facing the street. They stood at attention with hands clasped behind their backs, ready to perform their strong-arm crowd-control tactics at a moment's notice should the need arise.

To her surprise, Klara felt a strange sense of exhilaration and anticipation. Up until now, she'd only seen Hitler in person once—a year and a half ago when Vati took the family to the Berlin Sportpalast to hear the Führer's first speech as the newly appointed Chancellor of Germany. They'd stood on the floor of the stadium among the massive crowd, at least a hundred yards from the platform. Even at that distance, the loudspeakers had successfully conveyed the raw, emotional power in Hitler's voice as he hypnotized the audience with his bold vision for the German people. Today, though, the viewing should be even more impressive, since Klara was standing less than fifty feet from where the Führer's open limousine would pass.

Unable to restrain her building excitement, Klara left her parents and edged to the front row of the crowd, next to where Elke and her BDM friends had stationed themselves. She accepted a small swastika flag from a little girl and waved it along with the others. As she did so, she noticed three of the SA men in the middle of the street conferring with each other. They seemed worried about something, and they kept shooting nervous glances between the crowd and down the street toward where the motorcade should soon appear.

"Wonder what's eating them," mused an elderly gentleman next to Klara. "They look like they're expecting trouble."

Another man behind them was quick to respond. "Who could blame them? I just heard Goebbels[*] on the radio. He announced there

---

* Joseph Goebbels: Third Reich Minister of Propaganda

was some kind of attempted coup by the SA's national leaders. But he said it's been suppressed, and the traitors have been caught and 'dealt with.' You know what *that* means." He nodded emphatically. "Those men out on the street probably just heard, and they're wondering who's going to oversee all their SA rank and file now."

The older man crossed his arms and glowered. "Can't say I'm surprised. Those SA thugs have been getting out of hand lately. They've become almost an embarrassment to the Führer with their drunken antics. To hell with them. I hope they *all* get arrested and jailed."

Klara looked quizzically at the men, trying to make sense of what she was hearing.

Someone across the way pointed down the street and shouted. *"Here they come!"* Klara turned just in time to see a horizontal line of motorcycles turn the corner in orderly parade fashion. These were followed by an armored car and then an open-top limousine, flanked on each side by two rows of motorcycles. Slowly, the motorcade made its way in Klara's direction. The crowd flew into a frenzy of shouting, jumping up and down, and flag-waving. *"Heil Hitler! Heil Hitler!"* Like devoted worshippers of some powerful Hindu divinity, it seemed that everyone had the man's name on their lips.

As the Führer's vehicle neared, Elke and her BDM friends stood in line at rigid attention, their faces radiant and their arms outstretched in the fascist salute. A flash of jealousy struck Klara at the sight of the girls in their smart-looking uniforms comprising a dark blue skirt, a white, short-sleeved blouse, and a black neckerchief.

Without warning, a small child with a bouquet of flowers escaped from her mother's grasp and waddled into the street in front of the approaching line of motorcycles. The woman screamed, alerting a nearby SA stormtrooper. He jumped out from the curb, grabbed the little girl roughly and returned her to her relieved mother with a disapproving scowl.

The girl started wailing, prompting Elke to run over and ask the mother something. She nodded gratefully, and Klara watched in amazement as Elke took the bouquet and ran between the motorcycles toward Hitler's limousine. The SA man raced after her, shouting at her to halt. Seeing Elke's approach, one of the SS bodyguards standing on the vehicle's running board stepped down, preparing to block her.

The Führer rose from his seat and signaled the driver to stop. He motioned for the bodyguard to move aside and allow Elke to approach. A broad smile creased his face as he offered his hand to help her onto the running board. She placed the bouquet in Hitler's hand and, without hesitation, leaned over the door and planted a quick kiss on his cheek.

The crowd went wild. Hitler beamed with obvious delight and shook Elke's hand. After snapping his familiar half salute, he sat back in his seat, his eyes fixed upon her.

Like a queen on her wedding day, Elke was escorted to the curb by the SS guard. Instantly, she was mobbed by her BDM friends and other women around them, everyone weeping with delight and envy.

Klara, caught up in the moment of joy and admiration for her sister, couldn't help herself. As Hitler's motorcade resumed its journey and his car moved past her, she stood at attention and thrust her right arm out and up.

To her great surprise, the Führer spotted her. He smiled and waved.

"*Heil Hitler!*" Klara shouted as tears filled her eyes.

A few moments later, she felt a hand on her shoulder. "So, are you ready to join us now, Klara?" Elke asked softly.

CHAPTER 2

Berlin, Germany
July 8, 1934
(Later that afternoon)

Klara sat wedged between her brother Walther and his friend Heinz at the picnic table after the meal, tapping her feet impatiently. Across the table, a lively conversation was taking place between Elke and two of her admiring BDM subordinates whom she'd invited to join the family's lunch at Tiergarten Park.

"It was an experience that I'll cherish forever!" Elke repeated one more time to her captive audience, referring to her daring actions at the Führer's motorcade.

Klara glanced surreptitiously at her watch and sighed. *How long do I have to endure this?* If she didn't find some excuse to break away soon, she'd be late for the clandestine meeting near the Zoo that she'd arranged last week with Sophie and Jakob Friedmann, her two Jewish friends.

She was on the verge of telling Elke she was going to try and catch up with their parents, who'd just left on their own walk to the Zoo, when Heinz decided it was time for a little teasing.

"You BDM girls seem quite enthralled with the Führer," he observed. "And, of course, there are plenty of good reasons for that. But I was wondering... are you all *really* in full agreement with *every* single little thing he says?"

Elke's eyes narrowed. "What on earth are you getting at, Heinz?"

"I was just thinking about those 'proper roles' for all true German women that the Führer describes in *Mein Kampf*. Roles like: 'Women are the eternal companions of men,' 'the triumphant task of women is to bear and tend babies,' or, 'men are willing to fight, women must be there to nurse them.'"

"Yes? And what's wrong with those?" Elke retorted.

Heinz flashed a mischievous grin. "Well, would it not be possible that at least a *few* German women might be suited to more *intellectual* pursuits... beyond being solely a homemaker and baby-tender? Something more than just '*Kinder, Küche, Kirche** ?'"

Not waiting for Elke's response, he turned to Klara. "What's your opinion, little sister? I know you've expressed interest in a nursing career. Am I completely off base in suggesting something like this?"

Klara's face flushed scarlet. She'd always hated being asked to offer her views on the Führer's beliefs in the presence of Elke and her BDM friends. It seemed now as though everyone's eyes, especially Elke's, bored in on her, all waiting to judge her grand pronouncement. "Well, there are plenty of examples. We could point to women like that Polish Nobel Prize winner, Marie Curie—she discovered radium. Or that German woman, Bertha Benz. She helped her husband develop the first workable automobile. They both pursued their scientific interests while still raising families. There are plenty of other examples in different fields I could name..." She was about to suggest some but she trailed off as she noticed Elke shifting uncomfortably.

Heinz nodded approvingly. He turned toward Elke and smiled. "So, you see, my love? Can't you accept that it *is* possible for an honorable married woman to engage in worthwhile pursuits beyond the home?" He sighed wistfully and placed a hand over his heart. "Or perhaps, to embrace a *childless* life, romantically wandering the earth with a strong, handsome, charming lad such as myself?"

---

* Popular 19th Century German slogan for preferred roles for females. Translated as "Children, Kitchen, Church"

Elke glared at him with arms folded as the other girls attempted to stifle their giggles. "Heinz Schröder! You talk too much. Don't you *dare* try to hint that any ideas about German women, beyond those of our Führer, should ever be taken seriously. Especially yours! The only man *I* will ever consider marrying is one who respects our leader's views. A man who is willing to fight and die boldly on the battlefield for his wife, his children, his Führer, and the moral purity of our German nation."

Heinz, never lacking in self-confidence and highly aware of Elke's strong attraction to him underneath all her BDM bluster, shot her an amused smile. He leaned back, crossed his arms, and stuffed a large piece of mustard-dipped bratwurst into his mouth.

"*Ugh!*" Elke shook her head in disgust and rolled her eyes.

Walther leaned over and patted Heinz on the knee consolingly. "Well, my friend, it appears you've just reduced to zero any chance you had of winning the good graces of my sister today. Why don't the two of us take our own stroll to the Zoo? We can watch some *real* monkeys making monkeys out of themselves." The two youths set off down the path, content to leave Klara, Elke, and her friends behind to clean up and chat.

After a few minutes listening to the other girls drone on about silly things, Klara glanced at her watch again. She couldn't delay any longer if she was going to make that secret rendezvous with Sophie and Jakob.

She pulled Elke aside and spoke to her quietly. "I'm going to go meet up with Vati and Mama at the Zoo.

Elke eyed her suspiciously. "What, Klara? Is this because our conversation here isn't stimulating enough for you?"

Klara hesitated. If Elke knew the truth about why she wanted to leave—and whom she was *really* planning to meet with—it would prevent Elke from vouching for Klara if she ever decided to apply for membership in the antisemitic BDM.

"No, of course not. I'm just feeling a bit over-stuffed. I feel like stretching my legs and going to see the animals. It's been over five years since Vati last took us there."

Fortunately, Elke didn't press her any further. After apologizing to the other girls, Klara walked down the path in the direction of the Zoo.

⌒⌒⌒

"Klara! Over here!"

Klara peered through the low-hanging branches off the side of the path and saw Sophie Friedmann waving to her from a stone bench nestled within a hedge of bushes. As she approached, Klara noticed the worried look on her friend's face.

"We were afraid you wouldn't make it away from your family," Sophie said as she embraced Klara.

"I had to tell a fib to get away from Elke, and I don't have that much time before I need to go join my parents at the Zoo, but here I am for now. Where's your brother, and —*Sophie*, what's wrong? Your face looks like you've seen a ghost!"

Sophie gripped Klara's forearms. "Jakob and I were sitting here waiting for you, when we heard some men approaching on the other side of the hedge. We peeked through the bush and saw them. They were SA—three of them." She waved her hand disgustedly. "Drunk out of their minds, stumbling along and muttering obscenities at each other. One of them had a German Shepherd on a leash that he kept threatening to sic on the others if they didn't shut up. They passed by and didn't see us, thank God."

Klara's eyes widened. "Where's Jakob?"

"He went up the path a bit to see if any other Brownshirts are roaming around," Sophie said nervously, glancing from side to side. If so, we should probably move away from here."

"I just hope he's being careful. If any of them spot him and start questioning him, you know it could mean big trouble."

"Don't worry about *that*," Sophie said. "If anyone's learned to avoid tangling with Brownshirts, it's Jakob. Remember that beating he got last year? When he tried to argue with those two who kept shouting in his face about 'Jewish backstabbers like you who caused Germany to lose the Great War?' No, he'll be back safe and sound in a couple of minutes, I'm sure."

She motioned toward the bench. "But come and sit with me while we wait. I want to hear the latest happenings with the Neumann family."

Klara sighed as the girls sat down. "Oh, what's to tell that you don't already know or could've guessed already? Vati's absorbed with his rocket research, trying to resist the pressures on him to join the Party. Walther seems more interested in chasing girls than his university studies. Elke is head over heels for the Führer, and Mama's worried sick about all of it. Quite a motley crew, I'd say."

Sophie eyed her closely. "And what about my friend Klara? Is she still considering that plea from her sister to become a good Nazi girl and join her in the BDM?"

Klara looked down at her lap. She'd known Sophie would press her on this, and she wasn't eager to reveal her latest thoughts. Still, for all the years the two had played, studied, and shared secrets as school-mates, she owed Sophie the truth, along with at least an attempt at an explanation.

"I probably *will* join soon. I've heard from my father that to have any hopes of entering medical school in four years and training to become a nurse, I'll need to have all the right credentials on my application. Especially if Nazis are in charge of the admissions decisions by then, which it certainly looks like they will be."

"But Klara, what about—"

Klara placed her hand over Sophie's. "I don't believe all those horrible things the Nazis say about the Jewish people. And I promise I never will, no matter how many times they try to cram it down my throat in BDM. The only reason I'll join them is to check off the box for that future career you know I've been dreaming about. And hopefully have a little fun along the way with all those camping trips, hikes, and athletic things Elke tells me about."

Sophie shook her head. "Klara, I think you're fooling yourself, just like my father."

"What do you mean?"

"Papa keeps saying all this will eventually blow over. That there's no way the Nazis can keep on degrading and excluding us Jews from German society. Sooner or later, so he claims, the good German people will wake up and see what's going on. They'll realize how bad the economy will be hurt if we keep on being pushed out." Sophie's shoulders sagged. "Papa just can't believe that Jews like himself, who fought so valiantly for the Kaiser in the last war, would ever be shunned and persecuted by their own countrymen. And yet, meanwhile . . ." She cast her eyes to the ground.

"Meanwhile?" Klara prompted, squeezing her hand.

"Meanwhile, just last week Papa was fired from his job due to that law the Nazis passed last year. The one expelling Jews from the civil service—even though as a war veteran he was supposed to have an exemption. With his war injury, he'll have a tough time finding employment anywhere soon. And... and . . ." Sophie's eyes welled with tears.

"What is it, Sophie?"

"Yesterday, Mama received a visit from my little sister's doctor. He said that after careful observation and analysis, he'd diagnosed her deafness and signs of feeble-mindedness as being a hereditary condition. And because of that, he was obligated by that other new Nazi law for the 'Prevention of Genetically Diseased Offspring' to report Leah's case to the local Hereditary Health Court. Supposedly, they'll decide if Leah has to undergo forced sterilization . . ."

Seeing Sophie choked up, Klara grasped her hand, waiting patiently for her to continue.

"When my mother heard, she nearly fainted. She's convinced that Leah's going to be taken away from us soon. That they'll put her in an insane asylum somewhere and we won't be permitted to see her anymore. Or worse." Sophie shook her head sadly. "Mama's livid with Papa for not listening to his brother's warning last year. He urged Papa to get our family out of Germany and move with him to America before the Nazis make it impossible to live here. Oh, Klara, I just don't know what to—"

A voice from the other side of the bushes caused both girls to leap from the bench. "Sophie, it's me. Is that Klara with you?"

"Yes, Jakob, it's her," Sophie said with a sigh of relief. "What are you doing? Come and join us. Is everything all right?"

"It's fine. I'll be there in a few seconds."

Seeing Jakob for the first time in months, Klara was alarmed at how thin and unwell he looked. A year older than Sophie and Klara, the formerly athletic, irrepressible, fun-loving boy now walked with his neck craned forward, shoulders hunched, and eyes shifting warily from side to side. Klara wondered if the change might be connected with the taunting and bullying that Sophie said he was being subjected to by some Aryan schoolmates. Thankfully, when she went to embrace him, his voice sounded as confident and unconcerned as always.

"Hello, Klara. It's been too long! I hope Sophie hasn't been drowning you with all our family troubles."

Klara sighed. "Oh, Jakob, I can hardly believe what she's been telling me."

"Before we get into all that . . ." interjected Sophie, "Jakob, are we safe talking here?"

"Nothing to worry about. I tracked those SA men to a huge tent. A bunch of 'em are congregating there, listening to some Nazi official spouting the usual rhetoric against Communists and Jews. Didn't see any others wandering around, so we should be safe here for a while." Shoving his hands in his pockets, Jakob kicked a small stone along the ground. "It makes me sick that Sophie and I always feel the need to skulk around everywhere. But we never know if or when they'll pick us out and give us a hard time based on our supposed Jewish look." He grinned at Klara and tapped the side of his slightly aquiline nose. "But anyway, what has Sophie been telling you?"

Sophie groaned and rolled her eyes. "Oh, just like you guessed. All about our family troubles of late. But there's nothing any of us can do right now besides mope, so I'd rather change the subject to something lighter. Besides, Klara doesn't have much time. She's supposed to meet up with her parents at the Zoo."

Jakob's eyes lit up. "Hey, why don't all three of us walk on down there together? We can catch up along the way. Besides, I wouldn't mind seeing that special exhibit I hear they've set up for the Birds of Prey."

"Oh, that would be great!" Klara exclaimed. "I've heard some really great things about that. Especially the vultures." She held her arms wide, playfully flapping them as she cawed and pirouetted in a circle, ending with her hands held like claws posed to strike her eyerolling, laughing friends. "Did you know I am the highest-flying bird in the world? I've occasionally been spotted at 35,000 feet—higher than most airplanes!"

"But Jakob," Sophie objected after the merriment died down, "Are you sure we won't get spotted by—"

"*Sophie*! We can't keep trying to hide ourselves and who we are everywhere we go. It's ridiculous. Besides, any Brownshirts or Hitler Youth in this entire area will no doubt be attending that speech. There's nothing to worry about. And if it'll ease your mind, we can stay well off the main path on our way. Come on, let's go."

The three set off in the direction of the Zoo. As they ambled along, Klara was reminded how much she adored Jakob's intelligent speech. He always seemed to know *something* about any subject that was brought up. And for the first time since she'd known him, she noticed—to her delight—Jakob casting what she interpreted as several lingering, admiring glances in *her* direction.

After years consigned to my role as "beautiful Elke's cute, skinny little sister," maybe I'm finally coming into my own. It was an exhilarating thought, filled with enticing new possibilities.

⚍

Less than a couple of hundred yards from the Zoo's entrance, Sophie pulled up abruptly.

"Stormtroopers!" she whispered frantically, grabbing Jakob's arm and pointing discreetly toward two brown-uniformed men walking erratically along the path.

"It's all right," Jakob muttered. "Hopefully they're too drunk to notice us. Just keep walking and don't look at them when we pass."

The ruse didn't work.

"Hello, friends!" called out one of the Brownshirts. "A question for you." The two men left the path and crossed to where Klara, Jakob, and Sophie waited. Staggering up to Jakob, the man who'd hailed them stopped, drew himself up to full height, and puffed out his chest. He appeared to be in his mid-twenties, with the face and neck of a bulldog and reeking of schnapps.

"My comrade and I are from out of town and need some directions. Do you know where the big speech is being held?

"Do you mean the speech for the SA people, sir?" Jakob asked politely.

The man glared at him. "Of course. What other speech would be worth listening to, boy?"

"It's about a half mile ahead, straight up the main path. Then look for the big tent off to the left. You can't miss it. You're already heading in the right direction."

The man kept scrutinizing Jakob, his eyes squinting. He glanced at Sophie and Klara, then returned his gaze to Jakob. Mind made up, he turned to his comrade. "There's something funny about this one, Karl. Something tells me I'm smelling a Jew-boy here."

"Come on, Manfred," Karl said wearily. "We're already late for the speech. We don't have time for this."

Manfred snorted. "Nonsense. If we don't have time to expose and educate a Communist-sucking, backstabbing kike when we come across one in a public park, then we're failing in our duty as SA members."

Placing his hands on his hips, Manfred bent down and thrust his face within two inches of Jakob's, the brim of his cap touching the youth's forehead. "So how about it, my friend? Are you what I think you are?"

Please, Jakob, Klara thought, *don't say it. There's no need. Just lie to him and let's get out of here.*

Jakob straightened, pulled his shoulders back and drew a deep breath. "Yes, it's as you were thinking. And I'm not ashamed of it."

Sophie stepped beside him and grabbed his arm. "Nor am I, his sister!"

Manfred craned his head back and smiled. "Is that so? Looking at the two of you now, I suppose I shouldn't be surprised." He nodded toward Klara. "And what about *her*?"

Klara froze, her eyes darting back and forth between Manfred and Jakob. She wished she could melt into the ground and not have to face the wrath of these SA goons. But then she saw the desperate, pleading look on Sophie's face, and she knew she had no choice. *I can't abandon them now.*

"Th-These are my two best friends," she said, her voice shaking.

Manfred's eyes narrowed. "That's *not* what I was asking, *girl.*"

Klara opened her mouth to reply, but her tongue stuck to the roof of her mouth.

Jakob spoke up. "She *is* our friend, but she's not Jewish. Don't involve her in this."

"Involve her in *what*, Jew-boy? What exactly are we 'involved' in?"

Jakob didn't answer, but his gaze didn't waver from Manfred's sinister stare.

After several seconds, Manfred stood straight and backed away a step. "You're lucky, Jews. If we weren't late for the speech, I'd feel compelled to teach you both a lesson. As it is, I'll let you off with a small warning: don't let us catch you here when we come back. This park is too beautiful to be littered with garbage." Manfred turned and started to walk away with his comrade.

Klara breathed a sigh of relief. *This could have been so much worse.* But then she saw the defiant expression on Jakob's face and knew the worst was still to come.

"There is no law barring Jews from this park, sir," Jakob said.

Both Brownshirts froze in their tracks. Manfred whirled, his face livid. Rushing Jakob, he reared back and drove his huge fist against the boy's face. Jakob staggered backward two steps, blood spurting from his mouth and nose. He fell with a thud. Manfred was on top of him in an instant, kicking his legs, groin, and torso.

"*Dirty, rotten little piece of dung. Thought you could challenge me, huh?*"

"*Leave him alone!*" Sophie screamed. She grabbed hold of Manfred's waist, attempting to pull the much larger man away from her brother.

"*Karl!*" Manfred yelled to his comrade as he struggled to extricate himself from her grasp. "Get this Jew-bitch off me before I end up smashing her face, too." Karl ran over and grabbed Sophie by the neck, yanking her off Manfred. After shoving her to the ground, he stood over her and glared.

Realizing the futility of joining the fray, Klara raced toward the main path. Several onlookers stood there, gawking at the scene as if paralyzed. She rushed to a fit-looking man and grabbed his arm.

"Sir, please, help me stop them. Those SA men are drunk, and I'm afraid they're going to kill my friends."

The man looked at her uncertainly. "Jews?"

Klara nodded. The man turned to his companions, one of whom scowled and shook his head. "No doubt they deserve what they're getting."

Klara's heart froze as she looked back to see Manfred viciously pummeling Jakob while Karl struggled to keep Sophie at bay. "My God, won't *any* of you help?" she pleaded with the bystanders, all of whom remained unmoved.

"*Klara!*"

She nearly fainted with relief at the sound of her brother's voice. She spun around and spotted Walther and Heinz down the path, jostling other strollers out of their way. Running to meet them, she barely managed to stammer out what was happening. She pointed to the grassy area, where Jakob was attempting to curl himself into a protective position as Manfred continued to curse and deliver kicks to his torso.

Heinz took charge. "I'm familiar with these SA types. Come on, Walther. Klara, wait for us here. Your parents aren't far behind and should be here soon." The youths turned and hurried toward the fracas. Klara followed without hesitation.

Walther pulled up short and grabbed her forearms. "Klara... *no!* You may get hurt. Now, wait for Vati."

"No, Walther," Klara protested. "They're *my* friends."

"All right, come on. But stay behind us and don't say anything to upset those idiots even more."

The three approached Manfred cautiously. Thankfully, he seemed to have sapped most of his violent energy, as he was now straddling Jakob with hands on his hips.

Klara ran to put her arms around Sophie, who was kneeling and crying at Karl's feet.

Manfred looked up as Heinz and Walther drew closer. "Who are *you*?" he snarled.

"My friend and I are just a couple of university students trying to enjoy a day in the park, sir," Heinz said. He pointed at Klara. "And that's my friend's sister. She's known the boy and girl you've been dealing with since childhood. She begged us to ask you and your comrade to ease up on them and let them go on home. I promise we'll see to it that they leave the park immediately."

Manfred exchanged glances with Karl, then broke out in incredulous laughter.

"Karl, this *dummkopf* actually thinks we're willing to just turn these two Jews over, let him and his friends escort them home. Probably treat them to ice-cream cones along the way. *After what this little Yid said to me?* Now I can see why the Führer's becoming more and more disgusted with all these intellectual types. They have no backbone for what has to be done to clean up this country." He glowered down at Jakob, lifted his knee and stomped his face with the heel of his boot, drawing a cry of agony and a fresh spurt of blood.

"*Stop it, you brute!*" Klara screamed.

"*That's enough!*" Heinz shouted, his hands clenching as he took a step toward Manfred. "Get away from him, *now*."

Manfred's face turned crimson. He rushed at Heinz like a raging bull and drew back his fist. Stepping deftly aside, Heinz deflected the blow with his arm and delivered a powerful roundhouse to the side of Manfred's face. Manfred stumbled several steps before falling to one knee, holding his head in his hands. Heinz stared at him, seemingly stunned by what he'd just done.

Seeing his comrade down, Karl pulled a rubber club from his pocket and sprang from behind toward Heinz. He raised it to strike Heinz's head, but Walther's flying tackle intercepted him.

As Walther and Karl wrestled on the ground, Manfred pulled a pistol from his waistband. He kept it trained straight at Heinz as he stalked over to where Walther had Karl pinned. Grabbing Walther by the hair, he yanked him off his comrade and rolled him onto his back, then pressed the pistol against his forehead.

"*Apologize for interfering with us, you Jew-loving bastard,*" Manfred shouted at Heinz. "*Or your friend here will be the first to die. And you'll be the next!*"

Klara, who with Sophie had raced over to tend to Jakob, was certain her brother had only seconds to live. In pure desperation she looked toward the main path, praying to God that *someone* might empathize with them and come to their aid.

It was then that she saw him, boldly stepping forth from the mass of cowed onlookers—a tall, well-built man in a dark black uniform.

CHAPTER 3

Berlin, Germany
July 8, 1934

Klara would never forget her first impression of SS Major Gerhard Bremmer.

As he strode across the grass, the strange sensation of an approaching, powerful presence caused all involved in the struggle to stop and look his way. Passing by Klara and Sophie, he glanced at Jakob, lying bloodied on the ground in front of them. This gave Klara a brief but clear look at the man's face, which was shadowed beneath a black, visored cap displaying the Nazi eagle emblem.

His eyes were steely gray, set close together on his long, equine-like face featuring a narrow nose, wide but thin lips, and a pointed chin. A long, thin scar ran down his left cheek just above the jawline. Klara once heard that such a mark was considered a badge of honor for wealthy German military men who'd fenced during their school days.

The man wasted no time concerning himself with Jakob's plight. Without breaking stride, he walked directly to Manfred, who had already pulled his gun away from Walther's head and stuffed it back in his belt.

Manfred stood at attention and offered the Nazi salute. "Heil Hitler! Greetings, Sturmbannführer. Please allow me to explain. My comrade and I were on our way to the SA speech, when we happened to encounter that stinking little Jew and his sister over there. The boy made a vile remark about our National Socialist cause, and as you can see, we lit into him to teach him a lesson." He nodded derisively at Walther. "We were finished and about to move on when this Jew-sympathizer and his friend rushed up and tried to interfere. And so, we—"

The man in black had heard enough. With his right hand, he delivered a vicious slap to the already bruised side of Manfred's face, causing the brute to yelp and drop to one knee.

Klara and Sophie gasped and stared at each other in open-mouthed shock.

After a moment, Manfred peered up at the man in black with lips quivering. "Sturmbannführer, I-I don't understand. Are we not struggling for the same cause? Why did you—"

"*Shut up, you pig-faced lout!*" the man in black shouted, his fists clenched and poised to strike again. "You and your SA friends have become an absolute disgrace to the Führer—running around drunk, bragging about your past glories, picking fights you can't even finish. I saw it. If you didn't have your weapons on you, these two schoolboys would have totally cleaned your clocks. You uneducated, undisciplined, rebellious thugs are no longer worthy of the Führer's trust."

"Can you believe this?" Klara muttered to Sophie. The very idea of one Nazi paramilitary man turning on another in public was unheard of. Then she remembered the strange conversation she'd overheard at the Führer's motorcade earlier. Something about an attempted SA coup that had just been quashed. Could this have something do with that?

Who is this black-uniformed "Sturmbannführer?" Whoever he is, I think I'm starting to like him.

Manfred rose to his feet and stood straight, less than a foot away from the man in black. He lifted his chin defiantly and a slight smirk appeared on his lips. "Perhaps, *Sturmbannführer*, you will allow me to convey your personal complaint to our SA Chief of Staff—*Reichsleiter*

Ernst Röhm—whom I'm sure will be pleased to meet with you directly and correct your mistaken impression."

"*Röhm is dead, you blithering idiot*! Just like the rest of your national SA leaders across the country. All disposed of last week at the command of the Führer. Did you not hear Goebbels's speech on the radio today at noon? All you low-level SA skunks are now under the command of *Reichsführer-SS* Heinrich Himmler—to whom I am privileged to report directly."

Manfred's jaw dropped. He glanced at Karl, who appeared equally stunned. Manfred cocked his head, a frown of disbelief contorting his face. "I'm sorry, sir, but that could not possibly be. Reichsleiter Röhm would *never* allow such a travesty to occur."

In one swift motion, the man in black grabbed Manfred by the back of his collar and yanked him around. Placing the sole of his boot on the shorter man's posterior, he delivered a violent shove that sent Manfred stumbling onto all fours.

"Don't believe me? Then take your comrade, and crawl on like the insects that you are to your big SA speech. Maybe they'll be breaking the news by now, confirming everything I'm telling you about how the Führer has dealt with that homosexual pervert Röhm and his cabal of degenerate assistants. *Now go on, both of you, get out of my sight!*" The man in black watched with arms akimbo and a look of utter contempt on his face as the two Brownshirts took off running.

After a few seconds, he turned and sauntered back to where Walther, Heinz, Klara, and Sophie had gathered around Jakob. The youth was now sitting up, applying a handkerchief to his dazed, bloodied face as the girls tried to help.

Walther and Heinz jumped to their feet and saluted. After returning it, the man in black stuck out his hand—first to Heinz, then to Walther. "Well done, boys. You showed quick thinking, agility, and bravery today. And though I'm not entirely sure of your ultimate motivation, I must say I was quite impressed."

He glanced at Klara, whose arm supported Jakob's back. He cocked his head and flashed a quizzical smile. Klara returned it hesitantly, despite the odd chill that coursed through her entire body.

"Klara! Walther!"

Vati raced across the grass toward their location, the sight of him bringing relieved tears to Klara's eyes. After checking to see that Klara and Sophie were unhurt and that Jakob—though he clearly needed some medical attention—would recover, Vati walked over to the man in black, saluted and offered his hand.

"Thank you, sir, for your timely intervention. You may well have saved the life of my son and his friend. May I have the honor of learning your name?"

The man smiled. "Major Gerhard Bremmer, Liebstandarte SS Adolf Hitler. And you are?"

"Neumann. Erich Neumann, I teach and perform research at the Technical College of Berlin."

Major Bremmer eyed him. "*The* Erich Neumann? Professor of Physics and Rocketry, army research project leader, and doctoral thesis advisor for Wernher von Braun?"

Vati grinned and bowed his head. "I hope my reputation doesn't prejudice you against me."

"Oh, quite the contrary!" Bremmer said. "My nephew has attended several of your lectures at the college. He continues to rave over the depth of your technical knowledge and your eloquence in expressing it. I daresay our army and nation will soon have great need of the new rocket design ideas that people like you and von Braun are advancing.

"But that aside, I was just commending your son and his friend for their bold action. These are exactly the kind of soldierly young men our Führer is seeking to lead our resurgent national army, not to mention the SS and its subordinate organizations."

Walther and Heinz stared wide-eyed at each other with expansive grins before facing Bremmer and snapping to attention. For some reason, Klara cringed inwardly at the sight.

"Thank you, sir," said Heinz, his voice sounding at least a half-octave deeper than usual. "We could not be more honored."

Major Bremmer nodded. "Yes, yes. The only other qualification required would be the evidence of a deep understanding and unwavering commitment to National Socialist philosophy and policy. Tell me, boys, are you now—or were you ever—members of the Hitler Youth?"

In times past, Heinz and Walther would have bragged to all and sundry of their successful efforts to resist the peer pressure to join what they both considered to be a conformist organization for nonthinkers. Now, challenged by Bremmer, they could only hang their heads in embarrassment.

"I see," Bremmer murmured. "Well, it's disappointing to hear that your academic education took a higher priority. As our Führer says, the future of the Third Reich will lie in the hands of violently active, dominating, intrepid, brutal youth instilled with National Socialist passion and fervor. Not weak-kneed, overthinking intellectuals.

"However, boys, it's not too late. You are both at the perfect age to join one of the local Nazi Party organizations and learn how to redirect your college education to serve the Führer's cause." He turned to look at Vati. "But I presume your father here is already a member of the Party, and has already spoken to you of its benefits?"

Vati said nothing, merely looked down at the ground and shook his head.

Bremmer frowned. "Professor Neumann, may I have a word with you in private?"

Major Bremmer escorted Vati out of earshot and engaged with him for at least five minutes in what appeared to be a one-way conversation dominated by Bremmer. At least twice, the major pointed toward Klara, Sophie, and Jakob, leading Vati to nod in apparent agreement with whatever he'd said.

"What do you think they're saying about us?" Sophie whispered.

"I'm not sure, but I suspect I'll be finding out soon," Klara said.

Finally, Bremmer reached out to shake Vati's hand. The men saluted; then Major Bremmer spun on his heels and strode back to the path, disappearing into the crowd of onlookers as abruptly as he had first emerged.

"All right. Walther, Heinz, and Klara . . ." Vati called, "we've spent enough time here. It's time to go."

Klara glanced at Sophie and Jakob, immediately seeing their puzzled looks.

"Klara," Sophie pleaded, "will your father let you help me get Jakob to the doctor? I don't think he can walk on his own, and I'll need help supporting him."

Klara touched her arm. "Of course." She turned to call out to her father. "Vati, I'm going to help Sophie take Jakob to the doctor. I'll catch the trolley back home."

Her father's impatient retort caught her by surprise. "No, Klara. You will come with the rest of us. Now!"

"But Vati, I—"

"Klara! I will not argue with you. Sophie and Jakob can make it to the doctor on their own. Now come on. We've kept your mother waiting long enough."

Klara looked at her friends in disbelief. Sophie appeared on the verge of tears, unable to speak. Jakob simply closed his eyes and shook his head sadly. "Go on, Klara, it's no use. You must do what your father says."

⁜

On their way back up the path to the park entrance, Klara walked beside her parents, trying to keep her anger submerged. Several yards ahead, Elke and her BDM friends bounced along happily with Walther and Heinz. Elke clutched Heinz's arm and gazed adoringly at him as the boys recounted their manly exploits and the compliment they'd received from SS Major Bremmer.

Klara looked at her mother imploringly. "Mama, why did Vati prevent me from staying to help Jakob and Sophie? You know we've been friends for so long, and you and Vati have always liked them both and approved of my seeing them."

Mama sidled beside her and took hold of her hand. "Klara," she said quietly, a great heaviness in her voice. "Times are changing fast. We're all going to have to make a few painful changes in our habits if our family is to have any kind of future in this bold new world of the

Third Reich. Especially with SS Blackshirts like Major Bremmer lead-ing the way. In the end, I'm praying that your father is right and that the changes will be worth it. But for now, we need to just trust and obey him."

Klara turned her face toward the darkening groves of trees along the side of the path. Trusting Vati was one thing—she didn't doubt his deep love and best of intentions for her. Obeying him, however, could prove to be another matter altogether.

Yes, she would proceed with her previous plan to join Elke in the BDM to make her parents proud and gain the credentials she needed for medical school. But *never* would she allow her mind to be corrupted by the BDM's antisemitic stances, *and never again* would she leave her Jewish friends in the lurch as Vati had just made her do.

Not if she could help it.

PART II

CHOOSING SIDES

CHAPTER 4

Berlin, Germany
October 27, 1938
(Four Years Later)

Klara's stomach churned as the high-pitched voice of Professor Otto Gottschald resonated throughout the Berlin University Medical School lecture hall. His stentorian tone dared any of the first-year students to question his authority.

Pointing to the large screen on the wall behind him—where a silent film depicted scene after nauseating scene of insane or severely deformed asylum inmates struggling to perform basic life functions—Gottschald pronounced his verdict:

"*'Useless eaters: life unworthy of life!'* From the standpoint of our common humanity, I admit that the phrase first coined by a German psychiatrist in 1920 *does* seem a harsh thing to say. But the facts cannot be denied: people like the ones you are seeing in this film are little more than vegetables. They are, in fact, burdens on society, existing only to breathe and eat."

Gottschald paused and scanned his audience with arched eyebrows and a smug smile. "Can any of you claim that you would wish to be brought into this world, knowing you would be destined to live in such a despicable condition—without hope and without sense?" Receiving no response from the vast sea of grimacing faces and shaking heads, he shut the projector off and closed his argument. "We should all be thankful that our Führer created the sterilization laws which are finally bringing about an end to this madness. Not only for the good of Germany, but for the good of humanity!"

Seated in the balcony beside her classmate and friend, Heidi Schmidt, Klara could barely contain her fury. Amidst the strong applause, she leaned over to whisper in Heidi's ear. "This all just makes me want to throw up. They make it sound like mandatory sterilization is the only logical course of action for anyone with a hereditary disease. No concern at all for the dangers to the patient."

She would never forget the forced commitment of Sophie and Jakob's disabled little sister, Leah. It happened last year. She'd been sent to the Wittenau Sanatorium, where she'd been subsequently sterilized. Afterward, the doctors had informed the Friedmann family that the painful procedure had resulted in serious and long-lasting aftereffects to Leah's already fragile mental condition. The complications would almost certainly require a long-term, if not permanent, institutionalization and prevent the girl from returning home for anything other than the occasional, supervised visit. When Klara secretly went to visit the Friedmanns at their house last week, Sophie's mother had wept inconsolably over Leah's bleak prospects.

Heidi must have noticed the fierce gleam in Klara's eyes and guessed what she was about to do. She rested her hand on Klara's forearm. "Klara, don't," she pleaded. "You know they'll kick you out of the program if you voice the slightest criticism."

Klara smiled back at her confidently. "Don't worry. I'll behave myself. I just need to clarify something."

Her hand shot up in the air. "*Herr Professor!*"

Gottschald looked up from his lecture notes and peered over his spectacles. Seeing who'd created the disturbance, he cocked his head and smirked. No doubt, he was ready to pounce on the slightest sign of disrespect, considering Klara was one of the few females admitted to the program this year. "It seems we have an objection from the gallery. Yes, Fräulein?"

Klara stood at rigid attention, her mouth suddenly as dry as sandpaper. "No objection whatsoever, Herr Professor. You have shown us by this film and expressed what I'm sure most, if not all, of us are coming to believe in our hearts. We have just seen the inevitable, sad consequences of allowing these hereditary diseases to pass to future generations."

Encouraged by Gottschald's pleased expression and nod of approval, Klara continued. "My only question, Herr Professor, is this: for aspiring psychiatric nurses such as myself, what standard of care does the Reich Psychiatry Association envision for our institutionalized patients? Will it ever need to change?"

The professor shifted uncomfortably and crossed his arms as he glanced around the room at the other students, many of whom stared at Klara with puzzled expressions. "Fräulein, I think you, along with everyone else here, already know the answer to that question. Of course, the standard of care for institutionalized patients will remain as high as it always has been. Why would anything need to change?"

Klara hesitated. She needed to be very careful here. She didn't want to reveal her true feelings on this matter, but she also felt compelled to pose the *real* question that had simmered inside her for some time now. It was a question that had profound implications for people like Leah Friedmann.

"Well, sir, I assume the Association agrees with our Führer that people such as these are 'useless eaters' and burdens on society. So then, would it not be logical—in the case, God forbid, of future national economic distress and threat to our country's survival—to ration medical care in such a way that healthy, productive Germans are given priority?"

A deathly silence ensued. Klara snuck a hesitant glance at Heidi, who sat petrified with her eyes tightly closed. *Make my point, hurry up and get this over with*, Klara admonished herself.

"To put things directly, sir, does the Association feel that it is morally right to go to extraordinary and costly means to keep severely disabled people barely alive for decades? Even if doing so would require the reduction or elimination of government support for others who faithfully work for and defend our Fatherland?"

The collective gasp throughout the auditorium was accompanied by all heads craning to stare at the provocateur in the balcony. Klara's heart thumped wildly and her knees went weak as she worried that her bold attempt to put Professor Gottschald on the spot may have gone too far. She half expected him to demand that she leave the room immediately for her impertinence.

The professor strolled to the front of the stage's display desk and leaned casually against it with legs crossed. For several seconds, he stared down at the floor with his left arm folded across his abdomen and his right hand massaging his chin, as if contemplating how to deal patiently with a difficult child.

Finally, he looked up and addressed Klara in a surprisingly mild tone. "Fräulein, you pose a difficult, though mercifully hypothetical, question. It's been the subject of many scholarly debates on eugenics and population control over the past few decades. Not only in Germany, but also America and other developed countries. I can only tell you this: there has been no definitive position taken by our Führer or the Association on the matter of limiting care to the permanently disabled.

"And in any case, it would seem to be a moot point for the foreseeable future. No German citizen can look upon the glorious transformation of our society over the past five years under National Socialism without projecting anything but full confidence in our nation's prosperity and security. Intentional limiting of medical care to *anyone* should not be necessary."

Gottschald spread his arms wide with his palms up, ready to conclude the matter. "But Fräulein, even in the unlikely event that it one day becomes a necessity to limit care to the severely disabled, your responsibility as a psychiatric nurse would remain unchanged. *So long as the patient remains alive,* your obligation is to do everything in your power to ensure their comfort and care. After all, they did not ask to be born in their desolate condition. We must always pity them and treat them with kindness."

Klara wanted to press Gottschald with another question to clarify his last few statements but thought better of it. If she said anything more, she feared her voice would betray her raw emotions.

"Thank you, Herr Professor." She clicked her heels together and gave the Nazi salute, then took her seat. Her mind spinning with all manner of confusing thoughts, she didn't hear another word of the professor's lecture.

After the class concluded, Klara struggled to explain her concern to Heidi in the lobby. "It's not what he said. It's what he *didn't* say."

Heidi frowned. "What do you mean? I thought he was very clear. Our nursing care standards won't change."

"But that phrase he made a point of emphasizing, '*so long as they remain alive.*' What was *that* supposed to imply?"

"How about just what he said? As long as they're alive, they deserve the best nursing care we can offer." Heidi shrugged. "Why are you trying to read something into it beyond the obvious?"

Klara crossed her arms and scuffed the edge of a floor tile with her shoe. "I don't know. There just seemed something ominous about the way he said it, that's all."

"Well," Heidi said, her eyes widening as she looked over Klara's shoulder. "Maybe you'll get a chance to ask him yourself. Looks like he's coming this way."

Klara turned to see Professor Gottschald pushing through the milling students, clearly heading in their direction. His brows were furrowed, and he greeted the girls with a half salute and tight, formal smile. "Fräulein... *Neumann*, I believe?"

Too cowed to speak with the eyes of the other students upon her, Klara managed only to nod and stand at attention. *I went too far. He's going to boot me from the program.*

Gottschald looked politely at Heidi. "Please excuse me. May I have a brief word with Fräulein Neumann in private?"

"Of course, Herr Professor." Heidi left to join another nearby conversation, leaving Klara alone as she readied herself to receive bad news. Trembling inside, her discomfort must have been evident.

Gottschald reached out and touched her shoulder. "Please relax, Fräulein. I'm not here to condemn you. In fact, quite the opposite. I wanted to let you know how impressed I was with the boldness and clarity with which you advanced your question. I am not oblivious to the fact that our Führer's views and policies on the eugenics issue have raised a number of important considerations for our future medical professionals. Most are too timid to confront these questions head on, in public at least. You, however, are obviously different, and I greatly respect that."

Klara blinked several times. *Did I hear him right?* She sighed, overcome with relief. "Herr Professor, I am so grateful. I was afraid you would... well . . ."

Gottschald grinned. "Have you taken out and executed?"

Klara laughed awkwardly. "Well, perhaps not that bad, sir, but these days one never knows how honest, hard questions might get misinterpreted. I feared I had overstepped my bounds."

The professor's smile disappeared, and his face took on a hardened expression. "Indeed, I understand exactly what you mean." He glanced over both his shoulders, as if to confirm that no one was within earshot. "Fräulein Neumann, allow me to be direct. The reason I am approaching you is to inquire if you might be interested in applying to become one of my research assistants. I am always on the lookout for intelligent students who demonstrate an inquisitive, forward-looking, scientific spirit. Students who seek to understand and help achieve our National Socialist goals in the medical profession. If you would be interested, and if your background checks out, I am very disposed toward interviewing you for the job."

Klara's pulse raced as conflicting thoughts flashed through her mind.

A job offer from this arrogant Nazi professor was absolutely the *last* thing she would've expected after she'd challenged him in front of his class. In fact, given her disgust and anger after everything that had happened to poor Leah Friedmann, Klara knew she should come up with a polite excuse and refuse this opportunity—especially with a committed National Socialist like Gottschald.

And yet, a small voice inside her head cautioned her. *Maybe you should play along a bit and hear him out. Who knows how this might help your future career?*

"Oh, sir," she said in the most ingratiating tone she could muster. "It is such a wonderful honor to be considered by you for an RA position. But can you tell me anything about what the position would entail?"

Gottschald nodded and straightened his spectacles. "The research will involve something that I suspect will be very dear to your heart— assisting me in observing and recording impressions of psychiatric patients in a couple of our major Berlin asylums. The reports we generate will help the Psychiatric Association make important decisions regarding the use of future, more effective national therapies."

Klara barely suppressed her astonished gasp. *Major Berlin asylums?* Surely that would include the big one at Wittenau, where Leah was confined. She knew Leah's mother was allowed a half hour visit with the girl once per month, and the family was used to receiving a quarterly form letter that always said the same thing: "Your daughter is stable but showing no substantial signs of improvement." But those provided nowhere near enough insight. *This might give me a chance to check on Leah far more regularly, to comfort her and report back to Sophie and her family on how she's really...*

She did not even bother to complete the thought. Nothing else mattered; her decision was already made. Still, she had to play the game and remain calm. After all, she didn't want to arouse suspicion.

"Professor, that sounds exciting and *very* worthwhile. But may I ask, what would this mean for my school schedule and responsibilities?"

"Nothing to worry about in that regard, Fräulein, I can assure you. Your two, half-day visits to the asylums each week can be arranged so that you won't miss your school lectures. The additional hours that you'd spend on weekends writing your observations will be credited toward your academic requirements. In addition, you would receive a stipend for your efforts, helping to defray your total educational expenses. What would you say to that? Is it enough to interest you in a formal interview, at least?"

Klara gulped. It all sounded too good to be true. She could not imagine receiving a more attractive offer than this, especially so early in her university studies. *Don't let this slip away.* "Professor Gottschald, I would be delighted to apply for your RA position!"

A pleased smile lit up the professor's face. "Excellent! I am delighted to hear that. Then I will expect you in my office at 11 a.m. next Tuesday after my lecture, at which point we can conduct the interview. Until then, Fräulein Neumann . . ." He stepped back, drew himself to attention, and snapped the fascist salute, to which Klara responded in kind.

Gottschald started to walk away, then drew up short as he remembered something. "Fräulein Neumann, there was one other thing I meant to ask you."

"Yes, sir?"

"Your last name. I was wondering. Are you by any chance connected to the family of Professor Erich Neumann—the noted rocket scientist at the Technical College of Berlin?"

Klara nodded. "Yes, sir. I'm proud to say that Professor Neumann is my father."

"Ah!" Gottschald smiled warmly and offered a small bow. "I daresay, that is something that will enhance even further your chances for landing the RA position." He clicked his heels, spun around, and walked toward the lobby exit.

As soon as he was out of sight, Heidi rushed up, her eyes wide with curiosity and concern. "Well, what did he say? Did he answer your question?"

Klara stared at her for a long moment, trying to fathom everything that had transpired, and how much she should share with Heidi. Both girls had been members of the BDM for the last four years, and Heidi was well aware of, and even sympathetic to, Klara's general disenchantment with Nazi propaganda. But Klara had never let *anyone* know of her clandestine visits with the Friedmann family, or her concerns for Leah, and she was not about to start now—even with Heidi.

Finally, her face relaxed into a smile, and she grasped Heidi's hand. "Not exactly. I'll tell you all about it over coffee at the student lounge. Let's just say for now that I think I've really landed myself in the thick of things—in an unexpected but good way!"

CHAPTER 5

Berlin, Germany
October 27, 1938

When Erich Neumann finished saying grace at dinner, he began his usual round of inquiries to discover each family member's daily happenings.

Klara was eager to share her good news about the research position but, suspecting it would spark the most discussion, she decided to let the others go first.

"Oh, nothing much for me," Gertrude said. "The usual household chores, meeting with our neighbors to plan next year's Winter Relief Fund drive, and... oh, yes... and sprucing up the living room to receive your father's special guest after dinner tonight!" She glanced at her husband with a playful, reprimanding expression. "It would've been nice if I'd been given more than an hour's notice."

Walther paused, his spoonful of soup frozen just in front of his mouth. "Special guest? Who might that be, Father? Anyone we know?"

"Your mother knows, but I'm keeping it a surprise for the rest of you," Erich answered, a mysterious gleam in his eye. "Let's just say it's someone I think you will all very much enjoy meeting, and we'll leave it at that."

Klara, Elke, and Walther looked at each other with amused, puzzled expressions.

"Oh, come on, Mama," Elke pressed. "Give us a hint."

Mama tilted her head and smiled innocently, mimicking one of Elke's own favorite expressions. Glancing between the two of them, Klara was struck once again by their physical resemblance. Light blonde hair, blue eyes, angular facial contours: the typical features of a long line of women on her mother's side. On the other hand, Klara's and Walther's thin ovular faces, auburn hair and brown eyes clearly resembled their father's.

"Well, whoever it is," Walther ventured, "so long as it's not another one of those low-level functionaries come to bore us with his pleas for more contributions to the Party, I'll probably enjoy meeting them." He put his spoon down and cast a sly, sidelong glance at his sister. "Oh, and speaking of the Party, I was diligently performing my duties as accounting manager at the Gauleiter's office today when I overheard something that Elke might know a little about."

Elke stared at him suspiciously. "What's that?"

Walther shrugged innocently. "My supervisor heard from his wife that the Party's just formed some kind of national Faith and Beauty Society. It's apparently for girls aged seventeen to twenty-one, and it's supposed to help their transition from BDM to the National Socialist Women's League. Do you know anything about this, Elke?"

The question was met with her annoyed groan. "Oh! As if I hadn't already received ten earfuls on that subject in the past week from my own BDM area leader. I've been in my trainer role only since graduating from secondary school two years ago. And here she is, already wanting to make me one of the national chapter leaders for this new FBS. But after I saw one of their advertising posters, I told her I wasn't interested."

"It sounds like quite an honor to me," Walther observed. "Why would you immediately turn down a nice offer like that?"

Elke slammed her hand down on the table and glared at him. "Because I have no desire to participate in such silly frivolity. Honestly, parading around stadium tracks and performing gymnastics in a form-fitting, short, white tennis dress? It all seems designed to arouse the passions of all those lusty old army and political bigwigs in the stands. I wouldn't do it myself, and I'm even less interested in leading other girls in doing the same." She folded her arms defiantly and sat back in her chair.

Walther grinned. "Well, in that case I'm sure Heinz will be happy to know of your decision, since parading around in a short white dress in front of other men would certainly send him into a jealous rage. Especially now that he's joined the SS and thinks he's earned the right to transition from your steady boyfriend to your future husband."

"Ha!" Elke scoffed. "If that's what Heinz is thinking, he'll have to prove he's finally done with that aspiring actress he seems so enamored with. She keeps sending him invitations to her theatre performances—and he keeps accepting!" Elke uncrossed her arms and sat forward in her seat, her eyes flashing. "You're his best friend, Walther. You can tell him yourself. I will not compete with such trash. If Heinz really cares about me, he'll honor my commitment to the Führer's standards for the ideal Third Reich woman and stop patronizing that audacious little floozy—who, so I hear, still keeps the close company of a few degenerate Jewish artists and businessmen."

Mama started to protest, but her husband put a restraining hand on her forearm. "Let's not argue about this now. We have a guest arriving soon, and I'd like to enjoy my dinner."

The tempered reaction was yet another example, Klara recognized, of Vati's increasing tolerance for his eldest daughter's obsession with spouting Nazi propaganda to her own family. Ever since he'd finally caved and joined the Party last year, Vati had stopped voicing *any* personal objections to *anyone* about Nazi philosophy. No doubt, he feared that such objections could, either inadvertently or deliberately, get communicated back to his Party superiors and imperil his rocketry research position. Especially if they were reported by his own daughter, a respected BDM trainer.

Klara was baffled by Elke's obvious insecurity over her boyfriend's true motives for attending what she knew to be well-reviewed, Party-recommended German plays and movies. It certainly was difficult to reconcile *this* supercilious, faultfinding sister to the protective tigress who had boldly intervened in that dangerous situation Klara faced two years ago…

(Nazi Party Rally, Nuremberg, Germany: September 14, 1936)

"Oh, come on, Klara, it's our last night in Nuremberg for a whole year. Just another half hour. Then the three of us can walk back to camp."

"That's right, Klara. Remember? Our group captain said we don't have to report to our tents until midnight, and it's only quarter after eleven!"

So went the reasoning of Ingrid Richter and Helga Adler, two of Klara's BDM co-members, as they snuggled under blankets next to their newfound Hitler Youth beaus against the rear wall of an abandoned railroad supply shack just southeast of the city. Seated against the adjoining wall, Klara tried to keep her distance from a third, doughy-looking youth who kept casting lustful looks at her in between pulls from his beer stein.

Klara was in no mood to take the bait. "You two can stay longer if you wish," she told the other girls. She could barely make out their faces in the dim light afforded by a candle stub held in place by an empty beer bottle. "But we have to catch the train back to Berlin at eight tomorrow morning, and roll call's at six thirty. I'm exhausted, and I want to get some rest."

Helga rolled her eyes and groaned. "Oh, we forgot, Ingrid. Klara needs her 'purity sleep.'"

Draping his arm around her shoulders and pulling her closer to his side, Helga's companion cocked his head and grinned. "Purity sleep? What's that all about? Sounds rather ominous for poor, love-starved boys like us."

"Why Kris, didn't you know?" Helga giggled. "The Führer says all his BDM girls must get at least ten hours of sleep every night and eat the right balance of vitamins, minerals, and protein. He wants us bred like prize cattle, so one day we can have healthy babies with strong, handsome SS men and help create a pure, Aryan master race. Klara just wants to do her part!"

Klara shot Helga a look of disgust. Usually, she enjoyed and would play along with her friend's caustic honesty and witty remarks. But tonight, they'd all obviously had far too much to drink, and Helga was spouting disrespectful things that could easily get her kicked out of the BDM, or worse, if the wrong people heard her.

Actually, Klara was more disgusted with herself for allowing Ingrid and Helga to talk her into participating in this ridiculous tryst. They'd insisted it would be a fitting and relaxing end to their exhausting week of preparing for their special role in the festivities of the 1936 National Socialist Party Rally of Honor.

It was during a break at the dress rehearsal for Sunday's big event when the girls had encountered Kris, Jürgen, and Georg—three older boys from an Austrian Hitler Youth regiment. The six had struck up an enjoyable dialogue, and by the end of it, they'd made an agreement to meet on Monday night to celebrate the end of the event. Kris knew of a secluded little place just outside the camp boundaries that would serve the cause perfectly, and he'd said that the boys would be happy to bring some beverages suitable for the occasion. There would be no funny business, he promised; the girls' honor and wishes would be completely respected, and the boys would make sure they were back at their camp before the midnight curfew.

Despite Klara's concern that Elke, the girls' BDM section leader, would miss them at the after-rally bonfire and become alarmed, Helga and Ingrid had convinced her to join the party. Now, she was paying the price.

Her head spinning and her eyes heavy from the effects of two full steins of beer, she felt on the verge of vomiting. She needed to get out of this stuffy, dank-smelling shack—immediately.

"I'm sorry," she said, pushing herself up from the floor and standing on wobbly legs. "But I really want to go back. It was so nice to meet and talk with you gentlemen. And thank you for the beer. I'll see you girls back at the camp—and I'll tell Elke to expect you there soon."

Helga grimaced. "You're really going back... alone? At this time of night?"

"It's a straight road to the camp, it's mostly out in the open, and the moon's bright. Don't worry. I'll be fine. It's only a ten-minute walk."

Once outside, Klara realized her assumption that the moon would light her path had been misplaced. Low clouds had set in, and she flinched as several drops of rain landed in her hair. Within seconds, a hard steady drizzle was coming down. She was tempted to return to the party, but the thought of spending another half hour seated next to her chubby, drunken companion was insufferable. No, she would brave the short walk back to camp and retire to the tent she'd been quartered in with Elke and the other girls in the Charlottenburg BDM section.

Pulling a scarf from her sweater pocket, Klara wrapped it around her head to protect from the rain and took off at a fast walk. Thankfully, her nausea seemed to have passed, and her head was clearing rapidly. Vivid images of the past week's events flashed through her mind—especially today's awe-inspiring display of marching infantry, cavalry, Panzer tanks, and simulated bombing runs by siren-blaring dive bombers followed by wave after thunderous wave of heavy bombers. The only thing that had drawn a more ecstatic reaction from the thousands of spectators packed in the Zeppelin Arena was the Führer's concluding speech.

A few minutes later, Klara reached the edge of a narrow stretch of woods. The dirt road that passed through it led straight to a flat, open field where the Hitler Youth and BDM tents had been erected. Light from the camps' celebratory bonfires filtered through the trees ahead, along with the muffled sounds of singing.

She looked at her watch: eleven thirty. Plenty of time to cross the field and merge with the hundreds of other girls congregated around their bonfire, saying their goodbyes to friends from other sections.

Several steps into the wooded area, Klara realized she was not alone. To the left of the road, through the foliage, she could make out a flickering light with several shadowy figures huddled around it. A man's hearty laugh, followed by the raucous giggling of several females, confirmed that Klara and her friends were not the only ones partying beyond camp boundaries tonight.

A little farther along, she stopped short as a soft moaning sound reached her from somewhere behind a grove of trees. *Is someone in trouble?* She inclined her ear, soon realizing what was going on. The moaning transitioned to more frequent and louder sighs and gasps, accompanied by the deep-throated groans of unmistakable pleasure.

Klara winced and resumed her walk, discomfited by the sounds of passionate lovemaking. Thankfully, within seconds the orgiastic cries ceased, and Klara quickened her pace as her thoughts returned to more practical matters. Such as how to reenter the camp without causing a scene.

Approaching the end of the wooded area, she paused. Up the path, a small light bobbed up and down, drawing closer. Panic set in as she considered the possibility that it might be one of the camp security guards, sent out to discover and rope in any wayward partiers. If caught out here, Klara would certainly face questioning from her group captain, and she would likely be forced to betray the whereabouts of Helga and Ingrid. Suspension or even expulsion from the BDM could result for their deliberate violation of camp rules. She angled toward the side of the road and entered the woods. Spotting a thick tree about ten yards in, she hid behind it, hoping the trouble would pass. She screwed her eyes shut, her panic mounting with each passing second as she imagined being discovered and confronted by an angry, merciless guard.

After several minutes and no further sign of the bobbing light, Klara stepped tentatively from behind her hiding place. The light rain had stopped, and a break in the cloud cover permitted moonlight to dimly illuminate the road.

She'd taken two steps toward it when the sound of thudding footsteps behind her caused her to freeze. Before she could turn, a heavy arm crossed her chest and another her abdomen, drawing her body against the solid frame of her attacker. She barely managed a brief shriek before the assailant's hand clamped over her mouth and yanked her head back beside his.

"Don't fight, *Liebchen*, and all will go well." The voice was low and gravelly, the breath reeking of alcohol and stale tobacco.

Klara struggled frantically to free herself, but to no avail as the man's grip was ironclad. Realizing it was useless to resist, she went limp and allowed herself to be dragged a few more yards into the woods and behind a clump of thick bushes. With one hand still over her mouth, the man shoved the other underneath her sweater. Grabbing the top of her blouse, he attempted to rip it off. She lifted her foot and kicked backward against the man's kneecap with all her might. With a violent curse, he withdrew his hands and bent over in pain.

Klara took full advantage and broke free.

She didn't look back. She crashed through the underbrush onto the road, colliding with a dark figure. She screamed, fearing a second attacker had her in his grasp.

"*Klara?*"

She felt her face pinioned between two firm hands trying to get her to calm down and focus. Suddenly, she recognized the face behind the hands.

"*Elke!*" She grabbed her sister's wrists. "We need to get out of here. H-he tried to molest me and now he's coming after me!"

Elke cocked her head. "*Who's* coming after you, Klara? Look at me. What's going on, and why are—"

"*Ah… there you are!*"

Klara yanked her hands away from Elke and whirled to face her attacker. He stood at the tree line, his fists clenched, his chest heaving with labored breaths. She still couldn't make out his features in the shadows, but she could tell he was tall and solidly built.

"Who's that with you?" the man snarled.

She turned to run, but Elke grabbed her arm. Her voice sounded amazingly steady, unafraid. "No, Klara. We face this together. Here and now."

Elke bent to pick up the flashlight she'd dropped when Klara collided with her. She clicked it on and pointed the beam at the face of the assailant. Recoiling, he put his hands up to block the glare. For the first time, Klara saw who she'd been accosted by: a blond-haired man around forty in the uniform of a Wehrmacht* army soldier.

"Who are you, and what have you done to my BDM comrade?" Elke demanded.

"I didn't do anything to her, *Fräulein.* At least nothing she was objecting to. We were simply getting acquainted with each other, like everyone else in these woods tonight. And as for who I am... well, it's perfectly obvious, isn't it? I'm a loyal infantryman in the Führer's service. But since I can't see *you* with that damned light blinding me, perhaps a better question is: *who the hell are you?*"

Elke tilted the beam down slightly, permitting the man to lower his hands. "I am Elke Neumann, Charlottenburg Section Leader, BDM League of German Girls," she announced. "And *your* unit, sir?"

The man stared at her in disbelief. "You dare to demand identification from a German army officer, Section Leader Neumann? Thinking perhaps you'll deliver a complaint to my superior?"

Elke's face tightened. "The thought definitely crossed my mind."

"Ha! With the shenanigans that are no doubt taking place all around us this very moment between your eager BDM girls and randy Hitler Youths? Which one of us do you think will be believed, Fräulein Neumann? A *Wehrmacht* army officer, or a section leader for your League of German *Mattresses*? Come on! Your BDM's reputation at summer camps and events such as these is well understood and appreciated."

The man stretched his arms with palms open and took two cautious steps toward the girls. "But *Fräulein,* please, let's be reasonable. It's been a marvelous, but long, week for all of us. Why don't you and your pretty comrade simply relax and join me for a little—"

"*No closer, sir!*" Elke snapped, her face a mask of revulsion and anger. Once again, she tilted the beam directly into the man's eyes.

---

* Wehrmacht: Nazi Germany's "regular" armed forces (as distinct from SS and SA paramilitary forces)

"Arrogant bitch… give me that thing!" He lunged forward, grabbing the flashlight and struggling to wrest it from her left hand.

With lightning-fast dexterity, she reached into her skirt pocket with her other hand and extracted her seven-inch BDM dagger from its sheath. Stepping in close, she jammed the tip of the knife under the man's chin. He dropped his hands and stood at rigid attention as Elke pressed the blade as far as possible without puncturing his skin, causing him to grimace.

"Blink once—clearly—if you are truly sorry for bothering my comrade, who also happens to be my sister," Elke said softly, her left hand pointing the flashlight directly into his eyes—this time at point-blank range.

The man hesitated a few seconds, but then obeyed.

"Now, blink twice if you sincerely regret your insulting lies about the BDM and the brave, young girls who commit their lives to serving the Führer and the Fatherland."

No response.

"I said blink twice, you despicable oaf!" Elke shouted. *"Or I swear I'll shove this blade right through your mouth and into your nose."* She pressed the knife harder, this time drawing a drop of blood. The man grunted and quickly complied with her order.

"Good. Now leave us, and—"

The man jerked his head back. Knocking Elke's knife-wielding hand away from his chin, he whirled and raced back into the woods.

Elke returned the dagger and flashlight to her pockets, then turned to face her sister, who stood shaking in the middle of the road with her hand over her mouth. She embraced her, stroking the back of her head and shoulders.

After a few moments, she stepped back and grasped Klara's arms. "So, what are you doing out here, Klara?" she asked, eyes flashing. "You know good and well you went against our group leader's orders by going past camp boundaries. And look where your disobedience got you."

Klara stammered through her explanation, knowing at this point she would be wise to leave nothing out.

"And so," Elke pressed her, "Helga and Ingrid are still with those boys, no doubt disgracing themselves and helping prove those rumors about BDM depravity?"

Klara nodded and hung her head, ashamed and desperately wishing to put this all behind her. "They said they'd make curfew, so they should be coming up the road soon."

"I'll be right here waiting to receive them," Elke said, her voice stern. "You go on back to the camp now, Klara. We'll talk about this later. But never, *ever* do anything stupid like this again. Do you hear me? That soldier would have raped you. Or worse! And there wouldn't have been a blessed thing you could do about it. You're lucky I missed you at the bonfire and decided to come look for you."

Klara looked apprehensively at her sister, her lips trembling. "You're not going to report us to the group captain?"

Elke closed her eyes and sighed. "I'll be disobeying orders by *not* reporting all of you. But you are, after all, my sister. I don't want to see your future in the BDM ruined by one idiotic escapade. And if I don't report you, then I can't report the others."

Tears welled in Klara's eyes. "Thank you, Elke, for coming to find and rescue me." She moved to hug her sister, but thought better of it, opting instead to step back and snap the fascist salute.

Elke nodded, a faint smile on her lips. "Good. Enough sentimentality. And who knows? Maybe I'll require the same from you some day, sister." She returned the salute. "Now, get back and report in—quick, it's getting late. I'll go round up Helga and Ingrid."

Klara watched as Elke turned and strode off down the road, directing her flashlight beam from side to side into the bordering woods. She shook her head and smiled, filled with an unusually strong surge of admiration and affection for her sister.

Fearless mother tiger, protecting her young...

⸎

But that was then, Klara thought ruefully as she eyed Elke across the dining room table. Over the past two years, it seemed, Elke's attitude toward her BDM trainees and Klara had hardened. Now, any behavior or viewpoint that deviated from her understanding of the *Führer's will* was usually met with loathing and contempt.

Vati tried to break the tension. "Well, Klara, it's your turn. Anything new to report today?"

Klara hesitated. "Actually, Vati, there is." She proceeded to describe Professor Gottschald's offer of the research assistant position, and her decision to accept. She left out, of course, any mention of the true motivation behind her decision.

Vati, Mama, and Walther expressed their delight and offered their immediate congratulations, all in stark contrast to Elke's glaring reaction.

"Elke, dear, aren't you happy for your sister?" Mama prompted.

"To be perfectly honest," Elke said, "it strikes me as a selfish, unpatriotic choice to refuse the Führer's call by pursuing a profession better suited for men. And in fact, I'm amazed that this family—perhaps you, Mama, most of all—seem not to appreciate the Führer's observation that the proper role for us German women is to marry, tend the home, care for our husbands, and bear their children."

Vati had finally had enough. "*Daughter!*" he exploded. "You can quote the Führer all you wish, but in this matter, you're speaking from ignorance. The medical profession is a noble one with many notable examples of female contributions. *No one*—especially you—should disparage a capable woman's involvement in it. And in any case, the Führer certainly has not forbidden it."

Elke's face turned to stone. "Fine. Then, like the rest of my family, I'll eagerly await the great medical contributions my 'capable' sister will bring to support the Third Reich's advancement. Congratulations, Klara."

The biting exchange embarrassed everyone, and little was spoken for the rest of the meal. For Klara, it seemed but a confirmation of what she'd been suspecting for some time now. Elke's sisterly protection and support were things of the past; addiction to the Führer and Nazism had taken over her mind and heart.

Klara was relieved when the door chimes rang.

"Is he here already?" Mama fretted. "I need to clear the dishes!"

"He's a little early," Vati acknowledged. "But leave the dishes for now, dear, and let's all go greet him."

When Vati opened the door and stepped aside for his guest to enter, Klara caught her breath. She immediately recognized the sleekly handsome, tall, blond, and well-built man who looked to be in his mid-twenties. He'd been in the paper recently after being named the technical director for the German Army's new rocket development center at Peenemünde on the Baltic coast.

Vati draped his arm over the man's shoulder, grinning at his awe-struck audience.

"Dr. Wernher von Braun, allow me to introduce you to my family."

Klara fidgeted as von Braun shook hands with Mama, Elke, and Walther in turn, greeting each with a gracious smile and kind words of acknowledgement.

Reaching Klara, von Braun accepted her extended hand and held it in both of his, bowing slightly. "Fräulein Klara, it is my honor and pleasure. I've heard much from your proud father about your decision to enter medical school, and how well you are doing there. My congratulations, as I know how vital your services as a nurse will be to the future health and well-being of the German people."

Klara felt like melting on the spot from the tender touch and praise of such a highly respected and good-looking gentleman. "Th-thank you, sir, that is so kind of you to say," was all she could manage.

Glancing over his shoulder, Klara noticed her sister standing at attention with her hands folded behind her back.

Elke's eyes seemed to flash daggers as she glared at them.

Chapter 6

Berlin, Germany
October 27, 1938

After some light conversation with the family, Erich escorted von Braun to his private study for the main purpose of the visit. Before delving into the technical discussions that would certainly consume the next couple of hours, Erich poured his guest and himself small glasses of sweet Jägermeister and launched into an anecdote from more carefree times.

"I still remember hearing from your father about your famous first experiment with rocket propulsion, Wernher!" Erich laughed, raising his glass in a mock toast.

Von Braun rolled his eyes and groaned. "I doubt I'll ever live down the story of *that* fiasco."

"Yes, hmmm… let me see," Erich teased. "As I recall, it involved your deciding at the 'mature' age of twelve to lash six skyrockets to the rear of your coaster wagon, light the fuse, and then hop on for a wild ride down our elegant Tiergarten Strasse."

Wernher grimaced. "Father was none too pleased to have to pick me up at the police station afterward. Fortunately, he paid the fines, but I never heard the end of it when I got home. My enthusiasm for rocket experiments took quite a nosedive for a while."

"Yes, but who would have thought," Erich mused. "It was only three years later that you read that scientific article about an imaginary trip to the Moon, and it set that brilliant mind of yours on fire."

Wernher smiled and nodded. "I must admit, it certainly filled me with a romantic urge. Interplanetary travel! Now *that* was a task worth devoting my life to. Not to just stare through a telescope at the Moon and the planets, but to actually soar through the heavens and explore the universe."

Erich set his glass down and gestured toward his large desk, where he'd neatly laid out over twenty diagrams and data sheets. "Well, if you have hopes of making it to the Moon or planets in this lifetime, we should probably get started reviewing my post-flight analysis."

For the next hour, Erich led von Braun through a step-by-step review of flight data recordings and engineering assessments. They were all from last week's launch of the preliminary version of a new, 19-feet-long, 2.5-feet-wide liquid-fueled research missile—the "A5." The rocket had passed its test with no major anomalies, making it into the lower levels of the stratosphere.

The success had come as a huge relief for the Army's top brass. After four straight failures with the earlier "A3" rocket design, they had become extremely nervous. Perhaps, some were complaining, all that precious funding devoted to the support of von Braun's research would be better spent improving the Army's traditional artillery systems.

At the end of Erich's presentation, von Braun nodded and looked appreciatively at his former thesis advisor. "So, it appears your hunch was correct, Professor. As you suggested at the time, last year's failures were *not* the fault of the gyroscopes. The reason those A3 missiles tilted and went off course was due to the unexpected strength of those Baltic sea winds blowing in on our test-launch site. The control gear simply didn't have enough power to move the steel rudder vanes fast enough to correct the trajectory. I'm so glad we listened to you."

Erich nodded, folded his arms, and smiled coyly. "Even when I told you we'd need a *tenfold* increase in control actuator power to handle the winds, meaning that a major redesign would be required?"

Wernher closed his eyes and shook his head. "I must admit, I had some doubts whether the changes you suggested would work, and how much it would cost. Not to mention the schedule delay. But given the pressure we were under from our bosses to produce a bigger and faster missile, I'm so glad we went ahead with the changes. Especially with the fantastic results we achieved last week. Still, let's remember that was only a *prototype*. We're going to have to move very fast. The first test launch for an operational version is scheduled less than a year from now. And that test absolutely *must* succeed if we have any hope of convincing the Führer to keep the funding for the missile weapons program rolling our way."

At Erich's suggestion, the men moved away from the desk and settled themselves into the two plush-cushion guest chairs. After lighting up a cigarette, Wernher propped his elbow on the armrest and blew out a long puff of smoke.

"Professor Neumann, I have a proposal for you."

Erich arched an eyebrow. "What's that?"

Wernher peered at him intently. "I would love to have access to your tremendous wisdom and experience more regularly. How would you like to become an official member of my rocket weapons development team and join us at our Peenemünde test facility as an on-site technical consultant?"

"A *consultant*? For the A5 program?" Erich asked, his eyes nearly popping out of his head.

Wernher grinned. "Not only for the A5, but for the next bigger and better missile design. Hopefully, that one will have a chance of going into production for the Wehrmacht as a viable, fearsome, long-range weapon of war—should things ever come to that. And who knows? One day, maybe we'll all be able to direct our research and test results toward achieving what I and most of my team have always been striving for in our hearts—the peaceful use of rockets for interplanetary space exploration and travel!"

Erich's legs trembled with childlike excitement. This was the last thing he'd expected at this stage of his career; almost all von Braun's famous, high-powered team comprised young, ambitious experiment-ers in their early to mid-twenties. Thirties at most. Forty-four-year-old Erich with his staid professorial background and style would probably stand out like an ancient relic cast into a pond filled with modern technological wonders. Still, the idea of leaving behind the academic life—even if temporarily—to enter the unpredictable world of full-scale rocket development and testing was a dream come true. Not to mention the great honor of being personally invited by Wernher von Braun himself.

After a half hour of further discussion over the specific nature of the assignment and what it would mean for Erich's home life, his compensation, and future connections with the university, von Braun broached the inevitable question. "Well, Professor, what's the verdict?"

Erich bit his lip and looked at his lap for several seconds. When he raised his head, a huge smile lit up his face. "Assuming I can get Gertrude to agree to the move and to leaving our children in charge of the house here, you can count me in."

"Excellent!" Von Braun leaped to his feet and rushed over to shake Erich's hand. "I can't say how pleased I am to be working with you directly again, Professor."

Erich laughed. "I think this calls for another round of Jägermeister." He refilled both their glasses, and the two men toasted before returning to their chairs.

"By the way, Professor," said von Braun, "I can't leave here tonight without complimenting you on your beautiful family. I only hope to someday be blessed with a wife and children who display such genuine warmth and intelligence. They must make you very proud."

"Oh, *that* they certainly do. Though I must admit, these past few years have put quite a strain on all of us. Especially the children as they try to find their own places in our new Germany."

"Do you believe they're succeeding?" Wernher asked cautiously.

"Good question." Erich stared at his shot glass for several moments. "I suppose I'd say they definitely *are* succeeding, each according to their own idea of success."

Wernher tilted his head. "How do they differ, if I may ask?" He seemed genuinely interested.

Erich placed his glass on the side table, lit a cigarette, and settled back in his chair.

"Walther, my eldest, is the most traditional of the three. He comes from a long line on my side of mercantile traders and businessmen. His accounting job suits him perfectly for a stable future along that line. Although, ever since Hitler annexed Austria to Germany last March, my son has seemed a bit restless about his passive civilian role in the advancement of patriotic national goals. If a major war were to ever break out, I have no doubt he'd immediately quit his job and follow the example of his best friend Heinz—who's now Elke's steady boyfriend—and try to get more excitement in his life by joining the Wehrmacht. Or even the SS, as Heinz did last year.

"Elke, on the other hand, takes after her great-grandfather on my wife's side. He was one of Bismarck's generals in the Franco-Prussian war. Bold, headstrong, driven by visions of a perfect, regimented world led by a powerful, inspiring authoritarian. Elke's the quintessential BDM trainer with her magazine-quality Aryan looks and her accumulation of sporting awards and merit badges, not to mention her absolute dedication to the Führer's persona. Success for her is seeing every German girl under her wing become an outstanding model of National Socialist thought and behavior. *Including* her younger sister, Klara."

Von Braun raised his eyebrow. "Is there any question along *that* line? I must say I did detect a certain amount of tension between the two of them downstairs."

Erich smiled and nodded. "An astute observation on your part. Indeed, Klara's personal measure of success is far more tied to helping people in distress, even including some of her former Jewish classmates. This is much to the chagrin of her sister, who finds such sympathies to be entirely misplaced. Ever since Klara turned down the offer to follow in Elke's footsteps as a BDM trainer, the two have been constantly bickering over such things . . ."

He paused to flick an ash off his pant leg. "Occasionally, we'll observe one of them displaying flashes of tender concern for the other when they're upset over something. My wife and I just pray those deeper feelings will be enough to keep them from tearing out each other's throats over some disagreement about the Führer's desires and intentions. To be honest, though, we both think the surer solution would be to see them married off to strong, reliable partners to whom they can vent their frustrations. Assuming such can be found these days."

Wernher eyed him. "With the beauty and intelligence of them both, that should not be a long-term problem, should it?"

Erich shrugged. "We're expecting Heinz to propose to Elke any day now, and that should be an excellent match. Well, so long as Elke doesn't ruin things by insisting on National Socialist perfection in every tiny little thing he says and does. In Klara's case, we've yet to see her express interest in pursuing any serious relationship, though there've been quite a few requests and aborted attempts by suitors the past few years."

"It sounds like she's waiting for the right man to come along," Wernher suggested.

A sly grin spread across Erich's face. "Someone right like... perhaps... yourself, Wernher? I must say, she seemed quite enthralled by your presence and conversation tonight. Not that I would object on any grounds, mind you."

Wernher blushed and chuckled awkwardly. "Oh, Professor Neumann, you are most kind and trusting. And were it not for the incessant demands on my time and attention and a constant obsession with my beautiful, flaming rockets, I assure you I would be first in line to court your gorgeous daughter, Klara. But, for her sake as well as my own, it would not be right for me to stir the pot in that regard."

He paused for a moment. "That said, assuming you and your family are still planning on attending that ball at the American Embassy next week, there *is* someone who I think Klara might find very appealing.

A young man for whom I have great regard. I would love to introduce them."

Erich grinned and stroked his chin. "Now that sounds promising, though I dare not hint anything of it to Klara beforehand. She would balk at any attempt at matchmaking if she knew her father had anything to do with it."

The men had one more round of celebratory drinks and discussed plans for Erich to visit the rocket test-center at Peenemünde with Gertrude the second week of November to settle on their base housing arrangements. Satisfied with the agreement, Erich escorted Wernher to the front door and bid him goodnight.

What a productive evening, Erich thought. His A3 test flight analysis had not only been useful, but it had been commended by the nation's most revered rocket scientist. He'd been offered the job of his dreams. And who knew? By opening up to Wernher about his family, perhaps he'd sown a seed that could lead to his younger daughter finally meeting someone who could ensure her future marital happiness.

⦿

(Two nights later)

Less than fifteen minutes after entering the US Embassy ballroom with her parents, Klara desperately wished she'd obeyed her instincts to tell Vati she was coming down with a cold like her brother. That way she could have stayed at home with him, avoiding forced conversations with people she didn't know or care about. Besides, her interview with Professor Gottschald for the RA position was scheduled for tomorrow, and she'd much rather be spending a quiet evening at home preparing for it.

As it was, it didn't appear that anyone here tonight would have missed her presence.

Chewing her lip as she stood next to her father at the periphery of the dance floor, Klara directed her attention to the front stage. There, SS Lt. Colonel Gerhard Bremmer—Superintendent for the Berlin District of the National Criminal Investigative Police ("Kripo")[*]—had just been presented a certificate of appreciation from the US ambassador and was stepping up to the microphone.

It had been over four years since Bremmer's timely intervention in helping thwart the SA thugs' attack on Jakob Friedmann in Tiergarten Park. Shortly after that, according to Vati, Bremmer was promoted to his current role as the SS overseer of the Berlin Kripo. Ever since, his reputation had grown steadily in the eyes of the national SS hierarchy as they became increasingly impressed with Bremmer's ability to ruthlessly hunt, arrest, and extract confessions from those accused of serious crimes in Germany's capital city. And as Bremmer's notoriety and rank rose, so had the paramilitary career of Elke's boyfriend, Heinz Schröder.

After receiving Heinz's application three years ago and recalling his impressive actions in the Tiergarten incident, Bremmer had recruited him to the SS. Since then, he'd become something of an unofficial mentor and sponsor for Heinz. He'd checked frequently on his progress and offered some sage advice that had led Heinz to choose one of the newly formed, combat-focused *Waffen-SS* regiments for his future career path. In fact, Bremmer had been so delighted with the reports of Heinz's performance in basic combat training that he'd recommended and secured his protégé's promotion and acceptance into one of the elite national SS officer training schools. The two had become quite close, and Heinz and Elke frequently met with him for dinner and other social functions.

As Bremmer started to speak, Klara glanced across the dance floor where she spotted Elke standing close to Heinz, holding his arm affectionately with both hands.

Who wouldn't be proud of him? Klara asked herself with undeniable envy.

---

[*] The Kripo (criminal police) were responsible for investigating, arresting, and interrogating people accused of serious physical or moral crimes (rape, murder, arson, etc.). They often worked hand in hand with the Gestapo (secret state police), who were responsible for rounding up and interrogating Nazi political opponents and Jews.

"Herr Ambassador, Mayor Lippert, ladies and gentlemen," Bremmer began, addressing the mixed-nationality audience in German. "It is a great honor for our Berlin District Kripo office to be acknowledged by the US Embassy for our efforts to keep the streets, offices, and homes of our beloved city safe—not only for German citizens but also foreign diplomats and visitors. Indeed, I personally consider this recognition as a clear sign that, despite recent tensions, German-American diplomatic relations continue to thrive based on our mutual respect and commitment to maintaining a safe and peaceful world order."

Bremmer went on to laud the many shared values of Germans and Americans—including the desire for a bold national vision and a healthy, enlightened population eager to see its fulfilment.

"In conclusion," Bremmer pronounced, his arms outstretched in a grandiose fashion, "I would once again like to thank Ambassador Wilson and his staff for this wonderful ceremony. It is truly a celebration of our German-American friendship and our hopes for mutual cooperation and good relations in the future."

Klara spread her hands, anticipating the end of the speech and preparing to offer her applause along with the others. Unfortunately, Bremmer was not quite yet finished.

"And in that spirit of celebration," he went on. "I beg you to allow me, Herr Ambassador, to end my remarks tonight by publicly recognizing the formal engagement of an extraordinary young couple in our audience. Two people who, I believe, reflect the very best of what the German Third Reich has to offer to help ensure that we *all* will enjoy a secure, peaceful, and prosperous world in our future."

Bremmer didn't wait for the ambassador's permission to press on. "Lieutenant Heinz Schröder and your new fiancée, Fräulein Elke Neumann, would you both please step up here and accept our warm congratulations?"

What? Are Elke and Heinz officially engaged, and we're just now learning about it—along with the rest of the public—at a diplomatic ball? Klara stared open-mouthed at her father, who simply shrugged his shoulders, smiled gamely, and joined in the applause as Heinz and

Elke approached the stage arm in arm. Mama, both hands covering her mouth and her shoulders trembling, appeared to be weeping with joy.

Something is not right about this, Klara thought as she observed the strange scene of Bremmer standing between Elke and Heinz with his arms draped over their shoulders. As if he were the proud father of both. She bit her lip and joined the applause, trying her best not to reveal her annoyance. *Elke should have told her own family first. And if anyone, Vati should be the one to publicly announce the engagement of his eldest daughter.*

Klara listened with a growing sense of frustration and annoyance as Bremmer rambled on for several more minutes, first commending Heinz's choice of an SS career over more comfortable alternatives, then heaping praises over Elke's credentials as the Jungmädel's first national poster girl who became a BDM training leader. Heinz and Elke, Bremmer suggested, were shining examples of what youth in Germany, America, and everywhere should aspire to in their marriages and patriotic commitments.

Bremmer urged everyone to grab a champagne glass from the sidebars and join him in raising a toast to the happy couple. He then turned the microphone back over to Ambassador Wilson. The ambassador, his grim face clearly reflecting discomfort over Bremmer's audacious performance, thanked everyone before requesting that the orchestra begin its formal dance program. Erich grasped Klara's and Gertrude's arms and suggested they all go forward to congratulate Heinz and Elke. Klara, however, had endured quite enough.

"Vati, I'm not feeling too well. Please go ahead. I'll speak with Elke and Heinz before we leave tonight."

Erich flashed her a concerned look. "Klara, is everything all right?"

"Yes, Vati. I think I just need to step outside for a bit of fresh air."

After her father gave her a brief hug, Klara strolled across the rapidly filling dance floor toward the ladies' powder room. Her stomach was queasy, and her head spun with strange, disconcerting thoughts about Elke, Heinz, and their clearly blossoming friendship with SS Lt. Colonel Gerhardt Bremmer. Somehow, it all seemed just a bit... inappropriate.

Klara eventually made her way onto the rear balcony of the embassy dance floor where she stood alone, gazing over the balustrade at the darkening sky above the trees of Tiergarten Park. She'd managed to put aside—at least for the time being—her pique over Elke's apparent snub of the family, and her mind now shifted to churning over questions she thought Professor Gottschald might pose at tomorrow's interview.

A gentle hand touched her shoulder from behind. She whirled and gasped at the sight of Wernher von Braun.

"Dr. von Braun! What a pleasant surprise. I had no idea you were attending this evening."

He smiled warmly. "Fräulein Klara, forgive me. I spotted you and your parents earlier and was about to come greet you, but I got pulled into a conversation and was unable to extricate myself. At any rate, I'm so glad I'm catching you alone here, because there's someone I'd very much like to introduce you to. He's an American acquaintance of mine. And based on our conversation the other night, I think you'll find you share some common interests."

Klara, caught off guard by the abruptness of Wernher's suggestion, nervously reached up and touched the side of her hair to ensure it was still in place. "Oh, my. I hope I won't prove to be a disappointment. My English is quite limited."

Wernher laughed. "I am absolutely certain you needn't have any fear on *that* score." He turned and waved to someone who'd been conversing with a small group of people near the entrance doors to the balcony. The man waved back and made his way over to join Klara and Wernher.

The moment she first laid eyes on the gentleman approaching her, Klara confirmed beyond doubt that what she'd heard about those Hollywood romance movies was true. In terms of good looks, American men lacked nothing in comparison to the most attractive of their German counterparts—including even the debonair Dr. Wernher von Braun.

"Fräulein Klara Neumann, it's my honor to introduce you to Herr Joshua Peters. He's the son of the US Embassy's Deputy Chief of Missions, and a devoted American fan of rocket science. I can vouch for his credentials, since Joshua and I had the pleasure of dreaming together about space travel over countless cups of coffee after my recent guest lecture at the university."

"It is indeed a pleasure, Klara."

Klara's heart raced as Joshua bowed slightly and offered his hand, which was warm and smooth to the touch. Seemingly in his early twenties with wavy jet-black hair, hazel eyes, angular jawline, and tall, athletic physique enhanced by his midnight tuxedo, Joshua Peters was undoubtedly the best-looking man that Klara had ever met.

She self-consciously averted her eyes from his steady gaze so as not to reveal her instant attraction. "It's my pleasure as well, Herr Peters." She was still a bit uncertain as to why Wernher would be introducing him first to *her* and not to her father. After all, Joshua would likely have more in common with Vati given his rocketry interests.

Joshua seemed to recognize her confusion and hurried to explain. "When Dr. von Braun told me yesterday about your father's acceptance of the consulting position, he also spoke about meeting your wonderful family. He mentioned how impressed he was by your decision to pursue medical studies. Since I've considered becoming a psychiatrist someday myself, I was curious what might have led to your choice of the psychiatric nursing path. Wernher knew you'd be here tonight with your family, and he promised to introduce us so that I'd have a chance to hear your thinking on this—assuming you'd be willing to share."

Klara's eyes widened. Joshua's German was nearly flawless, with very little accent. And his apparent reason for wanting to meet her... well...

Am I imagining this?

"Herr Peters, I'd be delighted to talk with you about my career interests if you think it would help. But only if you promise to tell me about yours as well. I—"

Just then, someone hailed von Braun from the exit door. "Dr. von Braun, the ambassador would like to speak with you as soon as possible, if you're available."

Wernher grinned at Klara and Joshua. "Well, looks like I'll need to leave you two to get to know each other. But it sounds as if that will not be an issue. I'll look forward to rejoining you both before the night's over and they send us all home."

As Wernher walked inside, Joshua turned to Klara and grinned. "So… where should we start, Fräulein Neumann?"

Klara smiled back, surprised at the level of comfort she already felt in the presence of this intriguing young man. "Wherever you'd like, Herr Peters."

CHAPTER 7

Berlin, Germany
November 9, 1938
(One Week Later)

The Black Forest wall clock downstairs chimed six times, prompting Klara to throw her covers aside and bound out of bed. It had been a sleepless night of tossing and turning with anticipation. Today would be the first day at her new RA job, and later this evening she would enjoy her first official date with Joshua Peters.

As she washed and dressed, Klara's mind raced between pleasant memories of her all-too-brief time with Joshua at last week's diplomatic ball and her highly successful interview with Professor Gottschald the next morning...

The initial conversation on the embassy balcony with the twenty-one-year-old son of the deputy ambassador felt natural as each shared their backgrounds, motivations, and hopes for a career in medicine. He'd invited her inside to dance a waltz with him, and she'd eagerly agreed after making him promise to forgive her if she stepped on his toes. He'd proven to be an adept partner, leading her gently but confidently around the dance floor while occasionally offering an amusing remark to help her relax. Clearly, Joshua Peters was experienced in this role.

After the dance, Klara introduced Joshua to her parents, Elke, Heinz, and Lt. Colonel Bremmer. Joshua's connection with her father had been immediate when he mentioned his long-time fascination with rocketry and his admiration for Dr. von Braun and the German scientific community. Their animated discussion would no doubt have continued had Joshua not been interrupted by a junior embassy official. He was delivering an urgent message from the deputy ambassador requesting his son's presence. Taking Klara aside before leaving, Joshua expressed how much he'd enjoyed her company and asked if—with her parents' permission, of course—he could escort her to dinner at one of Berlin's finest restaurants. She'd accepted, and they'd set the date for the following week.

And if *that* had not been enough to celebrate, surely the next day's cordial interview with Professor Gottschald had topped things off. Gottschald had lauded Klara and her sister's pristine records with the BDM, her brother's and mother's support of National Socialist causes, and her father's sterling university reputation and Party membership. These were all strong confirmations, he'd declared, of Klara and her family's loyalty to the Führer and the Reich. As far as academic credentials, she'd already demonstrated through her superior course grades that she had all the technical knowledge required for the RA job. When he'd pressed her on her views of people with severe psychiatric disturbances or physical deformities and whether she felt she could emotionally tolerate the unpleasantries she would encounter in the asylums, she easily convinced him that she could.

Klara's excellent record and concise, confident responses to Gottschald's questions had sufficed for the professor to stand up, salute, and welcome her to his RA team. Her first assignment would be to visit the Wittenau Sanitorium eleven kilometers northwest of Berlin. She would meet and interview the asylum director there, observe some of the patients, talk with the staff, and take notes on her impressions. She and Gottschald would review those together a couple of days later.

In parting, although the professor had held their handshake a bit too long and gazed into her eyes a bit too fondly for Klara's comfort, she was of no mind to fret or complain. After all, without her even requesting it, Professor Gottschald had assigned her to visit the one asylum in the Berlin area that she was most interested in: the asylum where, she knew, Leah Friedmann was incarcerated.

Klara applied the finishing touches of makeup to her cheeks and eyes, then headed downstairs.

With her parents away on their search for base housing at the Peenemünde rocket center on the Baltic coast, she had thought she would simply slip into the kitchen this morning, enjoy her coffee in peace, then head off via taxi to Wittenau for her first day on the RA job. Walther would already have left for work, and Elke—home late after an evening out with Heinz—had the day off from her BDM duties and was presumably still sleeping.

As the light on in the kitchen indicated, however, a quick exit was not to be. When Klara entered, Elke looked up from her seat at the breakfast table and peered over the top of her favorite Nazi-sponsored newspaper: the *People's Observer*.

"I couldn't sleep," she muttered. "My mind kept swirling with thoughts about my wedding and where in the city Heinz and I should live." She returned her gaze to the paper. "Anyway, I left you some hot coffee in the pot."

"Thanks." Klara filled a small cup and sat down, hoping Elke would not commandeer the conversation this morning, as was often her habit. "So, what's new in the world?"

Elke grimaced. "Looks like some Jews across Germany could be in for a couple of rough days."

"How's that?"

"Well, do you remember we heard yesterday about that Jewish teenager who attempted to assassinate our German envoy in Paris? Shot him in cold blood in broad daylight at the embassy."

"Oh yes. I recall it had something to with the boy being angry over his parents and thousands of other Polish-German Jews being driven from their homes in Germany two weeks ago. Stripped of their belongings in the middle of the night and deported to the Polish border. And when the Polish government wouldn't accept them, they were supposedly just left there without any shelter or food." She grimaced. "What despicable treatment. I can certainly understand the boy being very upset, though he obviously didn't handle it the right way. And so?"

"And so," Elke continued, "it says here that many high-ranking Party officials are fed up with this kind of treachery and—especially if the envoy dies—they're urging the Führer to hold the entire Jewish population accountable and approve strong reprisals against them and their business and property interests across the nation."

A tightness spread inside Klara's throat as she thought about the Friedmann family. After all they'd been through with Herr Friedmann's job loss, Jakob's and Sophie's expulsions from public school, and Leah's sterilization and commitment to the asylum, the last thing they needed were more prospects of persecution.

"I suppose we'll know within the next day or two if anything's going to happen?"

"Yes, and it'll serve them right, if you ask me," Elke grumbled. She lowered the newspaper and flashed a tight smile. "So, today's the big day, is it not? The medical research career of our beloved Nurse Klara Neumann is to be launched and celebrated this evening over dinner with an incredibly handsome young man from the American embassy. Does life get any better than that?"

Klara laughed, glad the conversation had switched to lighter fare. "I'll let you know tomorrow after I've had a chance to reflect on it all. But I admit it's all very exciting, and a bit nerve-racking."

Elke nodded. "I can understand that. Especially having to deal directly with those asylum patients. I still can't get out of my mind that time when our BDM group toured one of the institutions. Most of the inmates could barely function at the level of animals and must have been suffering terribly." She gave Klara a strange look. "It's a wonder that our 'kind and caring, almighty God'—assuming he really is all of that—would allow poor creatures like those to even continue existing, don't you think? Why he wouldn't just decide to put them out of their misery and take them to Heaven immediately is beyond me."

Klara took a long sip of coffee, trying to hide her disgust over her sister's absurd suggestion, which Klara knew was intended only to bait her. Elke had forsaken the family's traditional Lutheran beliefs some time ago. Instead, she'd chosen to embrace the Nazi Party's concept of "Positive Christianity"—in which the enlightened Führer, not the "weak" Christ of ages past, was now seen as the herald of the new revelation to come.

"Somehow, I think the situation for many asylum patients is more hopeful than *that*, sister. There are a lot of new therapies that are helping, with more on the way. That's why I'm so committed to pursuing psychiatric nursing. I don't think God wants us to simply give up all hope and relegate disabled patients to the junk pile. Even the supposedly incurable ones that some people these days like to call 'useless eaters.'"

"Well." Elke shrugged. "All I can say is that your patients will certainly be lucky to have someone like *you* on their side, and I wish you well. I'm just not sure how many other Germans share your optimism and would be willing to pay the extra taxes for incurable, deformed people to eke out a degraded existence for *decades*."

Klara bit her tongue, knowing she didn't have time to vent her building fury. "I know I'm only one person, Elke, but I promise I'll do my best to help change those impressions," she said finally, as patiently as she could. She placed her empty cup in the saucer and rose from the table. "Thanks for the coffee. I suppose I won't see you until morning, since you'll no doubt be in bed by the time Joshua and I get home. I'll tell you all about my wonderful day then." As soon as she'd started walking away, Elke's commanding voice stopped her in her tracks.

"Klara, you need to be home no later than midnight."

Klara whirled to face her sister. Her face was scarlet. "*Excuse me?* Elke, you are *not* Mama or Vati! I'm eighteen, you're only two years older, and you're not my BDM section leader anymore. Who are *you* to be setting my curfew?"

Elke stood stone-faced with arms folded. "Klara, with Walther in and out so much, you know good and well Vati charged *me* with looking out for the house and you while they're gone. And just like he did with me and Heinz, Vati insisted you be back by midnight at the latest."

"It just seems so childish and ridiculous," Klara muttered as she yanked her topcoat off the post and shoved her arms into the sleeves.

"I hated it too, but you know they care about us, and our safety, and reputations. And... Klara... I . . ." Elke hesitated, gazing at the floor.

"What now?" Klara asked, her hand already on the doorknob.

"I just hope you *will* be careful with that man tonight. He is, after all—"

Klara finished her sentence. "An American?"

Elke nodded. "Not only that, but the son of the US deputy ambassador."

"What's wrong with that? Doesn't Germany have good relations with America? Don't we share many cultural values? Colonel Bremmer said as much in his speech. Why are you so worried about me going out on one date with Herr Peters?"

Elke frowned. "Don't be naïve, Klara. There's no country today that doesn't look upon Germany with envy. They see our progress under the Führer—and they either crave it for themselves or worry that we'll soon be powerful enough to impose our superior way on *them*. Should we choose to, of course. There's no country that wouldn't love to get their hands on Germany's scientific secrets or the weapons we're developing."

"So, what are you saying? That Joshua's an American spy who will try to use me to get to Vati and all his rocketry knowledge, or something like that? Elke, that is preposterous!"

"Not as 'preposterous' as you might think. Don't you remember hearing in BDM how America's well-known for its rich, spoon-fed playboys who love to prey on innocent girls for sex, money, or whatever else they can get out of them? I admit Herr Peters seems like a very nice gentleman, and I can't say he's deliberately out to exploit you. But a family of influence such as ours has to be very careful these days."

Klara rolled her eyes. "I promise I'll keep my dress buttoned, my purse zipped, and I won't be enticed into revealing any state secrets on my first date with him, Elke."

Her sister seemed completely unfazed by the obvious sarcasm. "And you'll be back by midnight, correct?"

Klara wanted to scream something nasty but held herself in check.

"I'll be back when I get back," she said in as mild a tone as she could muster. She stepped from the house but had taken only a few paces down the front walkway when the door opened behind her.

Elke's voice sounded oddly wistful. "You might not believe this, Klara Neumann, but you *are* my sister, and I do love you and care about you."

Klara drew up short. The memory of Elke at Nuremberg—the protective mother tigress—flashed in her mind. Why should she doubt that her Führer-obsessed sister meant what she'd said?

She sighed, turned, and waved goodbye.

"I'll see you this afternoon. Before my date with Joshua. And I promise we'll be back by midnight."

CHAPTER 8

Wittenau Sanatorium, Northwest of Berlin
November 9, 1938

Clutching a clipboard under her left arm, Klara stood nervously behind the middle-aged assistant nurse, waiting for an orderly to slide the bolt open on the other side of the steel door. Her pulse raced, knowing she was about to enter the male wing of the mental patients' ward for severe cases.

"He's taking forever," the nurse groused. "They're probably having to sedate someone." She knocked once again, still getting no response. Noticing Klara's raised eyebrows, she smiled grimly and shook her head. "Happens all the time in *this* ward! My apologies. We might have to wait a couple of more minutes."

Klara touched her arm. "It's no problem at all, Nurse Henckel. I'm just grateful to have *you* with me on my first tour of the facility. That was so kind of Direktor Bergmann to have you accompany me, especially when I know you have other duties to attend."

Nurse Henckel looked at her appraisingly, as if trying to decide how long Klara would last before begging for the tour to end. "Dr. Bergmann is a good man, and I'm glad to work under him . . ." She hesitated and lowered her eyes. "I just wish more of our younger staff were like him," she said softly.

"How's that?" Klara asked cautiously.

"Dr. Bergmann is of the old school. He really believes that measurable improvement is possible even for some of our chronic patients, in terms of their self-control and ability to contribute to society. Too many of our recent hires seem resigned to viewing and treating them as if—"

Before she could finish her sentence, the bolt clanged and the door was jerked partially open by a short, thin man in a light gray, collarless tunic and matching trousers. His ferret-like face wore an exasperated expression.

"What is it, Nurse? The doctor and ward nurse are busy with one of the insulin-therapy patients. They just came out of a treatment and are having some difficulties."

"I promise we won't disturb them, Herr Geld. Behind me here is Fräulein Klara Neumann. She's the new research assistant for Professor Gottschald at the university. Dr. Bergmann has directed me to escort her on a brief tour of our facilities so she can become familiar with our patients and procedures."

The orderly cocked his head, one side of his mouth curling with a sardonic smile. "Oh, of course. Here to take notes and acquire some ideas for new *miracle* cures." He cast an annoyed glance over his shoulder when a short, piercing shriek escaped the room behind him. "All right," he said finally, opening the door wider. "But please make it quick, and forgive me if I'm unable to accompany you. There's only the ward nurse, one assistant nurse, and four orderlies including me on duty today. And with over eighty urine, blood, and excrement-soiled bed coverings to strip and replace, I've got my hands full."

"I quite understand, Herr Geld," Nurse Henckel said. "We'll leave you to tend to the patients, and we'll be out of your hair in just a few minutes." She turned to Klara. "Brace yourself . . ."

Klara had thought herself well-prepared after all the films and psychiatric articles that she'd read. But upon entering the ward's large, whitewashed dayroom, the stark reality hit her like a sledgehammer.

An overpowering stench of urine hit her nostrils first, followed closely by the sting of bleach. At least thirty patients sat in wooden chairs that were anchored in various places near the walls, either alone or together in small clusters. Another fifteen or so stood against the wall or milled about the room, staring blankly with open mouths off into space.

Following Nurse Henckel closely on a slow, circuitous walk around the room, Klara struggled to record brief impressions on her clipboard as she observed the demented looks and random outbursts of shrill cries, screams, and mad laughter from many of the patients.

Nurse Henckel stepped back and whispered in Klara's ear. "A high proportion here are schizophrenics and epileptics."

As if to validate her comment, a man in one of the corners began to jerk and convulse as he lay on the floor, frothing at the mouth. Several patients around him screeched and jumped up and down, drawing the attention of two burly orderlies who rushed over to the scene.

"Shut up and get out of the way, you loony idiot!" one of the orderlies shouted at a patient who wouldn't stop trying to obstruct an assistant nurse from administering medication to the man on the floor. The interfering patient would not let go. With a curse, the orderly drew back his fist and crashed it square into the patient's face, driving him against the wall. He collapsed on the floor in a whimpering heap, his mouth bleeding. As the shrieks and crazed leaping of the other patients continued, the orderlies picked up the still-convulsing epileptic by his hands and feet and carried him to another room.

Klara stood as if paralyzed. She could hardly breathe, horrified as she was to observe such a ghastly scene. Thankfully, Nurse Henckel grasped her arm and led her through the audience of half-aware, vacantly staring patients.

"Is it *always* this disruptive?" Klara asked, trying to make some sense of the madness swirling all around her.

Nurse Henckel sighed. "I'm afraid these are the inevitable consequences of recent trends in our National Socialist policies. The need to build up our military and conserve monetary resources has forced many asylums to consolidate and conform more with Nazi philosophy.

"That means far more patients and less staffing in places like this. It's also meant a change in new-hire qualifications. New nurses and orderlies with no prior medical training or experience are often pulled from the pools of unemployed SA, Hitler Youth, or BDM members. Basically, we're hiring people with little empathy or patience for the suffering of others. Like those two manhandlers we watched back there."

She glanced warily at Klara. "Of course, I understand how difficult it must be for the Führer and the Party to decide on the proper course in such matters. And I'm sure the Führer understands and is saddened by the sufferings that weaker members of our society must inevitably bear in order to ensure the survival of the stronger ones."

Classic Darwinist thinking, Klara recognized. *The opposite of what Christ taught about leaving the flock behind to go in search of the single lost lamb.* She'd read portions of Hitler's *Mein Kampf* in BDM, and she had serious doubts about how saddened the Führer truly felt over the sufferings of asylum inmates like these. She started to voice her reservation but thought better of it and bit her lip.

The second stop on the tour of the basement floor was the therapy ward. Inside, over a dozen patients lay encased from neck to toe in warm water hydrotherapy pods meant to keep them calm. Behind a closed door in the Insulin and Electro-Convulsive Treatments Area, the doctor on duty was busy administering a third round of insulin to one of the more promising patients.

"We've had some great successes with this new insulin treatment," Nurse Henckel said. "You'll see some of the results once we get upstairs."

Indeed, stepping into the second-floor recovery dayroom for females, Klara was immediately heartened by the stark difference in patient demeanor and activity. The women sitting and conversing together in small groups or working together or alone at worktables on a variety of projects made a totally normal impression.

Walking with Klara through the room, Nurse Henckel halted and gestured to a girl who was sitting at the end of a small table with her back turned. "Look! That's Leah, one of the patients I was telling you about downstairs."

Klara caught her breath, trying hard to stop herself from simply rushing over and embracing the young teenager. In order not to raise suspicions about her personal connections with the Friedmann family, she had to make this appear like a chance encounter. "Oh, she seems so sweet."

"Yes, she is indeed. I'm so very proud of her. As I told you, she's extremely talented with her hands and is coming along very well with her mood control since the sterilization procedure."

Klara decided it was worth taking a risk. "Would it be all right if I sit and try to talk with her alone for just a bit? I'd like to observe how she responds to me."

Nurse Henckel hesitated and glanced around the room, apparently making sure they weren't being watched. "Well," she said finally, "we're really supposed to avoid fraternization with individual patients without a doctor present. But I don't suppose it will hurt if you keep it very short. Don't expect any real conversation, though. Leah's been deaf since birth, though she can read lips and utter simple phrases."

Approaching the table cautiously as Nurse Henckel watched at a distance, Klara pulled out a chair and sat across from Leah. The frail girl with close-cropped, dark black hair didn't bother to look up. She was obviously too absorbed in her intricate crochet project to notice or care about Klara's presence.

Klara placed both her hands on the table, just in front of the multi-colored shawl that Leah was working on. Suddenly, the girl stopped her work and looked up. Klara felt herself begin to choke up as she stared into her large brown eyes, one of which drooped. It had been at least five years since she'd last seen Leah, and her face had matured quite a bit—reminding Klara of Sophie at that age.

"Hello, Leah. Do you remember me?" Klara asked, hoping the girl would be able to read her lips.

Leah's mouth trembled slightly for a second, but her eyes showed no sign of recognition. After several seconds, she lowered her head and returned to her task.

Klara leaned in a bit farther and rested her hand on Leah's forearm. "Leah, it's me... Klara. Klara Neumann." The girl stared at her vacantly once again, shook her head and yanked her arm away from Klara's hand. She returned to her sewing task with a vengeance, her nimble fingers flashing furiously.

Klara leaned back and closed her eyes. She sensed that even basic communication with Leah could prove to be impossible. How could she break the news to Leah's parents and siblings? She rose from the chair and returned to Nurse Henckel.

"Finished already? How did it go?" the nurse asked kindly.

Klara started to shake her head when a sudden cry arose from behind her.

"*Ka-wa! Ka-wa!*"

Klara turned just in time to see Leah cast her sewing project on the floor, spring from her chair, and run toward Klara. She threw herself into Klara's arms and hugged her around the waist. Her body was trembling all over. Overwhelmed, Klara returned the embrace.

Leah cocked her head and looked into Klara's eyes "M-mummy? Where's M-mum . . .?"

"She'll be here to visit you next week, Liebchen, just like always. I'm—"

"*Nurse!*" screamed a strident female voice from across the room. Within seconds, an angry-looking woman, who from her uniform and badge appeared to be the ward's head nurse, stalked up to Klara and Nurse Henckel. She stared them both up and down as Klara and Leah held tightly to each other.

"Nurse Henckel, who *is* this person? And what does she think she's doing with that girl?"

"Please forgive me, Nurse Winkler. I should have been more watchful. This is Klara Neumann, our new RA student from the university who's been assigned weekly observations visits here. Dr. Bergmann requested me to provide her with a tour of our facilities. She was unaware of our rules, and when I'd turned away briefly to—"

The head nurse did not allow her to complete the alibi. Yanking Leah away, she grabbed her by the scruff of her collar and marched her back to the table. "Now you bend down, pick that thing you're working on off the floor, and sit down and finish it. Don't you want to be seen as making progress?"

Leah stamped her foot and let out a prolonged wail, prompting the head nurse to signal for an orderly who arrived within seconds. "Take her back to her room and tell her no dinner tonight. She must learn not to resist correction." Klara watched in horror as the orderly led Leah away, crying hysterically.

Striding back to Klara and Nurse Henckel, the head nurse stopped abruptly and glared at both.

"Nurse Winkler," Klara volunteered. "Please forgive me. Since I'm new, I was only trying to acclimate Leah to me. I had no idea she would—"

"Welcome to Wittenau, Fräulein Neumann. Hopefully you will learn our rules and procedures here and dutifully execute them in the future. They have been put in place for the good of all our patients. *Including* feebleminded, spoiled little Jewish princesses like the one you were just caressing. Unfortunately, we can't keep instilling people like these with the false notion that we will cater to their special whims and desires forever. The Führer has made that quite clear. Do you understand?"

Cowed to the core, Klara and Nurse Henckel clicked their heels together and saluted. After responding in kind, the head nurse stalked out of the room.

"In case you were wondering, Nurse Winkler was appointed to her position by the local SS health officer despite Dr. Bergmann's objection," Nurse Henckel whispered after the two women had finally collected themselves.

Klara nodded solemnly. It appeared that her assignment to observe things at Wittenau Sanitorium would not permit the easy interactions with Leah Friedmann that she'd originally anticipated.

The kindly, bespectacled Direktor Bergmann—whose white hair and Van Dyke beard made him appear to be in his sixties—seemed genuinely distressed as he peered across his desk at Klara. Most of her post-tour interview with the asylum director this morning had been devoted to a review of her initial impressions of the various wards. When she provided her account of the disturbing incidents and conditions she'd witnessed on the severe case floor, Dr. Bergmann sighed and nodded sadly.

"Unfortunately, in my view, the situation for asylums like ours is becoming quite dire in many respects. With all the cut backs in the quantity and quality of our nursing and orderly staff, reduced food rations, and other things, you have a recipe for a lowered standard of care. Even with the recent improvements in our therapeutic methods."

Klara blanched. *Lowered standard of patient care*? This was news. Had not Professor Gottschald stated to his students that this would likely *never* be something that could occur in Germany's foreseeable future under the glorious Third Reich?

What else might be on the horizon?

"Dr. Bergmann, if I may inquire, is there any mounting support in the medical community for the articles those two Nazi health officials recently wrote for the SS's newspaper? The ones suggesting the *euthanasia* of incurably disabled people— 'mercy killing,' I believe they called it—for the supposed good of both the patients and the Fatherland?"

Bergmann cast her a stony look. "I'm afraid I can't comment one way or the other on that. All I will say is this—I believe it is imperative that we do everything in our power here at Wittenau to help as many patients as possible to avoid being tagged with the 'life unworthy of life' label by our district health officials."

Klara shuddered at the sound of the degrading phrase. "But how do you draw the line for that?"

Bergmann folded his hands on his desk and seemed to study them as he shook his head. "The line seems more blurred every day. It depends on who's making the assessment. But most medical people agree that those patients deemed capable of regularly performing *some* kind of useful occupational work—either manual or intellectual— would seem to have a better chance of avoiding the label."

Klara's heart leaped. "So that would favor patients in the recovery ward who are capable of doing things like sewing or tending to the asylum's vegetable garden?"

"Yes, that would seem to be the case. Although it's unclear if even *that* would be enough to avoid the unworthy of life designation *if* the patient is still seen as having a truly incurable condition that requires the support of the asylum for decades to come."

Klara sat back in her chair, trying to process all the implications of what Dr. Bergmann had just revealed. It was clear that if Leah Friedmann was going to have any chance of getting out of Wittenau and making it back to her family, she would need to be seen by district health professionals as self-reliant and able to perform useful work despite her deafness. Otherwise…

Dr. Bergmann concluded the review session by complimenting Klara profusely on her first day's effort. He said he was looking forward to her future weekly observation visits. The two saluted and parted amicably.

On the taxi ride home, Klara tried unsuccessfully to put aside the disturbing recollections of the morning and her worries over what she should do to help Leah. She knew she needed to come up with some ideas, and the sooner the better. But she was too exhausted to think clearly now.

Fortunately, she could look forward to a long, refreshing nap this afternoon. After that, she'd still have plenty of time to prepare for a far more pleasant prospect: her first official date in the city with Joshua Peters.

CHAPTER 9

Berlin, Germany
November 9, 1938

By 10 p.m., Klara had finished her delicious dinner of marinated venison with potato dumplings and was halfway through a second glass of the 1928 vintage Bordeaux wine that Joshua had suggested. She already knew that this day would be etched in her memory forever. She didn't want it to end. Well, at least not this part of it.

Klara took a sip from her glass and glanced across their small table nestled in one of the secluded, candle-lit corners of Horcher's Restaurant on Luther-Strasse. Though she'd been on dinner dates with several young men before, none were as easy to look at and delightfully conversant as Joshua. He caught her eye and smiled, prompting her to blush and smile back awkwardly as she lowered her glass. She hoped he wouldn't misread her embarrassed reaction as that of a pretty but starstruck, goggle-eyed schoolgirl who wasn't yet ready for a mature relationship. *At least,* she tried to reassure herself, *I held my own by describing a little of my first day at the asylum. I don't think I bored him.*

Joshua's leaned forward, a concerned expression on his face. "Klara, I hope I didn't offend your sister when we were leaving your house."

Klara blinked. "Why would you think that?"

"Well, when I was opening the car door for you, she called out, 'Back by midnight… yes, Herr Peters?' I laughed and replied with some rather flippant remark to the effect of, 'Don't worry, you can trust us *American* men to honor our commitments.' I thought I detected a disapproving frown from her, as if I were suggesting that German men didn't deserve such trust."

"Oh, Joshua!" Klara laughed. "I truly appreciate your concern for my sister, but you're being far too sensitive. I know Elke well enough to tell she was quite impressed with your good manners and friendliness. In fact, as we walked out, she whispered to me, 'He seems like a good one. Don't mess things up.'"

Joshua exhaled with relief. "You're lucky to have a sister who cares about you like that."

"Yes, I need to keep remembering that. Though she *can* be very dictatorial in exhibiting her 'care and concern' for me at times—far more than even our mother. Especially when I disagree with her on something. Which seems to be happening more frequently these days . . ."

Joshua arched an eyebrow. "For any reason you'd be willing to share? Or maybe I should just mind my own business."

Klara lowered her eyes and took another sip of wine. "Better for another time. Right now, I want to hear more about you and your life here in Berlin as the deputy ambassador's son. Do you enjoy it, or find it as stifling as I do sometimes?" Her question broke the ice for the next half hour as the two shared stories of their experiences in the big city.

For her part, Klara recalled one of her childhood visits to the Berlin Zoo, during which her brother and sister had enjoyed mocking her supposed resemblance to some of the animals there. She concluded by speaking nostalgically of her deep wish to take a break from city life—her new RA job permitting. She wanted to revisit the countryside where her relatives owned a large farm surrounded by small lakes and beautiful walking trails.

Upon hearing this, Joshua's eyes lit up. He glanced around the room, then folded his arms on the table and leaned closer. "Klara," he said in a low voice, "May I ask you a personal question?"

She eyed him suspiciously. "That depends on what it is, Herr Peters. But I trust you won't embarrass me. So go ahead and ask, and I'll answer if I can."

Joshua gazed into her eyes intently. "Are you a believer?"

"A… believer? Do you mean in the religious sense?"

Joshua nodded.

Klara thought for a moment. *Where is he going with this?* "Well, yes, I mean… like my parents, I'm a Lutheran. I go to church regularly, take communion, believe in the Trinity, in Sola Scriptura, and that Christ alone can save us. Is that what you're asking?"

Joshua shook his head. "Those are all ceremonial practices or doctrinal beliefs. Very important, to be sure. And being a practicing Presbyterian myself, I subscribe to them. But what I'm trying to ask, Klara, is this . . ." He pressed his hand to his heart. "Do you ever, like me, have any curiosity about what it *really* means to be a true follower of Christ in our world today? And assuming that's what you truly desire to be, what it could imply for your life?"

Klara stared at him. "If you're talking about achieving some kind of sinless, holy perfection, I'm afraid I gave up any hope—and to be honest, even any real desire—for attaining *that* lofty status a long, long time ago."

"Oh, good heavens. No, I didn't mean *that*!" Joshua laughed, throwing his palms up defensively. "Thank God we can leave that burden to Jesus. And trust me, I'm no religious zealot. Far from it. What I'm talking about is something far more practical and relevant to the dangerous times we're living in."

Klara frowned, put her wine glass down, and leaned back in her chair. "Joshua, you'll have to educate me on what you're referring to."

"Ever heard of Bonhoeffer?" he whispered.

She tried to suppress her gasp. "*Dietrich* Bonhoeffer? The pastor?"

"One and the same," Joshua said. "What do you know about him?"

Now she understood why Joshua spoke in such hushed tones, and why she should keep her voice down as well. Fortunately, the restaurant was sparsely attended tonight, and no one was within earshot. Still, she'd heard rumors of hidden microphones planted in public dining places. To be safe, she leaned in toward him, her face only inches from his.

"I know he's a son of Karl Bonhoeffer, the chairman of the Psychiatry and Neurology Department at Charité Hospital. Professor Bonhoeffer lectured at a couple of my university classes last term. The main two things I've heard about Dietrich are that he's an excellent Lutheran theologian and one of the founding members of the Confessing Church movement. Which—so my father tells me—has been openly critical of the Führer and National Socialism." She glanced nervously over Joshua's shoulder to confirm their privacy before proceeding. "I also seem to recall hearing that Dietrich was banned from preaching in the Berlin area recently. But why do you mention him? And what does this have to do with your question about following Christ?"

Joshua smiled, his eyes gleaming as if Klara had finally asked the question he'd been waiting for all along. "A couple of months ago, I was on a hunting vacation in Eastern Pomerania. I had a chance to hear Dietrich speak on that very subject. I met with him for some brief conversation afterward, and he's everything you said as well as very kind and approachable. I recently read his latest book called *The Cost of Discipleship* on which he based his sermon that day. Personally, I think it's one of the most inspiring works I've read by a modern Christian author. Have you read it?"

Klara shook her head. "No. though I have heard of it, and it does sound very interesting." She grimaced. "Unfortunately, I fear that if my father—or even worse, my sister—were to catch me reading anything connected with the Confessing Church, I'd be ostracized as an anti-Nazi heretic for failing to support my own church's allegiance to the German Christians movement."

Joshua hesitated. "Klara, are you uncomfortable that we're talking about this?" he asked cautiously.

"Well, not really. Though I'm not sure why you're bringing all this up."

A sly grin spread across Joshua's face. "When you mentioned your past experience in the countryside, I had a vision."

Klara tilted her head. "A… vision?"

"When we spoke, Dietrich could sense my enthusiasm. He invited me to attend a two-day retreat he's offering in March for young pastors and their wives at his friend's country estate. Besides hearing him speak, there'll be time for some skiing and hiking. And so, after you mentioned your desire to get away from the city for a spell, I was wondering if you might like to join me as my guest."

"Oh, my!" Klara sat stunned, her heart beating wildly as she stared into his mesmerizing hazel eyes. She knew what she wanted her answer to be, but practical concerns dictated otherwise. "That sounds so wonderful, Joshua, but I… I really couldn't do that. First of all, I have no claim to be a pastor's wife. And second, unless I lied about the Bonhoeffer connection, I'm sure my father would strongly disapprove for reasons that I'm sure you can guess."

Joshua closed his eyes and nodded. "Well, on the first count, there'd be no issue since the retreat's open to more than just married couples. Single men and their female friends are welcome. The estate has separate facilities to accommodate either case. But of course, you're right about your father's concern, and I certainly don't want to cause trouble for you. I should've thought about that before I even raised the possibility."

Before she could stop herself, Klara touched his forearm. "Joshua, please don't apologize. It sounds delightful. I'm glad you asked, and if there were any possible way, I assure you I would—"

"No, Klara." He took her hand and cradled it between his. "Allow me to make a much safer suggestion. Would you consider accompanying me to the theatre next weekend? *After Midnight* is playing at the Schiller. It's a German drama based on the French film, *Nights of Princes*, and I hear it's excellent."

She accepted, of course, tingling with unfamiliar yet pleasurable sensations. She let her hand remain in his as their conversation continued.

Joshua glanced at his watch. "Uh-oh, the witching hour will soon arrive. I need to get you home so I can remain in the good graces of your sister."

Klara giggled. "Before your Mercedes turns into a pumpkin, and Cinderella ends up stuck here on the streets?"

"Actually," Joshua said, his eyebrow arched hopefully. "We still have enough time for a stroll down the Kurfürstendamm. It's right on our route back, and we can enjoy gazing into the display windows of those expensive shops . . ." He hesitated for a second before completing this thought. "The truth is, Klara, I've enjoyed our time together immensely, and I hate to let you go this evening."

Klara could hardly swallow, only smile and nod her excitement. Her memorable day was about to conclude on a perfect note. She couldn't have dreamed up a better ending.

Their car had barely turned the corner onto the Kurfürstendamm when Klara realized something was wrong. Dreadfully wrong.

Less than fifty yards ahead, several cars had pulled to the opposite side of the street and partially onto the sidewalk in front of a row of shops. Illuminated by the streetlights, men in civilian clothing poured out of the cars and stalked toward the shopfronts with various tools in their hands. A small crowd of onlookers converged around the cars, their eyes riveted on the scene.

Klara gripped the edge of her seat. "Joshua, what's going on?"

"I'm not sure," Joshua muttered, "but I have an idea." Slowing the Mercedes to avoid running into the traffic jam in their own lane, he glanced worriedly at her. "I heard on the embassy radio, just before I came to pick you up, that Ernst vom Rath—the German diplomat who was gunned down by that Jewish teenager in Paris—succumbed to his wounds and died late this afternoon. But even before that, Goebbels was screaming bloody murder. He said the wrath of the German people was bound to fall on what he called those 'sub-human, cowardly traitors who are trying once again to stab the Fatherland in the back.'"

Klara stared at him in dismay, remembering Elke's warning from earlier this morning. "And so, retribution against German Jews is now beginning?"

He nodded grimly. "Certainly looks like it. Here in Berlin, anyway."

"Joshua! Over there!" Klara gasped as she pointed to a high white wall separating two shops off to the left, upon which the words *Jude verrecke!* (Death to the Jews) had been scrawled over a huge swastika in thick red paint. A bit farther on, two men in civilian clothing ran up and smashed the front display window of a Jewish haberdashery shop with sledgehammers as several late-night strollers looked on in shock.

As their car approached the main disturbance, Klara saw that the windows of several other shops with Hebrew signage on both sides of the street had already been shattered—some apparently from the inside as evidenced by the countless shards of broken glass that covered the sidewalk and spilt out onto the street.

Joshua braked the car to a halt and rolled down his window. He called to a somewhat corpulent policeman who appeared to be doing nothing but standing alone on the sidewalk. His arms were folded over his ample stomach, calmly watching events unfold. "Sir, may we speak with you a moment?"

The policeman hesitated, then ambled over. He seemed to wobble as he walked. Reaching the car, he bent to place his hands on the bottom of the driver's window frame, clearly trying to steady himself. Even from her seat several feet away, Klara could smell the alcohol as he stuck his head through the window and peered over Joshua's lap and around the interior. Apparently satisfied, he pulled his head back. "You were asking?"

"Yes, officer, can you tell us what's happening up ahead? Is it safe to proceed?"

The man's fleshy face broke out in a twisted grin. "It seems that they finally have the excuse they've been waiting for."

"*They?* Who's '*they*?'" Joshua asked.

"Goebbels and his—*Whoa!*" A crash of glass just one storefront ahead caused the policeman to whirl and fumble for his baton. Klara watched with horror as flames licked up the back of the shop, silhouetting the figures of several men inside who were destroying the contents with axes and sledgehammers.

"*Officer!*" Joshua shouted. "Why are you and those other policemen not at least *trying* to put a stop to this carnage? This is beyond simple criminality—this is outright barbarity!"

The drunken policeman turned to face him. He wrung his baton nervously with both hands. "We *would* stop it, my friend, but..." he shrugged. "I'm afraid our hands have been tied."

"What? Your hands are *tied*?" Joshua challenged. "What in the world is preventing—"

The car behind Joshua blew its horn impatiently, jolting the policeman into his more familiar role.

"All right," he said firmly, pointing his baton in the direction of the once-again-moving line of cars. "Stop holding up traffic. Get going, stay well to the right and you'll be fine."

Joshua shook his head, muttered a curse, and rolled the window up in a fit of disgust. He shot Klara a concerned look. "Are you all right?"

"I think so. I just want to get out of here."

"We turn off the Kurfürstendamm in just about three blocks. Things should ease up soon. Hang on." He reached over to clasp her hand, which was trembling.

A half block ahead, Klara noticed a short man with skullcap and beard. He seemed to be pleading his case with two rough-looking hulks who were pushing and shoving him down the sidewalk. Suddenly, one of the assailants delivered a vicious punch to the bearded man's eye, causing him to stagger backward against the post of a streetlight. As they passed by only a few feet away, Klara got a good look at the man's face. She had no doubt who it was.

"*Oh, my God! Joshua!*" she shrieked. "That's Herr Friedmann, my friend's father. Stop the car now. We've got to help him!"

Joshua stared at her incredulously. "Klara, we can't stop here, we're—"

Klara grasped the doorhandle. "*Please, Joshua, stop the car. I'm positive that was Herr Friedmann. I'm getting out—*"

Joshua reached over and grabbed her left arm tightly. "Klara, wait, listen to me. I'll turn off at the next street. We'll park and go back to try and help.

CHAPTER 10

Berlin, Germany
November 9, 1938

After turning the corner and parking across the street from an unattended motorized police wagon, Joshua and Klara jumped out and ran back down the Kurfürstendamm.

Klara feared they might be too late. Her mind spinning, she wondered why Herr Friedmann would be in this area so late at night. But then she remembered Sophie telling her that after his dismissal from the civil service, her father had agreed to take over the management of the artisans' supply shop owned by his brother who'd recently emigrated to America. Sophie had said it was somewhere on the Kurfürstendamm, but she hadn't known exactly where. Now, it was only too apparent.

She clutched Joshua's hand as he led her up to the rear of another crowd of onlookers that had converged near the streetlight where she'd seen Herr Friedmann fall.

Jostling their way through the crowd, a mixture of sentiments bombarded them from all sides.

"The pig deserved it!"

"Every Yid does. They're all guilty."

"No, no. This is too much. As Germans and fellow human beings, we should be ashamed."

"*Ashamed?* The only one here to be ashamed is *you* for suggesting such traitorous, faint-hearted nonsense!"

Finally reaching the front edge of the crowd, Klara held her breath as she peered over the shoulder of a shorter lady to gain a glimpse of the man on the ground. He lay face up, perfectly still with his arms and legs splayed and his head covered in blood. Two men stood beside the obviously dead body, one with his arms folded and the other with his hands on his hips, both seemingly satisfied with the product of their work.

"Is it him?" Joshua whispered.

She stared intently at the body, her lips quivering, After a few seconds, she could tell that it wasn't Herr Friedmann. "No. It's someone else," was all she could manage before she collapsed into Joshua's embrace, shaking with both relief and anguish.

"Come on, let's get out of here," he said. "Hopefully, your friend got away." He put his arm around her shoulders and escorted her through the onlookers.

When they reached the back row, an attractive, well-attired woman holding the hand of a small boy wearing a brown SA kepi cap thrust her arm up and out toward the front of the crowd. "*Heil Hitler! Death to all Jews and other enemies of the Führer!*" she shouted, drawing the applause of many.

Klara noticed the boy observing her as she passed. He couldn't have been more than nine or ten. His round, cherubic face was lit with excitement as he smiled and waved tentatively at her. Klara looked away, disgusted. *How could any responsible mother allow her child to witness something like this?* she thought.

They'd taken but a few steps beyond the crowd when Joshua pointed at a darkened storefront up ahead. A prone figure was lying in a curled posture half on, half off the front step. She knew immediately—it was Herr Friedmann.

Racing to his side, they stooped and checked to see if he was alive. His painful groans and labored breathing were distressing, though welcome, signs of life. Lifting him by the backs of his arms, they helped him sit up and lean against the wall. It was then that Klara saw clearly his mangled lip, badly swollen eye, and blood trickling down his forehead. His eyes gradually focusing, he looked alternately at them in wide-eyed terror before trying weakly to squirm away.

Klara managed to restrain him with little effort. "Herr Friedmann, stop resisting. It's me, Klara Neumann. Sophie's friend. It's going to be all right, Herr Friedmann. My friend Joshua and I will take you back home and get help for you."

He stared at her blankly for a few seconds. "K-Kl-Klara?" he finally sputtered. She smiled and nodded, stroking his arm.

He looked at Klara with pleading eyes. "Jakob... my son?"

In her mind, an alarm was triggered. She peered at him intently. "Yes, yes. Jakob. Isn't he at home with Sophie and your wife?"

The elderly man shook his head as he struggled to speak. "He was with me... helping with accounting after we closed. Heard shouting in street... they came knocking... I told Jakob to get away through back door. He's... oh, I just don't know!"

Klara looked at Joshua, uncertain how to respond. Joshua shook his head. "We'll look for his son later. Right now, we've got to get this man to our car."

"Herr Friedmann," Joshua asked, "do you think you can stand if we help you?"

He nodded, and the two lifted him gently to his feet. They draped his arms around their shoulders to help him limp between them toward their parked car.

The sound of running footsteps from behind prompted Klara to look over her shoulder. She gasped at the sight of the little boy in the SA kepi cap, his cherubic face now transformed into a mask of satanic fury.

He closed in and started kicking at Herr Friedmann's legs. "*Dirty, rotten Jew!*" he screamed over and over, kicking away with all his might as Herr Friedmann cried out in pain.

Joshua, with Herr Friedmann's arm still draped over his shoulder, tried to shove the boy away with one hand. "Get out of here, kid. Leave this poor man alone!"

The boy stopped his attack for just a moment, then renewed his screeching, this time directed at Joshua and Klara.

"Jew helpers! Dirty Jew helpers! Shame! Shame!" He turned his head and looked back at the crowd, some of whom—including the boy's inattentive mother—were just now noticing what was going on behind them. He turned back and began attacking Klara, tugging on her skirt as she tried to move on with Joshua and Herr Friedmann. "Stop right now, you traitor!" he cried.

Klara had heard enough. She extricated herself from under Herr Friedmann's arm, whirled, and slapped the boy full force across the face. *"Go back to your mother, little man, and stop hounding us!"*

Stunned, the boy stood staring at her and holding his cheek. He looked as if he were about to cry. But then, he reached into his pants pocket and pulled out a small metal whistle. He turned toward the crowd and began blowing on it furiously, pointing at Klara, Joshua, and Herr Friedmann as they resumed their attempt at escape.

"They're getting away!" the boy screamed between his shrill whistle blasts. *"The stinking Jew and his helpers—they're getting away. Help!"*

Klara dared another glance. The boy's mother, screaming frantically for her son, had taken off in their direction with three men following behind.

She looked ahead. Only a few more yards to the intersection. With luck, they would just make it to their parked car, help Herr Friedmann into the back, and take off before their pursuers arrived.

They rounded the corner, the car now in sight only feet ahead.

"Halt! Where do you think you're going with that man?"

Two policemen approached rapidly with batons drawn and hands on their sidearms. Across the street, the formerly unattended police wagon was now a beehive of activity. At least ten disheveled men were lined up behind it, being unceremoniously hauled up one by one into the vehicle's rear open bed.

Still supporting Herr Friedmann, Joshua attempted a polite explanation to the policemen as Klara watched behind, expecting their pursuers to show up any second.

"Officers, as you can see, this man is injured, and we are trying to get him to the hospital."

"Yes, that's obvious," one policeman snapped. "But who is he? And why was he hurt?"

Joshua hesitated. "I'm not sure, sir. We just noticed him as we were—"

"*There they are!*" The three men who had followed the SA boy's mother rushed up, rubber truncheons drawn.

"*Officers, arrest this Jew and his helpers immediately!*" shouted one of the men.

The policemen shifted uncomfortably. "Says who?" one of them asked defiantly.

"Says SS Gruppenführer Reinhard Heydrich—our mutual boss, you stupid oaf. We three are members of the *Sturmabteilung*."

"SA, huh? Is that so?" the policeman challenged. He looked uncertainly at his comrade, who shrugged. "You're not in uniform. Show us some credentials."

The man cursed, drew out his wallet and pulled out a card that he held up in front of the policeman's face. "That enough for you?"

After scanning the card for a moment, the policeman took a step back and offered the fascist salute, prompting his partner to do the same. "Forgive us, sir. We were only trying to be cautious with our—"

"You police should be getting explicit formal instructions from Heydrich very soon that'll relieve your *ridiculous* hesitancy," the SA man spat. "At any rate, no more need for caution with these three pieces of vermin. Get them all into that wagon with the rest of the trash and take them to the station. They'll know exactly what to do with the Jew here. As for the other two, book them for interfering with police arrest of a criminal and physical assault of a helpless little boy. In fact, I think I'll accompany you to make sure you get this done right."

The policeman, completely cowed, nodded obediently and stepped forward to grab Herr Friedmann by the arm.

"Look here, sir," Joshua protested indignantly. "I'm the son of the United States deputy ambassador, and I object strongly to your treatment of this man and me and my lady friend here. I promise we will launch a formal protest to—"

He failed to finish his sentence over the harsh laughter and hoots of the SA men. "That's a good one," their de facto leader said. "You can tell that to the Gestapo, my friend, and see how they respond. All right, enough stalling. Let's go." He said something to his comrades, then led Joshua, Klara, and Herr Friedmann to the wagon as the two policemen followed meekly behind.

CHAPTER 11

Berlin, Germany
November 10, 1938

I *will stop whining and count my blessings. It could be worse.*
Klara sat on the edge of the undersized, wooden, straw-mattress-topped cot in her detention cell, holding her face in her hands and struggling mightily to stop the flow of tears.

With no window and the single bulb shining constantly from the low ceiling, she'd lost track of time, though it seemed like many hours had passed since she'd been yanked out of the wagon by the receiving guards at the police station...

Before they could recover their bearings, she and Joshua were pulled aside and escorted toward the station's main entrance. On the way, she'd watched in dismay as Herr Friedmann and the other Jewish detainees were brutally shoved, kicked, or dragged toward a high, iron-barred side gate that opened onto what appeared to be a brightly lit courtyard. She'd wanted desperately to cry out to him, to at least say goodbye, as she feared this could be the last time she would ever see him. But she'd stifled it, as Joshua had warned her it would only make things worse for everyone if the police suspected any intentional effort by an Aryan woman to help a Jewish friend escape National Socialist justice.

Once inside the station, Klara was separated from Joshua and led to one of the small desks at the rear of the crowded booking room. Behind it sat a plump, heavily mustached officer who'd taken down her personal data and asked one of her escorts to state the charges against her. When informed, the desk officer paused his writing and looked up at her. "Treating an old Jew better than a child of your own race, Fräulein? That's a serious charge." She'd merely stared back at him in silence, prompting the officer to shake his head and glare, his expression one of pure contempt. "Take her to the female wing, cell seventeen," he'd ordered. "Let her stew on things awhile before her interrogation."

At the door to Klara's cell, her escort turned her over to a surprisingly kind female guard. The young woman followed her inside and collected all her personal effects, though she didn't require her to strip down and allowed her to retain her coat.

The guard then handed Klara a wool blanket and explained what to expect. "The first night is always the toughest. There's no heat in here, and it will get quite cold. Best to keep walking around or doing little exercises as much as you can. Try to tire yourself out, because the light stays on all the time and it's hard to sleep. I've left some water in the jug along with a little bread on that stool in the corner. Knock if you want to be escorted to the toilet, but a bucket's in the other corner if you can't wait. Hopefully, you won't have to wait too long tomorrow before your interrogation, and if they find you innocent you'll be released immediately."

Klara had thanked the guard for her considerate treatment and watched forlornly when she exited and banged the iron door shut behind her. Left alone in the deafening silence, she'd fallen to her knees and bent over the cot, burying her face in her arms. She wept and prayed for several hours, trying to make sense of what was happening. Finally, a brief, fitful sleep overtook her...

Rising now from her cot, Klara managed to stand straight for only a few seconds before a sudden rush of dizziness forced her to sit back down.

Exhaustion, compounded by worry over Joshua and Herr Friedmann as well as her upcoming interrogation, had taken its toll. She could barely think straight, her mind vacillating between her immediate dilemma and the challenges awaiting beyond that: *How should I respond to the interrogator? Assuming they release me, how do I help Joshua? How can I get to Sophie, Jakob and their mother to let them know about Herr Friedmann and Leah?*

The more she ruminated, the more panicked she became. She forced herself to stand once again and, despite her dizziness, begin pacing furiously around the cell. After a few minutes, she felt as if she were on the verge of losing consciousness and collapsing.

God help me, I'm truly going crazy. They're going to kill me. I'm—

Suddenly, the door bolt clanged. Klara whirled, fearing the worst.

The kind female guard entered, a smile on her face. "Someone is here to see you."

The guard stepped aside to reveal Elke, standing in the doorway.

Dressed immaculately in her BDM trainer's uniform, her sister had never presented a more welcome sight to Klara's eyes, even in those dark woods at Nuremberg.

Elke strode briskly into the cell and turned to face the guard. "Thank you, Ilse."

The guard clicked her heels and saluted. "You are welcome, Fräulein Neumann. I will return in no more than twenty minutes."

Elke returned the salute and waited for the guard to shut the door before she turned back to her sister. Klara trembled under Elke's ferocious gaze, uncertain whether to be the first to speak or rather to simply hang her head and await the inevitable string of reprimands. All doubt disappeared when Elke's face softened and she extended her arms, spurring Klara to rush forward and embrace her. The girls clung to each other, saying nothing for several long seconds.

Finally, Elke extricated herself and took command as usual. "Sit on the edge of that cot, sister. We need to discuss some things, and we don't have much time." She removed the water jug from the stool, placed the stool directly in front of Klara, and sat down on it with her hands folded tightly in her lap, her eyes boring into her sister's.

"Joshua was released earlier this morning."

A choked sob of relief escaped Klara. "I-Is he all right?" she stammered after collecting herself.

Elke put a cautionary finger to her lips and leaned in closer, her face now only inches from Klara's. "Speak softly. There may be microphones," she whispered. "Joshua's fine. His people came and got him out after the police called the US embassy to verify his identity. He called me a couple of hours ago. Told me where you were and gave his version of things."

"But how were you able to get in here to visit me like this?" Klara asked.

"We have Colonel Bremmer to thank for that. I took a chance and called his office after speaking with Joshua. I was hoping I could rely on the colonel's high opinion and affection for Heinz and me. Of course, he was terribly busy dealing with all the chaos on the streets, but he took some of his valuable time to talk with me. His supervisor told him about Joshua's arrest and release, and he also knew the basics of your incident. Before he decided on whether to intervene in your case, he was waiting to see the formal report from the police. But in the meantime, he told me he would arrange a short visit for me to meet with you to make sure you're holding up all right."

Klara nodded and stared at her lap.

"Klara, look at me," Elke scolded, reaching out and lifting her sister's chin up. "If you want me to help you get out of here any time soon, I need you tell me the truth about *exactly* what happened out there. Don't lie to me, and leave nothing out, all right?"

Klara gulped, knowing what that would mean. *I'll cross that bridge when I get there.* She nodded, then proceeded to recount the events with Joshua.

"...And we tried to take the injured man to the car to get him to a hospital, but that's when that little Hitler Youth boy—"

Elke held her hand up. "Stop right there." She peered at Klara intently. "Did you recognize the man you were going to help *before* you insisted on stopping? Did you know he was a Jew?"

Klara's felt the blood drain from her face as she involuntarily blinked and averted her eyes. "Well... no... I–I didn't realize he was—"

Elke gripped both of Klara's knees. *"Klara, I said don't lie to me! I can always tell when you're lying, you know. You never could hide your little fibs. Not around me, anyway."*

Klara closed her eyes and released a slow exhale. Despite Joshua's warning, she knew it was hopeless to continue the charade; Elke had always shown a special knack for dragging things out of her. *Might as well get it all out now.*

She bit her lip, then opened up. "All right. As we passed by in the car, I did recognize his face. It was Herr Friedmann, Sophie's and Jakob's father."

"Herr... *Friedmann?*" Elke sat up straight, her eyes bulging. "Klara, did you tell any of the police that you knew him?"

"No. Joshua warned me not to."

Elke sighed with relief. "Well, if he couldn't stop your impetuous rescue attempt, I'm glad he at least had the good sense to advise *that.*"

Klara looked at her indignantly. "I don't understand, Elke. Why do you call it impetuous?"

Her sister's face contorted in exasperation. "Klara, was your first day at that asylum enough to drive *you* insane? Don't you realize what's going on out there?"

"Of course, I do. I was right in the thick of it."

Elke vehemently shook her head. "You only saw the beginning. The rest of the night and most of today, Jews across the entire country are finally getting what Goebbels said would happen—the German people simply won't lie down and take it anymore. Hundreds of synagogues have been torched, Jewish shops and homes raided and demolished. Jewish men seventeen and older are being arrested, paraded through the streets with 'I am guilty' signs around their necks before being hauled off to jail."

She paused to let her words sink in, then continued. "Harsh, I know. But this is clearly not the most opportune time for an Aryan to be seen showing acts of mercy to the people responsible for our country's hardships over the past decades."

"*Elke!*" Klara snapped. "I know what National Socialism has made *perfectly* clear to us these past few years, but how can *you* be so utterly callous? We used to love playing together with Sophie and Jakob, and Frau Friedmann was always so kind and would give us candy when we visited their house! And Herr Friedmann, with all his war medals for bravery, remember? What did they ever do to deserve this kind of treatment?"

Elke lowered her eyes and sighed. She seemed genuinely taken aback. "Well, I suppose there are a *few* decent Jews like them who I'd personally be willing to make an exception for in that regard." She shot Klara a pleading look. "But everything's changed now, sister. As of last night, most people in this country want the Jews to pay a severe penalty. And you know good and well that with our family's standing and reputation with the government, we can't be seen standing in the way of the people's will by taking chances like you did."

Klara knew further protest would be futile. "So, what's next for me?"

"I'll call Colonel Bremmer back, report that you are in stressful conditions here, and plead hard for him to get you a quick release. Hopefully you won't have to spend another night in here. I have no doubts that he'll wish to interview you personally beforehand, so expect that to happen. And Klara, I never dreamed I'd be admitting something like this, but your American friend was right. Whatever you say to the colonel, *do not* mention that you knew the man you helped."

Klara nodded. The knock on the cell door signaled their time was up, and the girls stood and wrapped each other in a hug.

"Thank you, Elke. And please thank the guard on your way out. She was very kind to me last night."

Elke smiled. "Ilse is a former BDM student of mine. I have more eyes and ears in this place than you might imagine." She started to turn toward the door, but stopped and leaned to whisper in Klara's ear.

"Promise me you'll stay away from the Friedmann family from now on. It's too dangerous."

Klara hesitated, knowing Elke had asked the impossible.

"I promise," she lied.

Elke looked at her dubiously. "That's good, sister, because I can't keep bailing you out of your deep waters forever."

Late that afternoon in his spacious office on the third floor of National Police Headquarters on Prinz-Albrecht Strasse, SS Lt. Colonel Gerhard Bremmer looked up from the bound sheaf of papers he was studying to observe his visitor. Putting the documents down, he stood and returned Klara's salute.

"Ah, Fräulein Neumann," he said genially, motioning to a chair in front of his desk. "Please, have a seat. And I beg your patience as I finish reviewing, once again, the last page of your arrest report. My apologies. If it weren't for all the extreme busyness of the last couple of days, I'd have already finished this before you arrived."

"Of course, sir, I understand completely. Thank you, sir." Trembling all over, Klara settled herself into the chair and stared straight ahead.

Apparently detecting her discomfort, Bremmer lowered his papers. "Would you care for a cigarette, Fräulein? Or perhaps a glass of water?"

"Oh, no thank you, sir. I don't smoke, but... well, yes... maybe some water, sir."

Bremmer smiled and nodded to a brown-uniformed aide at the side of the room. The man poured a tall glass of water from a pitcher and brought it to Klara. She accepted it gratefully, then proceeded to take little sips and scrutinize the high, wide wall behind Bremmer while he resumed his perusal of the report.

Between two red, black, and white swastika flag panels which extended from ceiling to floor, a gleaming steel Nazi war eagle spread its wings over a large colored portrait of Adolf Hitler. The Führer, dressed in a brown uniform with black belt, cross strap, and a cape draped over his shoulders, stood with one hand on his hip as he looked resolutely off into the distance. As Klara gazed at his portrait, she couldn't deny her sense of the supreme power and authority it seemed to convey to the entire room, in particular to the man seated directly in front of her: Lt. Colonel Bremmer.

Bremmer grunted softly and laid the report on his desk. He leaned back in his chair with his hands folded over his abdomen. "A very interesting tale. But I'd like to hear your own account, Fräulein Neumann."

Well prepared for this moment, Klara recited her version of events— confidently and flawlessly, she thought, including her explanation of discovering the "random stranger" injured and lying on the shop steps.

"Sir," she concluded, "I am regretful of my angry, irresponsible reaction to that little boy who I know was only trying to—"

Bremmer waved his hand impatiently. "No need to lose sleep over *that*. I probably would have swatted the stupid little brat myself if he'd kept pestering me like that." He grimaced and shook his head. "His irresponsible mother shouldn't have let him off his leash. We have enough SA hooligans running around this city trying to prove how tough they are without a small boy pretending to be one of them."

He leaned forward and folded his hands on top of the report. "What I'm far more curious about, Klara—if I may refer to you so informally— is, *why*?"

Klara stared at him, uncertain what he was after with his simple yet direct question paired with a penetrating gaze. "*Why*, sir?"

"Yes. Why was it that you felt compelled to leave the safety of your automobile and rush to the aid of a stranger whom you admitted you strongly suspected was Jewish?"

"I-I think I just felt compassion for another human being's obvious plight, sir. I really don't remember thinking at the time I should hold back because of his race."

Bremmer smiled and lifted an eyebrow. "You were playing the Good Samaritan, yes?"

Klara looked down at her lap. "I suppose, sir."

"Klara, like the rest of your family, you are a faithful Lutheran, are you not?"

She nodded. "I try my best, sir, though I know I often fall far short."

Bremmer shrugged. "No one's perfect. But I assume that, as a member of a Lutheran congregation that strongly advocates for the Positive Christianity philosophy of the German Christians movement, you have been instructed in the despicable, historical offenses of the Jews against Christian believers."

"I know well what we've often been reminded, sir. That it was Jews who were responsible for the murder of Jesus, Jewish cults that sacrificed Christian children to use their blood in religious rituals. In more recent times, it was primarily the Jews who caused our nation's defeat in the last war, and it is the international Jewish conspiracy that keeps attempting to poison society for Christians and other true Germans who strive to embrace the purity of our Aryan cultural roots, blood, and race."

Please, please don't ask me if I actually believe these things, Klara thought.

"Well said." Bremmer nodded his approval. "You've clearly been taught the ugly facts. Which is all the more reason why I'm puzzled by your choice to let sentimental feelings rule over your better judgment. Surely you understand the collective guilt of the Jewish race, so why not let the natural consequences prevail when it comes to individual cases?"

Tell him what he wants to hear. "That would seem to be the more logical course, sir, and I'm sorry I did not choose to follow it in this case."

Bremmer stared at her hard for several long moments, then his face relaxed into an easy smile. "Yes, I believe you now see the error of your decision, though I have no doubts it was well intended."

He closed the report, tossed it to the side of the desk and stood, prompting Klara to do the same. "Fräulein Neumann, I am happy to say that your responses have all been consistent with the officers' report, and that you appear properly contrite for your impulsive action last night. I will sign your release, and you can return to the police station to collect your things, after which you are completely free to return home and resume your normal activities."

"I am very grateful for your kindness and understanding, sir." The two saluted, then Klara spun around and walked toward the door held open by the aide.

"Oh, Fräulein Neumann. One last thing."

She froze and rotated back to face him. "Sir?"

"In regard to any future decisions and actions that testify of your commitment to National Socialism, I advise you strongly to stay away from Jews *and any other recognized troublemakers* who cause problems for our country. In fact, I believe you would do well to follow the excellent example of your sister, Elke, for whom I have the highest regard, as indeed I have for your entire family."

Klara forced a tepid smile. "I am honored, sir, and I will do my best." She clicked her heels and saluted one last time.

CHAPTER 12

Berlin, Germany
November 11, 1938

Despite his achievement, Lt. Colonel Gerhard Bremmer felt strangely dissatisfied.

Holding a glass of cognac in one hand and a cigarette in the other, he looked out the front window of his center-city apartment. The streets below now appeared calm, with no more sign of the long lines of police wagons. That was because earlier this afternoon, Goebbels had signaled all paramilitary units to stop their nation-wide, antisemitic riot incitement.

Job completed. Looks like I'll finally get some well-deserved sleep tonight. So, what am I still fretting about?

Gerhard knew he had every reason to feel proud of the performance of his Berlin District Kripo detectives over the past thirty-six hours.

After receiving preliminary orders just before midnight of the ninth from his boss—SS Senior Colonel Arthur Nebe, head of the national Kripo organization—Gerhard had faithfully issued his own directive to all his Berlin people:

"Actions against the Jews are about to commence in this city. They are not to be interfered with by our regular city police, firefighters, or

local Kripo detectives, except to prevent looting and other excesses. Our Kripo units should prepare to assist the Gestapo and regular city police in arresting up to ten thousand well-to-do Jews."

From the stream of reports Gerhard had received ever since, it was clear that his orders had generally been followed. Yes, there *were* some unfortunate excesses by the SA, including a few reports of Jewish men being beaten to death in the street or on the way to the Sachsenhausen concentration camp following their arrests. But on the whole, Gerhard thought his Kripo people had performed their jobs admirably. And as their overseer, he would certainly be commended by Senior Colonel Nebe.

It would be a nice tribute, to be sure. One that men of smaller ambition would certainly appreciate. But for a man of Gerhard's talents and stature, a few polite words of acknowledgement for a relatively minor personal accomplishment could never suffice to quell the persistent, gnawing hunger in his soul.

No wonder I'm still feeling dissatisfied tonight. Face it. What I crave is more than a nice tribute. What I really crave is to be promoted beyond this career-limiting city criminal investigation job and into the national-level SS ranks.

Gerhard knew that if he ever had any hopes of receiving that promotion, he would have to show Nebe's SS superiors (Heydrich and Himmler) that he was ready for something far more noteworthy than assisting the Gestapo in tracking down, arresting, and interrogating wealthy Berlin Jews. He would have to show them he could catch and fry bigger fish. The discovery and dismantling of a national sabotage ring, perhaps? Or maybe the foiling of an assassination plot against a high-ranking Nazi official?

Easier imagined than done. Gerhard sighed wearily. He took a drag on his cigarette, then turned away from the window and ambled over to sit on the settee facing the blazing logs in the fireplace. Placing his empty glass on the side table and extinguishing the cigarette, he picked up the framed portrait. He'd once sworn to destroy it because of the devastating sadness it inevitably produced. His throat caught as he held the frame tightly in his hands, savoring the image of his wife, five-year-old son, and three-year-old daughter standing together on the shore of Wannsee Lake. The photo had been taken nearly four years ago, a month before a tragic airplane accident cruelly ended the lives of all three.

He'd never forgiven himself for insisting they go on that Swiss vacation without him after learning just before departure that he'd been called to attend an urgent meeting with Nebe. On their return trip, they'd been flying through a thunderstorm when the right wing of the aircraft snapped off. He should've been there, trying his best to hold them close during those last seconds of terror as they all went down together.

His family's loss had sparked a prolonged period of deep depression and suicidal thoughts. It was only after selling their comfortable villa near the lakeside, taking this city apartment only a couple of blocks away from his office, and burying himself in his work that he'd been able to start recovering.

No doubt, that process was aided considerably by the friendly mentoring relationship that he'd developed with Heinz Schröder after the latter applied for membership in the SS three years ago. Heinz and his girlfriend, Elke Neumann, had quickly grown in his esteem and affections. They'd become almost like adult replacements for his deceased son and daughter as they joined him monthly for dinner at his apartment or a night at the theater or concert hall. They were the near-perfect Aryan couple in his eyes. Elke had especially intrigued him, not only with her physical attractiveness, but also with her zeal for the Führer and her father's reputation in the burgeoning rocket science business.

Gerhard set the picture of his family aside, stood, and walked over to the bar to refresh his drink. As he did so, a disturbing new thought clicked in his mind—a recollection from his earlier interview today with Elke's sister, Klara.

When he'd read the arrest reports just before Klara arrived, something jumped out at him: the identity of the man whom Klara and her friend had tried to help. "Herbert Friedmann: husband of Esther; father of Jakob, Sophie, Leah." It was the son's name that first caught his eye. *Jakob Friedmann.* The name sounded very familiar. Where had he heard it before?

He hadn't had time to probe the recesses of his memory then, but now, he certainly did. Returning to the settee, Gerhard settled back and stared intently at the fire. *Who* is *Jakob Friedmann?* Concentrating hard, he finally made the connection.

It all had to do with that incident in Tiergarten Park four years ago. The Jewish boy had been lying on the ground, being pummeled by those two SA thugs. Heinz and Elke's brother had valiantly fought to rescue the boy while Klara comforted his sister. After Gerhard boldly intervened and chased the thugs off, Klara's father told him that the Jewish boy's name was Jakob Friedmann. He'd also admitted that Klara had known and maintained a longtime friendship with Jakob, his sister, and *the entire Friedmann family* since her school days.

And so, it was clear. *Klara deliberately lied to the police, and to me, when she denied any knowledge of the identity of that old Jew.*

That was a very serious offense. In fact, it was a crime that could land the girl a hefty prison sentence should Gerhard ever decide to press a charge. Perhaps she decided to risk the lie so she could spare her family the embarrassment and complications of having her friendship with a Jewish family exposed to the police and their SS bosses.

If that were the only reason for her lie, I'd be willing to let things go, he thought. But the more he pondered the name, Jakob Friedmann, the more he became convinced that there might be something else compelling Klara to lie. Something far more sinister than simply preventing embarrassment and complications for her own family.

Gerhard lifted the brandy glass to his lips but paused halfway as the realization suddenly crystallized.

Jakob Friedmann, he recalled from a recent Gestapo report, was one of several names listed as having rumored involvement with an underground cell of local Communist sympathizers. They were printing and distributing anti-Nazi literature across the city, and they were proving difficult to catch. This was mainly because, in Gerhard's opinion, the Gestapo had other priorities and was not allocating sufficient detective resources to pursue all their potential leads.

Gerhard wondered: might *this* Jakob Friedmann and Klara's friend be one and the same? And if so, might Klara be aware of Jakob's involvement in the cell's activities, or possibly even involved herself? Now *that* could easily explain the reason why she'd falsely denied any recognition of Jakob's father.

This certainly presents a dilemma, he thought as he tapped his foot and considered the best course of action. He certainly didn't wish to be the cause of undeserved heartache and disrepute for the Neumann family—especially for Heinz's sweet fiancée Elke and her highly regarded father. On the other hand, becoming known for *personally* busting a local Communist literature-spreading cell that had been irritating Heydrich for quite a while now? Well, it wasn't exactly on the same level as breaking up a national sabotage ring. Still, it would be something *very* nice to add to his resumé. One more hole-punch on his ticket to a more prestigious realm of SS operations.

The best ploy for now, he decided finally, was to play things cautiously. Don't let Klara or anyone in her family know he was aware she'd lied to him, or about his suspicions concerning Jakob Friedmann. Keep loose tabs (using his network of casual civilian informers, since he didn't have the Kripo resources to spare for tighter, continual surveillance) on Klara's comings and goings. It made sense that, at some point soon, she'd try to visit Jakob and his family to let them know what had happened to the father. But after that, if the informants observed her continuing to visit the Friedmanns' house or meeting separately with Jakob, it could be an indication that her relationship with him went beyond mere friendship. Perhaps it could mean that she indeed had knowledge or even direct involvement with Jakob in this troublesome cell activity. If so, Lt Colonel Gerhard Bremmer would be prepared to pounce.

In the meantime, I have a phone call to make tomorrow. Erich Neumann, Klara's father, certainly would appreciate hearing directly from

Gerhard that he had decided to release his younger daughter without charges. Who knew how the appreciation of an esteemed national rocket scientist might one day pay off?

Gerhard closed his eyes and allowed his imagination to run wild. He saw himself seated at the head of a large table with Wernher von Braun, Erich Neumann, and their team of famous German rocket men and other secret weapons development experts. In his vision, these creative geniuses were all discussing their grand ideas and plans for protecting the nation under Bremmer's watchful political eye. As if he'd been personally assigned by SS Reichsführer Heinrich Himmler himself to monitor the scientists' loyalty and dedication to the true Nazi cause.

It was a big dream, he knew. But wasn't that what his aristocratic, war hero, Jew-hating Prussian father had always taught him?

Yes, indeed. I must always dream big, make my supreme effort, and let the chips fall where Providence decrees.

CHAPTER 13

Kummersdorf Army Firing Range: 30 Miles South of Berlin
March 23, 1939
(Four-and-a-half months later)

For impressing the Führer, a full-fledged rocket launch from the Peenemünde test facility on the Baltic coast would have been ideal. However, today's static-fire test of a horizontally suspended A5 rocket engine at the massive Kummersdorf Firing Range just south of Berlin certainly offered the next best alternative. After all, visitors who'd witnessed such demonstrations in the past had rarely failed to be left in a state of gasping admiration.

Or so went Professor Erich Neumann's thinking as he stood on the patio of the range's administration building together with Colonel Walter Dornberger (Wehrmacht rocket projects overseer), Dr. Wernher von Braun (technical director), and several other members of the vaunted Peenemünde rocket development team. They all anxiously watched as the Führer's motorcade proceeded up the long driveway in their direction.

Everyone on the team knew how critically important the Führer's reaction would be today. Bolstered by the Nazi invasion and seizure of Czechoslovakia just last week, Hitler's focus was on continuing preparations for expanded war using weapon systems that were already available. Gaining his personal audience for demonstrations of exotic new weapons was proving increasingly difficult. That was why everything had to go right. If this demonstration failed to impress the Führer, the A5 program could be in jeopardy.

The two leading cars in the motorcade pulled up beside the steps of the administration building as Hitler's vehicle and the others gradually closed in behind. Out of the first car sprang Lt. Colonel Gerhard Bremmer along with several SS officers and policemen. Bremmer hustled up the steps toward Colonel Dornberger as the other men fanned out to form an armed escort for the Führer and his entourage.

Erich was not surprised to see Bremmer here. The range administrative officer told him just last week that the Berlin Kripo chief had been ordered to personally organize and lead the security detail for this visit.

Bremmer saluted and shook hands with Dornberger, then turned to von Braun. "Greetings, Doctor! It is good to see you again, along with your esteemed colleagues."

Von Braun extended his hand. "A pleasure, Colonel. We all greatly enjoyed meeting you up at Peenemünde last month."

Bremmer looked at Erich, nodded and smiled. "I have Professor Neumann here to thank for arranging that, and I must say, I still have fond memories of my tour of your marvelous facility there."

Erich returned the compliment. "I think we were all quite impressed, Colonel, with your astute questions and obvious interest in the A5 program and rocketry in general. I'm very glad you accepted my invitation." Actually, he thought, it wasn't exactly clear who had invited whom.

The tour was proposed over four months ago when Bremmer phoned Erich just after the November riots. He'd advised him of his decision to clear Klara of all criminal charges, despite her indiscretion in trying to help some Jewish man (apparently unknown to her) escape from arrest.

Erich had expressed his deep gratitude and asked if there were anything he might do to repay his debt to Bremmer.

As a matter of fact, Bremmer had suggested, there was. Since his early school days, he'd taken an interest in the fascinating fields of ballistics and rocketry. He'd studied math and physics in college. He was especially intrigued with the ideas and experiments of Robert Goddard, von Braun, and others. He'd asked if it would be possible to work out a time to visit the famous Peenemünde site, where so much of the nation's future weapon systems research and testing was being conducted. Erich had been quick to offer his services, and the two-day visit, including a private tour and dinner with von Braun and his team, took place last month.

Bremmer glanced over his shoulder, then turned back and clapped his hands together. "Well, gentlemen, it looks like the Führer and his people are still gathering. We have a minute or so. I suggest we review the itinerary before they arrive."

The range administrator stepped forward. "Certainly sir, it's a fairly simple one. We will begin here with introductions, then take a walk through our small museum and photo gallery where I'll briefly explain the history and recent accomplishments of the range. Following that, we'll walk to the observation shed for the highlight of the day, the engine test-firing. Afterward, lunch will be served in the VIP dining room."

"Excellent." Bremmer whirled to salute the Führer who had reached the top of the steps. Beside him was General Brauchitsch—the German Army Commander in Chief.

"So, Colonel Bremmer," Hitler snapped, his face like a stone block beneath the distinctive, high-fronted visor cap. "How long will this take?"

"A little over an hour, my Führer."

Hitler looked at his watch impatiently. "Let's get on with it, then. I expect lunch no later than twelve thirty."

"Of course, my Führer."

The visitors were led to the museum, where Hitler barely seemed to pay attention as the firing range's history was recounted. He glanced at his watch again, prompting the range administrator to motion discreetly to the briefer to hurry things up.

After the entourage had finally been seated in the test-viewing area, Erich held his breath as the final countdown to ignition began. *This is it,* he thought, his eyes glued to the cylindrical rocket engine suspended by large steel claws on the other side of the thick glass observation window. With ten seconds to go, he tried to visualize the pressurized tubes as they fed liquid oxygen and alcohol from their respective tanks into the engine's combustion chamber. Soon, a wire-generated electric spark would unleash a massive expulsion of flame through the exhaust nozzle.

The lead test engineer called out the final sequence. "Five... four... three... two... one... *ignite!*"

Erich, who'd seen many such static firings, watched with his usual pride and awe as the long, bluish plume with yellow accents erupted. The earsplitting roar gained in intensity while the engine strained against its suspension frame. He looked around the room to observe the reactions of the first-time observers. As expected, many were slack-jawed, staring at each other with wide eyes as the entire room vibrated throughout the forty-five second firing.

When the plume flamed out and the engine roar diminished, the observation room was virtually silent as the visitors absorbed what they'd just witnessed. Within seconds, however, all were excitedly gabbing, gesticulating, and grinning at each other over the incredible display of A5 rocket engine power and its implications for future German military capabilities.

All, that is, except the Führer, Erich thought with alarm as he looked behind him.

Slumped back in his seat of honor between Colonel Dornberger and General Brauchitsch, Hitler merely stroked his chin and stared straight ahead as the two military men carried on animated conversations.

To Erich's horror, the Führer looked almost... bored.

A bit later in the VIP dining room, Erich sat at the Führer's large roundtable along with General Brauchitsch, Lt. Colonel Bremmer,

Colonel Dornberger, von Braun and several other key people from the Peenemünde and Kummersdorf rocket facilities. As they waited for the food to be served, Erich kept to himself, trying to take stock of the general tone of the chatter. Had the engine test left positive, lasting impressions? Or had it already been forgotten?

Hitler's mood seemed lighter. Seated between Brauchitsch and Bremmer, he smiled broadly and nodded at something that Bremmer was relating to him privately.

To Erich's shock, the Führer and Bremmer suddenly looked directly at him. Hitler's eyes were alight. "Professor Neumann, I believe?"

All the others at the table stopped their chatting and turned their attention to him.

Erich gulped. "Yes, my Führer?"

"Colonel Bremmer here reminded me of a delightful incident that took place one day several years ago. I was returning in my motorcade to the Chancellery when a beautiful young woman in a BDM uniform boldly approached my vehicle, handed me a bouquet, and pecked me on the cheek. Brightened my day after a very stressful week, as I recall. Bremmer tells me that you are the father of that girl—Elke, am I correct?—and that she's now admirably serving the Reich as a national BDM trainer?"

Erich's face flushed with a mixture of pride and hesitancy as all eyes shifted to him. "That's true, my Führer. And to this day, my daughter still speaks with great fondness and pride of that glorious experience. She says she'll never forget it. In fact, she speaks of it so often that my wife and I are convinced she'll never let *us* forget it, either!" The table erupted in laughter, mimicking the Führer's response to Erich's confession.

Hitler's face took on a serious, almost angry expression that instantly silenced the others. "You know, we need more German women like Elke Neumann. More women who will step up and embrace their natural roles as wives, mothers, and homemakers." The Führer's jaw twitched as he looked around the table. "I am sick and tired of the poisonous ideas that the Bolsheviks, the Jews, and their friends in the liberal western countries try to inject into the minds of our beautiful, pure, Aryan German women. And, speaking of the *Jews* . . ."

He shook his head emphatically and held up a single finger as he springboarded into another familiar accusation. "For one November night and the following day, German Jews experienced a little harassment and broken glass, expressions of the legitimate outrage of the true German people. But obviously, *that* was not enough of a lesson for our pampered German Jews. No. To this day, they continue resisting our government's legitimate demands for reparations for the damages to Aryan shop owners during the riots. They refuse opportunities to emigrate. They connive with Communists and common criminals to subvert our society with treasonous propaganda and filthy pornography."

Now apoplectic with self-generated rage, the Führer pounded the table with his fist. "I tell you, gentlemen, should a larger war break out, it will be the fault of the international Jewish conspiracy. Any Jews remaining in Germany will have to pay a price that they cannot imagine. In fact, should war break out, Germany will be forced not only to take extraordinary measures against the Jews who poison us, but also to reconsider our tolerance of *any* life deemed unworthy of life that perpetually drains our country's precious economic resources."

Hitler peered at the faces around the table one by one, each of which seemed to express complete agreement, or at least grim acceptance, of what they'd just heard.

His fury spent, the Führer's face relaxed as he sagged back in his chair and sighed. "Ach! Enough unpleasantries. I'm hungry. Where's our food?"

Catching the eye of Wernher von Braun across the table, Erich could sense that, like himself, his friend was not exactly thrilled with the Führer's demeanor. After all the effort to prepare for his visit, it appeared the man had not been impressed in the least. In fact, following dessert and with his head now drooping and his arms folded across his chest, he seemed on the verge of falling asleep.

As if he'd read their minds, the Führer lifted his head. *"Dr. von Braun!"* Once again, the entire table fell silent.

"Yes, my Führer?"

"An interesting display today. But I keep hearing you rocket people talk about this magnificent new A4 design. You say it's supposed to be the ultimate weapon for instilling panic and fear in our future enemies. It's able to deliver a one-ton warhead over two hundred miles, from what I was told. But what I want to know is: *when* will this wonderful rocket be ready for mass production and fielding? And why in the world are we testing an A5 engine *before* we test an A4 engine? Have we confused our sequence numbers?"

Wernher patiently attempted to explain that, although the A4 production design had been conceived and designated first, the A5 was actually a research rocket intended to test and work out bugs for some of the critical new aerodynamic and guidance ideas that the A4 would ultimately need to incorporate. To Erich's relief, Wernher was properly evasive in predicting when the A4 would be ready for wartime application.

"We hope within a few more years at most, my Führer," he said.

Hitler nodded, seeming only moderately satisfied. "Well, I hope it won't come too late. A few more years is a long time to wait for the A4, especially after the amount of time we've had to wait to arrive at *this* point of simply testing a research engine."

On the patio of the administration building after the meal, Erich and von Braun stood huddled with Colonel Dornberger, waiting for the Führer to complete his discussions with the test range director and his staff before the visiting entourage departed for Berlin. All three were downcast over Hitler's obvious lack of enthusiasm for today's test.

Dornberger shook his head in disgust. "He'd probably have me shot if he heard me say this, but it's clear to me that the Führer has no feeling for technological progress. Fortunately, we can take some consolation in General Brauchitsch's reaction. He told me right after the test that he was absolutely thrilled by what he'd seen, and he expressed his admiration and approval for what our Peenemünde team has been able to accomplish in so few years. I think he'll be a real ally for our program going forward."

"Well, that *is* at least one thing to be thankful for today," Erich said.

Von Braun cast him a sly grin. "Weren't you also thankful to have the Führer compliment you personally regarding your daughter Elke?"

Erich laughed. "I have our family friend Colonel Bremmer to thank for *that*."

Leaning back against the pillow he'd propped against the headboard, Erich cradled his wife Gertrude as she curled beside him with her arm draped over his abdomen. After several months in their small base residence at Peenemünde, it was nice to be spending one more night in the luxurious bedroom of their Berlin-Charlottenburg house. Especially after Erich's draining experience at the Kummersdorf range earlier today.

He looked around the room appreciatively, savoring the ashy smell emanating from the woodburning fireplace. *What a good job the children have done in keeping the place going in our absence!* He would definitely make it a point to thank them all at breakfast before he and Gertrude departed once again for Peenemünde. That was, if they were all able to rise early enough after their late dates tonight: Elke with Heinz; Klara with Joshua Peters; and Walther with... who knew?

"It sounds like a mixed success today," Gertrude muttered sleepily as she snuggled closer against her husband's side.

"Mmmm. I suppose. The test went as planned, the Führer didn't seem to care, and he complimented me about his memory of Elke and her famous bouquet-kiss."

Gertrude giggled and squeezed his side. "I wouldn't consider that last part to be a small thing. You should be very, very proud. Of *all* your children."

"Oh, that's not in question. It's just that . . ." His mind drifted back to the personal tour on which he'd led Colonel Bremmer last month at Peenemünde. At their private dinner the second evening, Bremmer had waxed effusively about his admiration for Erich's family, especially for Elke. But he'd also asked some rather strange, probing questions about

Klara that struck Erich as revealing an unusual amount of curiosity—perhaps even suspicion—regarding the nature of her political and religious beliefs, her relationship with Joshua Peters, and her current work with the asylums.

At the time, he'd attributed Bremmer's questions as something to be expected considering Klara's arrest. He was probably just checking to make sure she was properly behaving herself and that no further concerns were warranted. Now, though, he remembered something that Bremmer said just before he'd left Peenemünde for his train back to Berlin: "You are a wonderful father, Erich. And you'll do well to keep encouraging Klara to be careful about her associations and follow the excellent example of her sister in that regard. After all, Elke is clearly an outstanding model of German female service and loyalty to the Reich." Something about the obvious gap between Bremmer's undeniable admiration for Elke and his lingering concern over Klara's associations did not seem—

Gertrude interrupted his thoughts. "It's just that… what, Erich?" she prompted.

He sighed and related his experience with Bremmer to her. It was the first time they'd ever really discussed the man's rather strange concern for the comparative character development of their two daughters.

Gertrude said nothing for a several moments. "You know, Erich, as friendly and helpful as he's been to Heinz and Elke, there's always been something about that man that I've never completely trusted."

Erich chewed his lip. "I know exactly what you mean."

"Erich?" Gertrude turned her face to look at his with pleading eyes.

"Yes, dear?"

"Please be careful about talking to Klara about trying to live up to Elke's standard. You know how sensitive she is about such things. Not to mention the affection she has for you. You know how she's always looked up to you."

Erich looked at her, smiled, and kissed the top of her head. "I promise, dear."

CHAPTER 14

Berlin, Germany
March 25, 1939

Even in the dim light of the obscure beer cellar downtown where Klara had suggested they meet, she could clearly read the exhaustion on Sophie's drawn face.

It's been too long, she thought. *I can't even imagine what she's been going through these past four months, with both her father and brother missing and their fates still unknown.*

After the November riots and Colonel Bremmer's veiled warning to Klara to avoid future offerings of help to Jews, Klara had decided it wouldn't be wise to tempt fate by meeting at Sophie's house anymore. As a result, the two girls had been able to get together only one time since then. That extremely hurried encounter had occurred in early December in an isolated corner of Berlin's central subway station.

There, Klara had related to Sophie the details of her father's abduction and surmised that he'd probably been incarcerated in Sachsenhausen, the local concentration camp where many Jews were taken the night of the riots. Fortunately, she was able to partially offset that devastating news with the happier story of her weekly visits with Leah at the asylum, and her assurance that the girl appeared healthy, well-engaged with her daily activities, and not overly depressed.

Tonight, however, it was evident from the stressed look on Sophie's face that things were still in a state of turmoil.

Klara poured them both a glass of dark beer from the pitcher. "All right, so fill me in."

Sophie's eyes showed a spark of light. "Papa's home now, and Jakob's in hiding. But he's safe, for now at least."

"*Oh, thank God!* Sophie, what... how . . .?"

Sophie scanned the nearby tables to ensure no one was listening. "For weeks we heard nothing about them except for what you told me," she continued. "Then finally, one night last month, a miracle happened."

"Which was?" Klara prompted breathlessly.

"Papa walked in our front door without warning. We were so glad to see him, but . . ." Sophie's voice caught as she tried to speak. "Oh, Klara! it was heartbreaking as well. He didn't look like the same person we'd always known and loved. They'd shaved his head and beard, and he must've been subjected to hard manual labor; I could see it in the way he walked, in his stooped posture. When we tried to ask him anything about what he experienced, he just said, 'I'm fine, and I managed. Don't ask any more questions.' Of course, we should have known better, since we'd heard that before they were released, a prisoner had to sign an oath that on pain of death they would never reveal to anyone what had truly gone on in the camps . . ."

Sophie paused and glanced once again at the surrounding tables to confirm no one was observing. When she looked back at Klara, her eyes expressed defiance.

"Sophie, what is it?" Klara asked worriedly.

"Papa had no intention of keeping mum about his experience forever," Sophie said proudly. "It took him a few weeks, but he finally wrote down a few of the things he wanted the world to hear." She smiled and held her hand in front of her face with a small gap between her thumb and forefinger. "He got it all in tiny writing on both sides of a single page, then he wrote a copy. After he had Mama and me read the original, he hid it somewhere, though I have no idea where. Then he asked us if there was anyone, anywhere—someone not Jewish—whom we could trust enough to give them the copy and ask them, when they felt the time was right, to share it with any of their sympathetic Aryan acquaintances. Maybe even get it published anonymously in a foreign press someday."

Klara nodded tentatively and bit her lip, as she sensed what was coming next.

"Klara, you know whose name we all came up with together. Yours, of course. But only if you'd be willing."

Her whole body trembled. This was a huge and potentially very dangerous responsibility that Sophie was asking her to undertake. Especially with all the warnings she'd received after her arrest from Colonel Bremmer, her father, and her sister about future involvement in trying to directly assist Jews in any way. And yet, the plight of the Friedmann family and the trust they'd put in her melted her heart.

"All right, I can't promise anything except to do what I can if I see an opportunity. But how would I get hold of the copy?"

"Just keep looking at me and talking, and I'll hand a folded page to you under the table. Put it in your coat pocket, take it home, and read it when it's safe. I trust you'll know what to do with it at some point."

With the transaction completed successfully, the two girls smiled and raised their glasses to each other in a modest toast.

"Now, tell me about Jakob," Klara prompted eagerly.

Sophie shook her head. "We don't know all that much. After he escaped out the back of the shop that night in November, we had no word of him for over a month. We feared he was either dead or had been arrested and taken to Sachsenhausen like Papa.

"Then, one night—when I was returning with a few food items from the home of the only Aryan neighbors who'll still speak to us—a man sidled beside me and started talking in a low voice. He told me Jakob was alive and well, that he was hiding in the home of one of the members of some little group that he's been meeting with regularly for the past year. Jakob wasn't formally a part of the group, but he was sympathetic to its purpose and had agreed to run errands for them.

"The man said that after the riot, Jakob suspected he was on the Gestapo's close watch list, just like the rest of the group. And because of that, he decided not to risk coming home even for a visit, where he might be seen and reported by nosy neighbors. He knew my parents and I would be desperate for news from him, and that's why he asked the man to meet with me and let me know he'd survived and was safe. At least for now. When the time is right, the man said, Jakob will arrange to meet privately with me.

"That was the end of the conversation. The man walked away as quickly as he'd approached, and to this day, we haven't had any further word on my brother's fate or whereabouts. But at least we can now have hope, can't we, Klara?" She looked a Klara imploringly, as if seeking her reassurance.

Klara forced a confident smile. "I have no doubts, knowing Jakob, that he will soon be in touch, and you'll all get back together again."

Sophie nodded and sighed. "I hope so, because Mama is absolutely frantic at the thought of Jakob's peril, and Leah's constantly being at the mercy of 'those Nazi wolves at the asylum,' as she calls them. She's even threatening to take matters into her own hands and smuggle Leah out of the asylum herself. That is, if she can't get her released to come live with us. But Papa says there's absolutely no chance she'll succeed, and that our whole family would be as good as dead if Mama ever got caught trying something crazy like that."

Klara grimaced. "And so, your mother's only real hope now is for Leah to get released?"

Sophie nodded. "Yes, released or simply freed one way or another."

"*Freed?* You mean: helped to *escape?* Sophie, how in the world do you think something like *that* could be pulled off? And if not by your mother, then by whom?"

Sophie shrugged and gave Klara a tentative, mysterious look. Klara knew immediately what and whom her friend was hinting at.

Without much thought, she shook her head. "Sophie, listen to me. As desperately as I want to help you, something like that would be impossible. Even as an RA, there's simply no way I could sneak myself in *and* get out with her. The security is far too tight every minute of every day and night. Besides, if I were caught it would mean life imprisonment or worse for me, and it would definitely make things harder for . . ." She stopped in mid-sentence as she noticed Sophie's lips trembling and tears forming in her eyes.

Sophie looked down at the table. "Oh, Klara, that was so unfair of me to even make you have to *think* of doing something like that. You've done so much for me and my family already, and you've even agreed to help us transmit Papa's writing. I should've known better than to even *hint* that you should risk your life like that. It's just that Mama is feeling so utterly desolate about Leah, and I couldn't think of anything else."

Klara reached out and grabbed Sophie's hand in both of hers. "Don't apologize. I want you and your parents to know something. Although I can't help her escape, I promise, with all my heart, that I will do *everything* in my power to shield your sister from bad treatment, and to get the evaluation of her condition upgraded to the point where they will consider releasing her."

Sophie's lips trembled as struggled to find the right words. "Klara," she managed finally, "you are the very best friend—Jewish or Aryan—that I've ever had. You know my parents and I love you so much. Thank you, thank you!"

(Four days later)

Klara was grateful to be the sole occupant of a spacious berth on the two-hour train ride from Berlin to the Baltic seaport city of Stettin. With the curtain drawn, she rested both her feet on the facing seat as she gazed out the window at the snow-covered landscape racing by at over eighty miles per hour.

Only one more hour, and I'll see him again, Klara thought excitedly as she imagined Joshua standing on the platform, waiting to greet her with a passionate embrace and kiss as soon as she stepped from the passenger car. As full of activity as this weekend promised to be, she could only hope there would be time for at least one or two romantic interludes. Especially since these would be the last two days she'd see him before his departure for America. Joshua and most of the US Embassy staff would be leaving permanently—the consequence of US displeasure with the Nazi government over their purported instigation of the antisemitic riots in November.

It had been two weeks since their last date at the *Berlin Philharmonie* concert, following which he'd broken her heart with the news of his unexpected departure. He'd asked her to reconsider his invitation to attend this weekend's retreat in the countryside led by Dietrich Bonhoeffer. At first, she'd been quite miffed and had struggled not to voice her disappointment over his suggestion. She knew it was a ridiculous fantasy to think that Joshua would ask her to marry and accompany him to America. But why would he prefer to spend their last days together singing Christian hymns, praying, and listening to long sermons? Could he not come up with—or was he not interested in—a more romantic scenario? Didn't he realize she longed for some intimate time with him?

Joshua managed to convince her on his idea by mysteriously promising that it would be an experience she'd never forget. He said they could take an extra day alone together after the retreat to do some cross-country skiing or "whatever else we feel like doing" at a nearby resort. What exactly all *that* meant, she hadn't been sure, but it had sounded exciting, and she'd agreed to join him.

After securing several days off from her RA job and convincing her parents and Elke that she was going on a weekend ski-trip in the country with some nursing school friends, Klara had purchased her single ticket for the train ride and departed for Stettin first thing this morning. The plan was to meet Joshua at the station, then catch a taxi to the townhome of Bonhoeffer's good friend and supporter, Ruth von Kleist-Retzow. Later this afternoon, they would depart together in a car loaned by Ruth on a two-hour trip to the wealthy widow's country estate where the retreat was being held.

To help prepare her mind and heart for the event, Joshua had gifted Klara last week with a copy of Bonhoeffer's *Cost of Discipleship*. She'd read through it completely in only three evenings, and she'd come away deeply impacted by the challenges it posed to many of the watered-down, nazified doctrines of her current church. Doctrines which she knew her parents—especially her mother—were uncomfortable with, even if they never publicly expressed it. She could see why Joshua was so intrigued with Bonhoeffer, and she looked forward to meeting with the man and some of his followers over the weekend.

Secure behind the closed curtain of her compartment, Klara pulled the Nazi-banned theologian's book out of her bag and opened it on her lap. She perused the final chapters again, pondering Bonhoeffer's reminder to all believers that God's gifts of grace, forgiveness of sin, and eternal life did not come cheaply. That they required his only Son's sacrificial suffering and death on the cross. Therefore, every believer today who benefits from these gifts should, out of thanksgiving, feel a strong and compelling obligation to repent of their sin and strive to be a faithful disciple of Christ.

But how strongly do I truly feel and act boldly upon my own beliefs? she challenged herself. *How many times have I been perfectly content to take God's salvation for granted, as something I was owed based on my sincere conviction that Jesus alone is Lord? And then gone merrily along and said or done some sinful thing without the slightest concern for God's thoughts or feelings, as if I were ungrateful for his precious gift! And for that matter, how many times have I failed to say or do the things that I should have when I see others being abused or suffering?*

Such as four days ago, when she'd deliberately refused Sophie's desperate request, largely out of fear for her own safety. Looking up from her book and out the passenger car window once again, Klara once again pondered the nagging thought that had been regularly buzzing in her mind ever since her meeting with Sophie:

Why were you so quick to outright refuse your friend's plea to help Leah escape the asylum? Couldn't you have at least looked more seriously into the possibilities?

She looked down at the cover of the book and smiled wryly as the title stared back at her in big, bold letters: *The Cost of Discipleship.* Interesting, she thought. The cost of following Jesus, who'd willingly chosen the way of the cross, laying down his life for his friends and enemies alike. Was God trying to send her a message, or was it just the devil playing his usual tricks with her overly-sensitive conscience? She wondered what Dietrich Bonhoeffer might have advised or done himself in her situation, but then she quickly dismissed further speculation. *I'll be hearing enough from* him *this weekend.*

Sighing, she checked her watch. Only a half hour to Stettin and the warmth of Joshua's arms. She placed the book back in her bag and pulled from its lining the folded, two-sided page containing Herr Friedmann's poignant memoir of his experiences after being arrested and taken to the Alexanderplatz police station the night of November 9. She settled back in her seat and, for the third time, unfolded the page and read carefully:

Twenty of us arrested Jews were made to stand silently at attention for four hours in the freezing cold in the police station's courtyard, not knowing what was to come next. Finally, we were led into a second courtyard where we were pushed, kicked, and shoved into the back of a truck with a half-open canvas top. Standing packed together like sardines, we travelled past Berlin's sea of suburbs and bright lights, then down some dark country roads. At one point I looked out and saw a sign illuminated by the headlights of a vehicle behind us and realized immediately where we were heading—north, toward Oranienburg where the Sachsenhausen camp was located. Several minutes later, we passed some large electric arc lights and entered the iron gate of the camp.

Once inside, the truck screeched to a halt and we were assaulted with raucous voices shouting, *"Out, you Jewish swine, get down out of the truck! Why are you not down yet?"* As we were jumping down, SS men armed with batons and whips attacked us. Amid wild shouts and curses, they beat us mercilessly—on the back, legs, head and face. I got kicked in the back and fell to the ground, then I got another kick in the rear: *"Will you get a move on, you old Jewish pig?"* at the same time I was hit over the head with a riding whip. One man next to me remained lying on the ground with a large, gaping wound on his forehead from which blood was streaming.

We were made to run, hounded like a herd of sheep hunted by wolves for at least thirty minutes, back and forth over a large, open area lit by huge searchlights, bringing us all to a point of extreme exhaustion. Finally, they told us to stand still and form into columns, facing a wall about five yards high that surrounded the entire camp area. Electrified barbed wire had been strung along and in front of the wall, and every fifty paces a large sign had been put up on the grassy strip in front, showing a white skull and crossbones against a black background. At regular intervals stood large towers with searchlights and SS-men who pointed their machine guns at us, seeming to dare anyone to run and throw themselves in suicidal despair onto the electric wire.

They made us stand out in the cold like this, without food or water, for a total of at least twelve more hours! At some points, they would make us squat down for long periods and do other painful exercises. Many of the older, more sickly men could not endure the strain and would fall over, receiving curses and vicious kicks to the face and torso as their reward. Several died on the spot. At long last, well into the next afternoon, we were made to march to a large building, where we were ordered to strip down and take freezing cold showers as our naked bodies were pummeled by SS men with long canes. Next, on to a large room where our heads and beards were shaved and we were given our wretched, tattered, convicts' clothing. Finally, after still more hours standing in our new uniforms and responding to the constant, insulting questions of SS men trying to degrade our Jewish culture, we entered our barracks where steaming cauldrons of thin, hot soup awaited us. After slurping the broth down, we lay on the barren floor of our barracks exhausted, crammed together and with only a bit of straw to cushion our aching bodies. I soon fell into a deep and dreamless sleep, until a siren went off at about 4:00 a.m. the following morning. Another day of brutality and terror was about to begin... I cannot bear to describe the things that happened that next day and those following. Perhaps someday, in another writing.

Thoroughly sickened by what she'd just reread, Klara returned the memoir to the lining of her bag and tried to reorient her mind as she saw they were getting closer to the Stettin train station. Somehow, she sensed there was a deep connection between Herr Friedmann's experience, her last conversation with Sophie, and her upcoming weekend with Joshua and Dietrich Bonhoeffer. What exactly that connection was and how it would play out remained to be seen. For now, she was eager for one sight only: Joshua.

As the train reached the end of the platform, she kept her face glued to the window. *There he is!* She rose from the seat, grabbed her bag, and walked out of her berth toward the exit where a small line of passengers had formed, waiting impatiently as the train ground to a halt.

A strange sensation prompted her to turn and face the man behind her. Tall and clad in a brown overcoat and a wide-brimmed fedora pulled low over his forehead, he avoided her eyes. Not seeing anything of real concern, she turned back quickly, eager to dispel the eerie feeling she was receiving from the man's presence. Fortunately, it didn't last long. Her turn came, and she stepped down from the exit door. Just as she'd imagined, Joshua rushed forward and crushed her in his embrace.

"You don't know how much I've missed you after just one week apart, Klara," was all he said before delivering the most delicious, deep kiss she'd ever received.

CHAPTER 15

Eastern Pomeranian Countryside, Northern Germany
March 29, 1939

L ater that afternoon, following lunch at the Stettin townhome of Ruth von Kleist-Retzow, Klara and Joshua set out in Ruth's loaned car on the two-hour drive to the country village of Kiekow. It was there, at Ruth's large agricultural estate just outside town, that this weekend's retreat with Dietrich Bonhoeffer would be held.

A few miles outside Stettin, Joshua pointed over Klara's lap at something outside the automobile's front passenger window. "Look over there."

"What am I looking at?" Klara asked, observing what appeared to be nothing more than a dilapidated-looking house surrounded by several outbuildings in the distance.

"*Finkenwalde*," Joshua replied. "That's where it all started for Dietrich."

He went on to explain that Finkenwalde was the first seminary in the new, Bible-centric Confessing Church movement within Lutheranism that arose in opposition to the Nazi-bootlicking German Christians. Bonhoeffer, Joshua said, was called to be Finkenwalde's director in '35. By then, he was already being targeted by the Nazis for an earlier radio broadcast in which he'd warned the country against slipping into an idolatrous cult of worshipping the Führer as the leader of the German people rather than God.

"So, what happened to the seminary?" Klara asked. "It's closed now, isn't it?"

Joshua grimaced. "Yes, courtesy of the Gestapo. After they spied on an anti-Nazi sermon preached a couple of years ago in Dahlem by one of Dietrich's Confessing Church co-founders—Martin Niemöller—they'd had enough. They arrested Niemöller and many of his congregants. Then they came to Finkenwalde and closed it down in the summer of '37, sealing every door shut."

Klara nodded in admiration. "Hmmm. Thank God that Dietrich didn't just give up then and there, like most ordinary pastors would've. But how *did* he deal with the closure?" Klara asked.

Joshua smiled. "He came up with a creative way to circumvent the authorities. He went around to various churches in the remoter countryside towns and villages whose pastors were sympathetic to the Confessing Church. Placed several ordinands-in-training with each one. They'd be registered by the local police as assistant pastors, but they would continue their studies under Dietrich's clandestine direction while receiving support from the local congregations. These days, Dietrich makes regular rounds to these churches to check on everyone's progress. Occasionally, he'll invite selected ordinands to a small private retreat on Ruth's estate—just like the one we're having this weekend. It's all undercover, of course, and everyone must always be on guard for betrayal by the Gestapo. But so far, the strategy seems to have worked very well."

"I'm really excited to be attending, especially with you," Klara said.

Joshua grinned and grabbed her hand. "And *I* heartily second that!"

Klara felt drowsy and soon dozed off, awaking only when she heard gravel crunching noisily underneath the car wheels. Opening her eyes, she stared out the window as they pulled up to the entrance of what appeared to be a large manor house.

"Look!" Joshua exclaimed. "That's Dietrich out on the front patio, already greeting a couple of guests."

He pulled the car over to the side of the driveway.

"Hello, Herr Peters!" Dietrich Bonhoeffer's hardy voice resounded from the patio as soon as he spotted Joshua helping Klara out of the car. He bounded down the steps and strode over with arms open wide. "Allow me to welcome you to my good friend Ruth's famous countryside hotel!"

The two men embraced warmly.

"I am absolutely delighted that you made it," Dietrich said. "I'm so excited to have you join our discussions and prayers. And if you're up for it after our evening session tonight, a little table tennis perhaps?"

Joshua grinned. "That would be excellent, Pastor."

Dietrich peered over his shoulder. "And who's this beautiful lady behind you? Is this . . .?"

"Pastor Bonhoeffer, please meet Fräulein Klara Neumann, my friend from Berlin."

"Ah, yes! Welcome, welcome, Klara!"

Klara stepped forward and shook the warm hand of the tall, athletic, blue-eyed man with swept-back blond hair and wire-framed spectacles. His appearance came as quite a shock. Somehow, she had not imagined that the Confessing Church movement co-founder's physical features would measure up so uncannily well to Adolf Hitler's stereotypical model for the ideal Aryan male. "It's indeed a pleasure, sir," she said.

"Wonderful! Now let's get you two set up in your rooms, and then you can come down and join the rest of us for supper." He looked at Joshua. "And perhaps tomorrow after lunch, if you'd be willing, the three of us could take a stroll and get to know each other a little better."

Joshua and Klara exchanged astonished looks. "Oh, Pastor," Joshua said, "that would be superb, but we'd hate to take your time away from the others."

Bonhoeffer placed a reassuring hand on his shoulder. "I meet and talk with my students frequently throughout the year. The two of you are special guests and deserve a little extra attention from me. Besides, I'd love to hear your stories of recent happenings in the Berlin-Charlottenburg area. As you've probably heard, the Gestapo has severely limited my abilities to visit my childhood home there."

After supper, all twenty-five of the retreat's attendees gathered in the manor house's spacious and comfortable living room. Dietrich opened the session by playing the piano and leading everyone in song. Next, he encouraged short, freely offered prayers from anyone wishing to invite God's presence and blessing on the assembly. But then, instead of the formal sermon that Klara expected, Dietrich, after a very brief devotional reading, encouraged the attendees to voice what questions weighed most heavily on their heart. Almost immediately, one of the ordinands raised his hand.

"Pastor Dietrich," the man began in a surprisingly assertive tone. "I know many of us here are genuinely upset about the antisemitic riots last November, and we certainly don't condone them. But can we truly ignore the possibility that the ultimate reason behind the evils done to the Jews must reflect the curse that they historically bear for rejecting Christ?"

Klara was shocked by the question, even though she already knew that it reflected the thinking of not only the German Christians but even some in the Confessing Church as well. She held her breath as Bonhoeffer paused to consider his answer, seeming to bow his head in prayer before doing so.

After several interminable moments, he responded. "Armin, you know I love and respect you, and I know you are not antisemitic. But as Christ's Spirit instructs me, I have to firmly refute your interpretation since I believe it to be in error. The Jewish synagogues and shops that were burned across our nation, the homes that were destroyed, the people who were viciously assaulted and incarcerated in the camps… *they are God's own. For the Nazis or anyone else to lift their hands against the Jews is to lift their hand against God himself.* Why do I say this?"

He turned and picked up his pocket-sized Bible from the top of the piano, then held it up with one hand for all to see. "I say this because I know from the Scriptures—from the words of David, Zechariah, and the Apostle Paul in the Book of Romans—that Jesus came from the Jews, and he came to rescue them first. He has never abandoned them, but always longs to reach them. They were, and they still remain, the apple of our Lord's eye . . ." Dietrich paused to stare at the ceiling, clearly overcome with emotion. He put the Bible back down and took several moments to gather himself before continuing.

"We're infinitely fortunate that Christianity also came to us, the Gentiles. But we always need to remember what Paul wrote in Romans. That it came to us in part so that the Jews might eventually become jealous of the spiritual benefits we enjoy, and freely choose to receive Jesus for themselves. The fact that some of them helped to instigate Jesus's crucifixion doesn't negate the Messiah's love and hopes for them all."

He looked directly at his questioner, Armin, clearly wanting him to grasp his main point. "Nor should that fact prevent us from forbidding Jews of today—as the German Christians are currently doing—from becoming baptized and joining our churches. As Paul said, 'I am not ashamed of the gospel, because it is the power of God that brings salvation to *everyone* who believes: *first to the Jew, then to the Gentile*.'"

A grim silence fell over the room as the audience digested the uncompromising nature of Dietrich's words.

Klara felt her chest about to burst. She knew how tremendously comforting Dietrich's message would have been to Sophie, Jakob, and their parents. Not that they would necessarily ever desire to convert to Christianity. But surely it would encourage them to know that at least one major branch of German Lutheranism—the Confessing Church—was willing to fight the cowardly trends and speak out against Jewish persecution.

By the end of the evening session, Klara had no doubts as to why Joshua had become so enamored with the unique qualities of Pastor Dietrich Bonhoeffer.

⚓

(The next afternoon)

Klara sat alone on the patio bench, waiting patiently for Joshua and Dietrich to wrap up their conversation with one of the ordinands so they could begin Dietrich's promised private walk.

A hand gently grasped the top of her shoulder, jolting her out of her reverie.

"You look as if your mind had wandered off to another planet, Klara," Joshua joked. He and Dietrich stood behind the bench, grinning down at her.

Klara grabbed his hand and blushed. "Oh, you surprised me! But don't mind me. I was just thinking about some of the amazing things I've already learned at this retreat so far."

"Well," Dietrich said, "that's certainly encouraging to hear. Are you ready to take that stroll I promised? Who knows what else God might be wishing to teach the three of us this afternoon?"

The trio set off on Dietrich's favorite path on the entire estate, a three-mile trek through some fields and woods to the bank of a small creek and back. Klara had been warned by an ordinand's wife that Dietrich's strolls usually consisted of a fast sprint, with any unfortunate partners struggling to keep up. Today, thankfully, he seemed intent on a more leisurely pace, clearly viewing their conversation to be more important than the exercise.

A bit farther along, Dietrich spun the conversation from light bantering into a more serious direction. "So, Joshua, may I ask what your plans are once you return to America?"

Joshua looked at the ground and sighed. "Good question. Up until recently, I planned to follow the same general path as Klara and enter medical school in the psychiatry field. But over the past several months, I've been seriously reevaluating that option. With world tensions heating up after the Austrian and Czech takeovers—and especially after the November riots—I've been challenged by my father to put my German language proficiency and experience to use in my own country's foreign service. Possibly in the intelligence-gathering area." He cast a knowing glance at Klara. "In fact, I think I may have already received my first assignment in that regard. Should we explain, Klara?"

"Oh, uh . . ." Klara shot him a surprised look, uncertain whether it was safe to share with Pastor Bonhoeffer what she knew he was alluding to. Earlier at Ruth's townhome, she'd brought Joshua up to date on her deep worries about Leah's asylum situation and read him the account of Herr Friedmann's Sachsenhausen experience. Joshua had been appalled and angered, swearing that he felt like ripping the heart out of the next SA or SS man he encountered alone on the street. When Klara had asked if he'd be willing and able to smuggle the written account back to America and try to get it published in a major national news or magazine outlet, Joshua had gladly accepted the task.

Sensing her reluctance to talk about the sensitive matters, Joshua grasped her forearm and whispered in her ear. "It's all right, Klara. After all we've read about, heard, and seen from him this weekend, I'm absolutely sure that if there's *anyone* we can trust for their sound advice on all this from a godly perspective, it's Pastor Bonhoeffer."

Klara knew he was right. She looked at Dietrich apologetically. "I'm sorry for hesitating. I've been so used to hiding all this from my family and friends."

Dietrich gave her a reassuring smile. "I definitely understand, Klara. I would love to hear your story, but please, share only what you're comfortable with. You have my word that I won't do or say anything to compromise anyone involved. As you might guess, I've become quite the expert at keeping secrets lately."

Having reached the creek that was the halfway point of their walk, Dietrich led them both just off the path to a small, brightly lit area beside the bank where the snow had melted and the ground was dry. He pulled a blanket out of his backpack and suggested they sit and rest while listening to Klara.

She told him everything: about her longtime relationship with the Friedmanns, the night of the riots and her own arrest, the obligation to somehow get Herr Friedmann's story published, and her goal to protect Leah in the asylum. Finally, about her worries over compromising her own family—especially her father—if her activities with the Friedmanns were discovered by the Kripo.

Bonhoeffer absorbed it all quietly, nodding and grimacing occasionally as she related some of the painful details. When she finished, she asked for his thoughts and any advice. He reached out and placed his hand over hers.

"Klara, you're in a very difficult situation and it sounds to me like you're handling it admirably. I don't know what success Joshua will have in convincing the American press that Herr Friedmann's story is authentic, but it's certainly worth a try. It could have a hugely positive impact if the right people hear about this. As for your friend, Leah, I wish I could encourage you with a more hopeful outlook, but from what my father tells me, the situation for disabled people in asylums is getting more perilous every day. Asylum directors have already been put on notice that if a full-scale war ever breaks out, there could be some radical government policies implemented." He squeezed her hand. "The only thing I can suggest is to continue doing everything in your power with God's help to keep Leah off the list of incurables."

Klara nodded, her eyes moist with tears. "Oh, Pastor, I feel so guilty now about turning down Sophie's request to help Leah escape. I-I want so much to help, but I was just too afraid to put my own life on the line like that. And then I think of all you're risking for your faith, what Martin Luther did, Joan d'Arc, and all the Christian martyrs through-out history, and I feel so ashamed. Because unlike them, I just don't think my faith is strong enough to . . ." She paused, her gaze falling to the leaf-strewn ground.

Dietrich looked at her tenderly and smiled. "Klara, you're getting *way* ahead of yourself. There's absolutely no indication I can see that God is calling *you* to pursue some reckless strategy leading to martyrdom. Whether for Leah's sake, or anyone else's. God calls *very* few Christians to prove their faith that way. And those whom he does call . . ." Dietrich paused and stared off into the distance. When he resumed his statement, his voice had a strange catch to it. "Those he does call... I believe they'll know it beyond the shadow of a doubt. And they'll also have a sustaining peace, knowing that when their moment of trial arrives, God will grant them a special grace to bear the suffering and persevere, displaying their faith to the end."

When he faced her again after a few moments, she noticed his eyes were glistening. "Just keep asking for his wisdom and courage, and let God lead you one step at a time with all this, Klara. I know he'll never call you to face any trial that's beyond your capacity to endure it in faith, together with him.

After Dietrich, Joshua, and Klara prayed at length for each other, they rose and prepared to start the journey back. Dietrich stopped short, remembering something.

"Oh, Klara," he said, searching for something in his backpack. Producing a pencil and a small scrap of paper, he scrawled something on it and handed it to her.

"If you ever feel the need back in Berlin for a supportive ear and some safe, wise counsel on things, I can highly recommend my cousin, Arvid Harnack and his wife, Mildred. They live only a block from my parents' house, and not far from you. Mildred's from America, and I am sure you'd find her to be a warm and trustworthy companion, especially in Joshua's absence. Here's their address and phone number. If you'd like, the next time I see them, I'll be sure to mention you."

"Pastor, this is all so encouraging. You've been so gracious and helpful to me. I can't thank you enough!"

Dietrich Bonhoeffer grinned and draped his arm over Joshua's shoulder. "Glad you accepted this good man's invitation to come to our retreat this weekend?"

Klara laughed. "If I hadn't, he would've dragged me here. And now I know why."

CHAPTER 16

City of Stettin, Northern Germany
April 1, 1939
(Two days later)

*I*n half an hour, I have to step on that train and watch the love of my life fade into the distance.

As their taxi approached the Stettin station, Klara tried desperately to suppress the tears that threatened to burst forth at any moment. That was *not* how she wanted Joshua Peters to remember her.

Neither said a word as they huddled in the back seat, his arm around her shoulders and her head nestled under his chin. At least, she thought, she would always have the memory of these last three days to treasure.

Yesterday, finally alone with him on the cross-country skiing trail that traversed the snowy hills, she had unquestionably experienced the most thrilling, happiest moments of her life. Especially after she'd accidentally plowed into him at the bottom of a short but steep run, sending both tumbling over each other in a laughing, tangled mass of arms, legs, and skis...

⁂

She tried to extricate herself and stand up again, but Joshua grabbed hold of one of her ski poles and pulled her screaming and giggling on top of him.

Somehow managing to kick off their skis and throw their poles aside, he placed one hand behind her head and his other arm around her waist, pressing her much smaller body against his as he kissed her for what seemed a blissful eternity.

Finally, he let her break away for some air. "That'll teach you to stand at the top of a hill and proclaim that pretty German girls are always better skiers than red-blooded American males!"

Klara laughed and rolled off him onto her side, reclining on one elbow with her hand supporting her head and her other arm draped across his chest. "Well, we *are* better... unless some *dummkopf* American skier decides to stop in their tracks without warning."

She touched his lips with her finger and leaned in to kiss him on the cheek. "Now stop complaining about my obvious female superiority and tell me how you plan to remain faithful to me. And don't lie to me. Elke warned me about all those beautiful Hollywood starlets who'd no doubt love to throw themselves at somebody like you."

Joshua grabbed her wrist, his eyes sparkling. "Do you believe *everything* your sister tells you?"

"Well, certainly not everything. But when it comes to knowing the habits of fast girls, I consider her an oracle after hearing her constant gripes about the antics of that Berlin actress who she was convinced was after her fiancé, Heinz." She closed her eyes and sighed. "Never mind. Don't even try to answer my silly question. But will you at least promise to think of me? And write to me occasionally?"

"Klara, you know I will. And I also promise, as soon as I can find a way to weasel my way back into Germany again, I'll come knocking at your door. I'll even throw stones at your window, if it comes to that." He kissed her tenderly.

She snuggled closer and lay her head on his shoulder, not certain that he truly understood how much she was in love with him. If he were to ask her right now to spend their last night alone in some Stettin hotel instead of separate rooms in Ruth's townhome, she would be hard pressed to refuse him. Her mind couldn't help but envision the delectable possibilities.

Stop it, she scolded herself. *We're not married, and he hasn't even proposed. Besides, we're leaving on separate trains in the morning, and once we part, I'll probably never see him again. A final fling just wouldn't be right.*

Joshua's poignant question brought her crashing back to harsh reality. "Klara, will you promise me that you won't make rash decisions when it comes to helping the Friedmanns? I can't stand the thought of you being locked up in prison—or worse! And anyway, remember what Dietrich said, God doesn't condone self-appointed martyrs."

"Yes, I promise I'll remember all of Dietrich's advice."

Joshua turned his face toward hers, his expression conveying the feelings she knew he had for her without the need for words—the same love she had for him.

Their sweet, prolonged kiss was interrupted by a concerned voice calling from the top of the trail. *"Are you two all right?"*

Klara and Joshua looked up the slope. A man and his wife on skis stood gawking at them, obviously wondering if it was safe to proceed.

"Yes, we're fine, sir. Thank you for asking, and don't let us stop you," Joshua shouted back. *"We were just... uh... contemplating the beautiful scenery!"*

He made eye contact with Klara, and they both burst out laughing...

The line to purchase tickets back to Berlin was unusually long, but Klara cherished the delay as it allowed a few more precious minutes before her inevitable separation from Joshua. Neither spoke, both content simply to cling to each other as they approached the counter, shoving their suitcases along beside them.

Out of the corner of her eye, Klara spotted a vaguely familiar and discomforting figure standing near the entrance to the train platforms, reading a newspaper. She looked harder and was sure it was him: the same tall man in the brown overcoat and fedora whose presence behind her when exiting the train upon her arrival in Stettin had so unnerved her. Coincidence, or . . .? She started to say something to Joshua, but then the line started moving quickly, so she let it go.

They purchased their tickets then hurried toward the platform entrance. Klara's train would be leaving first—in only ten minutes. As they were about to pass through the door, Klara glanced at the brown-coated man who seemed to be absorbed in reading his newspaper only a few feet away.

Looks innocent enough. She breathed a small sigh of relief that was quickly overwhelmed by sadness over her imminent parting from Joshua.

Reaching the platform and finding her car, Joshua took her suitcases and loaded them into her compartment, which this time would be shared with two other women.

He returned to the platform and wrapped her in an embrace.

Time's up! She pulled his head down toward hers and whispered in his ear, her voice choking.

"You come back for me, do you hear, Joshua Peters? *Promise* me."

"I promise. As soon as I possibly can."

"I love you."

"I love you, too, Klara."

One last, passionate kiss. Then Klara broke away, turned, and walked toward her passenger car. She did not look back.

PART III

THE HARDER PATH

CHAPTER 17

Berlin, Germany
October 8, 1939
(Six Months Later)

"Yes, dear, I'll be down shortly."

As Eric Neumann prepared for tonight's formal dinner celebrating both the return of the newlyweds, Elke and Heinz, from their honeymoon and Walther's completion of basic infantry training for the Wehrmacht, he marveled at how needless his worries of late had been.

His private, gloomy predictions of a national catastrophe resulting from Germany's invasion of Poland had proven to be false. Yesterday's headlines announcing the capitulation of Warsaw and the final crushing of all Polish military resistance by the German Tenth Army had erased all doubt.

No longer did Erich fear that the declarations of war by England and France in response to the Polish invasion represented something more than empty bluster. It was the same hot air that the western allies had blown after the Führer's previous takeovers of Austria and Czechoslovakia. Once again, it was all quiet on the Western Front as the liberal democracies had refused to come to Poland's material aid. Yet another major peace deal with them seemed likely, which—together with the recently signed Russian-German Nonaggression Pact—should ensure that Germany could continue unhindered in its efforts to establish itself as the dominant European economic and military superpower.

For the first time since Hitler's formal recognition as the nation's dictator over five years ago, Erich's personal outlook for Germany under National Socialism had shifted from resigned acceptance to cautious optimism.

And as the nation's prospects look brighter, so too does the outlook for our rocket development program which I've been fretting over so much, he thought happily as he patted his face dry after shaving and stared at his image in the bathroom mirror. He wished that he could add to this evening's enjoyment by sharing his story of the launch success achieved at the Peenemünde test range just two days after the Polish invasion had commenced at the beginning of September. Unfortunately, the top secret nature of the work there prevented any casual disclosures.

Still, Erich couldn't help himself from reveling in the memory of that glorious late summer morning. He'd stood next to Colonel Dornberger and Wernher von Braun, watching the first full-scale A5 rocket lift from the firing platform. As the bright yellow and red missile rose vertically in the azure sky, the three men had held their breaths, the backs of their necks aching as they stared aloft. Would the new, beefier rudder design work properly with the gyroscopes and the new guidance and control algorithm to keep the bird on course despite the strong winds?

In little more than half an hour, they had their answer when the intact rocket body was recovered in the dark waters of the Baltic. The first full-fledged A5 had reached a height of over seven miles and achieved a range of eleven miles, leaving the entire Peenemünde rocket team rejoicing. Supreme Army Commander Brauchitsch had been so impressed that he'd personally guaranteed he would intervene with Hitler to ensure that funding for the A5 research program would continue. Also, that the development of the ultimate rocket weapon—the A4 model—would receive the highest priority going forward.

After combing his hair and putting on his dinner jacket, Erich gave himself one last look in the mirror. *No sign of gray hairs yet, and only the slightest traces of wrinkles across the forehead. Not bad, considering all the stress of these past few years. And with the future now so bright...*

He started down the steps to the living room, delighted by the mixed aromas of sauerkraut and Gertrude's traditional recipe for Maultaschen dumplings.

Halfway down, the front doorbell rang.

"*Vati!*" Elke called from the living room. "Colonel Bremmer is here."

Erich's throat tightened as he hurried down the remaining steps to greet tonight's guest of honor. It was Elke who had insisted on Bremmer's presence tonight. She and Heinz wanted to thank him for his continuing friendship with them, as well as his obvious regard and concern for the welfare of the entire Neumann family.

Why are Gertrude and I still hesitant about him? he chided himself. *After all the kindnesses he's shown to us, including getting Klara out of trouble after the riots last November? And honoring me by reminding the Führer of Elke's famous bouquet kiss? The man has repeatedly shown such genuine affection and concern for our entire family.*

As Erich placed his hand on the doorknob and prepared to offer his friendly greeting, he resolved to stop doubting what had by now become imminently clear:

Lt. Colonel Bremmer is on our side.

At the meal's conclusion, Erich and the others at the dining table watched with anticipation as Elke and Heinz finished unwrapping the package that Colonel Bremmer had just presented to them.

"Oh, Colonel!" Elke exclaimed. "I do believe this is the most beautiful gift you could have possibly blessed us with. It's just so thoughtful of you."

She dabbed at her eyes with a handkerchief as Heinz stood and held up the gold-framed, art-deco oil painting of a breathtaking Bavarian alpine landscape scene for all to admire.

Bremmer smiled at her fondly. "I only wish I could've been at your wedding to present it there, and to enjoy your special day together. *Ach!* The work of your city's Kripo chief never ceases to interfere with their preferred activities.

"But enough attention on me," Bremmer said firmly. "This is an evening to celebrate the good fortune and accomplishments of the Neumann family and Heinz Schröder, their new son- and brother-in-law."

He lifted his wine glass to propose a long-winded, grandiloquent toast. "To the lifelong happiness of Elke and Heinz. To the wonderful contributions that Erich and Klara are making to the fields of rocket science and psychiatric nursing. To the excellent models that Gertrude and Elke provide for National Socialist mothers and wives. And last but not least, to the courageous examples of Walther and Heinz who will soon be leaving to defend our country from the forces of Bolshevism and international Jewry that have long oppressed us... May the protection and blessings of Providence abound for all."

"And here's to you and the SS, Colonel Bremmer," Heinz interjected, his voice choked with emotion. "For showing me the true meaning of all-out commitment to one's Fatherland and Führer. *Zum Wohl, and Heil Hitler!*"

All raised their glasses. "*Zum Wohl, and Heil Hitler!*"

Erich took a long sip, wondering if Bremmer had noticed that Klara was the only one who hadn't voiced the words of the toast. If so, he hoped he would not take offense. *She seems unusually tense and out of sorts tonight.*

Bremmer leaned toward Heinz and placed his hand on his shoulder as he arched a teasing eyebrow in Walther's direction. "Maybe someday, Heinz, we'll convince your best friend to graduate from the Wehrmacht and join you in the SS. Walther, have you heard about all those wonderful reports we're hearing of the performance of our new *Waffen-SS* combat units in Poland?"

Walther grinned hesitantly. "Yes, I have heard *some* of the reports, Colonel."

"Good! Then you must admit that all those old, conservative army generals who doubted the ability of the SS to engage in full-scale military operations—the ones who said we were good for nothing more than fighting paramilitary street battles, overseeing state security police, and guarding concentration camps—they were badly mistaken."

Walther looked as if he were about to say something, but he merely nodded and studied his plate. Erich sensed that for some reason his son was not in full agreement with Bremmer's rosy assessment of SS combat capabilities.

An awkward silence ensued for several moments.

"Well," Elke spoke up, "I, for one, am thankful for all that SS leaders like you, Colonel, have done to help our Gestapo and Kripo police rid this city of Communists and violent criminals. I saw the statistics recently, and it's amazing what's been achieved."

Bremmer leaned back in his chair, nodded, and folded his arms. "Yes, we've made excellent strides in those regards. My hope is that in a year or so, we'll have most of the remaining garbage removed. I just hope our efforts won't be sabotaged by the religious fanatics and other so-called humanists in this country. Men like that Catholic priest von Galen, and the Lutheran Confessing Church pastor, Dietrich Bonhoeffer, who we banned from preaching his nonsense in Berlin. Weak men like these are always objecting to the tough measures called for."

He cast a brief glance at Klara, who held her face in a frozen smile.

"But have no doubts," Bremmer continued, his voice taking on an ominous tone as he addressed the entire table. "With war now unleashed, we've entered a new era. Enemies of the state will no longer find any safe haven. Certainly not in this city, at least. Sooner or later, they will *all* be flushed out and dealt with. I personally guarantee it."

A stunned, cowed silence gripped his audience.

Hope we'll always stay on his *good side*, Erich thought.

Later that evening, Klara grasped her brother's arm as they strolled together on the paved path beside the bank of the Spree River which threaded its way through Charlottenburg and into the heart of Berlin. During dinner, she'd sensed that Walther was troubled by something. Knowing that he'd be departing Berlin tomorrow to join his new army unit posted near the French border, she wondered if it might have to do with his natural trepidations over the possibility of experiencing lethal combat for the first time. Concerned, she'd suggested the river walk as a familiar, private venue for sharing what she suspected might be on his heart.

After some light cajoling, Walther confessed to what was really bothering him. "It's something Colonel Bremmer said, Klara."

"About . . .?" she prompted.

"About the supposed accomplishments of those new Waffen-SS units in Poland. Colonel Bremmer conveniently left out part of the story."

"What do you mean?"

Walther said nothing for several seconds. In the dim light afforded by the regularly spaced walkway lamps, Klara could see that his face looked strained. He motioned to a small bench by the side of the path and suggested they sit.

After waiting for two casual strollers to pass by and checking around to ensure their privacy, Walther leaned in close and spoke softly. "Apparently, it wasn't just Waffen-SS combat units that were sent to Poland. There were special SS follow-up units called *Einsatzgruppen* that were sent behind the main forces."

Klara stared at him blankly. "So, what was their purpose?"

Walther stared at her with widened eyes. "They were *death squads*, Klara. Assigned to systematically identify and immediately execute all Polish intelligentsia, clergy members, teachers, members of the nobility, and political leaders. Especially Jews. Basically, anyone connected with the Polish national identity, which Hitler's decided to erase from the face of the earth. From the stories I've heard, they accomplished their mission quite well. Tens of thousands of civilians, shot and buried in mass graves. Cases of dozens of Jews locked up in their synagogues and burnt alive or shot while they tried to escape." He paused and stared down at his lap. "There. You asked, and now you know what was bothering me."

His words struck Klara like a thunderbolt. It took several seconds to recover from her mind-reeling, stomach-knotting revulsion and face the implications of what she'd just heard.

"Walther, does Heinz know about this? And if so, how can he... how can *you*... possibly keep serving in—"

Walther placed his other hand over hers and took a deep breath. "I know what you're about to ask, Klara. I can't speak for Heinz. Before tonight, it'd been quite a while since we'd last seen each other, and I'm not even sure he's aware of everything. Although, you'd think with his Waffen-SS officers' training nearly complete and his connection with Bremmer, that he would know far more about this than I do. If so, he doesn't seem to be showing any stress about it.

"As for me . . ." He shook his head. "It sickens me to think that a civilized country like ours could allow, let alone command, a part of its armed forces to commit atrocities like that. I'm still holding out some hope we'll eventually find all these stories were untrue, or at least greatly exaggerated. But assuming they are true, there's only one thing that can keep my conscience clear enough to follow through on my army commitment . . ."

"And what's that?"

"Knowing it's my duty to defend Germany from the Bolsheviks and those arrogant western nations who keep rubbing our noses in the dirt after World War I."

Klara squeezed his hand and nodded. After reading Herr Friedmann's account of Sachsenhausen, she had no doubts what the SS were capable of when it came to atrocities. For a moment, she considered sharing with Walther the story of his experience, but she quickly thought better of it. Walther had no idea of her continuing involvement with Sophie, and at this point, she had no desire to burden him further with concerns over her own dangerous actions of late. *He'll be gone tomorrow, and who knows if or when I'll see him again? I should just give him whatever comfort and encouragement I can.*

"Walther, I'm so proud of you for wanting to defend our country without turning a blind eye to its faults. I know you have a good heart and would never allow yourself to be cajoled into murdering or abusing innocent civilians. And I'd certainly hope the same would be true for Heinz, if not Colonel Bremmer."

"Yes, one would hope so." Walther grimaced and shook his head. "Heinz, Elke, Colonel Bremmer... what a trio. They seem so... oh, I shouldn't even say it." He paused and bit his lip. "Klara, what do *you* think of Bremmer?"

She hesitated, wanting to be careful in her answer. "Well, the man is certainly impressive in both his appearance and reputation. It's true that he does seem overly affectionate toward Heinz and Elke for my own personal tastes, but I must admit he's shown kindness to all of us. Especially to me, when he went out of his way to get me released from jail after the riots. He could just as easily have let them charge me and keep me locked up."

Walther shrugged. "All I can say is, I'd never want to do anything to provoke him. Heinz once told me Bremmer's an absolute *terror* when it comes to tracking down and extracting confessions from violent criminals. Heinz said he's so effective, that even the Gestapo will occasionally send one of their political prisoners over to his special interrogation cell so he can wring the truth out of them. He can't stand it when suspects lie to him, especially enemies of the state. He takes their lies very personally."

A chill coursed through Klara's body. She recalled the strange look Bremmer had cast her way as he'd mentioned Dietrich Bonhoeffer's name at dinner. It was as if he somehow knew of Klara's attendance at Bonhoeffer's retreat last March and was testing her reaction to his accusation against the man. After all, the main condition for his decision to release her from jail last November had been her agreement to avoid future contact with Jews and other troublemakers.

Oh, stop imagining things, she scolded herself. *It's been months since Joshua and I saw Pastor Bonhoeffer. Months since I last met with*

Sophie. If Colonel Bremmer wanted to arrest and interrogate me over either of those connections, he would've done so already.

Walther checked his watch. "It's getting late. We'd better get back. Father wanted to talk with me tonight since he and Mama are leaving early tomorrow for Peenemünde... and this is the last I'll see them for quite a while." His voice quavered as he spoke the last few words, prompting Klara to wrap her arms around him.

CHAPTER 18

Eglfing-Haar Asylum, Southwest of Munich
October 31, 1939

The public tour of the children's ward at the Eglfing Asylum had begun less than two minutes ago. But already, Klara's reaction to the director's opening remarks was one of utter disgust. She wondered if any of the twenty-some visitors, most with nonmedical backgrounds, felt the same way.

Standing beside two of the asylum's female nursing assistants, Klara could only close her eyes, bite her tongue, and barely keep herself from shaking her head with revulsion as Direktor Hermann Pfannmüller droned on.

What a far cry from the modest, respectful approach of Dr. Bergmann at the Wittenau Sanitorium, she thought. No doubt, this was one of the reasons Klara's RA advisor, Professor Gottschald, had insisted she travel the six hours by train from Berlin to spend a week at Eglfing with Pfanmüller and his staff. He wanted her to observe and gather data on the differences in methods, patient responsiveness, and leadership styles at the two institutions.

"Overall, I think you will agree that our facilities are immaculately clean and well cared for," proclaimed the obese, bespectacled Pfannmüller as he pointed over the shoulders of his audience toward the ward's fifteen beds of severely disabled children. Each one was only between the ages of one and five. "But with our nation now on a war footing, it's important to be truthful about the difficulties we are facing and how we are effectively and humanely dealing with them. Here, allow me to illustrate . . ."

Pfannmüller broke off his speech and strode through the awed group of visitors, which had separated to create a path like the Red Sea parting for Moses. Reaching the first bed on the left, he motioned for one of the assistant nurses to come help. Together, they pulled a little boy with both forearms missing out of the bed. Pfannmüller sat on a tall stool and positioned the child in front of himself. He then held the tiny, emaciated boy up in the air by the back of his collar, displaying him like a dead hare to the gaping audience.

"As a National Socialist and member of the SA, creatures like this naturally represent to me an unbearable burden—not only to themselves, but also upon the health of our entire nation. And so, how can we relieve this burden? Well, we certainly wouldn't want to relieve it through extreme, artificial measures such as poisons or injections, since that would only give the foreign press yet more propaganda material against our nation. No. As you see, our approach here is simpler and more natural."

With a knowing look and a cynical smile, Pfannmüller set the child, his head sagging, down on the floor. "This one will last another two or three days." Pfanmüller went on to quickly clarify that his asylum was not being so inhumane as to *completely* withdraw food from the children; it was merely gradually reducing their rations.

The sight of the fat, grinning director with the whimpering skeleton at his feet, surrounded by other obviously malnourished children, made Klara want to retch. She could only ascribe the crass way Pfannmüller displayed his cruel methods to some devilish combination of narcissism, sadism, and foolishness.

Seeking at least a hint of confirmation for her own sense of alarm, she leaned over and muttered to the nursing assistant next to her. "Did

I hear him right? They're intentionally *starving* these poor children to death here?"

The nurse looked at her with a cold stare. "There's really no other logical choice. We are doing the best we can. I suggest you get used to it."

Klara barely managed to stuff a horrified, furious retort. *Not here. Save it for my report to Professor Gottschald.* She simply nodded, then turned and followed the rest of the tour group out of the ward. On her way, she couldn't stop thinking about what she'd just witnessed and heard: the barely disguised practice of child starvation at Eglfing-Haar.

It was a practice that, in light of the Nazi government's recent rhetoric, did not bode well for Leah Friedmann.

(Two Days Later: Berlin University Medical School)

"Klara, I can only imagine how difficult it must have been for you to observe what you did. I so admire your concern and compassion for that poor child. Your honest report has been extremely illuminating. It will no doubt help me raise some legitimate concerns with my superiors at the university, and also with the city's public health commission. I'm so proud of you, and I can't thank you enough."

Never had Klara felt so understood, so appreciated by Professor Otto Gottschald. Yes, he had always exhibited great respect for her industriousness and intelligence and had often seemed to eye her with a strong hint of tender affection.

Today, however, after sitting in front of his university office desk and pouring out her heart, Klara believed she may have finally found the professional ally she had craved for so long. A highly learned man who shared her passion for both the scientific and humanitarian dimensions of psychiatry, who truly understood the unique pressures faced by a female medical student under the authority of National Socialism. A man willing to report the truth to a higher authority, despite the potential dangers.

Klara looked at him, her eyes glistening. "Oh, Professor, I am so glad to be working for you. You've treated me very kindly, and I feel I've learned so much of value through this RA appointment. I-I just wish . . ." Her voice trailed off at the thought of Leah and the peril she would certainly face if the Eglfing-Haar method became widespread among the nation's asylums. *Is now the time to share my concern for her with Gottschald?*

Gottschald's voice sounded concerned, soothing. "What? What is it that you hope for, Klara? Please, tell me."

A small voice in her head advised her to avoid revealing too much. "I just wish that our asylums might find some other way to serve the national cause besides starving innocent children."

Gottschald nodded sympathetically. "Yes, I definitely agree. That does seem to be an excessively harsh solution to an admittedly tough problem. Fortunately, I know there are other people in the medical community who are arguing for alternative, kinder strategies for dealing with the economic necessities that have been thrust upon us. I'm not at liberty to discuss those right now, but I can assure you that important discussions are taking place at the highest levels. We can remain hopeful. In any case, rest assured that I will carefully consider your observations of Eglfing-Haar. They will certainly inform my future discussions with colleagues and superiors. You have done well, Klara."

"Thank you, sir."

With the interview over, Klara stood to salute as Gottschald did the same. Before she could raise her arm, however, the built-up tension and emotion from the last several days erupted. Her entire body shook as she brought both hands up to her mouth.

Seeing her distress, Gottschald immediately swept around his desk and took her in his arms. "There, there, Klara. I know how hard it must be with all you've been through." His arms felt warm and comforting. She closed her eyes and allowed him to lay her head against his chest and tenderly stroke the side of her face and hair. A tiny sense of alarm pinged in her mind, but she brushed it off, preferring to accept the consolation she so desperately needed. It helped to imagine that it was

Joshua embracing her, rather than her well-meaning professor and RA supervisor.

"Klara, look at me," Gottschald said suddenly.

Confused, she pulled her head back and lifted her eyes to meet his. In an instant, she knew that Gottschald's embrace was motivated by something more than simple heartfelt compassion. She now recalled he was single, and that Heidi—her student-friend—had once hinted at his involvement with another student.

"Everything will be all right, I promise." He closed his eyes and tilted his head toward hers, obviously intending to kiss her on the lips. At the last moment, she turned her face slightly so that his kiss just missed the corner of her mouth, landing on the bottom of her cheek. Shocked, she allowed it to linger, responding in kind with her own—a feigned gesture of polite acknowledgement, belying the sudden spasm of revulsion that chorused through her body as he tightened his grip around her waist and pressed her head harder against his lips.

After several interminable seconds, he pulled his face away. His eyes gradually came into focus, and he smiled awkwardly as he released his grip and took a step back. He seemed to be panting slightly. "Forgive me, Klara. I meant no disrespect… I wished only to—"

Klara was quick to alleviate his concern. She could not afford to lose Gottschald's sponsorship and support. "Oh, no sir, I took no offense. You were just being gracious at a time when I very much needed it. Thank you." Anxious to get away, she took a step back, snapped to attention and saluted. Gottschald did not return the salute, but merely smiled and nodded.

She moved to walk out of the office and had just reached the door when Gottschald's icy voice brought her to an abrupt halt. "Oh, Fräulein Neumann."

She turned again to face him, unsure what to expect.

"I strongly advise you to keep everything you experienced at Eglfing-Haar and what we discussed in this office strictly confidential. There are far too many interested parties beyond these walls who may be inclined to misinterpret things in a counterproductive and malicious way. Please trust me to handle the concerns you've raised in a proper manner. Remember, starting vicious rumors could harm many people, including yourself. Will you do that?"

Klara knew she was not being offered a choice. "Of course, sir. You can rely on me."

CHAPTER 19

Berlin, Germany
December 6, 1939
(Five weeks later)

Klara glanced once more at the small piece of paper with the address, wondering briefly if Sophie's messenger had made a mistake.

Surely, she thought, Sophie could not have meant the rundown apartment building that now faced her from across the street. Even by the unpretentious standards of Berlin's inner city, working-class Neukölln district, the dilapidated, sagging wooden structure appeared to be on the verge of collapsing at any moment.

Then again, why should I be expecting anything else? Wasn't it me who asked Sophie to suggest an unassuming, safe meeting place—one unlikely to warrant observation by Colonel Bremmer's roving Kripo agents? Given Bremmer's reprimand about offering her help to Jews, discovery of this meeting by the Kripo was the last thing she needed.

Klara checked her watch and saw that she was twenty minutes early for the meeting. With the day being unusually warm for December, she walked to a nearby bench and sat down. She closed her eyes and inclined her face gratefully toward the bright, early afternoon sun.

What a relief to be alone and unwatched, away from the standing-room-only crowd on the U-Bahn train she'd taken to get here. It wasn't easy to get away from prying eyes and ears these days, and the thought of finally being able to let her guard down with her best friend was a pleasant one.

The girls had met once in Tiergarten Park last June, shortly after Joshua's departure for America. Klara had sensed that someone had been watching them, though nothing had come of it. Both had agreed, however, that communication by mail would be safer for a while at least. Since then, they'd exchanged occasional short letters and messages relayed by a former mutual schoolmate. Today's secretive meeting would be their first communication since Klara's experience at Eglfing-Haar. With all that had happened recently, Klara knew the next two hours would be dominated by family news and highly emotional displays of both laughter and tears.

Of course, Sophie and the Friedmann family's situation would provide the chief topics of conversation. Klara considered how much she should reveal about her mounting worries for Leah in view of her Eglfing-Haar discovery, and, perhaps even more disconcerting, the private conversation she'd had last week with Dr. Bergmann at the Wittenau Sanitorium.

Bergmann had delivered some alarming news regarding some new order from the Reich Health Commission requiring the registration of the names of *all* inmates with certain specified hereditary disabilities. Current capacity for performing useful work was to be indicated, and any non-Aryans on the list were to be specially denoted. Unfortunately, despite Leah's impressive improvements in her moods, mental alertness and ability to work alone in her sewing and asylum gardening tasks, Bergmann had been obligated to include her name on the list. He wasn't sure what it would lead to, but he thought it possible that those on the list might eventually be transferred to cheaper facilities where they'd receive basic care but no further treatment for their condition.

No, Klara resolved. *I won't destroy Sophie's hope by scaring her with all this. What can either of us do about it, anyway? I'll just try to keep her spirits up with my stories of Leah's progress.* She checked the address once again, rose from the bench and walked across the street.

Before exiting the building's rickety, barely functioning elevator on the third floor, Klara peered down the corridor to ensure no one was present. Hurrying to the door at the far end, she knocked four times—the pre-arranged signal. The door opened almost instantly to reveal Sophie, who reached out and pulled Klara inside.

The girls stood for a moment simply facing each other, both at a loss for words. Sophie appeared thinner, her face even more pinched than the last time they'd met. Fortunately, she still had that bright fire of determination in her eyes that Klara had always admired and treasured.

Sophie smiled at Klara's concerned look. "I know. It's this drab outfit that I keep having to wear over and over. Thanks to Herr Hitler, most of us Jews don't have enough money to buy new clothes anymore. Don't fret though, at least I trouble myself to wash them once in a great while." Bursting with laughter, the girls fell into each other's arms, embracing for the first time in months.

"My, how did you settle on *this* place?" Klara asked, peering dubiously around the small living room. The room's walls were entirely barren, and it was furnished only with several cheap wooden armchairs facing a small sofa across a low coffee table.

"The building's owned by the father of a trusted Aryan friend of mine. She knew this apartment had been vacated by a renter recently. She asked her father if she could use it occasionally for weekend meetings with some literary club friends she has in this area, at least until another renter was found. He agreed, she gave me a spare key, and... *voilà!*"

Sophie brought in a pot of tea and some cups from the kitchen. The girls sat together on the couch drinking their tea and nibbling on pieces of a braided, honey-sweetened egg bread loaf that Sophie had brought in her purse for the occasion. After sharing some family anecdotes, Klara updated her friend on the good news about Leah's progress and general spirit. The conversation took a depressing turn as Sophie described the menial, odd jobs that she and her parents had been forced to take as a result of the latest slew of anti-Jewish decrees passed by the government.

"They pay barely enough to make our rent and keep food on the table, and we—"

Four quick knocks on the door interrupted her sentence. Klara stared at her in wide-eyed terror. Had their safe house somehow been discovered?

Sophie smiled and placed her hand on Klara's forearm. "Nothing to worry about. I was expecting a guest."

"A *guest*?"

"Yes, someone I'd like you to meet." Sophie arose from the couch and grasped Klara's hand as the two walked toward the door.

Sophie leaned her head close to the door frame. "Who is it?" she whispered.

"It's me... Franz," responded a baritone voice on the other side.

"Oh, good." Undoing the chain lock and opening the door, Sophie stepped aside to allow a man in a dark overcoat with scarf and fedora to enter the room. After hugging him briefly, Sophie pulled away and gestured toward Klara behind her.

"Franz Brockhaus, please allow me to introduce my good friend, Klara Neumann."

"Very pleased to meet you, Fräulein," he said in a friendly, vaguely familiar voice.

Klara accepted the man's proffered hand and shyly lifted her eyes to meet his. With his wide, walrus-style mustache and thick-lensed glasses, it was difficult to make any preliminary judgments of his character. His name didn't sound Jewish, but...

The man held on to her hand longer than expected, and she began to feel uncomfortable. He leaned in a bit closer. "Don't recognize me yet, Klara?"

She drew back and looked at Sophie, who stood beside him with her hand covering her mouth, clearly trying to contain her laughter.

Klara peered back at him, confused. "No, I . . ." She stopped talking as the man released her hand and took a step back. He removed his glasses, then peeled off his false mustache. Letting them drop to the ground, he grinned and lifted his hat.

"*Jakob!*" Klara cried, throwing herself into his arms. It had been over two years since she'd last seen him, and she knew from Sophie that he'd been in hiding ever since those November riots.

"Looks like my disguise is working pretty well, Sophie." Jakob laughed. "Did you mistake Franz for a Gestapo detective, Klara?"

"Oh, you!" Klara chided him, slapping his arm. In an instant, her expression turned serious. She took his hand and led him to one of the armchairs facing the couch, then she made him sit as she poured him a cup of tea and Sophie tore off a thick slice of egg bread for him.

Leaning forward with hands folded across her knees on the edge of the couch, Klara studied him. "Tell me everything, Jakob."

Jakob rolled his eyes and groaned. "That would take an entire week, and I only have an hour or so. But I'll give you the highlights, if you want to call them that."

Klara sat mesmerized as Jakob related the harrowing tale of his illicit activities and constant efforts to avoid discovery.

It had started a few months before the November '38 riots. Feeling outraged and helpless against the Nazis' antisemitic legislation and increasingly violent acts of persecution, he'd sought the solace of several other Jewish friends who had banded together under the inspirational leadership of a Berlin electrician named Herbert Baum. Baum also happened to be a member of the outlawed German Communist Party, whose ranks had been decimated over the past several years by arrests, incarcerations, and executions.

At first, their group had focused on weekly meetings to discuss German antisemitism along with a variety of esoteric philosophy books and theoretical Marxist-Leninist tracts. Soon, though, Baum had encouraged them to consider taking on a more active role against the Nazis. By the time of the November riots, Jakob and some others had become involved in the distribution of leaflets arguing against National Socialism.

"We were still small at that point, but we'd definitely made ourselves a nuisance to the Berlin Kripo, who were thankfully busy with other things," Jakob recalled. "A couple of days before the riots, I heard someone had accidentally dropped my name along with a couple others in our group to a possible Gestapo informer, hinting that we might be Jewish-Communist sympathizers. You can imagine my panic on riot night when the SA men pounded on our shop door. I thought it was the Gestapo... after me, specifically. Fortunately, I'd already thought about an exit plan in case of emergency, and I escaped out the back. I eventually made it by foot to an Aryan friend's house in the Mitte district. He agreed to take me in for a few days to let things settle down before trying to return home."

Jakob shook his head sadly. "When I learned that Papa had been arrested, I decided to stay in hiding to avoid putting the rest of the family at risk. And that's what I've been doing ever since, moving from one safe place to another, wearing this silly disguise whenever I go out. I had a friend contact Sophie to let the family know I was alive and well, and just two weeks ago I met her here." He looked at her and smiled fondly. "It was the first time in over a year that I'd seen anyone in the family. She told me about what Papa had gone through at Sachsenhausen . . ."

He stared down at his lap, unable to continue for several moments. He finally focused on her and resumed, his voice choked. "And about your brave agreement to take the copy of Papa's memoir and ask your boyfriend to smuggle it to America. I—we—can't thank you enough for that, Klara."

She sighed. "I only wish I had more good news to report about Joshua's efforts to get it published. In his last cryptic letter I got just before the war started, I was able to decipher that he'd received interest from a couple of magazines. But there was still some doubt about its authenticity and appropriateness for publication. He said he wouldn't stop trying, though, and I know he won't."

Jakob closed his eyes and nodded. "When it comes to exposing the Nazis' crimes, *trying* is about all that can be expected from anyone these days. At least that's what our leader, Herbert Baum, keeps telling us."

"*What?*" Klara eyed him with alarm. "Jakob, are you *still* in contact with that group? What about your family? If you get caught, you know things would come down hard on them as well!" She glanced at Sophie, baffled to think that she and her parents could be at peace with Jakob's choice.

Jakob touched her forearm. "I'm not leaving them to the wolves, Klara. For that very reason, Herbert encouraged us to do everything we can to help our family members emigrate as soon as possible."

"*Emigrate?*" Klara frowned. "I thought other countries weren't accepting Jewish refugees from Germany anymore."

Jakob and Sophie exchanged knowing glances.

"We have a special contact," Jakob explained. "Herbert put us in touch a while back. She's the American wife of an important official in the Reich Ministry of Economics. The man's a Nazi party member, but he's secretly anti-Hitler, and he and his wife are both sympathetic to the plight of Jews in Germany. As it turns out, the wife has connections with an American Jewish emigration organization that's helping German Jews to resettle in special farming communities in the Dominican Republic."

He motioned for Sophie to complete the story.

"It was amazing, Klara! The wife, Frau Harnack, went all out for us. Thanks to her efforts, we're expecting visas to come through soon for my parents, me, and Leah. Assuming we get those and my parents make a final decision to go through with things, we'll be able to book passage by train to Lisbon, Portugal and from there on a neutral ship bound for the DR. But it all depends on those visas coming through."

Klara cocked her head back. *Frau Harnack? American wife?* Was this the same American woman whom Dietrich Bonhoeffer had spoken of so warmly? "Excuse me, Jakob. Is Frau Harnack the wife of *Arvid?*"

He tilted his head in surprise. "Yes, do you know them?"

"I haven't met them, but someone I know who's definitely anti-Nazi told me about them. He suggested I meet them if I ever felt the need for support and encouragement given my own less-than-ecstatic views of National Socialism."

Jakob cast a knowing glance at his sister. "I'd say you would get more than support and encouragement from the Harnacks, Klara, were you to meet them. You'd get a whole new perspective on things that *all* of us who have to remain in Germany could be doing at some point in the near future. In fact, if you'd like, I'd be happy to escort you to their house one evening and introduce you!"

"Well," Klara demurred, "I'm not sure I'm quite ready for *that*, yet. But I'll certainly keep your offer in mind."

Jakob nodded. "Whenever you're ready."

After several more minutes of discussing Leah's situation and how to stay in touch, the three stood and embraced as Jakob voiced a traditional Jewish prayer asking for blessing and protection. *Strange,* Klara thought as he was doing so. *Before today, I never knew him to even pretend he believed in anything religious.*

Exiting through the rear of the apartment building at Jakob's suggestion, Klara returned to the street and headed toward the U-Bahn station. She'd travelled less than a block when, out of the corner of her eye, she noticed a tall man standing just ahead in the alcove of a shop entrance. He was smoking a cigarette, and his eyes briefly met hers as she passed by. She wracked her brain for a moment, trying to place him.

Oh, my God. Different-colored coat and fedora, but I'm sure... it's him! The same man who'd given her such chills upon her arrival and departure at the train station in Stettin.

Klara quickened her pace and looked over her shoulder. Fortunately, just as at Stettin, the man did not seem interested in following or even observing her any further. Still, she couldn't help but wonder: might these sightings reflect something more than mere coincidence?

As she approached the U-Bahn, she couldn't get rid of the disturbing thought of herself as a small mouse that had unwittingly stepped into a trap. A trap that was about to spring.

CHAPTER 20

Wittenau Sanatorium, Northwest of Berlin
January 19, 1940
(Six weeks later)

Klara grasped the tiny, malformed hand of eight-year-old Ingrid Mayer as the two stood in line with the other patients and escorts. All were waiting for the bus to appear around the corner of the asylum's main building.

"Any minute now, Ingrid," Klara tried to reassure her young charge who, unable to speak intelligibly, stared up at her with a mixture of confusion and fear. "And once we're on, I promise I'll sit beside you the whole way. There's nothing to worry about."

What a brazen lie, Klara thought. In fact, she herself was anxious and trembling inside over what she feared the day would bring. If her hunch was correct, Ingrid and the other severely disabled patients in line could well be embarking on a one-way journey to permanent, hopeless exile in an institution offering only the barest of life-support functions.

She'd only found out about this difficult assignment yesterday morning at the end of Dr. Bergmann's review of her weekly observations.

"Klara, I need you to do something a bit different tomorrow," Bergmann had said mysteriously.

"Of course, Herr Direktor."

"It seems we're just beginning to understand the true purposes behind that patient registration I spoke to you about last month. I received a call last night from the Reich Health Commission. Tomorrow morning, the first group of ten patients—the ones whose names I submitted—are to be picked up and transported to an unnamed, nearby facility. They assured me the patients will be well cared for there and, in fact, will be eligible for some new, experimental therapies. That may well be, but I'd like to have a better understanding of what kind of facility this is, and how they handle incoming new patients. They were unwilling to explain these things over the phone, but they told me I could assign a few trusted staff to escort the children to keep them calm on the bus and during the admission procedures at the facility."

He'd then looked at her pointedly. "Klara, I want *you* to be one of the escorts for the three children that will be included with this group. The children all know and trust you, and I know I can rely on you to provide me with an honest and thorough assessment of everything. You certainly won't learn everything about the place, though you'll detect a lot from first impressions. Whatever you can find out will help my future decisions."

Klara had not pressed Bergmann on exactly what future decisions he was referring to. But she sensed he was clearly on the side of his patients—that he would do everything he could to prevent them from being transferred to a poorly managed, inadequately staffed facility that would treat them no better than animals at a zoo.

"*Look! Look! Bus!*" shouted one of the adult patients, sparking frenzied jumping and excited moans and shrieks. Thankfully, there were no indications of panic, and the attendants were able to quickly settle them down. No doubt, this was the intended result of each patient having been given a sedative with breakfast and repeatedly told by staff that the new facility would be able to take much better care of them.

Klara's throat tightened as the large, gray-painted vehicle with darkened windows advanced slowly and pulled to a stop at the front of the line of patients. This did not look at all like the gaily-colored busses that had occasionally been used to transport some of the patients on short field trips.

The bus doors opened and the first adult patients in line were helped in by two staff assistants, who then handed each patient's allotted suitcase to the bus driver for storage in a special compartment. When their turn came, Ingrid started crying and grabbed hold of Klara's waist.

"Get her up here, Nurse. The ones behind you are starting to act out, and we haven't got all day," one of the assistants growled impatiently.

Klara glared at him. "Please allow us just a few moments, sir." Without waiting for a reply, she pulled Ingrid aside and knelt in front of her. "It's all right, *Schätzchen*," she whispered, cradling the girl's face between her palms. Somehow, she could tell Ingrid understood that things were not going to get better, but worse. Her heart breaking and having no further words to comfort her with, Klara simply pulled her close and hugged her tightly. The two then boarded the bus together.

The ride lasted only about thirty minutes but, unable to see out the darkened windows, Klara had no idea where they were heading. She managed to keep Ingrid occupied with a small doll until, halfway through the journey, a gray-uniformed female assistant from the transport organization stood in the aisle at the front of the bus.

"All right, everybody," she began cheerily. "We've only a short time left before we arrive, and I thought it would be fun for everyone to join me in a little singing to put us all in good mood. Would you like that?" Her suggestion was greeted by a mixture of blank stares, lolling heads, tentative claps, and a few unintelligible cries. The woman produced a small accordion and led the group in several short songs praising the Fatherland, the Führer, and National Socialism. None of the patients knew the words, but a few managed to hum or moan loudly along. At the end of one of the tunes, one tiny man, who appeared to have dwarfism, became so inspired as to stand in the aisle and thrust his arm out in the fascist salute. This drew raucous laughter, shouts of approval, and clapping from the other patients.

Upon arrival, the adult patients filed out of the bus first, followed by the three children with their escorts. Clutching Ingrid's hand as they stepped down to the pavement, Klara was struck immediately by her surroundings. She appeared to be in some unfamiliar, small city. Directly facing her was a complex of buildings dominated by a massive, rectangular brick structure with a gabled roof, many small windows and an iron entrance door. Absent from the entire complex was any evidence of grassy walking areas and benches for patients, or any signs of the current patients themselves. *It looks far more like a prison than an asylum*, she thought.

But that was not her only disturbing impression. An odd, nauseating odor permeated the cold, damp air. At first, she thought it might be fumes from the bus. But as the group was herded by several uniformed male officials toward the main-building's entrance, the foul aroma became more intense. She glanced over her shoulder at the escort behind her. The woman was obviously noticing as well and appeared equally puzzled. She wrinkled her nose, smiled uncertainly and shrugged.

Klara and Ingrid entered the building and were ushered through a small lobby into a large, high-ceilinged receiving room. The room was empty of furnishings save for three desks spaced evenly near the rear wall, each attended by a white-uniformed staff member. Erected along each side wall were six curtained-off booths where Klara assumed preliminary examinations would be conducted. In the far corner was an opened door, beside which stood two hulky attendants who waited to escort the registered, examined patients into the interior of the building.

Arriving at their indicated registration desk, Klara started to offer Ingrid's name but was cut off by the attendant. "We cannot afford to make mistakes, here, Nurse," he said in an impatient, haughty voice. He then directed Klara to turn the little girl around so that he could personally read the full name taped onto her back. "Ingrid Mayer. Good. You may turn and face me again." Holding a single-page form in his hands, his eyes darted between the paper and Ingrid as he tried to match the words with the patient. He muttered to himself as he checked off the items on his list: "Eight-years-old, one parent Jewish, diagnosed at three with hereditary encephalitis, clear signs of feeblemindedness, severe deformity of right hand, future work potential deemed very low."

The man shook his head slightly then looked up at Ingrid with a cold, scornful stare. "You're in the right place now, little girl." He turned to the side and summoned one of the staff's female nurses who were standing at attention next to the booths. When she arrived at the desk, he stamped the form and handed it to her. "This one's ready. No discrepancies noted." She nodded, took the form and indicated for Klara and Ingrid to follow her to one of the booths. Once there, she yanked aside the white curtain and beckoned both to step inside. The small, enclosed area contained nothing but an examining table and a suitcase in the corner that Klara recognized as Ingrid's.

"Strip off all of her clothes," the nurse demanded coldly.

Klara hesitated. "Is there a blanket or at least a sheet she could—"

"*No*, Nurse, I'm afraid there is not," the woman snapped. "As soon as her examination is finished, the girl will be given a standard gown and escorted inside to the dormitory. The doctor will be here momentarily, so please get her clothes off and we'll get her up on the table." Ingrid did not resist as Klara helped her undress. She seemed lethargic, probably due to the sedative that all the patients had been given. Klara and the nurse helped her sit up, shivering, on the linen covered table.

Moments later, the doctor swept the curtain open and entered. He was obviously in a great hurry. Without looking at or saying a word to Klara or the nurse, he grabbed the form handed to him by the nurse, scanned it briefly, and nodded. "All right, let's begin. Lay her down, please, and hold her still."

To Klara's dismay, it took the doctor less than two minutes to complete his examination, which began with taking measurements of her skull and body. He looked cursorily at her ears, nose, eyes, and the inside of her mouth, then pushed a probe up her vagina, a seemingly pointless action that caused Ingrid to squeal with discomfort.

"This girl has passed her examination, Nurse," he pronounced curtly. "Please hand me the form and I'll sign off. Then have her put on a gown and take her to the escorts."

"What about her suitcase, Doctor?" Klara asked. "It has all her regular clothes and toys in it. Should I carry it for her and hand it to the escort?"

The doctor looked at her strangely. "She won't be needing that. Everything she needs from here on will be provided by the facility staff. They'll take her suitcase and store it in a safe location." With that, he swept the curtain aside and left the booth.

As Ingrid sat dazed, naked, and shivering with Klara's arm around her shoulders, the nurse pulled a gray, formless, floor-length cloth gown from a box under the table and motioned for Klara to put it on the girl. She then peeked out the curtain, appearing to be looking for some signal. Finally, after several seconds: "Our turn."

Exiting the booth with Klara and the nurse each holding of one of Ingrid's hands, the three walked toward the door leading to the dormitory. There was no line to wait in; it seemed the two male attendants had been escorting the patients away one at a time as soon as they finished their examinations. The men had returned to their station, and one was motioning impatiently for Ingrid to be brought to them.

Klara sensed Ingrid's rapidly mounting fear. She looked pleadingly at the nurse. "May I accompany her to the dormitory?"

She shook her head firmly. "No. Only facility staff are allowed to accompany patients beyond this point."

As they neared the attendants, Ingrid stopped in her tracks and began wailing. When the nurse spoke harshly to her, Ingrid instinctively yanked her hand away and turned to grab Klara around the waist.

"Could I have just a few moments alone to the side with her before they take her?" Klara suggested. "I think it would help to calm her down."

The nurse again refused. "That would only make her more agitated. It's best to make these partings quick and emotionless. It will make their transition easier." She motioned to one of the attendants for help. He hurried over and peeled Ingrid away from Klara's sheltering arms. Lifting her up roughly, he carried her toward and through the door. She screamed the entire way, stretching her arms out for Klara.

Klara rushed to the doorway to wave goodbye, but the other attendant stood in the entrance, his large frame partially blocking her sight. The only thing she was able to see over his shoulder was a narrow passageway, with steps leading downward.

The restaurant waitress cocked her head back and looked at Klara strangely, obviously wondering why anyone would need to ask what city they were in.

"Brandenburg an der Havel," she answered as she escorted Klara into the nearly full dining area. "Are you just passing through our little town here? From the looks of your uniform, I thought you were a nurse from that asylum down the street. We get a lot of their staff coming here for supper or drinks at the end of their day."

"No, I don't work there," Klara said. "I'm a nursing research assistant from Berlin University. I was helping to transfer some patients on a bus today from Wittenau Sanitorium to the asylum here. For some reason, when we boarded the bus, no one bothered to tell us what city the asylum was in, and we were all too busy tending the patients to ask."

After seating Klara at a small table for one, the waitress handed her a menu. "My apologies for our limited selection tonight. Our main cook is taking a vacation, and so we're only offering a couple of our most popular dishes."

"Oh, that's all right. I need to leave to catch my bus back to Berlin in an hour and I'm not very hungry anyway. A stein of your local pilsner and a small order of potato pancakes will be fine."

The waitress nodded and was just starting to walk away with the order when Klara stopped her. "Fräulein, I was just wondering, do you know if the asylum has been operating here a long time?"

"I just moved here myself only two years ago, but from what I've heard it used to be a regular prison until Hitler came to power and they converted it into a concentration camp. It was only this past year that they turned the old prison's main building and some other new ones they've constructed around it into what the city's calling the Brandenburg State Hospital and Nursing Home."

She grimaced and shook her head. "I know they're trying to help the unfortunates, but for the life of me, I can't understand what's going on there. This past month or so, there's been such a stench in the air around here."

Klara gasped. "I noticed that as soon as I stepped off the bus earlier. Pretty awful. But as soon as I got inside the main building, I didn't notice it anymore. Are you sure it has something to do with the asylum?"

The waitress nodded emphatically. "I was out walking with some friends after a movie one night and we passed near the place. Must have been around midnight. The smell was getting very strong and one of my friends pointed to one of the new, smaller buildings that had just been constructed. Its chimney was belching flame and smoke. We figured that *had* to be the source."

"That's very strange," Klara said. "I can't imagine what—" She stopped herself mid-sentence as the memory of Ingrid being carried down the steps by the asylum attendant flashed in her mind. She suddenly felt sick and looked away.

"Are you all right, ma'am?" the waitress asked worriedly.

Klara recovered quickly. "Yes, yes, I'm fine. Just a passing dizziness. Happens to me every now and then. But thank you for asking. And please bring my beer first."

The waitress laughed. "After what you've no doubt had to deal with today, I can understand that. I'll be back with it shortly."

Klara stared straight ahead, seeing nothing in her mind but a wall of flame and a huge, dark shadow of a man casting Ingrid—alive and screaming—into the middle of it, her small body flailing in agony, its flesh gradually becoming charred and the smoke going up, up...

She shook her head to clear it. *Stop. That's ridiculous. Even at Eglfing-Haar, I saw no indication of plans to eliminate a helpless, disabled child through an excruciatingly painful death by fire. There must be another explanation for whatever they were burning in that building. Unless . . ."*

Yet another horrifying possibility had just begun to form in her mind when the waitress returned and set the beer stein down in front of her.

"I'm afraid you'll have some pretty rowdy company to contend with." She nodded toward the thin cloth divider separating her table from the one beside her, where three men with boisterous voices had just been seated. It was obvious they'd already had too much to drink this evening.

Klara rolled her eyes and offered a weary smile. "I'll manage somehow. Thank you for the warning."

After the waitress left, she took a long pull from the stein, not anxious to reengage with her highly unsettling train of thought. Fortunately, the men on the other side of the divider provided a timely diversion. Whether they knew it or not, Klara could hear practically every word.

"Hey, Klaus, I hear you knocked some Hitler Youth's teeth out last week. What was *that* all about?"

Grateful for the temporary distraction, Klara listened as whoever Klaus was proceeded to brag about his self-described courageous action. He said he'd "rescued" an attractive woman who was being pestered and insulted at a local bar by two drunken Hitler Youths. His efforts on her behalf had supposedly been rewarded later that night with "far more than a polite kiss."

His story sparked laughter, jeers, and a flurry of off-color remarks from his comrades as the waitress brought their drinks. Klara was rapidly losing interest in trying to follow their crazy chatter, when a comment by one of the men caused her to perk her ears and lean closer to the divider.

"...still stinking bad again today down there. What the hell are they *doing* at that place?"

A momentary pause, then: "You *really* want to know?"

"Of course, we'd like to know, Dieter. But what could *you* possibly have to offer in that regard?"

"Not me directly. This is from a friend of mine. He has a relative who works on staff there. The two were out getting soused the other night and, at some point, the man started blabbing about a lot of things he shouldn't have."

"Such as?"

"Seems the guy—let's call him Fritz—is a formerly unemployed hospital aide who's a dedicated Nazi and member of the SA. He was recruited by the asylum director just last month. Right after he started working, they asked if he'd be interested in making a higher salary in exchange for taking on some additional confidential tasks. Fritz was desperate to support his family, so he agreed to the offer without knowing exactly what he was getting himself into.

"After he signed an oath to keep his mouth shut, they told him a secret new program called *Aktion T4* was being rolled out at selected asylums across the country by the Reich Health Commission, starting here at Brandenburg. They told Fritz his new tasks would involve helping out with some special new therapeutical procedures on incoming patients . . .'

"Uh-oh," one of the story-teller's friends groaned. "I can already guess where this is heading. But don't let me stop you now, Dieter. This is getting too exciting!"

Dieter continued. "So just two weeks ago, a bus arrived from another asylum carrying about twenty disabled loonies, both adults and children. Fritz was ordered to escort them from the processing area down to the basement, where he helped a couple of other nurses strip off their gowns. Then he walked them all into a small room where, they were told, they'd be receiving a shower. After Fritz exited, the doctor in charge slammed the room's steel door shut and announced to several other doctors and other officials who were apparently there to observe things that they were ready to begin. Then he signaled to another man standing behind the glass window of a nearby booth with some machinery and a large metal cylinder. The guy nodded and turned a tap, and there was a loud hissing sound. The doctor told everyone—*get this!*—that 'it should only take about ten minutes for the gas to do its job,' and he invited several officials to take turns looking through a peephole in the door. Whatever it was they were seeing happen inside that room, they each nodded and seemed satisfied . . ."

Klara clutched her throat and held her breath as a dead silence dropped on the other side of the curtain. "So, what happened next, Dieter?" someone finally prompted.

"So, after twenty minutes, the doctor opened the door. Fritz said he nearly collapsed on the floor when the doctor ordered him and several other male attendants who'd just arrived to go inside, collect the bodies, and stack them on some empty carts that were waiting in a nearby corridor. 'We'll have them moved to the new crematorium building and have our first trial of that later tonight,' the doctor said. According to Fritz, anyway."

A long pause ensued before anyone spoke.

"Dieter, you *can't* be serious. This has got to be the tallest tale concocted by mankind."

"Don't believe me then, dummkopf. I'm only telling you what I heard."

Klara had heard enough. Her stomach roiling with nausea, she rose from her seat and walked to the cashier. "No need for the waitress to bring my pancakes. Here's the money to cover the full bill. I need to leave immediately."

"Of course, ma'am," the cashier said graciously. "My apologies for your loud table neighbors. I hope you weren't too offended."

Klara waved her hand, "Oh, not at all. In fact, they were more helpful than they could possibly know."

Exiting the restaurant, she checked her watch and hurried across the street to the bus stop.

There's no way I'm going home before letting Dr. Bergmann know what I found out here, she resolved as she sat down on the bench to await the bus's arrival. She shook her head, scoffing at her own naïvely understated fears of earlier today.

There was now no way of avoiding the full, ugly truth. That facility at Brandenburg an der Havel was *not* an asylum offering helpful, new, life-improving therapies. Nor was it a starvation camp intended merely to keep chronically disabled people barely sustained at the lowest, cheapest possible level until they gradually succumbed.

No, the Brandenburg State Hospital and Nursing Home was worse than Eglfing-Haar. It seemed to have but one primary purpose: to function as a regional center for the rapid, systematic killing and disposal of anyone the Nazis considered human garbage, contaminating the racial purity and straining the economic resources of the Third Reich.

CHAPTER 21

Wittenau Sanatorium, Northwest of Berlin
January 31, 1940
(Two weeks later)

Leah Friedmann struggled to articulate her words as she handed the small, paper-wrapped box to Klara, who sat next to her on the asylum garden's bench.

"F-For you, Ka-wa," she managed finally after several stuttering attempts.

Klara stared at her in astonishment. *Is this what I think it is?* She carefully tore off the paper and opened the box's lid.

"Oh, Leah… oh, Leah," she murmured in amazement as she lifted out the exquisitely brocaded silk scarf and held it up by its corners. "I knew you could sew, but *this*?" This was not the work of some amateur hobbyist, she realized. The intricately woven starburst design with its brilliant, variegated coloring had the appearance of something from a professional seamstress.

"So now I finally know why you kept asking me to bring you all those different colored spools of thread. I knew you were working on something, but every time I asked, you'd just shake your head and refuse to answer."

Leah giggled. "I wanted… to sur-surprise." She motioned excitedly for Klara to wrap it around her neck.

"Oh, this is just so absolutely gorgeous," Klara murmured as she traced the outline of the brocaded image admiringly with her fingers. "Leah, how did you ever manage to get this done so quickly? You were always working on other sewing projects whenever I'd visit."

"I knew you coming, so I-I hide this in box under table… pretend work on something else. Then pull it out after you leave."

Klara reached out and hugged Leah tightly, then drew back and cradled the girl's face in her hands. "No one will ever give me a more beautiful, perfect gift," she whispered, articulating her words clearly so that Leah could not possibly misread her lips.

Folding the scarf carefully, Klara laid it back in the box and replaced the lid. "I'm going to put this in my purse and take it home with me. And you know what? My sister Elke and I are going out to a restaurant for dinner tonight, and I'm going to wear this. I can't wait for her to see this on me!"

I have to show this to Dr. Bergmann as soon as he gets back from his vacation next week, Klara thought.

Two weeks ago, when Bergmann listened to her report on her experience at the Brandenburg facility, he'd shaken his head with horror and disgust. "I've long heard whispers from some colleagues that things were heading in a very bad direction, but *never* anything of *this* degree and scope." Seeming genuinely distressed, he'd confided to Klara that he felt obligated by God to raise some important questions with his superiors on the Reich Health Commission. Were they *really* fully aware and consenting to the procedures at Brandenburg? If so, why had he not been informed?

In the meantime, he'd told her, he was committed to doing what he possibly could to protect his patients from having their names added to the *Aktion T4* transport lists. The most important criteria for exemption from these would almost certainly be the patient's assessed capacity for useful work and evidence thereof. In that regard, he'd assured Klara that Leah should be safe. He'd already indicated her high potential for agricultural work on her RHC registration form, and just last week he'd made arrangements for Leah and several other patients to work a day per week starting next week at a local nursery.

And once he sees this amazing scarf, any residual doubts he might entertain concerning Leah's work capacity will be completely erased.

"Want to walk for a bit before I have to leave?" Klara asked.

"All right." Leah looked at her sadly. "Ka-wa?"

"Yes?"

"I wish you d-don't have to go."

Klara hugged her again. "I know, Liebchen. Me too."

The two strolled hand in hand around the garden boundary. They'd almost completed one circuit when Klara spotted an assistant nurse waving frantically to her from a rear doorway to the administrative offices. Grasping Leah's hand tighter, she led her quickly to their beckoner who had now been joined by a male attendant.

"Fräulein Neumann, something's come up. I need to speak with you privately. Kurt here will escort Leah back to the patient's wardroom."

"Don't worry, Leah," Klara said, sensing the girl's confusion and alarm as the attendant led her away by the arm. "I'll come say goodbye before I leave. I promise. And remember, your mother's scheduled to visit tomorrow."

The nurse pulled Klara just inside the door. Her face had a frightened look, and she spoke quickly in a low, nervous tone.

"Some people from the Community Patients Transport Service arrived about an hour ago. They barged into the reception office, and their doctor in charge demanded to know where were the twelve patients on their transport list for today—why weren't they already outside with their attendants, waiting to board the bus to Brandenburg?

"Our reception nurse told him there must be some mistake. The next transport wasn't scheduled on Wittenau's calendar until next week when Dr. Bergmann would be back from vacation. The doctor insisted she was wrong. He demanded she find someone in authority who could round up and prepare the twelve patients for transit within a half-hour. Otherwise, he said his transport service would do the job themselves.

"The receptionist immediately called for Dr. Bergmann's assistant and Head Nurse Winkler. They came down and tried to reach Dr. Bergmann at his home phone, but he wasn't there. So, they told the transport people that the best they could do was to prepare ten of the twelve patients on the list for transport, since the other two are currently in sickbay isolation cells. 'Not good enough,' they were told. 'Our orders require *twelve,* and we will not leave here today with fewer than that. If you have any issue with that, you can argue with our two, armed SS guards outside.'"

Klara stared at her in wide-eyed disbelief. "So where do things stand now? And why am I being involved?"

The nurse bit her lip and looked at her hesitantly. "They've already got the ten healthy patients lined up outside, starting to board the bus. As for the other two, Nurse Winkler needs your help with those, and she told me to come get you."

Klara felt the blood drain from her face at the mention of Nurse Winkler's request. She could already guess where this was going. Pulling herself together, she rushed to the reception room where Head Nurse Winkler and Dr. Bergmann's assistant director stood with the transport service doctor. They appeared to be looking over a patient's file.

"Nurse Winkler, I heard you were—"

The craggy-faced head nurse looked up and cut her off impatiently. "Fräulein Neumann. Finally. I was wondering if you'd ever get here. We need to prepare Leah Friedmann for transport to Brandenburg immediately. Since you have been close to Leah ever since you've been here, and she is so comfortable around you, you are the logical person to help her get ready. She is allowed one suitcase. The bus leaves in fifteen minutes. Please proceed."

Klara stood frozen, trying to absorb what she'd just been ordered to do.

"*Nurse, did you hear what I said*?" Winkler demanded angrily.

"Nurse Winkler, may I speak with you alone for just a moment?" Klara asked, trying to keep her voice from betraying the rage building within her.

Winkler glanced at the transport doctor for approval. "All right," he said after sighing and looking at his watch. "But make it quick."

In the far corner of the room, Klara faced the woman who had so rudely objected to her effort to engage with Leah that first day of her RA assignment at Wittenau.

"Nurse Winkler, why is Leah being selected for transport?"

"That is not a question for someone in your position to ask. In Direktor Bergmann's absence, it is the decision of his assistant director as advised by me."

"But Leah is clearly making outstanding progress, and she has been identified as having very high capacity for useful work!"

"*Identified*? By who, Nurse? *You*?" Winkler hissed. "A research assistant with an obvious penchant for allowing sympathy for her favorite patients to cloud her better judgment?"

Klara stopped herself just in time from revealing indignantly that it was Dr. Bergmann himself who had confided to her concerning the high rating he'd given Leah on the RHC registration form.

"Yes, by *me*, unqualified as you say I am. But Nurse Winkler, surely, you've seen for yourself what Leah is capable of. You've seen the special ability she's displayed with her sewing projects, her diligence and effectiveness with her gardening tasks. How can you *possibly* deny those things?"

"I don't deny them," Winkler huffed. "But they are not the only criteria for deciding if someone is eligible for transport."

"What other criteria are there?" Klara pressed.

Winkler shifted nervously. "A number of factors. The incurability of their congenital condition. Their lack of ability to communicate and follow directions without raising idiotic, temperamental fits—something Leah constantly demonstrates in my own interactions with her. Other things . . ."

Klara's eyes narrowed. "Such as the one thing you haven't mentioned yet?"

"What are you referring to, Nurse?"

"The fact that she's Jewish."

Winkler's entire body stiffened. "Fräulein Neumann, I am not going to stand here any longer and argue with you over the transport service's selection criteria. It is beyond my control. Now I am ordering you—*get Leah prepared and down here in fifteen minutes*, or I will assign someone else who won't pamper her as much as you."

Klara stared at her, tears forming in her eyes. "You've always hated her, haven't you, Nurse Winkler? And now, you'll finally be rid of her forever. Do you have any idea of what they're doing to patients at Brandenburg?"

"*That's enough, you insolent bitch*!" Winkler snapped. "I have absolutely no idea what you're raving about. Now are you going to get Leah, or not?"

Klara knew there was now no other option. Her face burning and her heart beating wildly, she turned and walked toward the patient dormitory. Whatever she said to Leah, she knew it would be the biggest lie she'd ever told.

❧

"We're about two minutes from the gate," Dr. Horst Bergmann said tensely to Klara, who was seated beside him in the front passenger seat of Bergmann's Opel sedan. "If we're lucky, their bus would have arrived no more than twenty minutes ago and hopefully they're still in processing." He looked at her sharply. "Make sure you have your identification ready for the guard. We can't waste any time with them."

Klara nodded and reached into her purse to pull her badge out, her hand trembling violently as she did so. She knew every passing second could mean the difference between Leah Friedmann's survival and her extermination. There was no time for misunderstandings with the Brandenburg facility's guards or receiving room attendants.

It was only by sheer miracle, Klara knew, that she and Dr. Bergmann had even the smallest possibility for rescuing Leah from a hideous fate. Were it not for Bergmann's last-second decision to forego filling his car's gas tank on his way home from the airport, he would have missed Klara's frantic call.

She'd recounted to him with lightning speed all that had happened at the asylum over the past two hours. That the transport bus had just left with Leah on it, crying inconsolably despite a sedative and Klara's best efforts to calm and reassure her.

Bergmann, after initial expressions of shock and fury, had wasted no more time on detailed explanations or recriminations. Instructing Klara to remain by the pay phone, he'd immediately placed a call on a separate line to the Brandenburg facility director but for some reason had been unable to get through. Knowing he was taking a huge risk, he'd then called a personal acquaintance—an executive assistant to Colonel Bremmer at the Berlin Kripo office—to report a kidnapping of one of Bergmann's highly functioning patients by a community transport service that had obviously exceeded its authority.

Since Bremmer was a member of the Reich Health Commission's board of advisors, Bergmann had requested the assistant to put him in touch so he could alert Bremmer to the situation. The assistant had said he would pass the concern on directly to Lt. Colonel Bremmer as soon as he was out of his meeting.

Realizing there was no more time for delay, Dr. Bergmann had requested that Bremmer call him back at the Brandenburg facility. He'd then told Klara on the other line that he would pick her up at the front gate of Wittenau. They would drive together to Brandenburg. Hopefully, they would arrive in time to confront and appeal to the asylum director—*before* the valve was opened to release the deadly poison.

"There's the gate, just ahead," Bergmann said. He pulled next to the guardhouse that was tended by two men in SS uniform, one with a submachine gun.

"What's your business here, sir?" the unarmed guard asked gruffly, peering suspiciously through the open driver's window at Klara.

"Direktor Horst Bergmann and my chief assistant nurse, Klara Neumann from Wittenau Sanitorium," he said as the two held up their badges. "We are here to see Direktor Kempler on a matter of extreme urgency and importance."

"Is he expecting you?"

"Hopefully he has received a call by now from the Berlin Kripo office, alerting him to the reason for our visit. If he has not received it yet, please assure him that he will very soon."

"Wait here," the guard ordered. "I'll have to call. Your badges, please." Bergmann handed them over and the man disappeared inside the shack.

Klara held her breath and checked her watch. If the timing of her previous visit here was any indication, Leah would be standing in line at the registration desk, about to undergo her sham of a physical examination. There were only a few minutes left before she would be led down that narrow passageway to the hellish end that awaited her. Klara could not bring herself to imagine the confusion, terror and heartache she must be experiencing, especially without Klara there to offer what comfort she could. That possibility had been smashed when Nurse Winkler had insisted that another attendant accompany Leah on the bus, since Klara was "obviously too emotionally attached." In retrospect though, Klara knew that if she'd been allowed on the bus, there would have been no way for her to contact Dr. Bergmann in time to attempt Leah's rescue.

The wait continued for another interminable minute. The guard finally exited the shack and stepped up to the window. "You may proceed," he said curtly as he handed back the badges. "Second small white building to the left of the main reception building straight ahead."

The guard with the submachine gun slung the weapon over his shoulder and lifted the gate, permitting their car to pass through and speed down the lane.

"What is the meaning of this, Bergmann?" railed the Brandenburg facility director as he stood at his desk, glaring across it at the two intruders from Wittenau Sanitorium. "You arrive unannounced, you threaten some kind of call from the Kripo, and meanwhile you delay me from completing the tasks I'm obligated to accomplish today." He pointed at the row of phones lining the front edge of his desk. "In less than twenty minutes, I expect to receive a call from our operations center requesting my presence there. That is all the time I have to discuss your concern."

"Then let me get straight to the point, Herr Direktor," Bergmann shot back. He proceeded to explain what had transpired earlier at Wittenau. How it was only by Klara's timely recognition of the transport service's terrible mistake in forcing the selection of a high-performing, work-capable patient that he had come to be alerted to the situation.

Direktor Kempler glared at Klara. "And what medical credentials does this person bring to her judgment of such matters?" he asked, his voice dripping with condescension.

Bergmann jumped to her defense. "Fräulein Neumann is a first-rate research assistant sponsored by Professor Otto Gottschald at Berlin University. She's been assigned for the past year and half to Wittenau to observe the treatment and progress of our patients. She has never failed to impress me with the thoroughness and accuracy of her observations. Besides myself, I consider her the one most knowledgeable about the true capabilities of the patient in question, and so I brought her with me. Klara, would you please give Direktor Kempler a couple of brief examples of what you've—"

"You can stop right there," Kempler interrupted. "I know Gottschald, and I'll be checking with him later to validate her credentials. But I do not want to hear the opinions of your junior assistant right now. I am nearly out of time, and unless you can give me some good reason as to why I should overturn the recommendation of your own head nurse to the transport service and release this patient back to you right now, then I must insist that we conclude this interview."

Bergmann didn't hesitate. "Allow me to put forth a good reason, Herr Diretktor—the integrity and legality of your *Aktion T4* procedures here."

Kempler stiffened as if he'd been struck by a lightning bolt. "Aktion T4? What do you know about that?" he asked, eyes narrowed.

"Only what I conveyed to the Berlin Kripo office just before leaving to come here. I'm rather surprised they haven't contacted you yet."

Kempler stared at him uncertainly for a few moments, then reached to pick up a phone and began dialing a number. "Lt. Colonel Bremmer, please. This is Kempler at Brandenburg. Possible *Aktion* issue here… I see… well, please tell him if I don't hear back in ten minutes, I will proceed with the next round as planned."

He hung up the phone and sat down without inviting Klara or Bergmann to do the same. "So, we'll wait to see if the Kripo places any priority on this legal concern of yours. In any case, may I know what you have heard about Aktion T4?"

Bergmann nodded to Klara, who then related her experience escorting Ingrid Mayer to the Brandenburg facility and what she'd overheard in the restaurant afterward.

When she finished, Kempler simply shook his head and flashed a sympathetic smile at Dr. Bergmann. "Your assistant may be a shrewd observer of her patients' behaviors, but when it comes to recognizing the ridiculous fairytales and idle gossip of drunken men for what they are, she is sadly deficient. And I'm surprised that you, Dr. Bergmann, could also fall so easily for such nonsense."

"So, there is no such thing as Aktion T4?" Bergmann challenged. "If that's the case, why did you just mention it in your call to the Kripo?"

Kempler leaned back in his chair and sighed. "It's true that Aktion T4 is the code-name for a new therapeutic procedure that we are trialing here at Brandenburg at the request of the Reich Health Commission. I do not know how the name was leaked to those men your nurse overheard—and we will certainly be looking into that." He spread his palms and smiled innocently. "But I assure you the therapy itself does *not* involve sending poisonous gas into a sealed chamber with disabled patients. And though I'm not at liberty to describe it until the RHC gives me permission, and we've had a chance to evaluate its full effectiveness, I can say that its purpose is to *help*—not harm—the patients who receive it."

Klara knew without a doubt in her mind and heart that Kempler was telling a blatant lie. She opened her mouth to challenge him when one of the phones on Kempler's desk sprang to life with a shrill ring.

The phone was painted red, unlike the black phone he'd used moments ago to call the Kripo.

Kempler looked at his watch and nodded. "Right on time." He picked up the receiver. "Kempler here… Yes, it is safe to proceed. Please begin, and I will join you in a minute." He replaced the receiver and stood. "My regrets. But since we have not heard back from the Kripo, I must be present in the operations center to observe the next administration of our new procedure."

"*But Dr. Kempler, what about my patient?*" Bergmann protested. "This is a travesty!"

"First of all, Bergmann, the girl is not *your* patient. She is a patient in the custody of the National Socialist state. Secondly, as such, she was legitimately selected by the RHC's transport service doctor—on the advice of your own head nurse, I might add—for delivery to our facility. If you wish to object further, I suggest you take it up directly with the RHC. This interview is over."

Seeing that further effort would be useless, Bergmann clicked his heels and saluted, prompting Klara to reluctantly follow suit.

As she turned and accompanied Bergmann toward the door, she nearly vomited at the thought of Leah sitting naked and shaking on a gas-chamber bench, squeezed between other terrified, disoriented patients, all of them wondering what was coming next.

Her hope now gone, she and Bergmann were about to pass through the door when a phone rang behind them.

"*Wait!*"

CHAPTER 22

Brandenburg Facility, Northwest of Berlin
January 31, 1940

"Yes, Colonel, I understand . . ."

Klara and Dr. Bergmann stood next to each other, staring in suspense at Direktor Kempler. His face had turned chalky white over whatever instructions he had just received from his caller.

"Yes, I will act immediately and prepare for your arrival. *Heil Hitler!*" Kempler banged the black phone down and immediately grabbed the red phone to his operations center.

"Where do we stand?...*What?*...All right, shut it down *now!*... *I don't care, dammit, I said shut it down now and get them all out!* I'm coming now."

Kempler had the look of a scared rat as he struggled to get his arms into his white lab coat while sweeping past Klara and Bergmann on his way to the door.

"Make yourselves comfortable. The Berlin Kripo chief will be here in forty-five minutes."

When she first saw Lt. Colonel Gerhard Bremmer flanked by two SS-men and stepping through Direktor Kempler's office door, Klara was not sure how to react beyond standing and offering the expected fascist salute with the others in the room. From here on, she decided it would be best to take her cues from him.

Without looking left or right, Bremmer strode directly to Kempler's desk, shook his hand, and exchanged a quick word of greeting. Kempler promptly offered his chair and stepped aside.

Bremmer then turned to face the others who stood in a rough semicircle around the desk. "Please, relax and be seated. We may be here awhile, as I will need to hear both sides of this situation." After seating himself, he scanned his audience from left to right, stopping momentarily to familiarize himself with each face. When his eyes met Klara's, to her great surprise and disappointment, he displayed no sign of recognition.

"This is the girl in question, I presume?" he asked, pointing to Leah Friedmann, who sat supported by an assistant doctor and nurse on the other side of the semicircle from Klara and Bergmann. She was dressed in a gown and appeared barely coherent, her eyes glazed and her head sagging to the side. Occasionally, she would grimace and cough lightly as spittle trickled down her chin.

"Yes, Colonel," Kempler confirmed. "We were able to stop the procedure just in time."

"So, this is her normal state?"

"Exactly as we have observed her since she stepped off the bus here earlier today," Kempler asserted.

Dr. Bergmann nearly exploded with indignation. "*Colonel, I assure you this is not her normal—*"

Bremmer held his hand up. "You will speak when it is your turn, Doctor. All right, I want to hear the whole story from both sides starting with you, Direktor Kempler. To begin with, why was there a misunderstanding as to the pick-up date?"

For the next twenty minutes, Bremmer listened patiently to the impassioned arguments of the two directors, occasionally stopping them to interject a question. When Bergmann finished, Bremmer stared at him, rubbing his chin.

"Direktor Kempler," he asked, "what is the status of your current procedure?"

"The patients are in the waiting room, Colonel, no doubt becoming quite agitated. We must make a decision soon if this is to happen today."

"Hmmm." Bremmer continued to ponder. "As far as this girl is concerned, it is clear to me that any final decision must hinge on clear, indisputable evidence of her current capability for performing work of use to the Third Reich. I do understand Dr. Bergmann has marked her as "high potential" on her RHC form, and he has indicated some capacity for sewing and gardening. However, I fail to see from her visible condition here how she could possibly have merited such an optimistic assessment… at least one sufficient to outweigh the other factors working against her."

Klara knew she couldn't keep silent any longer. She reached into her purse and pulled out the small box. "Colonel, if I may . . .?"

He looked at her and smiled slightly—his first sign of any recognition. "Yes, Fräulein?"

She stood and approached his desk, holding Leah's beautifully brocaded scarf up by the corners for all to see. "If *this* is not sufficient evidence of an *exceptional* capacity for performing useful work, then I can't imagine what would be."

She handed it over to Bremmer, who examined the article closely. "This is indeed exquisite," he said as he looked in amazement at Leah, who now appeared to be dozing off, her head sagging even farther toward her chest. "And you're telling me that *she* made this?"

"Oh yes, sir, I—"

"*Colonel!*" Kempler broke in. "Surely, we can't simply take the claim of this student nurse at face value. As I've already indicated, her emotions and sympathies are obviously highly prejudiced in favor of restoring the girl to her own personal care at Wittenau. Who's to say she didn't purchase that item somewhere else for herself, and is now simply using it to make a show?"

Klara smiled to herself, knowing that she'd prepared ahead for this possibility. "Colonel, there is more proof. May I?"

Bremmer nodded, an amused expression creeping onto his face.

Klara returned to the chair and reached into her purse for the knitting pad, the two- foot length of white silk, and the three, color-threaded needles that she'd had the foresight to grab from Leah's sewing box and bring with her—just in case.

She walked to Leah and asked the attending doctor and nurse to move aside and let her sit down next to the dozing girl.

She put her hands on Leah's shoulders and jostled her gently.

After a moment the girl's head stirred and she lifted it slowly. She opened her eyes, at first blinking at the harsh light but then finally focusing in on Klara's face, which was only inches from hers.

"Liebchen, it's me, Klara. Please, wake up. It's all right, I promise."

"K-Ka-wa!" she stuttered, the light in her eyes gradually returning as a small smile formed on her lips and a tear began to roll down her cheek.

Klara gently wiped the tear away with her thumb and took Leah's hand in her own. "Leah, listen to me," she said softly. "I want you to do something for me. I'd like you to just pretend for a minute that you and I are sitting at your usual sewing table, and you're showing me how you would start to make me another scarf. I brought your sewing kit along, and you just need to show me how you do it so I can watch and learn. Will you do that for me?"

Leah looked over Klara's shoulder, suddenly seeming to realize they were not alone. "W-who are they?"

Klara placed the knitting pad on Leah's lap and held her face between her hands. "Leah, don't worry about them. They know you're good and just want to watch you like me. Just keep your head down and pretend you're all alone as usual." She laid the silk over the pad and placed the three threaded needles on top. "There," she said, "it's all here for you, Leah. Show me how you do it."

The girl looked at her as if she were about to cry.

"Please, Liebchen, just for me."

Slowly, Leah picked up two of the needles and began to thread them through the silk. One over the other. Then the third, crossing over the other two. Within seconds, her hands were moving at a blindingly fast pace, weaving all three threads in and out to form a multicolored embroidered strip. Leah was in her own world, oblivious to anything else.

Klara stepped away to allow the others to watch the incredible scene unfolding before them. Colonel Bremmer stood and walked over for a closer look as the others watched in amazement at the sheer speed and accuracy with which Leah worked. Klara stood beside the girl with arms folded. She cast a quick glance at Bremmer and smiled tentatively, her throat choked with emotion. He caught her eye and nodded, the movement slight enough that only she would notice.

After two minutes, Bremmer had seen enough. "You can stop, Fraülein. You have proven your nurse's point, and you've proven it well." He turned to Kempler. "Small, agile hands like that would perform very well in an army uniform repair or munitions assembly factory. Those are two things I'm sure we'll have an extraordinarily heavy demand for soon, wouldn't you agree, Direktor?"

Kempler was not done yet. "There's no denying her sewing skill, Colonel. But I know I need not remind you there are *additional criteria* that the RHC has been directed by the Führer to consider in these cases. And in those regards, the girl rates worse than some of the others who have already been treated here."

Bremmer nodded. "It's true there are several important factors at play here. I will need to make a couple of private calls to the RHC and my own SS superior. If I may borrow the phone in your adjoining conference room, Direktor Kempler, I should be able to return shortly and announce my decision."

"Of course, Colonel. We shall all anxiously await, as will the patients who are still awaiting the procedure to resume."

The wait was less than fifteen minutes. Bremmer reentered the room with an expression that brooked no possibility of question.

Klara held her breath, praying for the outcome she craved.

Bremmer addressed Kempler first. "Direktor, you may resume the procedure immediately."

Klara gasped, her hand flying to her mouth. *She's lost.*

"However," Bremmer continued, "the girl is exempt. She will return to Wittenau with Dr. Bergmann and his assistant after I speak with them in the conference room. Dr. Bergmann, I will see you first. Direktor Kempler and the rest of you, please return to your duties, and thank you for your understanding and help in this matter. That is all."

All stood, clicked their heels, and saluted.

Direktor Kempler and his assistants hurried out of the room to complete their deadly procedure.

Klara raced to Leah and took her in her arms. There was no longer any need to hide her tears of relief and joy.

"So, Klara, it seems we meet again. My apologies for not revealing that I knew you in front of the others. I feared it would create too much confusion."

"Oh, Colonel Bremmer, I truly understand. And I can't thank you enough for allowing me the chance to prove Leah's exceptional capabilities. I know you could easily have decided otherwise."

Bremmer peered across the small conference table into Klara's eyes for several long seconds. Finally, he smiled and nodded, then leaned back in his chair and took a long drag on his cigarette. "That is true. But I must say I was extremely impressed—and I daresay, even quite touched—by the boldness and determination you showed in trying to defend the girl.

"In fact," he continued, his eyebrow arched. "It all rather reminds me of an occasion one night in November of '38 when a certain tender-hearted young woman named Klara Neumann rushed to the aid of an elderly Jewish man who'd been beaten by an angry mob."

Klara blushed, recalling her vow to Bremmer at the time to do her best to honor his advice to avoid future misplaced attempts to rescue Jews from the so-called natural consequences of their sins against the German nation.

She lowered her eyes. "I admit I still struggle at times to separate my emotions from more practical considerations, Colonel," she said, her tone sheepish despite her true feelings.

"Yes, well, in this case, you certainly did the right thing by proving the girl's potential work value to the Reich. With that in mind, with the approval of the RHC I have directed Dr. Bergmann to reinstate the girl at Wittenau and proceed to engage her in the work program he signed her up for. Also, as discipline for their lack of attention to the transport schedule and their poor decision in selecting Leah, I have ordered the demotion and transfer of Bergmann's assistant director and head nurse to another asylum. The girl should not have to face more threats like the kind she was subjected to today... so long as she continues to prove herself fit for the Reich's workforce."

Klara sat stunned, hardly believing her ears. She suppressed a crazy impulse to jump from her chair, lean over the desk, and hug Colonel Bremmer. For the first time, she sensed what it was about him that Elke had always seemed so charmed by. As for Nurse Winkler's fate, Klara didn't even bother resisting the temptation to gloat.

"There is no outcome I could be more pleased with, sir."

"I thought you would like it. Now there is another, related matter that I need to address with you—just as I already have with Dr. Bergmann."

Klara nodded as a chill went up her spine. "Of course, sir, I expected there might be."

"It concerns the fact that both of you have obviously become aware of the existence and essential nature of the Aktion T4 program. It is unfortunate that you had to learn about it from the mouth of a treasonous rumormonger, but that is beside the point. In order to preserve the program's integrity and effectiveness, the RHC insists that both of you must now be officially informed of Aktion's purpose and scope and sign an oath of secrecy regarding them."

Bremmer produced a paper from his inner jacket pocket and set it on the table in front of Klara.

"Please read this over carefully. Once you sign, failure to strictly observe its terms will result in long-term confinement in a concentration camp and possibly a death sentence. Do you understand, Klara?"

"Yes, Colonel."

The document revealed nothing specific about the actual procedures to be employed by Aktion T4. It stated only that the program was approved by Adolf Hitler, who had entrusted certain doctors and facilities designated by the RHC with the authority to identify and grant a "merciful death" to disabled adults or children who were considered incurable. The final line committed the signee to strict secrecy about the project in recognition of their loyalty to the Führer and the state.

Klara was still too giddy with relief over Bremmer's decision regarding Leah to give much thought to what she had just read. *This is only a confirmation of what I'd already suspected was the case*, she thought. *Besides, at this point, I really don't have a choice. They are aware I know far too much.*

"I'll sign, Colonel," she said without further questioning.

"Good." He handed her a pen, and she affixed her signature to the bottom of the form.

He took the form, folded it and placed it back in his pocket. "Oh, Klara, there is one other thing I'd like to ask before you leave—a favor, in fact."

"Of course, sir, how may I help?"

Bremmer stamped his cigarette out in the ashtray, then clasped his hands together in the middle of the table. A pleasant smile on his face, he looked Klara directly in the eye. "I was wondering: is it possible that you'd have any information as to the whereabouts of a man named Jakob Friedmann?"

Stunned by the unexpected question, Klara tried to recover her bearings. How much did Bremmer already know? How much should she reveal? She realized the dangerous position she was in. One careless statement could spell catastrophe, not just for Jakob but for herself as well. There was no time to think, only to stall and hope for the best.

"Jakob... Friedmann?" she asked hesitantly.

"Yes, do you know him, or know anything about him?"

Play it safe. "Why yes, sir. If it's the same man you're referring to, Jakob Friedmann and his sister Sophie were former schoolmates of mine."

"And have you seen him since your schooldays?"

Klara realized the trap that Bremmer was trying to set. Bremmer knew good and well she had seen Jakob since then at least once. She decided to turn the tables.

"I don't know if you recall it, sir, but the last time I saw Jakob, *you* were there as well, and I thank God that you were. It was that incident six years ago in the Tiergarten, when you came to the rescue of my brother and Heinz when those SA thugs were threatening them. That Jewish boy who'd already been beaten by them and was lying on the ground next to me when you arrived was my old schoolmate, *Jakob Friedmann*. Perhaps you never took note of his name then, or simply forgot, sir. In fact, sir, as it turns out, he's the brother of Leah!"

Bremmer's expression softened. "Congratulations, Klara. You have passed the basic truth test that I was obligated to administer. Yes, I do remember that incident as well as the name of that injured Jewish boy you were so concerned about. If you'd denied knowing him or about his relation to Leah, I would know instantly that you were lying to me."

Klara laughed nervously. "Well, sir, I am glad to have removed that concern for you."

"Yes, yes," Bremmer said soothingly. "So, tell me, Klara, have you had any occasion to speak with or see Jakob Friedmann in recent times, say over the past couple of months?"

Another trap. This time, she knew there was only one way to respond if Jakob and his anti-fascist friends were to have any chance of avoiding discovery and arrest.

"Oh, no, sir. I haven't personally seen him since that day in the Tiergarten."

"Not at all?"

Klara hesitated. "No, sir. Not that I can remember, anyway."

Bremmer lowered his head for a few seconds, as if debating how to phrase his next question. He looked up again with a slight smile and stared at her, his steel-gray eyes boring into the depths of her brain.

"You would not lie to me about this, would you Klara? You see, I believe Jakob may have some information that could help me with a particularly tough case I'm working on, and I would very much like to talk with him."

He's leaving me no choice. "Colonel Bremmer, my family and I are indebted to you. I would not lie to you about Jakob."

The colonel's eyes narrowed as he continued to stare at her for several more interminable seconds. Finally, his face relaxed and his voice took on a more genial tone.

"Good. And you will inform me immediately if you happen to come across him or hear of him in the future? I hope you realize the lengths I went to today to convince the RHC and my SS superior to spare Leah. It was a risky career move on my part—there is not much sympathy in the SS these days for a police chief's advocating for a disabled Jewish girl. But you know how highly I think of you and your family, and I truly wanted to aid your personal effort to rescue her. And so, once again, can I count on you?"

"Yes, sir, you have my word."

Bremmer smiled and extended his hand. "I believe you, Klara. Thank you, that is all. Enjoy your ride home with Dr. Bergmann and Leah."

Klara stood and saluted. Her knees felt like buckling as she walked out of the conference room past the two SS guards and into the fresh air. She looked across the narrow driveway and spotted Dr. Bergmann waving to her from the parking lot where he stood next to his idling car with his arm around Leah's shoulder.

She waved back and made her way toward them, thanking God for his mercies and praying that her blatant lies to Colonel Bremmer would not come back to haunt her.

CHAPTER 23

Berlin, Germany
February 27, 1940
(One month later)

Gerhard Bremmer was tired of his role in this part of the Kripo's enhanced interrogation process. It was too messy. Too brutish. Clearly beneath his dignity as a university graduate and high-ranking SS official.

The problem was, he had become very good at it. So good in fact that, up to now, his superiors had been reluctant to promote him to a more genteel position. At least twenty times over the past five years, they'd sent some of the Gestapo's most resistant Communist suspects to be finally broken in one of the specially equipped cells in the basement of Bremmer's Kripo headquarters. It was here that he'd worked with some of his more sadistically minded assistants to perfect their ruthless techniques. Rarely had these failed to extract a confession to support a sham trial in one of Hitler's special, extra-judicial courts that were dedicated to quickly sentencing major political or civil crime suspects to concentration camp or execution. Especially a suspect like the man in front of him today, who was alleged to be both a Communist and a child rapist-murderer.

"You would not lie to me about this, now would you, Herr Glöckner?"

Bremmer stood directly in front of the bloodied suspect. His wrists were manacled behind his back and attached to a rope swung over a ceiling pulley, ready to be yanked up by one of Bremmer's three assistants whenever the signal was given.

So far, Bremmer had spoken in soothing tones to his victim, but his patience was running out. He moved in closer, his face now only inches from the man's. "You know, Glöckner, I hate liars. Especially liars who waste the Kripo's time by luring us down a bunch of rabbit trails. Now tell me the truth, and all your suffering today will be over. *You* were the one who violated that poor little boy over and over, then slit his throat afterward. Am I correct?"

After his beating, the man was barely able to sputter the words through his mangled lips. "N-no, Colonel… I swear… I was home with my family that night… Please, I—"

"*I don't believe you, you lying, perverted, Communist rat!*" Bremmer shouted. "Maybe you need a little drink to help you remember things correctly." He grabbed the man's hair and yanked his head back. One of the other two assistants who were gripping the suspect by his upper arms handed Bremmer a full bottle of rye whisky, the neck of which he proceeded to ram through the man's gaping mouth and part way down his throat. The man writhed, gurgled, and choked as the excess liquid spilled out over his mouth and chin. After half the bottle had been emptied, Bremmer finally pulled it out and yanked the victim's head upright again. It took a full minute or more for his vomiting, coughing, and spitting to finally subside.

"*Now* are you able to remember your part in this despicable crime a bit more clearly?" Bremmer growled. The man stared at him blankly for several seconds before slowly shaking his head from side to side.

Bremmer closed his eyes and sighed, knowing what was coming next. This was the part he was growing to despise the most. He wondered how *anyone* could endure such agony for so long, simply to postpone for a few days a nearly inevitable date with the guillotine. He doubted that he himself could.

After nodding to the assistant holding the rope, Bremmer turned away and began walking toward the cell door as the victim's screams assaulted his ears.

Fifteen minutes. That was all the time Bremmer would have in his office upstairs to relax and collect his senses before returning for what would assuredly be the final round of questioning. No suspect could realistically hope to hold out beyond this gut-and kidney-punching stage. Especially while strung up from the back by their wrists, their shoulders gradually dislocating.

Reaching his office, Gerhard plopped down in his comfortable leather chair. He reached into one of the drawers, pulled out the bottle of his favorite brandy, and poured himself a tumbler. Draining it, he didn't have to wait long for its soothing effect to take hold. Some of the most profound reflections of his life had taken place during these moments of in-between. Today was no exception.

God in Heaven, how he looked forward to the day when Reichsführer-SS Himmler would call him into his office and congratulate him, Gerhard Bremmer, on his well-deserved promotion. He would then be placed in a position truly compatible with his education, capabilities, and natural interests. A position that would have made his still-beloved deceased wife and children proud of him.

True, he hadn't yet pinpointed what that ideal position would be. But for some reason, ever since his tour of the Peenemünde rocket facility with von Braun, Erich Neumann, and the other rocket men last year, the imaginary title of something like "SS Overseer of Reich Secret Weapons Development" had often flashed in his mind. Now *that* would be a job worthy of his background. He may not be a brilliant rocketry expert, but he did have a university degree in math and physics, and he *had* impressed von Braun and the others with his technical questions about the A5.

Oh, what a reward and honor it would be to oversee the military-related technical goals and political loyalties of those world-class

Peenemünde rocket men! Certainly, if this crazy Sitzkrieg[*] phase ended soon and actual hot war broke out against England and France, an SS overseer for the development of secret weapons like the A5 would be seen as one of the most important roles in the Reich.

In the meantime, Gerhard thought, *it won't hurt to maintain my strong, friendly personal connections with Erich Neumann and his family.* Indeed, one never knew when a favorable word from Erich might trickle through the rocket community at Peenemünde, further enhancing the possibilities of Gerhard's connections.

Fortunately, with Erich, Gertrude, and especially with Elke, keeping their relationships going should be easy. Over the past six years, Gerhard had come to know and appreciate each of them for who they were: friendly, gracious, and—especially in Elke's case—deeply committed to National Socialism.

Which reminds me, I need to start preparing my guest lecture for Elke's BDM class next week, he thought. Perhaps, he might even ask her out for coffee afterward. She must be feeling a bit lonely with Heinz away at the front. Besides, he'd always found Elke a joy to converse with.

With Klara, the situation was far more complicated. Despite Gerhard's best efforts to be friendly and rescue her from her own lapses of judgment, he knew Klara was continuing to flout his advice and withhold the truth from him. He wasn't sure yet what motivated her lies and suspicious behavior, but those were certainly making it impossible to relate to her as he did with the rest of the family.

The incident at the Brandenburg asylum was only the latest example. Gerhard had hoped that, after the kindness he'd extended by convincing his boss to spare that disabled girl, Klara would have rewarded him by volunteering information on the current whereabouts of Jakob Friedmann.

Unfortunately, the calculated ploy had backfired, and Gerhard's superior, Senior Colonel Nebe, was furious when he learned about it

---

* Sitzkrieg (Sitting War): The long (8-month) period following formal declarations of war by England and France against Germany when there was very limited military combat occurring between the two sides.

the next day. With Jakob's name rapidly rising on the Gestapo's wanted list due to his rumored anti-Nazi graffiti and leaflet-spreading activities, Nebe himself was under pressure to find and arrest the youth *now*. Since Klara had not given Gerhard any useful information, Nebe had immediately retracted his support of Gerhard's request to ensure long-term protection for Leah at Wittenau. Instead, Nebe was now going to turn Leah's fate back over to the RHC and let them punish Dr. Bergmann and Klara for all the trouble they'd created.

Poor Klara, Gerhard thought. *She should be getting the bad news today or tomorrow. If only she hadn't feigned total ignorance and instead had provided me with some morsel of information on Jakob, I could've saved her a lot of trouble.*

But there was something else about Klara's behavior that bothered him.

Gerhard's informants had told him about spotting Klara at the Stettin train station last March in the company of her American diplomat friend, Joshua Peters. They had stayed overnight at the home of Ruth von Kleist-Rostow, a supporter of Dietrich Bonhoeffer. Several months later, Klara was seen walking alone in the Neukölln district of Berlin—a known haven for Communist sympathizers.

Both of these locations seemed far removed from Klara's normal orbits. Might there be something nefarious afoot? Was all this strange behavior indicative of some ideologically-driven, pro-Jewish, anti-fascist agenda, supportive of the treasonous activities of people like Bonhoeffer and Jakob Friedmann?

All things considered, when it came to Klara Neumann, Gerhard had to admit he still couldn't put things together. Obviously, he did not have enough evidence to confront her with anything specific. The most he could do was patiently track her movements through his informants. Wait and see if she eventually made a mistake that would reveal what she'd really been up to with her strange journeys and with her involvement with the Friedmann family, especially with Jakob. Klara must know *something* about Jakob's whereabouts. But if she didn't reveal it to Gerhard soon, of her own accord, Senior Colonel Nebe would be furious. Gerhard's promotion and that dream job as overseer of the Peenemünde rocket men could then be in dire jeopardy.

Gerhard looked at his watch. Time was up. He poured himself another half-tumbler of brandy and downed it in a few gulps. As he walked down the stairs to the basement, he could already envision the horrific sight he would encounter once he opened the cell door. Like the others before him, Herr Glöckner would be begging to end the torture by confessing his crime. Sad, Gerhard thought, that it had to be such an ordeal for all concerned. But if vile criminals like these insisted on being broken, then that was exactly what SS Lt. Colonel Gerhard Bremmer aimed to do for them.

(Two weeks later)

Klara sat on the U-Bahn bench, anxiously waiting for Sophie to arrive for their planned meeting. She wondered if this would be the last time she'd see her friend.

If so, it would be for a good cause. In the note Sophie had sent requesting the meeting, she'd mentioned that the Dominican Republic visas had finally come through for herself and her parents, but unfortunately not for Leah. Although her parents had decided against going and leaving Leah behind, they'd insisted that Sophie take advantage of what would undoubtedly be the last opportunity for *any* member of the family to escape the ever-increasing Jewish persecution. Her passage on a train to Lisbon and thence on to the DR by ship had been booked for late April.

Klara looked forward to hearing Sophie's plans for a new life in the Dominican Republic. It would be a huge transition from urban to agricultural life, and she would naturally dread leaving her family behind. Still, knowing Sophie, Klara anticipated she would be immensely excited about the prospect for such a bold, new life-adventure.

At least one of us should have some hopeful news to report today, Klara thought. For herself, the report could hardly be more depressing.

Five days after helping to save Leah from the Brandenburg gas chamber and accompanying her back to Wittenau, she'd been summoned to Professor Gottschald's office for a private meeting. As soon as she'd entered the room and observed his pinched expression, she could tell that his increasingly fawning, adoring attitude toward her had taken a distinctly colder turn.

"Fräulein Neumann," he'd begun without even waiting for her usual salute. "I am deeply disappointed by what I learned yesterday from my friend Direktor Kempler at the Brandenburg asylum. He told me what happened with Leah Friedmann."

Gottschald had gone on to complain that it was not Klara's place as a student RA to interfere with patient selection and transport matters. Instead of Dr. Bergmann, she should have called *him*, her official supervisor, to obtain the proper advice on how to deal with the situation with Leah. Gottschald knew Kempler and other RHC people quite well. He could have explained the situation to them, and they would have listened without involving the Kripo. This would have spared everyone a lot of trouble. But since she'd decided to take matters into her own hands without consulting him, she'd embarrassed the Berlin University Medical School's reputation with the RHC and him personally. In fact, he had come close to dismissing her outright from the student nursing program. It was only his high regard for her skills and excellent performance up until now that had prevented him. Unfortunately, though, he couldn't prevent the *other* inevitable consequences of her actions.

"What other consequences?" she'd asked.

That was when Gottschald had dropped the hammer, telling her of the RHC's decisions countermanding Colonel Bremmer's promises concerning Dr. Bergmann, Klara, and Leah.

The idea of Bergmann getting fired was bad enough. But to hear that she herself would no longer be able to work at asylums for the remaining eighteen months of her RA contract? That Leah would no longer be guaranteed protection from Aktion T4 mandates? *That* had brought her to a state of indignation and helpless rage. Rage at the RHC for maligning her reputation and obstructing her career. Rage at

Gottschald for refusing to defend her. Rage at the entire Nazi health care system that clearly sanctioned murder of the disabled.

Seeing her reaction, Gottschald had been quick to shift his tone, putting on his tender, empathetic mask. He'd put his arm around her shoulders, suggesting they go have dinner at a nice restaurant so he could console her and offer some possibilities for alternative RA assignments.

Thoroughly sickened by the obvious romantic ploy, Klara had slipped out from under his arm. She'd crossed her arms and looked him coldly in the eye. "I'd prefer to discuss those options here, right now, Professor."

Chastened, he'd returned to his desk and said he would have to think about some things before making any decisions. Then he'd abruptly dismissed her.

The following day, Gottschald sent Klara a notice explaining that her new RA assignment would consist exclusively of routine research and reporting on medical journal articles. For the time being, there would be no further hands-on activities in the university laboratory or in classroom instructional support.

Ever since, Klara had struggled to keep her spirits up. Cut off from seeing Leah and her other patients, she felt like the heart of her day had been ripped away. She hoped that seeing Sophie again would help to cheer her up, at least for an hour or so.

After what felt like an eternity, Klara spotted Sophie at the bottom of the platform steps. Her friend didn't return Klara's wave, merely walked over and sat down next to her on the bench. It was clear that something was terribly wrong. Sophie's whole body trembled, and her eyes were downcast. She looked like she'd been crying.

"Sophie, what is it? Your trip . . .?"

Sophie shook her head slowly. "It's off, Klara. I can't leave my parents now."

"*Off*? Why?"

Sophie reached into her purse and handed a folded form letter to Klara.

27 February 1940

Dear Herr and Frau Friedmann:

On 15 February 1940, your daughter Leah was transferred to our asylum at Brandenburg an der Havel in accordance with a ministerial decree issued on the instructions of the Reich Health Commission. This measure took place in the context of the national situation which requires consolidation of our public and private health-care facilities.

We regret to inform you that the patient died suddenly and unexpectedly of acute meningitis on 26 February 1940.

Since your daughter suffered from a grave and incurable mental illness, you must regard her death as a form of deliverance.

To prevent the possibility of spreading infectious diseases (which experience shows us is often the case with mental patients), the RHC ordered the immediate cremation of the body. Your consent is superfluous in cases like this.

If you would like to inter the urn with the remains in a cemetery or family burial plot near your home, please let us have proof of the acquisition or possession of the burial place within fourteen days. We will then send the urn free of charge to the cemetery concerned. Otherwise, we will bury the urn ourselves.

We enclose two death certificates which you should keep safe for presentation to the authorities.

Heil Hitler.

Johann Kempler, Direktor
Brandenburg State Hospital and Nursing Home

After finishing, Klara couldn't take her eyes off the page, shaking her head in utter shock and disbelief. She looked up at Sophie and gazed into her friend's glistening eyes. Strange that at this moment, she would shed no tears of her own. No, the only thing she felt was a burning sensation in her chest, rising to her throat. She handed the letter back to Sophie and took her friend's face between her hands, not caring at all who might be looking.

"Sophie, I am so sorry. I wish I could have done more to—"

Sophie gripped her wrists tightly. "No, Klara. Mama had a short visit with Leah the day after you rescued her from Brandenburg. She told Mama what you'd done. You did everything you possibly could."

Klara hugged Sophie, not knowing what the future held for either of them. She prayed for some kind of guidance.

Within seconds, she knew immediately what she had to do—just as Dietrich Bonhoeffer had suggested.

CHAPTER 24

Berlin, Germany
April 15, 1940
(Six weeks later)

Just before the start of the polka band's next tune, a waiter rushed to the outdoor stage of the Prater Beer Garden and handed a message to the leader. The man scanned it and grinned. He held his arms up in an attempt to get the noisy, merry-making crowd to settle down for a few seconds.

Erich Neumann cast a fond smile at his wife Gertrude as she conversed with Elke on the other side of their private family table. Gertrude, like Elke and Klara, had no idea what was coming, and he couldn't wait to see their reactions.

"Ladies and gentlemen," the band leader announced. "We have much to celebrate tonight. Not only have our German troops and airmen performed magnificently in the Norwegian campaign that started six days ago . . ."

At this, practically the entire audience, at least half of whom were men dressed in brown or black uniforms, rose in unison and cheered wildly. News of Hitler's successful invasions of Denmark and Norway had clearly stirred the patriotic sentiments of the vast majority of the

German populace. The beer garden's owner had tried to capture the mood by heavily decorating the stage and surrounding pavilion with swastika flags and other Nazi regalia.

The band leader raised his hands once again and motioned everyone to be seated. "Yes, not only that, but we also can celebrate something much closer to hearth and home—in honor of two lovely people who are here with us tonight. Ladies and gentlemen, please join me in lifting a toast and offering congratulations to Professor Erich Neumann and his wife Gertrude on the occasion of their *twenty-fifth wedding anniversary!*"

Another hearty round of cheers and applause was soon overtaken by the pounding of beer mugs on tables and a loud chorus of, *"Kiss! Kiss! Kiss!"*

Erich turned toward his shocked wife and grinned. "Shall we oblige them?"

Gertrude laughed. "Do I have a choice?"

Erich threw his arms around her and proceeded to plant a longer-than-normal kiss on her lips as the crowd cheered them on. Finally, Gertrude decided it was time to pull away for some air and show a bit of decorum. She rumpled his hair, her obvious signal drawing delighted laughs from the crowd as the band launched into its next tune.

"My, Mama and Vati!" Elke laughed as she raised her stein to them. "I never knew you two to be our modern-day Romeo and Juliet!"

Gertrude blushed. "Some things are not meant for the eyes of one's children," she joked. With one arm draped over her shoulders, Erich took a long pull from his stein before putting it down and gazing across the table at his two daughters. How proud he was of them both!

Despite Heinz being away for over six months with his SS unit in Poland, Elke looked radiant, a more mature version of the beautiful, vivacious fourteen-year-old who'd once graced the *Jungmädel* posters. Erich had received so many compliments from local party members and their wives about the positive impact of Elke's BDM training classes on their teenage daughters. There was no question she was the picture of the perfect young German woman that the Führer had envisioned.

And although Klara had seemed strangely quiet and perplexed when he and Gertrude had returned home from Peenemünde last month, tonight she seemed like her old self. It was as if a silent burden had been lifted, and she now appeared eager to engage with the general atmosphere of celebration. *It was probably just a case of some stress over her university studies, or maybe a case of angst over missing her American boyfriend,* Erich thought. At any rate, he couldn't be prouder of her burgeoning medical career and how well she was acquitting herself in her RA work.

Yes, it appeared that he and Gertrude had raised both girls well in these volatile, changing times. Most of the credit for that went to Gertrude, of course; his own role had consisted mainly of being the family's breadwinner and decision-maker. The stringent demands of his rocket science career had left him little time or energy for anything else.

Thankfully, that career had paid off quite handsomely for everyone so far. *And if the Norway invasion is any indication of Hitler's future intentions,* he thought, *my future income from supporting military rocketry programs should be assured for at least the next two decades, if not beyond.* What a thrilling journey it was shaping up to be. If the A5 program continued to maintain the string of successful test flights seen so far, within two years Germany should be fielding the world's most powerful, long range artillery weapon of mass destruction. And within twenty—if von Braun's ultimate dream were to pan out—that same weapon could be adapted to the peaceful and glorious purpose of delivering a German man to land on the Moon!

A fifteen-minute break was announced by the band leader, finally permitting conversations to drop to a normal volume.

"I only wish Heinz and Walther could be here to celebrate with us," Gertrude lamented.

"Oh, Mama," Elke groaned. "You *would* have to go and remind me how much I miss my husband, now wouldn't you!"

"I'm sorry, dear. We *all* miss them both terribly. But at least we received notes of congratulations from each of them. And we also received a beautiful card from our friend, Colonel Bremmer. He wanted to be with us tonight, but he had another pressing engagement."

Elke's eyes widened. "I wish you all could have heard the talk Colonel Bremmer gave my BDM class two days ago. He was explaining what was happening in Norway, and why it was so strategically important to keep the British from occupying it first. He also made an excellent point about the common racial bonds between Norwegians and Germans. In fact, he said the Führer believes that while Germany has developed the more superior culture, Norwegians overall are even more racially pure Aryans than Germans."

She gripped her mug with both hands and leaned forward in her seat, her eyes sparkling. "And so, Colonel Bremmer says the Führer has two long-term objectives. He wants to help the Norwegians develop their culture along German lines. But because of Germany's declining birth rate, he also wants to recruit and pay unmarried, racially pure Norwegian women to have babies by German SS-men. The babies will be brought to Germany and raised here as part of the national *Lebensborn* program that Reichsführer Himmler set up a few years ago. Oh, you wouldn't believe how Colonel Bremmer had all the girls in my class on the edge of their seats, hanging on his every word!"

Erich noticed that the whole time Elke was talking, Klara stared at her with an odd expression. It was one that could suggest either intense interest or disguised disgust—he wasn't sure which. At Elke's last remark, she drew back slightly, her face seeming to turn pale.

"Klara, are you all right?" Erich asked.

She recovered quickly, shaking her head as if to clear it and flashing the relaxed, happy smile that she'd displayed before Elke's discourse. "Oh, it's nothing, Vati. I was just thinking about what Elke said, and realized how much my own views have been changing lately. In fact, I have an announcement in that regard."

Everyone stared at her in curious anticipation.

"I informed Professor Gottschald last week that I'm resigning from the psychiatric nursing RA program."

A collective gasp. "*What*? *Klara!* Oh, my Lord!"

"Why, Klara?" Erich asked softly. "You were doing so well."

"I've finally come to realize how naïve and overly sentimental my vision for helping rehabilitate severely disabled people has been, now that I've, in fact, experienced it. I had no idea how much effort and resources it takes just to keep a patient like that barely alive, doing little more than breathing and eating. I do truly feel sorry for them, but I can't justify wasting my time on people like that anymore. Especially when our country has so many more curable people who could truly benefit from the resources and care that are now being devoted to incurables."

"So," Elke asked cautiously. "What does this all mean? Are you finished with nursing now?"

"Oh no, not at all. I'm just switching tracks from psychiatric to general nursing for the remaining months of my studies. I won't receive the RA stipend anymore, but I've been promised by my curriculum advisor that I can get some of the money back by assisting at Charité Hospital a couple of evenings a week. And for the rest of it . . ." Klara glanced coyly at Elke.

"Come on sister. Don't keep us in suspense," Elke begged.

"For the rest of it, I've decided it's high time I joined the ranks of German women honoring the Führer's wishes to raise our children in the spirit of our Third Reich. And so, to cover the remainder of my school tuition, I'll be providing child-care for a private school biology teacher two afternoons a week."

It took a few moments for everyone to digest and react to what they'd just heard. Elke's eyes grew moist. Gertrude simply continued to stare. Erich looked at his daughter, trying to keep his emotions in check. "Klara, are you sure this is what you want?"

"Yes, Vati, I'm absolutely sure. I've thought about this a lot, and I believe it's the right direction for me now."

Elke wiped her eyes, then threw her arms around her sister. "Oh, Klara, I am so very, very proud of you. I know how you've struggled to fully embrace some of the things you learned in BDM, and I don't doubt you've always had good intentions. But now you've finally come to see the light!"

Klara returned the embrace, smiling and patting Elke's back. "I have *you* to thank for at least part of that, Elke. You've always looked out for me and been such a role model. I guess I've just been too proud and stubborn to see it all until recently."

Erich exchanged glances with his wife. Gertrude seemed perplexed to say the least. He himself wasn't sure what to make of all this. On the surface, it sounded like an impetuous and possibly ill-conceived decision. But then again, as he observed how resolved and content Klara seemed to be... who was to say?

"Ladies and gentlemen," the polka band leader called out. "In honor of the great victories being achieved by our troops in Denmark and Norway—and with thanksgiving to our Führer for his wisdom in sending them there—we now bid you all to rise and join us in the singing of our German National Anthem."

Erich and Gertrude stood together, flanked by their daughters on either side. All held their hands over their hearts as the band struck up the stirring tune and the crowd's voices began to rise:

> *Germany, Germany above all*
> *Above all in the world*
> *When, always, for protection and defense*
> *We stand together as brothers,*
> *Germany, Germany above all...*

Perhaps it was the thought of his son Walther and son-in-law Heinz in uniform, standing boldly at the nation's borders as they prepared to defend the German way of life. Perhaps it was simply the two steins of beer he'd already consumed. But for the first time since Hitler's rise to power, Erich felt a surge of pride in his nation and the man leading it. Hitler may have some odd personality quirks and disconcerting views on racial purity, but when it came to national economic and foreign policies, his achievements could not be denied.

German women, German loyalty,
German wine and German song,
Shall retain, through the world,
Their old, respected fame...

Erich closed his eyes. He wrapped his free arm around his wife's waist and considered his amazingly good fortune. When it came to German women, he knew God had gifted him with the very best. He thought of Gertrude, her love, loyalty, and support of him all these years, her faithful charity work at their church and with the National Socialist Women's League. He thought of Elke and the honor she had brought to their home through her loyalty to the Führer and her work with the BDM.

But then, when he thought of Klara who was standing next to him, his heart was overwhelmed with tenderness. He turned to glance at her. When he saw her with her hand over her own heart and smiling affectionately up at him, he could not stop the tears from clouding his eyes.

Unity and Justice and Freedom
For the German Fatherland!
After these let us all strive together...
Flourish, German Fatherland!

We're already flourishing, Erich Neumann thought. *What a great time to be alive.*

"*Heil Hitler!*" the crowd roared. Everyone, including Klara, thrust their right arm up in the fascist salute.

⚍

(One week later)

Klara was walking along the sidewalk in the Tiergarten quarter of Berlin's Mitte district when she saw the man in the fedora and dark trench coat approaching in the dim light. Her immediate inclination was to turn and run. But as he drew closer, she recognized him and nearly burst out laughing.

"Haven't you worn out that silly disguise yet, Franz?" she chided as he stopped in front of her.

Jakob Friedmann grinned, twisted the end of his false mustache, and lifted his hat. "I just wanted to see if you remembered. Are you ready? We need to be there in ten minutes."

Klara nodded, trying to think of something to say to hide her nerves. She didn't want Jakob to think she was having second thoughts. "As my father might say, let the countdown begin."

"Spoken like the faithful and true daughter of a famous German rocket man." Jakob discretely grasped her upper arm and led her down the sidewalk in the direction from which he'd come.

They walked for about five minutes, passing only an elderly couple the entire time. Finally arriving at a seven-story building on Woyrsch Strasse, they entered and headed to the base of an elevator shaft where Jakob pushed the up-signal button. While they waited for the passenger compartment to arrive, he peered at Klara.

"There's nothing to worry about. I've already briefed them thoroughly on your background, motivation, and qualifications. And that's in addition to the letter they'd already received from Pastor Bonhoeffer concerning you. This is just a friendly face-to-face introduction and pep talk."

Klara nodded. "Thank you, Jakob." She knew that without his help, this meeting would never have happened.

"How is your family?" he asked cautiously. No doubt he knew this would be the most sensitive issue for her.

"They're fine. They don't suspect anything, but I didn't enjoy lying about my true beliefs to them, especially to my father." She looked at him plaintively. "I do still love each of them, Jakob."

"You wouldn't be the same girl I've always known and respected if you didn't, Klara. But there comes a point when we all must make our own decision, no?"

Arriving on the fifth floor, the two walked to the end of the corridor. Before knocking on the last door, he looked at Klara and smiled. "Shall I?"

She took a deep breath, let it out and nodded. "Go ahead."

A few seconds later the door was opened by a tall, striking woman with a swan-like neck. Her long blond hair was tied in a braided knot against the back of her head and stood out dramatically against the black velvet robe she was wearing. "Right on time!"

Jakob laughed softly. "Would you expect anything less from Franz Brockhaus and his wife?"

"Come in. Come in, you two!"

Once safely inside, the door closed securely behind them. Jakob made the introduction. "Mildred Harnack, please meet my good friend, Klara Neumann."

The woman smiled and extended both her hands. "Klara, what a pleasure! Arvid and I were wondering if we'd ever get to meet you. We've heard so many good things."

"I'm just sorry I waited so long to contact you," Klara said. She was already feeling much more at ease.

Mildred waved her hand. "This is perfect timing. Both Arvid and I have been travelling the last couple of months. And, speaking of Arvid . . ."

She turned and gestured toward a side door where a tall, blond, blue-eyed and bespectacled man in his forties had made his appearance. Klara could easily make out the resemblance between Arvid Harnack and his cousin Dietrich Bonhoeffer. His greeting, while a bit more reserved than Mildred's, was nonetheless gracious and welcoming.

"Well, Mildred," Arvid said after the initial pleasantries. "I suspect Klara is as anxious as we are to have her meet the rest of our little group. So why don't the three of us spend a couple of minutes alone so we can properly orient her? Jakob, you can go on in. Everyone is here and waiting in the study room. I know they'll be happy to hear about your thoughts on our favorite subject. We'll join you shortly."

Mildred escorted Klara to the sofa and offered her some hot tea which Klara politely refused. Mildred and Arvid then sat down in two armchairs facing her.

Arvid got straight to the point, his voice taking on a hardened edge.

"Klara, I know Jakob has already explained to you what we are about here. And we know what we need to know, both from Dietrich's letter and from Jakob, about your own capabilities and motivation. So, if you truly want to learn more about us, and perhaps join our effort, *now* is the time to decide. The second we walk you through that door and introduce you to the others by your new alias—*Gretchen*—you will have placed yourself on a path more dangerous than any you've traversed in life. You will constantly have to be on guard as far as your words and movements. You will need to continue the patriotic front with your family and with whomever you're working at the hospital. Any mistakes could mean prison, concentration camp, or death for yourself or the others here. Do you understand?"

He paused for several seconds to let her digest what he'd said. Klara swallowed hard. She felt as if she were standing on the precipice of a steep cliff, about to take the plunge into a bottomless pit. *Why am I hesitating to answer him? I knew this was coming.* She closed her eyes and took a deep breath. Her last memory of Leah Friedmann's sweet face helped to steel her nerves.

"Yes, sir, I definitely understand," she said finally.

Arvid leaned forward with his hands clasped tightly between his knees. He continued, his gaze intense. "And maybe the hardest thing of all, Klara, will be the inevitable discouragements and disappointments you'll experience. Your efforts will feel trivial and fruitless at times. Like David facing Goliath without a slingshot. This is a long-term proposition. It could last for years, and we have no guarantee that it will produce the general uprising we all crave. The only thing we *can* guarantee is the satisfaction of knowing that we did our best to warn our countrymen and the rest of the world of the apocalypse to come."

Arvid leaned back in his chair and folded his arms. "And so, Klara, with that 'rosy' picture in mind, would you like a few minutes alone to consider things one last time? No one would blame you for backing out at this point."

This time, she did not stall. "No, Herr Harnack, I have no desire to turn back now."

"Excellent! Then… shall we?"

Arvid and Mildred stood, prompting Klara to do the same. Each took her by the hand and escorted her through the side door.

Three women and six men including Jakob stood, waiting to greet her.

Mildred placed her hand gently on her back.

"Welcome to the Circle, Gretchen."

Klara sat on an aisle seat of the nearly deserted U-Bahn passenger car. Only two more stops until Charlottenburg. Looking at her watch, she saw she had plenty of time to make it home before Elke, meaning she would avoid the inevitable inquisition.

She closed her eyes and imagined Joshua Peters sitting beside her, his hand enfolded in both of hers. It had been months since she'd received his last letter—before the Polish invasion. She missed him terribly. But she knew he would be immensely proud of her decision at the Harnacks' tonight. She hoped that one day, she would be able to see him again and tell him all about it.

Arvid was right. This was going to be a long, hard path. And after hearing of the exploits and dangers faced by the others she'd met tonight, she could only pray that God would give her the strength to endure whatever lay ahead.

Reaching into her purse, she pulled out the beautiful scarf that Leah Friedmann had made just for her and wrapped it carefully around her neck.

Now it's my turn, Leah.

PART IV

RESISTING GOLIATH

CHAPTER 25

Berlin, Germany
July 10, 1942
(Two years later)

"All right, Hans. Enough fooling around. Your mother will be home in an hour. She'll expect you to be fast asleep."

Klara kissed the five-year-old son of Wolfgang and Lina Freitag on the cheek. She made sure he was at least pretending to have his eyes closed before she turned off his light and stepped out, softly closing the door behind her.

Finally! She let out a deep sigh of relief. Hans was quite a handful to be sure, but he certainly was lovable. Besides that, the money she received from this child-sitting job was a crucial supplement to income from her post-RA nursing position at the Charité. Together, these jobs had supported her daily living needs, as well as her clandestine efforts with the Circle over the past two years.

Klara went into the kitchen of the small, fourth-story apartment rented by Herr Freitag, a middle-aged, secondary school biology teacher. Heating up some coffee, she looked at the wall clock. A quarter to three. Perfect. Enough time to sit and gather her thoughts before the start of the daily, 3 p.m. political and military news broadcasts from the BBC on Herr Freitag's radio. Listening and taking notes on these Nazi-outlawed foreign programs was one of her most important tasks in support of the Circle. Considering the consequences she could face if somehow discovered and reported to Nazi authorities, it was also one of the most dangerous.

Filled coffee cup in hand, Klara walked down the short hallway into the living room and sat on the couch. She took a sip from her drink, then leaned back on the cushion, breathed deeply and closed her eyes. *What a nerve-racking, exhausting day so far...*

Her early morning nursing shift in the long-term recovery ward at the Charité had ended at ten, but not before she'd held the hand of that adorable, boyish Wehrmacht soldier and watched him draw his last, gasping breath. He'd been recuperating well from the severe abdominal wound he'd sustained in Rommel's North Africa campaign a few weeks ago, but a septic infection from his most recent surgery had set in overnight and caused his vital organs to start shutting down. Klara had been the only nurse on the ward at the time she discovered him panting heavily, and it was too late to call for help from the doctors. She would never forget the haunting look in the youth's feverish eyes as he stared at her, unable to express the agony and terror of his last moments without any family members present.

Sadly, there'd been no time to recoup from that heart-wrenching incident. Immediately after her shift ended, she hurried home to pick up the stack of twenty sealed envelopes that she'd locked in her bedroom desk. Each envelope contained an anti-fascist propaganda leaflet authored by associates of the Circle, and was marked for posting to a random address pulled from a phonebook for wealthy Berlin neighborhoods. For the last two years, Klara's weekly task was to deliver a set of envelopes with faked return addresses to the general mailbox in the lobby of the local post office—without drawing attention to herself. Usually, this hadn't posed too much of a challenge. Today, though, she noticed one of the postal clerks staring at her oddly from behind his window. Caution had prevailed and she'd left quickly left without depositing the envelopes, greatly worried that her longtime routine may have finally come under suspicion.

After a rushed, anxiety-burdened lunch alone at a nearby tavern, she'd taken a short bus ride to check in on Sophie Friedmann and her parents. Ever since last September, when Hitler ordered the round up and deportation of all remaining Jews in Berlin to ghettos in Eastern Europe, the three had been hiding out in the basement of Frau Adelberg, a kind, elderly Aryan woman who was a friend of Arvid and Mildred Harnack. When the deportations had begun, Mildred had immediately pointed Klara to the widowed former teacher who was also a staunch Circle sympathizer. Frau Adelberg had readily agreed to take the Jewish family in. She'd also offered to help provide for their food and basic needs with extra ration coupons purchased on the black-market.

Though Klara knew the Friedmanns were extremely grateful for the generosity that Frau Adelberg had shown them, she also knew their confinement was taking a fearful toll. At the end of today's visit, Sophie had pulled her aside and said she didn't know how much longer her mother could survive the emotional pain of Leah's loss, Jakob's continuing absence, and her family's constant isolation. With very few opportunities to leave what was effectively their basement prison, Sophie herself looked and sounded to be at the end of her rope, Klara thought. It tore her heart out to say goodbye to her friend until they could all arrange the next secret visit.

By the time her bus had finally arrived at the Freitags around one-thirty, she'd wondered how she could possibly handle any more stress in one day. And yet, she'd had no choice but to press on, knowing that her most demanding work still lay ahead...

⸎

Rising wearily from the couch at 3 p.m., Klara sat down on the stool in front of the small table that supported Herr Freitag's prized RCA Victor radio receiver. She could still remember the pride the man had taken in demonstrating the set's wide reception range to her over two years ago when she'd first come to take care of Hans. He'd even bragged of its ability to pick up German language BBC broadcasts from London, while of course denying that he'd ever consider using it himself for such an illegal purpose.

At the time, Klara had not really appreciated all the possibilities. But once she told Mildred and Arvid about the radio and its ability to access the BBC, they'd asked her if she'd be willing, as part of her work with the Circle, to incorporate it into her regular childcare routine at the Freitags'. Klara had at first been reluctant, knowing that foreign broadcast listeners were always exposed to the danger of being discovered and reported to the Kripo or the Gestapo. Were that to happen, it would almost certainly guarantee a quick arrest followed by a long-term prison sentence. However, she'd eventually agreed to accept the risk.

Reaching for her purse, Klara pulled out a pencil and small notepad on which to record a few brief words and phrases from today's broadcasts. These would help jog her memory when reporting at tonight's bi-weekly Circle meeting at the Harnacks' residence. She turned the set's power on and adjusted the dial to the distinctly marked Nazi Party channel.

Always need to suffer through the usual boring bluster first, she thought resignedly. The static cleared quickly, as did Klara's false preconceptions of what she'd be hearing from Joseph Goebbels today.

"We are now receiving reports confirming that the major port of Sevastapol has fallen!" screeched the high-pitched, excited voice of the Nazi propaganda minister. *"All Soviet Army resistance in the Crimea has finally crumbled under the relentless onslaught of our heroic Wehrmacht soldiers and airmen. The drive toward Stalingrad and the capture of vital oil reserves in the Caucasus region is now underway!"*

Klara perked up her ears. This announcement seemed to signify a momentous new development in the direction of the war, at least on the Russian front. Klara tried to imagine the implications for both Walther and Heinz. Last June, when Hitler had turned on Stalin, his former ally, and launched the massive Nazi invasion of the Soviet

Union, both men had been transferred to the eastern theatre. Each were now captains of their units, and both had been involved in the heavy fighting in December near Moscow. Would they soon be leaving behind their "spring vacation"—as Walther had described it in his last letter home—and joining the Stalingrad offensive? She said a quick prayer, not only for their physical safety but also for the protection of their souls from the corrupting influence of all the unspeakable evils they were no doubt witnessing.

As Goebbels rambled on with his typical invective against Jews, Bolsheviks, Poles, and the decadent Western liberal democracies, Klara realized it was time to commence the far more valuable—though illegal—portion of her listening task. She fiddled with the dial. Seconds later, she detected the faint voice of someone speaking in German in an English accent. The signal was unusually weak, and she had to turn up the volume quite a bit to hear the phrases that only came through in fragments:

". . . confirm... Sevastapol... fallen after a six-month siege... severe loss for the Soviet Army and nation... BBC correspondents report better news... North Africa... British Eighth Army tanks and troops under General... holding fast at El Alamein against Panzer tanks of Rommel's Afrika Corps... preventing Nazi capture of Egyptian port cities . . ."

It was about all she could make out from the military news segment before the signal faded out. When it returned after a minute or so, the programming had transitioned to classical music.

Well, that certainly wasn't much from the BBC today, Klara thought. Some days the signal was stronger and the reporting more extensive than others. Still, she wasn't too disappointed, since she knew that *any* tidbits of information on the true state of the war from an anti-Nazi perspective would always be welcomed with gratitude by her friends in the Circle. Especially as they all knew that obtaining such information came with a significant risk.

Klara carefully adjusted the dial back to the innocuous channel to which the set had been originally tuned, then shut off the power. Frau Freitag would be returning soon from her secretarial job. No doubt, she would pursue her familiar pattern of settling down to listen to her favorite music and entertainment programs. She would be completely unaware of Klara's illicit activity while her son slept. The process had worked flawlessly for over a year and a half, and Klara was highly confident it was a safe arrangement for all concerned.

Stashing the few notes she'd taken from the broadcasts into the lining of her purse, Klara settled back on the couch to await Frau Freitag's arrival. To pass the time, she began to organize her thoughts in preparation for tonight's meeting. There would be quite a bit to report about her experiences over the past two weeks. Also, she'd want to mention the revealing discussions she'd had last week while nursing a wounded soldier at the hospital. She would need to keep her report very succinct, allowing time for the others to ask questions and contribute their own brief updates.

Tonight's main topic of interest, she was sure, would revolve around whatever Arvid might have learned concerning the fate of Herbert Baum. Baum—the inspirational leader of the Jewish anti-fascist resistance cell to which Jakob Friedmann had become attached several years ago—had recently made a catastrophic mistake from Arvid's perspective.

Two months ago, Baum and several of his cohorts had ignored Arvid's personal warning and followed through on their own scheme to sabotage the anti-Communist propaganda exhibit—mockingly named "The Soviet Paradise"—that Goebbels had set up in the center of Berlin.

Unfortunately, most of the Baum group's planted explosives had failed to detonate properly, resulting in only minor damage to a couple of display booths. The German press had not even bothered to report the incident. Hitler, however, was livid over the sheer audacity of the attempt, and the Gestapo and the Berlin Kripo had quickly launched a furious search for the culprits. In late May, according to Arvid, Herbert Baum had been betrayed as the leader of the Paradise attack by a careless co-worker at the electrical plant where Baum worked. He'd been arrested and taken away, but there'd been no reliable word of his fate. Everyone in the Harnack Circle had been on edge, wondering if Baum would reveal his co-conspirators and their various contacts, possibly leading to some in the Circle itself.

For Klara, Baum's arrest raised some more specific and terrifying concerns. Would it lead to the discovery and arrest of Baum's part-time helper, Jakob Friedmann? If so, what would that mean for Sophie and her parents? Would Jakob be coerced into revealing their hideout? What would happen to Jakob himself?

She desperately hoped that tonight Arvid would be able to offer some more clarity on the whole situation with Baum and the implications for Jakob. The devastation of losing Leah Friedmann to Nazi cruelty had been bad enough, but the possibility of now losing Jakob, Sophie, and their parents as an indirect result of the Baum incident made her sick with worry. Somehow, they had all become as precious to her as her own family.

Please Arvid, bring some good news for me tonight.

⌘

Arvid Harnack grasped his wife's hand as he stood with head bowed, preparing to address Klara along with the other Circle members who had just finished seating themselves around the living room. After several moments, he lifted his head and began to speak.

"This afternoon, I met with one of my police contacts and he gave me some disturbing information. Herbert Baum was declared a suicide by hanging by the state prosecutor on June 11. In fact, according to my source, he was tortured to death by the Gestapo."

The collective gasp of horror was followed immediately by soft cries and groans from several of those present. Klara sat stunned, trying to absorb what she'd just heard.

Arvid continued. "To Herbert's everlasting glory and credit, he refused to divulge the names of anyone else, even after being beaten severely and taken to the plant where he worked to force him to identify others. Unfortunately, within a couple of weeks the Gestapo still somehow tracked down and arrested more than twenty people in Baum's group. It's likely they'll all soon be executed, and the Gestapo are hungry to arrest others they may have identified during their interrogations."

More gasps and groans. "What does this mean for Jakob Friedmann?" asked one man.

Arvid glanced at Klara and nodded. "Yes, about Jakob. As most of you know, after the Paradise fiasco, I told Jakob I thought it best that he not attend our Circle meetings for several months. I didn't want to take the risk of his being caught up in the Gestapo sweep and inadvertently setting them onto our trail. He agreed, and no one that I know of, including Gretchen here, has had any contact with him since then. I don't think he's been arrested yet, but the Gestapo are certainly not finished with their search for Baum supporters. At this point, all we can do is pray for his safety and protection."

Klara lowered her head. This was not the good news she had been hoping for. If Jakob got caught, it would almost certainly mean—

No, I can't allow myself to think about that.

With a supreme effort of self-control, Klara forced herself to remain attentive through the rest of the meeting and deliver her own update when called upon.

Afterward, as she was about to leave with the others, Mildred Harnack pulled her aside and addressed her by her true name. "Klara, may Arvid and I have a word with you?"

Mildred escorted her into a small den and invited her to sit next to her on the settee. Arvid soon joined them, bringing a pot of hot coffee and three mugs. After they'd settled themselves and begun sipping their drinks, Mildred opened the conversation, her voice tinged with concern as she looked closely at Klara.

"Klara, your update was very helpful. We continue to be very impressed with how diligent you've been in carrying out the tasks we've assigned you over these past couple of years. But we couldn't help noticing how strained you seemed after Arvid mentioned the news about Herbert and Jakob. We know how close you've been with Jakob and his family, and so it's not surprising that you'd react the way you did. But we just wanted to check, is everything all right with Jakob's family? I would imagine you're very worried about them."

Klara's voice caught as she tried to speak. "I am so thankful to both of you for what you did by introducing me to that dear Frau Adelberg who agreed to hide them in her basement. I only see Sophie once in a great while now, and . . ." At this point, she nearly broke down. "Oh, Mildred, I'd be lying if I pretended I wasn't sick with despair over what I know the constant confinement is doing to Sophie. She used to be so vibrant and full of life, and now, well, the truth is, she and her parents have nothing to do but sit and worry incessantly about Jakob and their own discovery, deportation, or worse. Added to their devastation over Leah's murder, I think it's all slowly killing them."

Mildred took Klara into her arms and spoke to her tenderly. "It's all right, dear, it's all right. You've been holding this in a long time, I know." After a few moments, she looked at her husband. "Arvid, can we . . .?" Klara lifted her head from Mildred's shoulder, confused about what she was referring to.

Arvid rose from his chair and came over to kneel beside her. He placed his hand on her arm. "Klara, I can't promise anything yet, but there may be a way to get Sophie and her parents—or at least Sophie—out of the country soon."

Klara blinked, her heart leaping. "Out of the *country*? But how, Arvid? I thought the Nazis shut down *all* emigration possibilities a while back. And besides that, no countries—including even the Dominican Republic—are accepting German Jewish refugees anymore, right?"

Arvid smiled. "It's not easy. But there are exceptions to the rule if one knows the right people. And, as it turns out, my cousin Dietrich Bonhoeffer and his brother-in-law happen to know quite a few of these right people."

Klara had the clear sense this was not the time to ask for too many specific details about the plan itself. "So, what do Sophie and her parents need to do?"

"We still have all their personal information and the photos you gave us for those DR visa applications two years ago. We'll send all that to Dietrich, and it should be enough to get some false papers drawn up when the time's right. But in the meantime, don't tell the Friedmanns anything until I get confirmation of the details. It may take a few weeks, and I don't want to falsely raise their hopes. The only reason I'm telling *you* now is to offer you something to help keep your own spirits up. We know how hard and dangerous your work with us has been, and we may soon need your help on something else. If you're willing."

Klara reached out and hugged him. "Arvid, you know I am always willing."

For the first time since the news of Leah Friedmann's death, Klara could sense a tiny glimmer of light breaking through her seemingly ever-present cloud of gloom and despair.

CHAPTER 26

Berlin, Germany
July 31, 1942
(Three weeks later)

When Gerhard Bremmer entered the top-floor office of SS Senior Colonel Arthur Nebe, he discovered his superior standing with hands folded behind his back, staring out the window at the Berlin skyline.

Nebe turned and acknowledged Bremmer's salute, an unusually pleasant smile lighting up his dour face. "Ah, Gerhard. I was just taking a few moments to enjoy the view of our beloved city. I suppose we should count ourselves fortunate that it's still so relatively unmarred. Seems our Luftwaffe's[*] fighter planes are doing a good job of scaring off the British air force. Hard to believe it's been nine months since the last RAF bombing raid here, yes?"

Gerhard nodded respectfully. "We'll need our flyboys to keep up their recent trends, especially with the Americans joining against us after Pearl Harbor."

"Hmmm." Nebe grunted in agreement. "Have a seat, Gerhard. We have some matters to discuss."

---

[*] *Luftwaffe*: Formal name for the German Air Force headed by Reichsführer Hermann Göring

Taking the chair in front of Nebe's desk, Gerhard faced his boss with pulse racing. He already had a suspicion of what this meeting was going to be about.

The head of the national Kripo organization began by extending his hand. "First, Lieutenant Colonel Bremmer, please accept my congratulations on what you and your Berlin people have accomplished in connection with this Herbert Baum matter. Baum and twenty of his Jew-dogs have been caught and either executed, or they will be soon. The Führer is pleased, and Reichsführer Himmler is quite impressed with how you've handled things."

"Thank you, sir. I am deeply honored." *And even more honored if Himmler would finally grant me that promotion he's been hinting at for three years*, Gerhard thought. *What more do I need to do?*

Nebe leaned back in his chair and stroked his chin. He seemed to have read Gerhard's thoughts. "You know, Gerhard, I count myself fortunate to have had your services in this role for such a long period of time. Your policing of Berlin has certainly made my own job easier. But there's no question in *my* mind that you're ready to have the oak leaves of a full SS colonel sewn onto your collars. As you know, I submitted my recommendation to Himmler earlier this month."

"Yes, sir, I am definitely in your debt regarding that," Gerhard offered humbly.

Nebe shook his head. "No need for modesty. You have long deserved it. When I spoke with Himmler just yesterday, he seemed to be in general agreement, though he said his hands are tied until he can clearly convince the Führer that this Berlin business has been totally cleaned up once and for all. The Führer wants Himmler's guarantee that *absolutely none* of Baum's associates or supporters are still roaming the city, scrawling their graffiti and distributing their treasonous leaflets."

Gerhard smiled. "That shouldn't be a problem, Senior Colonel. We're down to the last five rumored Baum associates, and we expect to have them all nabbed by the end of this week."

"Yes, so I've heard, and that's very good." Nebe formed a pyramid with his hands and rested his chin on them. "But Gerhard, Reichsführer

Himmler feels there's one Baum collaborator in particular whom he fears we may have forgotten about, or perhaps simply been remiss in following up on."

"Who is that, Senior Colonel?"

"Our old friend, Jakob Friedmann."

Gerhard blinked and cocked his head. "But Senior Colonel, did we not agree that Friedmann had effectively disappeared from the scene long ago, that he wasn't a serious threat, and that it wasn't worth expending resources trying to track him down anymore?"

"That was indeed our decision at the time, especially after you were unable to extract any information from Professor Neumann's daughter concerning his whereabouts. But some new information has come to light."

"New information?"

"The Gestapo put the press to one of the captured Baum people last week and got him to reveal a couple of unexpected things. Apparently, Jakob Friedmann has *not* disappeared or been inactive. He and another Baum supporter—some friend of Jakob's with the unforgettable name of *Aaron Bierwagen*—have been moving between various safe-houses, hiding behind aliases and disguises the entire time. The suspect said both of those men were involved in that graffiti-painting action at the "Soviet Paradise" exhibit the day before Baum's sabotage attempt. And that's not all."

"Sir?" Gerhard shifted uncomfortably, his mind already wrestling with the implications.

Nebe peered at him intently. "What I'm about to reveal is highest classification, top secret information that I received a few days ago from the *Abwehr*[*], and I'll expect you to treat it as such."

"Of course, sir." Gerhard sat rigidly on the edge of his seat as Nebe continued in soft tones.

"Two weeks ago, our Abwehr agents finally succeeded in deciphering a strange, encrypted radio message they'd intercepted eight months

---

[*] *Abwehr*: German military intelligence organization

ago. The message was sent from the Soviets' main intelligence agency in Moscow to a network of spies in Germany and the occupied countries. The spies have been causing us a lot of headaches, including the transmission of Wehrmacht capabilities and operational plans to the Russians.

"Our Abwehr people have labelled the group "The Red Orchestra," and they're now hot on their tails in both Belgium and Germany. The message they deciphered revealed the names and addresses of three suspected Orchestra leaders and their wives who've been working out of Berlin. Turns out one of the men—Arvid Harnack—is highly placed in the Reich economics ministry."

"Were we aware of him previously, sir?" Gerhard asked cautiously.

Nebe shook his head. "The Gestapo had some dealings with him quite a few years ago in connection with some other matters, but they eventually let him off, and his career certainly never suffered. In the meantime, we've had some indications that he and his wife have been spreading anti-fascist leaflets along the lines of the Baum group. But if this international charge against Harnack pans out, that's an entirely different level of treason. We now have him under surveillance."

"And may I ask, sir, how Jakob Friedmann fits into this picture?"

"Under torture, the Baum supporter gave up not only detailed descriptions of Friedmann's and Bierwagen's disguises, but also his recollections of hearing Friedmann brag about his supposed connections with another Berlin resistance group led by—guess who?—a man named Arvid Harnack. Unfortunately, the Gestapo couldn't get anything else out of him, including where Friedmann or Bierwagen are hiding.

"And *that*, Lieutenant Colonel, is the only thing that Himmler feels is separating you from your well-deserved promotion. He needs you to help the Gestapo find the last of those Baum Jews and get them off the streets—especially Jakob Friedmann. And, of course, force Friedmann to reveal his knowledge of *all* Harnack's activities. Once that whole Red Orchestra resistance nest is uncovered and demolished, the Führer will certainly have several major rewards to pass out, including yours."

Nebe broke into a wide grin. "Who knows? Maybe you'll finally land that new job I know you've been thinking about for quite a while—riding herd for our SS over the fabulous Peenemünde rocket men."

Gerhard stood, clicked his heels and saluted. "You can count on me and my Berlin Kripo to finish the job, Senior Colonel."

Indeed. And I know exactly where to start.

"It's been far too long, Professor!" Gerhard lifted his wine glass in a toast to Erich Neumann, the man who now, in more ways than one, held the key to Gerhard's future.

"Yes, it certainly has, Colonel," Erich responded with equal alacrity. "Gertrude and I have missed having you over for dinner at our home, but we know how busy everyone has been these past couple of years. And on these rare occasions when Gertrude and I are able to get away from Peenemünde, it seems there's hardly time to catch up with anyone besides our two girls. So, thank you for inviting me tonight. You chose an excellent spot for our reunion."

Gerhard smiled as he glanced around at the mostly empty tables in the quiet but elegant Italian restaurant near his former family home on the shore of Wannsee Lake. "I was determined to choose *someplace* where I could don my civilian clothes and not be recognized as 'Lt. Colonel Bremmer' for a change. I'm glad you approve! And I hope your wife and daughters are not too offended that I made this a one-on-one."

"Well, they *were* a bit disappointed at first not to have been invited. But I managed to soothe their feelings by insisting this would be primarily a business meeting—and that the topics of our conversation would likely bore them all to death. They seemed content to know that I would tell you hello and invite you to dinner the next time Gertrude and I visit Berlin."

Bremmer laughed. "Good thinking, Erich! You can tell them I heartily accept their invitation. So, tell me, Professor—to the extent you can talk about it—how are things in the world of our Peenemünde miracle weapons?"

Erich's eyes lit up like a child who'd just been handed a piece of candy. For the next quarter hour, he expounded on the recent testing successes achieved by the new A4 rocket design, while bemoaning the funding competition from a new pilotless aircraft weapon known as the "buzz bomb." It was being developed by the Luftwaffe and had recently caught the Führer's interest.

"Hmmm." Gerhard nodded sympathetically, "I'd personally hate to see the A4 project usurped by unworthy rivals." He then eyed Erich with a sly smile. "Perhaps the von Braun rocket team would benefit from a little more high-level support from the SS? I realize von Braun himself joined the SS a couple of years ago, but everyone knows that was only done as a symbolic gesture to appease Himmler. Von Braun's low rank as a junior SS stormtrooper leader certainly doesn't carry much weight with the Führer."

Erich laughed. A bit nervously, Gerhard thought.

"Well," Erich said. "If by high-level support you mean having some unschooled SS administrator who'd try to go around Colonel Dornberger, our Wehrmacht rocket projects manager, and dictate our development processes and schedules—*that* would not be viewed very positively by anyone on our team. In fact, it would be seen as quite dangerous.

"But, on the other hand," he continued with a twinkle in his eye. "If you mean having a scientifically knowledgeable and empathetic SS liaison officer—someone such as yourself, perhaps?—who would work with us and Colonel Dornberger to strongly advocate our cause with the Führer, then I think most if not all of our team would be quite grateful for that."

I can't believe it... Erich just expressed my own dream in a nutshell! Gerhard thought with barely disguised elation. He grinned broadly, then bowed his head in a display of mock humility.

"Oh, you flatter me, Professor, but I will nonetheless revel in your compliment. A position like that would certainly be to my liking someday, but it's totally out of my hands at this point." *Well, not exactly,* he thought. *It depends largely on how the professor responds to the main question I had for him tonight. Now's the time to ask.*

Bremmer took a long sip of wine and glanced around the room to ensure no one was within earshot. "Erich, I would like to switch the subject to another matter, with your permission."

"Certainly, Colonel."

"Do you remember the first time we met? That incident in the Tiergarten?"

"Of course. *That* would be difficult to forget. It's where our friendship started."

"Yes, and do you remember the name of that Jewish boy who'd been beaten by those SA thugs?"

Erich thought for a moment. "Oh... I believe that was... oh, yes. That was Jakob Friedmann. He and his sister Sophie were former schoolmates of Klara. I still remember the advice you gave me, urging me to tell Klara to stop associating with them in the future. To the best of my knowledge, she heeded my warning. Is there a problem with him?" He peered nervously over the top of his glass.

Gerhard could barely keep a straight face. *Oh, if only Erich knew.*

"Well, I'm not sure yet. My Kripo office has some questions we'd like to ask Jakob in connection with some important matters, but unfortunately, he seems to have disappeared from the area, as has the rest of his family. In fact, no one has seen Jakob since the '38 riots, nor any of the rest of his family since they vacated their house about four months ago."

Erich nodded. "Trying to escape deportation?"

"Most probably. Their names were on the list. But it's Jakob we're most interested in finding right now." Gerhard cleared his throat. "Erich, I know it's been a very long time, but would you possibly have *any* idea of where he might be found? Any places you can recall Klara saying he liked to frequent, either alone, or with his family? I know I could ask her directly, but given her friendship with them, I don't want to put her in an uncomfortable position if I can avoid it."

Besides, Gerhard thought, *she's already denied any recent connections with the Friedmanns. Why should I expect anything new from her?*

Erich closed his eyes and stared down at his glass for several long moments, clearly trying to recollect any memory of relevance. Finally, he shook his head.

"I'm sorry, Colonel, but I just can't think of any place in particular where Jakob would be found. In fact, the only places I recall Klara telling us where she would ever see him or Sophie were either at their house or at Tiergarten Park once in a while. And, as I said, I don't believe she's seen any of them in quite a long time."

Gerhard sighed and leaned back in his chair. *Here we go again.* Another dead end. Without any insights from Klara or her father, Gerhard's search for Jakob Friedmann was essentially dead in the water. And without Jakob Friedmann in his grasp, Gerhard's chances for meeting Himmler's promotion criteria were—

"Wait a minute!" Erich exclaimed. "I *do* remember something Klara said to me once. I think it was about three weeks after that Tiergarten incident. She was still very upset about the whole thing—and angry that I'd told her to stop seeing Jakob and Sophie. She said something about not understanding how a Christian family like ours could turn our backs on our good friends, even if they were Jewish. She begged me to allow her to go see Sophie and Jakob one last time to apologize and say a proper goodbye.

"I relented that one time and permitted her to go see them, but I remember demanding that she tell me where they'd be meeting. She said they'd probably end up taking a walk along 'Jakob's favorite running path' in the Tiergarten."

Gerhart sat bolt upright. *Could this be the clue he was seeking?*

"And did she give any more details about where this path might be located within the Tiergarten?" he asked sharply. "That's over five hundred acres."

"I vaguely remember her saying that it passed by the Composers' Memorial monument, where Jakob and some Jewish friend of his—I seem to recall he had some funny last name like Bierwagen, or something like that—liked to take a break and sit for a spell after a run." Erich cast a skeptical look. "Of course, it seems rather doubtful that Jakob or his friend would still be treading that same ground today, given the prohibition against Jews in parks and public places."

Unless they were very confident wearing those great disguises mentioned by Nebe! Bremmer thought excitedly. What Erich had just suggested was a long shot, but it was one that was certainly worth checking out.

For the remainder of their dinner, Gerhart barely paid attention to anything else Erich said. The possibility of finally capturing the elusive Jakob Friedmann and his friend Aaron Bierwagen under a monument to Beethoven was all he could think about.

CHAPTER 27

Berlin, Germany
August 21, 1942
(Three weeks later)

Klara had initially been hesitant to accept Elke's invitation to join her and Trudi Schuster, Elke's favorite BDM trainee, for apple cider and Bundt cake this afternoon in the Neumann residence courtyard. With no further word from Arvid Harnack over the past six weeks concerning either the whereabouts of Jakob Friedmann or the status of Arvid's plan to smuggle Sophie and her parents out of the country, she was feeling increasingly stressed and had lost all desire for idle socializing.

But there was also a more pressing reason for her reluctance. It had to do with her new weekly task. In the absence of news of any additional Gestapo or Kripo arrests of Herbert Baum supporters, Circle members had voted to continue with their anti-Nazi leaflet distribution efforts. Mildred Harnack had asked Klara if she would be willing to graduate from her prior role as a leaflet mailer and become a dropper instead. This would involve discretely stashing several of the recently printed leaflets in parks, telephone booths and subway stations around the city. Deeply committed to doing whatever she could to help the cause, Klara had agreed. And having already prepared to make a drop this afternoon, it was not a task she was inclined to put off.

Elke had been persistent, though, explaining that Trudi had expressed interest in serving as an assistant nurse in lieu of working on a country farm to fulfil her obligatory, one-year Land Service duty for the BDM. The girl had been looking forward to meeting Klara and talking to her about the nursing field, and Elke was interested in getting Klara's general impressions of Trudi's aptitude for such an undertaking. Couldn't Klara spare just an hour between two and three to chat with them?

Deciding that her secret errand could wait one more day, Klara had relented. By two-fifteen, the three women were nestled in cushioned chairs under the shade of the courtyard's large oak tree, sipping their cider as they engaged in lighthearted conversation.

"Speaking of talent, Klara," Elke said proudly, "did you know that Trudi here has already earned more BDM merit badges than either of us managed to achieve before graduation? And to think she still has almost a year left!"

"That's very impressive, Trudi," Klara acknowledged. "What's your secret?"

The petite, fresh-faced girl with long, dark brown hair pinned in plaits around her forehead and the back of her neck blushed and lowered her eyes. She then looked fondly across the garden table at Elke. "I think it was having a teacher and mentor like your sister, who took such an interest in me when I first joined BDM. She kept encouraging me to try a lot of different activities that I never dreamed I could be good at, like learning French, leading girls' gymnastics sessions, or conducting meetings on worldview matters."

Elke smiled and nodded approvingly. "I saw the natural leader in you from the very beginning, Trudi. And you forgot to mention your recent work with the BDM's air raid defense support association and your new part-time job." She looked at Klara and sighed. "Oh, how this war has changed things since Klara and I were members."

"What's your part-time job, may I ask, Trudi?" Klara inquired.

Trudi looked at Elke and smiled gratefully. "Thanks to Frau Schröder, I work three mornings a week as a receptionist at the Berlin Kripo office."

Klara barely suppressed a gasp of shock and alarm. She glanced back and forth between Trudi and Elke. "The *Kripo* office?"

"Oh, it's nothing much," Trudi said. "Just routine filing and greeting visitors in the outer lobby mainly. But I'm excited to learn a few things about how criminal police detectives work, and it's very interesting getting a chance to read some of the old case files."

"My, that sounds exciting. But how did you get the job? Did Elke help you?"

"Definitely. She knew I was looking for some work this coming year, and so she invited me to join her and Colonel Bremmer for lunch one day a few weeks back. I was a bit intimidated, knowing his position, but your sister insisted and I'm glad I accepted. He seemed like a very nice man. I can see why he's become such a good friend of your family. Anyway, we got around to talking about my desire for part-time work, and Colonel Bremmer offered me the clerical job on the spot."

A thousand thoughts raced through Klara's mind as she tried to process what she'd just heard. It had been over two and a half years since her last encounter with Bremmer at the Brandenburg asylum. She'd lied to him then about her lack of knowledge regarding Jakob Friedmann or his family. And up until six weeks ago—when Arvid Harnack had broken the news that Jakob might once again be at the forefront of the Kripo's search list—she'd been at peace, figuring that Bremmer would have no cause to question her again about anything. Since Arvid's report, though, she'd lived in a constant state of tension. Sooner or later, Bremmer could track Jakob down and force him to reveal both his and Klara's connections to the Harnack Circle. What exactly might Trudi's job at Bremmer's office portend for any of this? Klara couldn't say, but there was something unsettling about the timing of it. Not to mention the revelation of Elke's continuing contact with the colonel during her husband's absence at the front.

"Klara, are you all right?" Elke prompted.

"Of course, why?"

"You looked like you were in a trance there for a few seconds."

"Oh, I was just remembering that first time our family met Colonel Bremmer. It wasn't under the most pleasant of circumstances."

Elke smiled grimly. "No, it certainly wasn't. But it turned out well for our family, didn't it? I've already told Trudi the story. She's—"

Just then, the phone inside the house rang.

"Probably the BDM national training leader. I was expecting to hear from her today." Elke excused herself and rushed inside.

Klara attempted to change the subject to less sensitive matters.

"So, tell me about your nursing interest, Trudi. Where did that come from? I want to hear all your thoughts on switching out agricultural work in favor of assistant nursing for your Land Service project."

Trudi had just launched into an enthusiastic telling of how she'd taken care of her grandfather during his lengthy illness when an agonized scream pierced the air.

"*Elke?*" Klara shouted as the two girls jumped from their chairs and ran toward the back door.

Rushing into the living room, they drew up short at the sight of Elke standing like a statue by the telephone. She'd already replaced the receiver, and she stood staring at the wall with her arms clutched around her waist. Her face was white, and her lips were trembling. Klara had never seen her so distraught.

"Elke," Klara pleaded. "What's wrong? What is it?"

Elke turned to face her. "Heinz was severely injured at Sevastapol. They're transporting him to the SS military hospital south of Berlin. He's arriving this afternoon. I've got to get ready to go see him."

Klara grabbed her sister's forearms. "I'm coming with you."

(Beelitz-Heilstätten SS Military Hospital – 30 miles Southwest of Berlin)

"I just don't understand. Why did it take over a month for the SS to notify me that my husband was injured and on his way home?"

Klara gripped Elke's hand as they sat together in the hospital waiting room, expecting at any moment to be summoned in to see Heinz. "I don't know. I'm sure we'll find out soon."

Out of concern for her sister's fragile state, she decided not to voice what she'd learned from her experience treating wounded soldiers at the Charité. Only those soldiers with permanently disabling wounds were sent home. The others were treated in hospitals near the front and eventually returned to the fighting.

Having no more comforting words to offer, Klara gazed blankly at the large picture hanging on the wall behind the reception desk. It was a photograph of a younger Adolf Hitler in patient garb, posing with other soldiers who, like him, were recovering at Beelitz from their wounds suffered in the 1916 Battle of the Somme.

The Führer's mustache was a lot wider and certainly styled much better then, she thought idly. *I wonder why he decided to change it.*

A dark-haired man in a white medical coat and black necktie entered the room from a connecting hallway. He approached and stopped in front of them.

"Frau Elke Schröder?" he inquired gently.

"Yes, and this is my sister, Klara."

"My name is Dr. Fritz Dahlke. I am the SS medical intern who had the honor of accompanying your brave husband, Captain Schröder, on his journey from Sevastapol to Berlin."

Elke gasped and sprang from the bench, her hands covering her chest. "Oh, Doctor, is he . . .?"

Dahlke smiled slightly and placed his hand on her forearm. "Yes, he will survive, and he's doing as well as can be expected."

"Can we go see him?" Elke pleaded.

"Yes, in just little while, after the head doctor has completed his examination. In the meantime, I am to inform you of the circumstances of your husband's injuries and prepare you for what you can expect."

Klara felt her heart sink as Elke let out a soft cry and grabbed hold of her arm. After several moments, she'd gathered herself enough to signal Dahlke she was ready for him to proceed.

"I suggest we first move to the conference room down the hallway," Dahlke said. Once there, he closed the door and offered the women seats across the table. He held Elke's gaze steadily in the eye as he spoke in a gentle, though matter of fact, tone.

"From the battlefield reports, it seems that your husband was leading a unit of twenty SS infantrymen in chasing down a group of Soviet soldiers. Captain Schröder and his men were lured into a heavily wooded area outside the city and ambushed. Six of them were killed immediately. Five others were wounded and unable to move on their own. As the fight proceeded, the wounded became cut off from the rest, including your husband, who were trying to make it back to the city under heavy fire.

"Captain Schröder refused to leave his wounded men behind. Together with his corporal, he returned to the woods to retrieve the wounded one at a time and help them back to the main group. They managed to get four men back safely, but just as they were exiting the woods with the fifth man under the cover of friendly fire, a Russian sniper opened up with deadly accuracy. The corporal and the wounded man were killed immediately, and your husband took a shot in the back of his upper right thigh. He whirled around and started shooting back, but he took another shot above the right knee and collapsed . . ."

Dahlke paused and lowered his head in deference as Elke gripped the edge of the desk with both hands. "Go on, Doctor," she said, her voice barely a whisper.

"The sniper got off three more carefully placed shots—two to the left leg and another to the upper left arm, each spaced about a minute apart. It was clear the intent was to inflict more pain rather than killing your husband immediately. Finally, the SS men located the sniper and set up a heavy machine gun. They blasted her out of the tree and chased her away, allowing them to retrieve Heinz and carry him back to the city hospital."

Elke shook her head as if she wasn't processing something. She wiped her eyes and stared at Dahlke in puzzled amazement. "Did I hear you say, *her*? Are you saying it was a *female* Russian sniper who sat in that tree, torturing my husband with her pot shots? And she managed to get away?"

"Yes, it appears that was the case."

Klara glanced at Elke, whose whole body now appeared to be trembling, her eyes squeezed shut and her mouth quivering in helpless fury. After several moments, she seemed to settle a bit and took a deep breath. "Finish, please."

"The hospital doctors did all they could, and they succeeded in saving your husband's life, but . . ." Dahlke lowered his head once again. "Unfortunately, to do so they were forced to amputate his left arm and both legs above the knee."

"*No!*" Elke jumped from her chair, her hands flying to her mouth. Klara rose quickly and wrapped her arms around her, doing her best to calm her violent shaking.

"I can only imagine how hard this is. I will leave the two of you to have a few private moments before we go in to see your husband," Dahlke said softly as he stood and moved to exit the room. Seeming to remember something, he paused.

"Frau Schröder, I know this might come as small consolation right now. But you should know that Heinz has been recommended to receive the Knights Cross with Oak Leaves and Swords for his brave and selfless actions under extreme combat conditions. He is a true hero of the Fatherland. Certainly, in my eyes."

It was several minutes before Elke was finally ready to sit down again. A nurse appeared at the door. "Frau Schröder? You may see your husband now."

By the time Klara and Elke entered through the door of the officers' recovery ward, Elke had somehow found her bearings. An expression of stoic calm was on her face as the two women approached the bed where Heinz lay, clutching each other's arms. As they drew beside him, Heinz, bandaged heavily from the chest down, turned his head, opened his eyes and attempted to smile. His face appeared thinner, but as handsome as Klara had ever remembered it. A small tear formed in his eye.

Elke broke completely. "Oh, Heinz, Heinz…" She leaned over, cupped her hands around his face and kissed him tenderly on the lips.

Klara, choked with emotion, grasped Heinz's uninjured hand and kissed it. What a disparity, she thought, between the solid evidence of personal bravery she was witnessing now and the sordid stories of SS atrocities as told by Jakob and Sophie's father, her own brother Walther, and the wounded army sergeant she'd treated at the Charité weeks ago.

For the first time since joining the Circle, she experienced an unfamiliar pang of guilt over her actions with them—actions that could easily be construed as aiding the mortal enemies of the Fatherland's brave soldiers like Captain Heinz Schröder, who had nobly fought and sacrificed himself to save the lives of his comrades.

Chapter 28

Berlin, Germany
September 3, 1942
(Two weeks later)

Alone in her bedroom this morning after Elke had left to visit Heinz at the hospital, Klara sat at her study desk, rereading the key lines she'd underlined on her sample copy of the Harnack Circle's latest leaflet:

The People are Troubled about Germany's Future

Time and again, Propaganda Minister Goebbels attempts, in vain, to scatter new sand in our eyes. But no one can deny any longer that the catastrophe of National Socialist policy threatens us all.

The major military successes of the early war years have not yielded decisive results. Despite the Wehrmacht High Command's fabrications, the number of German war casualties is rising to millions. Almost every German house is in mourning.

Let those who are too weak to learn the truth continue to swallow the lies. Let those who are too idle to seek the truth remain passive. All responsible people ought to reckon with the facts that a final victory is no longer possible for National Socialist Germany and that Hitler will founder in Russia, just as Napoleon foundered. Anyone continuing to equate the future of the nation with Hitler's fate is committing a crime. Germany must live, even when Adolf Hitler's star falls.

That is the truth, and the truth will no longer be suppressed. It must find its way to the people.

So let no opportunity pass by to counter the propaganda. Pass on letters from the Russian Front. They give the lie to the hypocritical Nazi propaganda. They show what war really looks like. Write to your soldiers in the field about what is happening at home! Send this letter out into the world as often as you can! Pass it on to friends and workmates! You are not alone! Start fighting as an individual, then in groups.

TOMORROW GERMANY WILL BE OURS!

Klara had no illusions. Should she be caught by the authorities distributing such a scathing document calling for active public resistance, she would almost certainly be convicted and executed for high treason.

When Mildred had shown her a sample of this most recent Circle creation two days ago, she'd asked if Klara still felt up to participating in the leaflet-dropping task. It definitely carried more risks of discovery than the Circle's more standard distribution method of mailing letters anonymously. If desired, Klara could revert to this safer method, no questions asked.

Klara had almost yielded to her recent emotions and accepted Mildred's offer—even to the point of saying she wished to decline *any* further participation in the Circle's leaflet spreading efforts. It was not a question of her safety; she'd made over seven drops now, and she felt confident she could continue making them without attracting suspicion. Rather, it had to do with last week's heart-wrenching experience at the SS hospital with Elke and her heroic husband Heinz. How could she keep praying for God's protection of the same servicemen whose efforts she and the Circle were clearly and directly condemning and trying to undermine?

After listening to her concern, Mildred sought to reassure her. "Klara, it's *not* hypocritical to desire the safety in battle of individual German soldiers who may unwittingly be fighting for a cause they haven't yet fully understood as being evil and accepted as such. That's why we desire this latest leaflet to be passed on to our soldiers at the front as well as to the general German populace—to wake them to the terrible truth of what they are in reality fighting for. For those who do awaken, the hope is that they'll become motivated in one way or another to help us resist and eventually bring down this evil government and the fanatical, hateful despot who leads it. So, Klara, there is really *no conflict* between your prayers for soldiers like Heinz or your brother, Walther, and your efforts to help bring an end to this National Socialist nightmare."

Klara's conscience had been put at ease by the argument, and she'd agreed to continue making the drops. She'd left Mildred's apartment with a stack of a hundred leaflets wrapped in brown paper and strapped to her lower back, hidden inside her slip. By the time she arrived home, her confidence and commitment to her mission were completely restored...

The downstairs clock struck ten. *Time to move.*

Eager to get going, she stashed the sample leaflet behind the lining of her purse along with the nine other copies she planned to distribute today. After placing the remaining stack of ninety copies in the small, decorative, storage box that her parents had gifted her years ago, she closed the lid and locked it. She walked to her closet and returned the box to a shelf in the rear that was well-hidden behind layers of hanging clothes and stacks of heavy medical schoolbooks.

She'd taken two steps out the front door with her precious cargo when she heard the phone ring. Thinking it might be Elke calling from the hospital, she went back inside and picked up the receiver. "Hello? Klara Neumann speaking."

"Good morning, Klara. It's Nurse Wagner. We're experiencing a shortage today and need you to report early for your emergency room shift. Can you make it in by noon?"

Klara recognized the coded message and its original source immediately. Arvid and Mildred had long ago stopped communicating with their supporters by phone to avoid being tapped. They'd worked out a system of intermediary contacts and coded messages tailored to the unique home or working situation of each Circle supporter. In this case, "Nurse" meant the message was from Mildred, and "emergency room" meant that a personal meeting was requested to discuss a highly urgent matter. The meeting would take place at a prearranged location in the Mitte district at the indicated time.

"Yes, Nurse, I would be happy to come in early. I will be there at noon."

Placing the receiver down, Klara debated whether she would have ample time to complete her planned drops at the Zoo and several other isolated spots in Tiergarten Park before catching the U-Bahn to Mitte. She glanced at her watch. It would be close, but she decided to press ahead. Better to have today's task behind her so her mind would be clear for whatever Mildred had to say. These days, urgent meeting requests from the Harnacks were usually not a good sign.

Klara sighed with relief. *One of the smoothest runs I've had... and finished a half-hour early!*

It was her last deposit of the day: a single leaflet, folded into quarters and deftly transferred from her purse into the crease of the newspaper she'd pretended to read while sitting by herself on a bench in the waiting room of the Charlottenburg U-Bahn station. Rising to go purchase a cup of coffee, she intentionally left the paper behind on the empty seat next to her and began walking toward the waiting room's small café beside the stairway leading down to the trains.

She realized that what she'd just done was little more than a tiny symbolic gesture. And yet, when added to the nine other deposits she'd already made today at various strategic locations plus the ninety others she planned to make in the days to come—and with this total being multiplied at least twenty times by the similar actions of other leaflet-droppers across the city—she knew her small action was an essential part of something much bigger. It was *her* contribution to the public expression of collective outrage and defiance against the Nazi regime that she and a small but growing number of other German citizens had privately come to loathe from the depths of their souls. Who knew what a single leaflet—somehow finding its way into the hands of just one talented, committed patriot with the right resources and connections—might do to sway that person into taking actions against the regime that could help change the course of history for the better?

Finishing her coffee quickly, she grew restless and decided to wait by the tracks for the U-Bahn's next scheduled departure for Mitte in fifteen minutes. She walked down the stairs and took a seat on an empty bench against the tunnel wall. Her thoughts quickly drifted to her upcoming meeting with Mildred. What could have prompted her to ask for it? Something to do with the escape plan for Sophie and her parents, perhaps? It had been weeks since Arvid had first mentioned the possibility. Since then, he'd had no more news on the subject, or at least none that he was ready to share up until now. Or maybe—

She sensed trouble the moment she noticed the tall, lanky man with an etched, birdlike face shuffling directly toward her.

"May I?" he asked, pointing to a spot near the end of her bench.

Klara nodded curtly, then turned her head away. She began fiddling in her purse for something to read or otherwise occupy herself with. *Anything* to avoid giving the impression she was open to casual conversation.

To her horror, the man sat down and immediately scooted closer to her—far too close for comfort. Before she could object, he reached into his jacket pocket and pulled out a folded newspaper which he laid between them on the bench.

"Did you leave something behind, Fräulein?" he asked in a low voice, a sinister-looking smile playing on his lips.

Klara's heart froze. She knew immediately that she'd been discovered. She also knew the protocol for such an event: *deny, deny, deny.* Her pulse racing, she tried to maintain an innocent tone.

"The newspaper, sir? Oh, no... that wasn't mine. But thank you anyway."

"Are you certain about that, Fräulein?" the man persisted. "I could have sworn it was *you* who I saw as I passed behind your bench in the waiting room. Happened to look over your shoulder at just the right time, I suppose, and couldn't help noticing how fast you moved something from your purse into the crease of the newspaper right before you got up and left it on the bench. Struck me as a little odd, and so I waited a couple of minutes before I decided to go back and investigate. And, lo and behold, guess what I found?"

He slowly moved his hand to lift up a corner of the newspaper, far enough to clearly reveal a portion of the now unfolded illegal leaflet.

"I must say that made for some very interesting reading," he said as he covered it once again. He looked at her with cocked eyebrow. "The kind of reading that could cause a great deal of trouble for anyone caught with it in their hands. And even more trouble for someone trying to intentionally pass it on. I debated with myself what I should do with this, but when I spotted you exiting the café I finally decided I should bring it to your attention. I thought... perhaps... we could work out a little agreement."

Klara stared at him blankly, now completely uncertain as to who this man was or what he wanted. He didn't present himself like the Gestapo or Kripo agent she'd originally feared, but in any case she knew there was no longer any point in further denying her culpability.

"*Agreement,* sir?"

The man looked around at the sound of a large group of passengers suddenly entering the platform from the base of the stairwell. Several sauntered over to the adjoining benches and took their seats. A uni-formed city policeman took up his position next to the stairwell, presumably to ensure that no shenanigans took place during the passenger debarkation/boarding process when the train to Mitte arrived in about five minutes.

"Time's running short, Fräulein," the man said nervously, his voice almost a whisper as he leaned even closer to her. "And so I'll get to the point. You see, the truth is, I really don't like Hitler any more than you do. Just got out after six months in prison for saying some tiny thing against the Nazis. I can't get a job, and I have a sick wife and three small kids to feed."

"I'm very sorry to hear that, sir. But I—"

"I need a bit more than your sympathy right now, Fräulein."

"I'm not sure what you're suggesting, sir."

The man nodded toward her purse. "A hundred Reichsmarks will allow you to have this newspaper back."

Klara gasped. "A *hundred*? I don't have anywhere near that much in my purse."

"Then give me whatever you have, including any ration cards. Just do it fast."

"And if I don't?"

He jerked his head toward the policeman, who was now looking casually in their direction. "Then I'll show it to *him* and point you out. I can always get a few Reichsmarks from the Gestapo for turning in traitors."

Klara hesitated, now wondering if the man might be bluffing. "I could just as easily tell that policeman you're lying. That it's *your* leaflet and that you were just trying to extort me."

His jaw tightened as he peered at her intently with narrowed eyes. "I don't think you'd really want to do that, Fräulein. The Gestapo already know me, and after what they've already put me through, they know I wouldn't dare take a chance lying about something as blatant as this."

The incoming train signal switched to yellow, indicating arrival in two minutes.

"What's it going to be, Fräulein?"

She glanced down the track, debating whether to comply with the man's demand or simply get up, walk quickly down the platform and board the train.

Too late. The man shrugged, picked up the newspaper and started to stand.

Klara grabbed hold of his arm. "*Wait, please!*"

He took his seat again, waiting expectantly.

Klara reached into her purse. Hands shaking, she quickly withdrew the entire contents of her billfold totaling nearly fifty Reichsmarks along with three ration cards.

The man took them and pocketed them in his jacket. "Good decision. Thank you, Fräulein." He shot her a strangely sympathetic smile. "Next time, maybe you'll take a little more care to see who might be prowling around behind you." He stood and walked quickly toward the stairwell, tipping his cap politely to the policeman as he passed by. In another moment, he was gone from sight.

Her mind numb and heart pounding, Klara grabbed the folded newspaper and tucked it in her purse. She tried to stand as the first car of the train pulled up in front of her, but she suddenly felt faint and had to sit back down for a few moments to get her bearings. Finally, she rose to join the other passengers lining up to board the second car. Once in her seat, she closed her eyes and breathed deeply for what seemed the first time since the man had first approached her.

Careless idiot! She berated herself. *You almost lost everything today.*

Her nerves frayed after escaping her near-disaster at the U-Bahn station, Klara could only hope that she would be emotionally prepared for whatever Mildred Harnack might have to say at the emergency meeting she'd called.

The moment she entered the Mitte apartment and saw Mildred's unusually tense expression, she knew something very serious was up.

"Klara, Jakob Friedmann may be on the verge of being arrested."

"*What?* Klara stared at Mildred with her mouth agape "How do you know? Has something happened?"

"We just got word that Jakob's close friend, Aaron Bierwagen, was snatched by the Kripo in Tiergarten Park last week."

It took only a moment for Klara to grasp the implications. Though she didn't know Bierwagen personally, she was aware of his long-time association with Jakob. "So, depending on what the Kripo are able to squeeze out of Bierwagen, Jakob might be next?"

"That would only make sense," Mildred replied. "And if Jakob is caught, you know what that could mean, not only for him, but for all of us in the Circle."

Klara nodded pensively. She also knew well what it could mean for Sophie and her parents. "I should tell Sophie so she and her parents can prepare themselves, just in case the worst happens with Jakob. Every so often, I know he visits them at their hideout."

Mildred put her hand on her Klara's arm. "Before you do that, there's something else you need to know."

"What's that?"

"We finally have news from Dietrich on his brother-in-law's escape operation. It's on, and Sophie's been accepted as one of the passengers."

Klara stared at her blankly, the possibility of Jakob's capture still weighing heavily on her heart despite this promising new development. "And her parents?"

Mildred shook her head sadly. "Unfortunately, getting the false papers for them proved too difficult. I know it will be hard for Sophie to leave them and her brother behind. Do you think she will?"

Klara looked down at her lap. "I really can't say. When is this escape going to happen?"

"In a couple of weeks, supposedly. But here's the thing, Klara. This is going to be an unusual and dangerous operation. Sophie will no doubt need some convincing that it'll work. And given the very short time frame, Dietrich feels that will most likely happen if you meet with her to explain things and convey the false papers that she'll need."

"But how am I going to find out what's involved so I can explain it?"

"You'll need to travel to Stettin this coming Saturday, to Ruth von Kleist-Retzow's townhome in the city. I've already purchased the train tickets for you. Dietrich and the trip leader will be there. They'll tell you all the details and give you everything that you'll need to help convince Sophie and get her prepared."

"And what if she decides not to go after I talk to her?"

Mildred nodded. "The trip leader will assume that was her final choice if he doesn't see her at the departure point at the scheduled time. They won't be waiting around for anyone. But Klara, you'll have to convey to Sophie that, as a Jew, this will no doubt be her last chance to get out of Germany alive.

"In fact, since we can't be sure whether Jakob will be caught and forced to reveal everything he knows, *all* of us associated with the Circle should be preparing ourselves with some escape or hiding plan should the worst happen. Next week, Arvid and I are taking a vacation in Lithuania to discuss just that. We both think it would be good for you to start thinking along those lines as well."

Overwhelmed by a sudden wave of exhaustion, sorrow, and trepidation over the dangers ahead, Klara closed her eyes and let out a long sigh. "You warned me in the beginning that it might one day come to this."

Mildred smiled, though Klara could clearly detect the weariness in her face and voice. "Yes, we did. But that day isn't here yet. And there's still a lot of work to do."

CHAPTER 29

Beelitz-Heilstätten SS Military Hospital
September 6, 1942
(Three days later)

What's taking them so long?

Waiting anxiously for Elke to complete her consultation with her husband's doctor and join her in the hospital garden, Klara prayed that the initial report they'd received of Heinz's mental breakdown had been exaggerated.

"Please come to the hospital immediately, Frau Schröder," the nurse had demanded in the phone call to Elke two hours ago. "Your husband experienced a serious psychotic episode overnight. The doctor feels your presence is required immediately." Elke had called for a taxi and made the thirty-mile drive to the hospital with Klara, wondering what could possibly have triggered such an occurrence.

It was only yesterday that Elke had seen him on her regular afternoon visit. Heinz had seemed more alert and content than at any time since his return—although he *did* react very strangely when one of the nurses stopped by to express gratitude for his service. Instead of thanking her, he'd merely stared at her coldly. His lips had trembled as if he wanted to say something but couldn't. The nurse had walked away, embarrassed, and Elke had felt terrible for her. But afterward, Heinz had assured Elke that the nurse had simply had the misfortune of provoking the horrific memory of the deaths of his comrades. After asking Elke to apologize for his rudeness, he'd brightened up once again, saying he looked forward to a visit later in the evening from Lt Colonel Bremmer. The colonel had promised to bring a box of Bavarian chocolates and some reading materials. Elke had left without a hint of the impending nighttime crisis.

Finally! Klara leaped from her bench at the first sight of her sister walking through the garden's entrance gate. As she drew closer, it was clear that the news on Heinz was not good.

"Elke, how is he?" Klara asked cautiously.

Elke appeared to have been crying, but her face was now taut, almost angry. She did not look at Klara directly; rather, her eyes seemed focused on something over Klara's shoulder. It was as if she were replaying some horrific imaginary scene in her mind.

"Let's walk," she said firmly. "I need to process some things."

Klara waited with bated breath for Elke to initiate the conversation as the two strolled along the pebbled path around the garden.

"When I first saw him, they'd moved his bed to an isolation room. His doctor and a couple of assistants were hovering over him. They stepped aside and I saw his arm strapped to the bed's siderail, another strap across his forehead, and one more across his waist. He'd woken in the middle of the night, screaming and pounding his head with his fist over and over. They said he seemed to be hallucinating. He kept shouting, '*Leave them! Leave them, dammit... No! No!*' He wouldn't stop yelling, and he woke up the entire officers' ward. The assistants gave him some strong sedatives and finally managed to calm him down. He was just coming out of his daze when I walked in."

"Was it a memory of the sniper attack?" Klara asked. "I've treated several wounded soldiers at the Charité who've had recurring nightmares over their last battle. It's not so uncommon."

Elke nodded. "That's what I thought at first. But the doctor pulled me aside and told me he wasn't so sure. He thought there might be something else that was disturbing him."

"Why would he think that?"

Elke hesitated. "He said Heinz had, at a couple of points, screamed out something about a little Jew boy. The doctor couldn't figure out what he was referring to, but it didn't fit in with the sniper battle. He urged me to see if I could get Heinz to tell me more about what might be really bothering him."

"So did you?"

Elke suddenly stopped, sighed and bit her lip. She pointed at a small bench just ahead of them by the path. "Let's sit for a minute."

As soon as they did so, she pulled a crumpled handkerchief out of her purse and dabbed at her eyes. "I was alone with him for an hour. He was really agitated, kept shifting his head from side to side, until I finally grabbed it and got him to focus on me. He said he needed to get some things off his conscience, and he asked if I really was willing to listen. I said yes, and he told me some things. Things I'm still having a hard time believing."

Klara peered at her closely. "Things like… what?"

Elke said nothing for several seconds, then began to speak. Her voice was trembling and barely audible. "Heinz said that two days before the sniper incident, his commander ordered Heinz's SS unit to raid a tiny Crimean village that had supposedly been hiding some wounded Soviet soldiers. 'If you find any, shoot them and their aid-givers on sight,' he was told. 'Then go house-to-house, round up all the village leaders and all the Jewish men over sixteen you can identify, and hang the lot of them in the public square.'"

Klara gasped, her hand touching her throat. This sounded exactly like the kind of atrocities their brother Walther said had been committed by those specialized Einsatzgruppe*n*-SS units in the immediate aftermath of the '39 Polish invasion. The same type of monstrous cleanup that other Einsatzgruppen units were performing in support of Hitler's invasion of western Russia, according to some of her fellow Circle members. Up until now, Klara had hoped that the combat-focused *Waffen*-SS units like the one Heinz commanded would not be directly involved in perpetrating such barbarous reprisal actions against civilians.

"And did they follow through?"

Elke nodded, both hands now wringing her handkerchief.

"Heinz tried to protest to his commander that he had not thought *that* sort of action was the responsibility of frontline SS troops like his. But the commander told him he'd better get used to it, because the war wasn't going smoothly, and Himmler's expectations of *all* his SS men were changing fast. And unless he was willing to face a court-martial and probable execution for insubordination, he had no choice but to obey.

"When he and his men got to the village, they found nine wounded Russian men being tended to by villagers. All were shot immediately along with those helping them. Twenty other male villagers were hanged in the square as their wives and mothers and children watched. And that's not all."

Klara touched her sister's arm. "What else, Elke?"

"They wrapped up the raid and were preparing to leave the village, when an old Jewish woman ran up to Heinz. She told him a couple of his men were lingering in her house, torturing her daughter and her infant grandson. She begged him to put a stop to it. He took a couple of his junior officers, and they ran to the house. They entered just in time to see one of the soldiers forcing himself on a woman he'd pinned down on the dining table. His comrade stood dangling the woman's small, screaming baby boy upside down by one leg over her face, obviously taunting her.

"Heinz was livid. He pulled his pistol and ordered the men to release the woman and her son and stand with their backs against the wall. He demanded to know why they'd disobeyed his specific orders to leave all women and children alone. One of the men said she had called him and his comrade cowardly Nazi trash as they passed the house on their way to rejoin the others. He insisted that he and his partner were not about to allow a filthy Jew to insult them like that—especially a woman.

"Heinz was so disgusted by the men's animalistic behavior and by everything else he'd been ordered to do that he just lost it. He yelled at them, '*I ordered everyone in our unit to leave them—leave the women and children alone, dammit. Both of you clearly disobeyed a direct order from your commanding officer, and now you're going to pay the price.'"*

Elke's head sagged. She barely managed to choke out her next words: "Then he—he walked over and... shot each of the men... point-blank in the forehead."

Shocked to the core, Klara draped her arm around her sister's shaking shoulders, patiently waiting for her to continue.

"Heinz told me he knew he shouldn't have executed those men. He believes he wrongfully murdered them. He should have placed them in custody, taken them back to the city, and recommended a court-martial. Even though his junior officers assured him that they believed the two men had always been unruly, disrespectful troublemakers for the unit, and that they deserved what they got. Despite their support, Heinz has been carrying a lot of personal guilt over the whole affair. He's even thinking that what happened to himself afterward might have been divine punishment for his sin. He was determined to hide the story and his true feelings about the incident from me and everybody else. At least until last night, when the memory came surging back in his terrible nightmare."

"So how did you respond to what he told you?" Klara asked softly.

Elke's face tightened, her eyes taking on a hard, angry look. "I tried to reason with him. I held his hand and looked into his eyes. I *pleaded* with him to realize that he had absolutely no reason to feel guilty about anything. He'd faithfully carried out the orders his commander had given him on how to conduct the raid. The two men he'd shot had blatantly disobeyed *his* orders and behaved like vile pigs in the process. For God's sake, he more than proved his integrity and bravery by his heroic performance two days later. I told him that I am proud of him and that he has *nothing* to be ashamed of, and the medal he's going to receive proves it." She shook her head vigorously and slapped the arm of the bench. "But nothing I said seemed to convince him. He just seems so determined to wallow in his false sense of guilt."

Klara stared at her in alarm. "Elke, you sound almost angry at Heinz."

Elke jumped up from the bench as if stung by a bee. She whirled and faced her sister with eyes flashing fire.

"I am not angry at Heinz, Klara," she hissed. "I *will* tell you who I'm angry at. I'm angry at that Russian *sniper-bitch* who took it upon herself to torture my poor husband when he was lying defenseless on the ground. I swear to you—if I could just get my hands on that little Bolshevik insect, I'd squeeze her neck so tight her ugly, stupid-looking Slavic head would pop off! And I'd do it slowly so she could suffer just like Heinz, whom she happily managed to turn into a triple amputee and prevent us from ever having children together—"

Elke's crossed her arms over her stomach as she burst out in sobs.

Klara sat speechless, unsure of what to say or do. She definitely understood Elke's reaction, though she wondered how the Russian sniper woman might have felt knowing some of her own family members had been shot or hung in that village public square on Heinz's orders. Still, Elke faced a formidable future with her disabled husband, and Klara wanted to avoid any hint of doubting Heinz's motivations.

Elke swallowed hard and took several deep breaths, her shoulders rising with each one. "Let's go. I need to walk some more," she said finally.

The women walked silently around the remainder of the pathway. As they neared the end, Elke stopped and peered cautiously at her sister.

"I don't know if I should be telling you all this, Klara. But I can't tell anyone else, and if I don't get it off my chest, I think I'll go crazy."

"What is it, Elke?"

"There's someone else I'm very angry at right now."

"Who's that?"

"Colonel Bremmer."

Klara stared at her in disbelief. "*Colonel Bremmer?* But I thought you said he'd been incredibly supportive, and—"

Elke held up her hand. "I know, I know. Yes, he has been all that and more. At least up until last night when he visited Heinz."

"Why? What happened?"

"Heinz told me he said something—probably meaning it as an innocent joke—that made Heinz feel even more terrible about himself. In fact, I have no doubt that it contributed to his experience last night and his continuing depression today."

"So, what did he say?"

"The two of them were joking about possible work Heinz could take on in the future. Colonel Bremmer told Heinz that he shouldn't worry at all because in his condition he would be 'highly sought after and paid well by national circuses as one of the most highly honored and decorated *useless eaters* in all of Germany.'"

Klara recoiled. "Are you serious? He actually said *that*?"

"As I said, Heinz was sure the colonel meant it only as a joke. But it obviously didn't sit well, and Heinz was too embarrassed and ashamed to make a fuss about it."

"Oh Elke, that is one of the most crass, insensitive remarks I've ever heard. Don't you think you should mention this to Colonel Bremmer, ask him to at least apologize to Heinz, if not to you?"

Elke grimaced. "I probably should. But it seems so unlike him, and he's been so good to Heinz and me over the years. I just can't understand why he would say something so hurtful like that. Well, anyway, if he's truly a friend I suppose it's my responsibility to bring it to his attention when we meet for lunch next week."

Klara looked at her askance. "Lunch with *Colonel Bremmer?*"

"Oh, I assure you Klara," Elke responded quickly. "It's entirely innocent. I've been meeting with him for lunch about once a month, both during Heinz's deployment and since his return. Heinz knows about our meetings and heartily approves as he trusts the colonel's intentions and knows our talks have been a great emotional support to me. I just hope the colonel will continue to be in his elevated mood when I see him, so he'll take my complaint the right way."

"What's causing his elevated mood, may I ask?" Klara asked nervously.

"He couldn't say much about it as it has to do with his work. But he did share with me the last time we met just two days ago that he was very proud of his Berlin Kripo unit. They'd just succeeded in helping to finally bust that ring of Jewish-Communists led by Herbert Baum who tried to sabotage the Soviet Paradise exhibit last May." She nodded approvingly. "On that score, I told him I heartily shared his joy. *Anyone*—Jew or otherwise—who busies themselves with spreading hateful propaganda and lies about the Führer or our brave soldiers in the field like Heinz *deserves* to be arrested and executed."

"Well," Klara said, dismayed but not surprised to hear her sister's blanket condemnation of anti-Hitler voices. "I certainly hope the colonel feels at peace with all the chips falling into place for him and his Berlin Kripo as far as this Baum business is concerned."

Elke nodded. "Yes, and he said it was only a matter of days before something far bigger and more exciting would be breaking due to his Kripo's excellent interrogation work with those Baum criminals. He really wished he could tell me about it, but of course he couldn't."

"Our Berlin Kripo Chief's work never gets dull, does it?" Klara said, her insides swirling with a mixture of fear and nausea. Could Bremmer's comment be an indication that the Kripo was on the verge of catching Jakob and exposing the Circle?

Elke smiled faintly as the women resumed their walk toward the garden gate. "No, I suppose it doesn't. I only hope he'll still be in a good mood when I try to tell him how he offended Heinz."

Klara nodded sympathetically, though she realized that if Colonel Bremmer was still in a good mood at Elke's next meeting, it *could* well be the result of Jakob's arrest. The Gestapo, together with Colonel Bremmer and his Kripo people, were undoubtedly closing in on their new leads from the Baum group's confessions and whatever other information they had on Jakob and the Circle. They could strike like a cobra at any time.

I have to help Sophie get out of the country. Now.

CHAPTER 30

Ruth von Kleist-Retzow's Townhome: Stettin, Germany
September 9, 1942
(Three days later)

"You expect Sophie Friedmann to pose as the daughter of a *Nazi Abwehr agent*? How is that possible?"

Klara stared in open-mouthed disbelief across the dining room table at Dietrich Bonhoeffer and Friedrich Arnold—a short, balding man of about fifty whom Dietrich had just introduced as the leader of the escape effort. It was an audacious plan, which had been over a year in the making and involved sympathetic Nazi government officials at the highest levels.

How will I ever convince Sophie that this ridiculous-sounding scheme for Herr Arnold to shepherd his wife, his fictitious daughter, and ten other Jews on a fake intelligence mission across the Swiss border has any chance of succeeding?

Dietrich exchanged quick, knowing smiles with Friedrich. "Seems that we get the same initial reaction from everyone involved, no?"

Friedrich smiled grimly and reached to pull several official-looking documents from his briefcase which he then spread on the table in front of Klara. "Before I explain the mission process and the purpose of these items, Fräulein Klara, allow me to first clarify who I am and my role. I am a Jewish ex-lawyer from Berlin whose family—just like the Friedmanns—has suffered terribly under the Nazi persecutions.

"Fortunately, I have a longtime Aryan friend who also just happens to be the Chief of the *Abwehr*. This man—Admiral Canaris—is highly respected and exerts great power within the Nazi hierarchy. But he is secretly opposed to Hitler's efforts to exterminate Jews and Russian prisoners of war, and he's been seeking ways to undermine those efforts. As it turns out, Dietrich here has become one of Canaris's most trusted secret allies in this endeavor."

Klara's jaw dropped. *Dietrich Bonhoeffer—the leader of the Nazi-hating Confessing Church—teaming up with the head of the German armed forces intelligence organization? Am I hearing things correctly?*

Dietrich, noticing her surprise and look of dismay, hurried to explain. "Please don't panic, Klara. I assure you that we all, including Admiral Canaris, are very much on the same side, passionately opposed to what Hitler and the Nazis are doing to the Jews. And so, my secret alliance with him is not a betrayal of my faith. In belief and practice, I'm the same Confessing Church pastor and anti-Nazi theologian you've always known. Does that set your mind at ease, Klara?"

"Hmmm." She passed a finger back and forth across her lips. "Yes, I suppose it does, but I must say, you seem to be living in a tangled web of intrigue."

Dietrich chuckled. "That's putting it mildly. But enough about me... please continue, Friedrich, with your side of our story."

Friedrich nodded and picked up where he'd left off. "Admiral Canaris was very sympathetic to the plight faced by my own family as well as another Jewish family we know, especially after the Berlin deportations began. Working with Dietrich and his brother-in-law, Hans Dohnanyi—who's actually one of Canaris's senior Abwehr advisors—he came up with a scheme to help our two families, plus several other Jews, escape to Switzerland.

"The basic idea is for each of us to be formally documented as being either an Abwehr agent or one of their family members. As a group, we'll be assigned a special Abwehr mission that will enable us to receive permission from the SS to cross the border. Once we're safely in Switzerland, the ruse will end. That's because Dietrich is secretly arranging for us all to be taken into protective custody as legitimate political refugees by Swiss government and church leaders. We'll be free to stay under church protection in Switzerland or to pursue further emigration opportunities. Canaris has even promised we will receive funds to support our initial living expenses there."

This whole scheme sounds complicated and risky, Klara thought. *What if the Jews' true identities are somehow discovered by Nazi guards at the border crossing?*

After a few more minutes of patient explanation and reassurance by Herr Arnold, she finally agreed that the general plan, though treacherous, at least seemed feasible. And anyway, with Sophie facing discovery, deportation, and death if she remained in hiding, there really was no other viable alternative.

"So, what's next? What do I need to do to help?" she asked the men.

Friedrich pointed to the documents on the table. "These are the special Abwehr identification cards, support papers, passport, and visa that Dietrich and others worked very hard to create for Sophie—my pretend daughter—using the information supplied to us previously by Frau Harnack. You will go meet with Sophie at her hideout later this week and attempt to convince her to accept the terms. If she does, then you'll leave the documents with her. If not, you'll destroy them."

He studied her for a few moments before continuing. "The plan is to convene the entire group, fourteen of us in all, at the Berlin Zoo train station on the night of our departure. You, Klara, will need to escort Sophie by taxi to the station that night, and make sure she gets there at least forty-five minutes before the scheduled departure time. Once you help her find me, then she and I can go through customs together. As far as a departure date, we are aiming for some time during the week of September 22–29. However, there are still some important details that Dietrich is working out with the Swiss church people who will be vouching for us as legitimate refugees. If for some reason we're unable to resolve any remaining differences by September 29, then the entire operation must be called off, as the passport window will expire after that."

Dietrich shook his head. "Let's all pray that will not be the case. We'll only get one chance at this."

"Amen to that," Friedrich said. "At any rate, I will need you to check in with me every day during that week at 1 p.m. using a pay phone to determine if it's a go for that evening. That will give you about five hours to let Sophie know so she'll be ready for you to pick her up. If all goes as planned, she'll be on the train to freedom by 8:15, and you can then go home and celebrate with a few glasses of vintage wine."

"But Herr Arnold," Klara objected, "how will Sophie's parents explain her absence to the Gestapo if they happen to discover their hideout after she's left?"

Friedrich smiled. "We've thought of that scenario. The thing that you must instruct them to do in that case is to lie. They are to tell the police that Sophie joined a small number of other Jews who were planning an escape out of Germany through Denmark to Sweden. They are to claim that Sophie didn't reveal any of the details or her contacts— simply that one day she said it was time, packed her suitcase, kissed them goodbye, and off she went. This is not unheard of these days. The Gestapo should find it a credible alibi for Sophie's absence. Of course, we can only hope and pray that Sophie's parents won't reveal their knowledge of or connections with *this* operation. If they do, it could easily spell disaster for a lot of people, including Dietrich and you."

Friedrich Arnold took a deep breath and reached out to place his hand over Klara's. "Do you have any more questions? I know this is a tremendous amount to absorb, and you are being very generous and brave to take on this role on behalf of Sophie."

Klara nodded but said nothing as she struggled with the full realization of what she would need to do.

Dietrich placed his arm around Herr Arnold's shoulders. "Friedrich, would you mind if Klara and I shared a few moments alone?" he whispered.

"Of course not. Take your time. I'll be waiting in the living room with Ruth."

After Friedrich left, Dietrich removed his spectacles and placed his elbows on the table, chin in hands. "Never in your wildest dreams did you imagine yourself involved in such a complex escapade, am I correct?"

Klara sighed wearily. "Yes, that's certainly true. But if it succeeds in getting Sophie safely out of this National Socialist hell on earth, then it will have been more than worth it."

"It's been a very lonely and hard journey for you these past few years, hasn't it Klara?" Dietrich said softly. "Without your boyfriend Joshua, very little contact with Sophie, worried about discovery by the authorities, having to constantly pretend you're someone who you are not around your family . . ."

The mention of her family unleashed the emotion that had been building over the past several days. She told Dietrich about the situation with Heinz and Elke and how it was tearing her apart to see what Nazism had done, and was still doing, to destroy the bodies and souls of loved ones caught in the web of its unfathomably evil lies.

"There are times, Pastor," she confessed, "when I'm tempted to openly explode at Elke over her inability—or maybe it's just her obstinate refusal?—to see Hitler for the monster that he is. But if I did that, I fear it could easily do more harm than good. In fact, I'm not sure I could trust her not to report me to the authorities. Sometimes, as much as I care about her, I feel that I'm losing hope that she'll ever be able or even want to change her mindset."

Dietrich folded his hands together on the table. "Like so many others in this country, the devil certainly seems to have used Hitler to keep Elke firmly in his clutches and prevent her from seeing the light. But Klara, you must never give up hope for your sister. You never know how or when or who God might use to provide the spark that will turn Elke's mind and heart away from blindly following her Führer to following God's ways. That spark might not happen until the last second of her life, but it is always possible. Remember the thief on the cross?"

Klara nodded and smiled. "It's one of my most treasured stories from the Bible. I remember Elke also really loved it when we first heard it in church. But I wouldn't mind hearing it again from *you* right now, if you don't mind."

Dietrich grinned. "I'd be delighted. I always love telling it. Remember, it starts with the two thieves who were being crucified next to Jesus. One thief knew that his own life of following the devil and his ways deserved death. But as he looked at Jesus, something changed inside him. He recognized Jesus as purely righteous, as someone who held the power of God to forgive his sins and grant him eternal life in Heaven, despite his wicked past. In his last breath, he simply and humbly asked Jesus, 'Please remember me when you come into your kingdom.' Jesus, recognizing the man's sincere change of heart, assured him, 'I tell you the truth, today you will be with me in Paradise.'"

Klara looked down at her lap. "I just pray I'll have the privilege of seeing that spark of recognition happen for Elke—hopefully *way* before the last second of her life. And if there's anything *I* can say or do to help make it happen, I hope God will show me."

Dietrich cocked an eyebrow. "Be prepared, Klara. Someday, he might just do that. In the meantime, you've got enough work on your hands with Sophie."

CHAPTER 31

Berlin, Germany
September 29, 1942
(Three weeks later)

Heart thumping, Klara approached the pay phone down the street from the Charité Hospital. *This is it.* The last chance to receive the coded signal before the window closed for the border escape operation. Everything hinged on whether Dietrich had finally succeeded in persuading the reluctant Swiss church officials to circumvent official government policy and accept Jewish refugees.

Each day for the past week, the contact's terse message had translated to the same, "not tonight." Each morning, Klara's hopes for Sophie had started sky-high, only to be dashed by yet another dose of reality at 1 p.m. It would be devastating if the operation had to be cancelled. Especially after the tremendous effort Klara had expended to convince Sophie and her parents that the escape plan was worth the risk.

Klara placed the coin in the slot and dialed the familiar number with a trembling finger. After four rings, the receiver clicked as it was lifted on the other end.

"Hello?"

"This is Frau Steinmann. I'm calling to check on the status of my orders," Klara said, using her alias.

"Yes, I'll check. One moment please," the male voice responded.

Klara bit her knuckle, waiting for the final verdict. Seconds later, it came.

"Frau Steinmann?"

"Yes?"

"I'm happy to say we have your most recent order ready. You may pick it up before closing time at seven-thirty."

Klara was speechless for several seconds, stunned as she was with a mixture of relief and elation.

"*Oh!* That is wonderful news! Thank you ever so much. I will be there by then."

It's on! Now, to alert Sophie…

She was about to hang up when the voice on the other end spoke again.

"Frau Steinmann, I also wanted to let you know we are having some major shipment issues with the company that took your previous order. We just received notice that the two large items and several of the smaller ones were damaged in transit. I sincerely regret this, and we will let you know as soon as possible how you can reorder or collect a refund."

What? Klara nearly dropped the phone. In an instant, her elation switched to stomach-dropping alarm over the news that Arvid and Mildred Harnack (the two large items) and some other members of the Circle had been arrested (damaged) by the Gestapo. Advice on what to do might come, but there was no hint as to how, when, or from whom it would be provided. She knew the rules for this dreaded scenario. Unless someone contacted her with more information, she would need to lie low and rely on herself to evade the Gestapo.

"Yes, I understand, and I'll look forward to whatever instructions you can provide whenever you have them. I will see you at seven-thirty to pick up my current order." She slammed the phone down and remained in the booth, trying desperately to fight off her panic. Who had exposed the Harnacks? Had Jakob been arrested and been forced to reveal his connection to them? Was Klara next?

Calm down. First things first—think of Sophie. She needed to call Frau Adelberg, the woman who was hiding the Friedmanns in her basement, and tell her to inform Sophie that the operation was on. Next, take the bus to her childcare duties at Herr Freitag's apartment. Then, home by five to prepare a dinner for herself and Elke. Finally, tell Elke she was going to see a movie with one of her colleagues and take a taxi to the bus stop nearest Sophie's location.

Sophie should be waiting to join her with her suitcase; together they would travel on to the Berlin Zoo station. Friedrich Arnold should be there to greet and accompany Sophie through the customs inspection, after which the girls would say their last goodbyes before the train departed.

After placing the call to Frau Adelberg, Klara exited the phone booth and made her way to the bus stop. With the plan now in motion, her thoughts inevitably returned to fears for herself.

Would Arvid, Mildred, or any of the others arrested crack under the pressure of interrogation and reveal Klara's name? If so, her own arrest could happen at any time, anywhere. Even, God forbid, at the train station.

Her options were limited. It was too late to try to go into hiding. Besides, there was really no place she knew of that would be safe. Her only recourse was to get rid of the only evidence that could clearly link her to anti-Nazi activities: the ten or so undistributed Circle leaflets she'd left in the lockbox in her bedroom. If discovered, those would certainly be used as evidence against her. The likely outcome would then be a formal charge of high treason followed by torture, a sham trial and death sentence. Not to mention the overwhelming trouble and disgrace she would bring her own family. But without the leaflets as supporting evidence of her guilt, she might be able to avoid conviction on the most serious charges.

Fortunately, she should have about an hour alone at home before Elke's return. That would allow time to retrieve the remaining leaflets, burn them in the fireplace, and dispose of the ashes. At the very least, her mind would be settled on *that* score by the time she left to meet Sophie...

⚮

The moment Klara walked through the front door of her house she knew her plan to destroy the leaflets had misfired.

"Elke! What are you doing home so early?"

Elke looked up from the magazine she'd immersed herself in while sitting on the living room couch. It was clear something was bothering her.

"I received a call at work this morning from the SS hospital," she said, throwing the magazine on the coffee table. "Heinz experienced yet another episode last night. It's his third since they started. The doctor said . . ." She paused and took a deep breath. "He said if Heinz has any more of these, they may need to consider moving him to a psychiatric ward."

Putting aside her own pressing worries for the moment, Klara sat beside her sister. "Elke, I am so sorry. I thought he'd been improving."

Elke shook her head, eyes downcast and brows pulled together. "His wounds are healing well, according to the doctor. But his depression and nighttime anxiety are worsening. I could see it in his face when I saw him yesterday afternoon." Tears began to roll down her cheeks. "His eyes seemed glazed and unfocused. He kept trying to look at me, but then he'd quickly look away as if ashamed and mutter something like, 'Elke, I am so, so sorry.' I held his hand and kept trying to console him. But I can tell he's still having terrible guilt over killing those two subordinates in Russia, and because of his amputations, he's despairing that he can't be a legitimate husband for me anymore."

"Did he actually say that?" Klara asked softly.

"Yes, in so many words. I- I told him that he would *always* be my husband and that I was proud of him and that I would *never* stop loving him, no matter how . . ." Elke covered her face with her hands.

Klara reached out and embraced her. "In sickness and in health, until death separates… right?" she whispered in her ear. "I can't imagine how hard this must be for you, sister."

Elke nodded. She pulled away to dab at her eyes with her handkerchief. "If I only knew what to say, what to do for Heinz that would help him feel better about himself."

"Did Colonel Bremmer ever apologize to you and Heinz for that idiotic joke he made about Heinz's condition?" Klara asked cautiously.

Elke grimaced and rolled her eyes. "Oh! I wish you hadn't even asked about *him*."

"Why?"

"I finally had that lunch with him a couple of days ago. He took me to a nice restaurant, and he seemed to be in an extraordinarily good mood to start. Said that his Kripo people had successfully wrapped up some big investigation recently and—since it was now all over and the suspects rounded up—he was looking forward to taking a two-week vacation in southern Germany. He said he'd be leaving next week."

Klara's heart leaped. *Investigation over? All suspects rounded up? Bremmer leaving on vacation?* Wouldn't that imply that her own name had *not* been disclosed by the other arrested Circle members and that she was now out of immediate danger? The prospect caused a huge, surge of relief to course through her body. "That sounds like a promising start to your conversation," she said innocently.

"Yes, it was. Until he slyly asked if I would like to accompany him on his vacation."

"*What?* Are you serious?"

"Well, he did suggest it in a teasing tone, but I could tell he meant it even though I'm sure he'd deny it." Elke shook her head angrily. "I was disgusted. It reminded me of the way he'd spoken to Heinz, and I confronted him on it. I told him how hurt Heinz had been by his *useless eater* comment, and I asked if he'd be willing to apologize."

"Good for you! And what did he say?"

"He seemed genuinely taken aback, and said he *would* tell Heinz that he was sorry if he had offended him. He thought Heinz would have been able to recognize it for the silly joke that it was. Then he seemed to turn almost angry, and he went on to complain about Heinz's 'pathetically weak, self-flagellating' view of his actions in Russia. He said no self-respecting SS man should ever experience regrets over carrying out his superior officer's orders—no matter the circumstances. Nor should they feel guilt over punishing subordinates for refusing to obey *their* orders. Obedience to orders is always paramount, according to Colonel Bremmer—no matter what those orders are. Heinz acted correctly along both those lines. So why, the colonel wanted to know, is he so intent on destroying himself by wallowing in this false guilt?

"When I suggested that Heinz had not entered the Waffen-SS thinking that mass murder of innocent civilians would become part of his job requirement, and that perhaps *that* was contributing to some of his depression, I saw the colonel's face harden. Then I went even further and said I didn't believe the Führer himself would approve of anything like that."

Klara stared at her sister in amazement. How could Elke possibly believe that Hitler wasn't capable of permitting, or even directly ordering, such atrocities to be carried out by the SS? There could be only one reason: Elke still viewed the Führer through an ideal lens, one that would not allow any stain to be associated with him. Any disreputable actions had to stem from the corrupt moral choices of his subordinates—certainly not the orders of her beloved Führer.

"How did the colonel react to *that* one?" she asked.

"He just shot me a patronizing smile and said that I've got a lot to learn about the realities of war and the evolving plans of the Führer— whatever *that* was supposed to mean."

Indeed, Klara thought wryly, thinking of her Aktion T4 experience. *Oh, how I wish I could just open up and tell her the truth about everything I know. But she's clearly not ready.*

Elke continued, "Then the colonel ended the conversation, paid the bill, and drove me back to my class while hardly speaking another word. I must say, I left with a distinctly sour tang in my mouth for the first time since we've known him. I just hope he apologizes to Heinz the next time he visits. Heinz so desperately needs encouragement now. I'll have another chance when I go visit him tomorrow."

The sisters talked a while longer about Heinz's perilous physical and emotional state, as well as the personal struggles Elke faced as she considered the bleak, long-term prospects. Aware of her own time crunch, Klara waited for a convenient pause in the conversation, then looked at her watch.

"I really need to start getting dinner ready. I'm going to see a movie in the city tonight with another nurse from the Charité, and a taxi's coming to pick me up at seven."

Elke seemed to welcome the change of subject to lighter matters. "That sounds delightful. What are you seeing?"

"*Beloved World*," Klara lied. "It's that new romantic comedy everyone's been talking about."

"Oh, that sounds like something I'd love to see with you if I wasn't so depressed about Heinz. But wouldn't it be better to see with a handsome gentleman rather than a fellow nurse?" Elke asked as she followed Klara into the kitchen. "Someone like your American boyfriend from the embassy. *Joshua Peters*, wasn't that his name? Are you sure you're not fibbing about who you're going out with tonight, Klara? You know I'll squeeze the truth out of you, sooner or later."

Klara laughed nervously. "Oh, Elke, do you never stop? No, I promise you it's just a good *female* friend of mine that I knew from nursing school."

She busied herself with preparing the meal, knowing she needed to start concentrating on getting Sophie safely to the train station. Thankfully, with Elke's news of Colonel Bremmer's completed investigation and his upcoming vacation, she no longer had to contend with the crushing fear that her own arrest was imminent. There were now only two tasks separating her from being able to enjoy more or less complete peace of mind:

Tonight—send Sophie off to Switzerland and freedom.

Tomorrow evening—come home after work and secure my own freedom, at least from fear, by destroying those remaining leaflets while Elke visits Heinz.

For the first time since waking, Klara started to breathe normally.

"When you get to Hollywood eventually," Klara teased Sophie. "Make sure you wear that hat and dress. People could easily mistake you for Hedy Lamarr."

"Oh, sure," Sophie scoffed. "You *would* have to pick the world's most beautiful, seductive, Austrian Jewish actress to compare me with now, wouldn't you?"

The girls' light banter disguised their nerves as they walked toward the entrance of the Berlin Zoo train station. Everything had gone smoothly since the taxi picked Klara up from her house. A quarter hour later she'd been joined by Sophie who'd been waiting, suitcase in hand, at the bus stop nearest Frau Adelberg's residence. The taxi driver had been a bit too nosy for Klara's taste, glancing in his rearview mirror at his passengers, perking up his ears anytime one would venture a quiet remark to the other. But they'd reached their destination on time at seven-thirty and started their last walk to the terminal.

Klara's only role from this point was to escort Sophie inside and help her locate her Abwehr "father," Friedrich Arnold. Once that was done, the pair would go through the customs booth together. Assuming there were no hitches, they would pass through the gate to the platform and board their train before it was scheduled to leave at eight-fifteen for the eight-hour journey to Basel, Switzerland.

Her optimism building, Klara focused on the large sign over the entrance doors about thirty yards ahead. The sign contained the familiar subtitle reflecting the harsh requirement for all German public transportation in the year 1942: *"Juden Verboten."* She leaned toward Sophie walking beside her and started to say quietly: "Won't you be ecstatic when—"

A shrill whistle sounded from somewhere up ahead.

Klara and Sophie drew to a halt. A uniformed policeman waved for people to form a line behind a portable wooden barrier that two workers were placing on the sidewalk in front of the entrance.

"Klara, what is it?" Sophie asked frantically, setting her suitcase down and clutching Klara's arm.

"I'm not sure. It looks like a checkpoint," Klara said, her voice trembling. Was this merely an untimely recurrence of the random screenings by the regular police to prevent suspected criminals, army deserters, and the like from escaping the city by train? Or was it something far more threatening—*such as a Gestapo net being cast for a specific individual such as Sophie or myself?*

Klara looked wildly all around but could see no evidence of any police forming anywhere behind her or to the sides. *A good sign. Probably just a typical screening,* she thought. Still, the checkpoint presented a major obstacle. Time was running short. The train would depart in thirty-five minutes, and it would probably take at least fifteen once inside the terminal to locate Friedrich, pass through customs, and get to the boarding platform.

"Come on, we've got to get in that line fast," Klara said firmly.

"But what about—"

"Sophie, don't argue, just pick up your suitcase and let's go."

By the time they joined the line in front of the barrier, there were at least ten people ahead of them. The first man took nearly a minute to have his papers checked and respond to a couple of questions. At this rate, they would make it inside the terminal with only about twenty minutes to spare. Unfortunately, that wasn't the only concern. Her own identification papers should be in good order, but would Sophie's special Abwehr pass be recognized by these city policemen? Or would they become confused and challenge her identity?

"If they give you any trouble, just insist that they call the number on your pass," Klara whispered into Sophie's ear as she stood behind her in line. "It's one they'll recognize as associated with national SS headquarters. Tell them to give the number on the card to whoever answers the phone, and you should be cleared to pass through. We can't talk or recognize each other from here on."

Sophie nodded, though Klara could tell she was struggling not to panic and run.

Klara held her breath as Sophie stepped up to the barrier.

"Papers?" the policeman demanded.

Sophie handed him the special pass. He scrutinized it for several seconds, frowning. "What's this?"

Klara's heart sank. *My worst fears realized.*

"A special pass, sir," Sophie said, her voice shaking slightly.

"Special pass? From who? Are you trying to bluff me, woman?" He peered at her closely, then looked back down at the false, Aryan name on the pass. He stared at her again. "Are you a Jew?"

Sophie shook her head vigorously. "No, absolutely not, sir. And if you doubt what I'm saying I suggest you call—"

The policeman cut her off. "Schmitz!" he motioned to one of his assistants standing off to the side. "We may have caught one here. Check her out."

The assistant hurried over and grabbed Sophie by the arm and scooped up her suitcase. He escorted her to a small table with a phone and made her sit on a stool while he examined her pass.

"Next. Papers?" the policeman growled at Klara. She stepped forward, trying to avoid looking him in the eyes as she tried to answer his standard questions without betraying the slightest concern in her voice. To her great relief, he handed them back to her and motioned for her to proceed on through the entrance.

She hastened through, knowing that she had but one mission now—and that was to find Friedrich Arnold and beg him to wait a few more minutes on the chance that Sophie might be able to clear the checkpoint. She looked at the station clock: a minute or so past eight— less than fifteen minutes before the train departed. She searched the crowded terminal floor, looking for Friedrich. *There he is, waiting by the customs window!* She rushed over to him.

"Klara, where's Sophie?" he asked, extreme urgency in his voice. "We need to go through customs and get out to the train *now!*"

Klara rushed to explain what happened and pleaded for them to wait five more minutes, though every bone in her body told her there was no hope... Sophie was lost, with no way out.

After the time had passed, Friedrich looked at her compassionately. "Klara, I know how hard this is, but you know I can't wait any longer. The others are depending on me to shepherd them through at the other end, and I can't—"

"*Klara!*"

Klara whirled at the sound of Sophie's voice. Her mouth fell open as she saw Sophie running toward them with her suitcase, waving frantically. Klara rushed to greet and hug her briefly.

"The pass must have worked!" she whispered in her ear.

Sophie nodded, a huge grin of relief on her face. She quickly grabbed Friedrich's arm and strode with him up to the customs window as Klara stood aside and observed. *Please God, let them through.*

This time, there was no challenge. Klara joined Sophie and Friedrich as they strode toward the gate where they paused for one last goodbye.

"Klara," Sophie said, her eyes filled with tears. "You don't know how much you've meant to me. I love you, Klara. Please take care of my parents and tell them and Jakob that I'll always love them and I'll never, ever forget them."

"I promise, Sophie. I know I'll see you again someday. And remember, if you ever get to New York . . ."

"Yes, I promise, too."

After a final embrace, Sophie passed through the gate with Friedrich—the gate to freedom.

Hidden well in the lining of Sophie's suitcase was a short, handwritten note that Klara had penned to the man who had captured her heart at that embassy diplomatic ball, and who would always have a place with her fondest memories.

Dear Joshua: I am doing well, as I hope and pray you are, too.
I'm still waiting. Love... K.

CHAPTER 32

Berlin, Germany
September 30, 1942
(The next day)

I f there was a day in the past ten years when she had felt more at peace with herself despite the circumstances, Klara Neumann could not remember it.

She settled back with her eyes closed in the comfortable chaise lounge in Herr Freitag's living room after putting Hans down for his nap. As she did, the hand-wringing, last-minute victory of Sophie's successful departure resonated in her mind.

Oh, how I needed that. All the heartache and stress of the past two years—Joshua's leaving, Leah's death, being fired from her RA position, constantly risking arrest with her Circle activities—had taken a huge toll, causing her to wonder if she had the emotional strength to keep on resisting the Nazi regime. But somehow, the sight of Sophie passing through that station gate to freedom made all these troubles and frustrations fade into oblivion. For once, her resistance efforts had been rewarded.

So where from here? she wondered.

The immediate concern was the lingering possibility that she might be identified as a lower-echelon supporter of the Circle. But the more she thought about it, the more optimistic she became. Arvid and Mildred were the only two people in the group who knew her real name and background. She was known to everyone else she'd met at Circle meetings only by her alias, Gretchen. And she could not imagine Arvid or Mildred volunteering *anything* about Klara and her relatively minor role in the group, even under severe Gestapo pressure.

Her mind now clearer and more settled as far as the short-term dangers went, Klara rose from the lounge chair and walked into the kitchen to refill her glass of tea. Her thoughts gradually shifted to the longer-term implications. Certainly, with the arrest of the Harnacks and other leading Circle members, her time as an active supporter of *that* branch of the German resistance effort was over. There was no one to report to for orders. So, what should she do with herself? What would be her new, driving purpose for living each day?

Maybe just take a well-deserved break for a few weeks and read an interesting book or two, she thought wearily. She walked back into the living room. Out of habit, she sat down on the stool beside the side table and switched on Herr Freitag's RCA-Victor radio receiver. She tuned the dial to the standard Nazi news channel, anxiously wondering if she would hear the worst—that a train to Switzerland had been stopped at the border and fourteen escaping Jews apprehended.

Fortunately, the 3 p.m. headlines seemed to offer nothing more than the never-ending blabber of optimistic projections for the Stalingrad offensive. Goebbels seemed to be in an unusually effusive mood today:

"Carpet bombing over the past two weeks by our vaunted Luftwaffe aircraft has reduced Stalin's prized city to a heap of smoldering ruins. Our Wehrmacht soldiers have now occupied the city's industrial center, and the badly diminished and demoralized Soviet troops are holed up in an ever-tightening enclave in the eastern part of the city near the Volga River. Final victory is imminent!"

Klara could only stomach a few more seconds of Goebbels's rant before yielding to her usual pattern of switching the dial to the German-language BBC station. For once, she would be able to simply listen with her own curious ears without needing to record notes for an upcoming Circle meeting.

She turned up the volume a bit to pick up the announcer's deep voice over the static. For some reason, the signal was stronger than usual.

"Soviet forces are still showing amazing resilience despite concerted Nazi air and ground attacks on their beleaguered forces in Stalingrad. Latest reports indicate that a new German offensive in the area has been thwarted by heavy casualties... Our Moscow correspondent tells us that Russian morale in the capital city is high despite the perilous situation around Stalingrad. Spirits in Moscow are aided by the many inspiring stories that continue to trickle in of the Soviet peoples' heroic efforts to resist the horrific siege of Leningrad for the past year . . ."

Klara sat mesmerized for several minutes as the announcer recounted one of the astounding tales from a civilian who'd managed to avoid starvation and escape the Nazi cordon around Leningrad by traversing several frozen lakes in the middle of winter. *And I thought my life was hard,* she thought, a twinge of guilt pricking at her stomach. *To think what those poor people are having to endure in—*

Her ears perked up at what sounded like a light knock on the front door. She turned the volume down and inclined her ear. Another knock—three light raps.

Nothing to panic over, she thought. It sounded like the mailwoman's knock. It had happened before when she'd needed to sign a receipt for delivery of some official letter to Herr Freitag.

She immediately switched off the receiver and walked toward the door.

"Yes? Who is it?"

"It's the post office lady, Fräulein Neumann. I have another letter for you to sign for Herr Freitag. He seems to be getting more than his share of these lately," she said lightly.

"Oh, certainly." Klara opened the door a crack, allowing the smiling mailwoman to hand a sealed envelope to her. "Thank you."

"Oh, Fräulein Neumann?"

"Yes?"

"There are some gentlemen here who would like to speak with you."

Before Klara could react, three men pushed the mailwoman aside, shoving their way through the door and into the apartment entryway. Klara recognized one of the men as the landlord from downstairs; the other two had the appearance and demeanor of plainclothes detectives.

She stood, surrounded by the landlord and one of the other men with her back against the wall, dazed and wondering what was happening. The landlord said nothing, simply glared at her as the third man strode to the side table with the radio set and switched it on, turning up the volume.

Klara's heart nearly stopped. *I forgot to switch the channel back!*

The German-speaking voice with a heavy English accent continued to enthusiastically narrate the tale of Soviet heroism, loud and clear.

The landlord's face broke into a sinister, triumphant smile. "Seems the German-language BBC is indeed one of your favorite stations, Fräulein." He turned to the man beside him. "Detective, she's all yours."

The man pulled a badge from his coat and flashed it front of Klara's eyes.

"Detective Wagner, Berlin Kripo." He returned the badge to his pocket and pulled out a set of handcuffs. "Fräulein Klara Neumann, you are hereby placed under arrest."

Terrified, Klara was unable to utter a word of either question or protest as the man pulled her hands behind her back and locked the cuffs around her wrists.

"Good work, Herr Detzel. The Kripo thanks you."

Detzel, the landlord, smiled grimly as he glared at Klara. "I wish I could take all the credit, Detective. But as I've already told you, and I'd now *love* for Fräulein Neumann to hear as well, the accolades should be reserved primarily for Herr Freitag's next-door neighbor."

He recounted how he'd been working to repair the wall of his son's bedroom several weeks ago and had detected some strange sounds coming through it. Listening more closely, he thought it sounded like someone speaking with an accent on a foreign radio station. He checked his watch and recalled that this was the time period when

Fräulein Neumann was supposed to be there alone, watching over the Freitags' little boy. He bored a small hole almost entirely through the wall to hear things more clearly and listened several more times over the next two weeks with the same result.

"Once I was made aware of the situation by my tenant," Detzel concluded triumphantly, "that's when I contacted your office."

Detective Wagner nodded approvingly. "You did exactly the right thing, Herr Detzel. I'm sure you will be receiving a reward from our office soon."

Detzel grunted. "The only reward I desire, Detective, is to know that a despicable traitor like this has been dealt with according to the laws of our National Socialist state." He shook his head in disbelief. "Honestly! A woman who would repeatedly betray her own employer's trust by committing a crime in the confines of his own house, while his child sleeps in the bedroom? Disgusting. Absolutely disgusting."

"We will certainly try to see that she receives what she's due," Wagner assured him. He motioned to his helper. "Let's go. It's getting late, and we've still got a thorough search of her house to perform with her help."

House search? Klara nearly fainted. She knew immediately the implications.

The Circle leaflets! If they find those, I'm as good as dead.

Klara's head throbbed and her legs wobbled as Detective Wagner and his assistant walked her up the pathway to her house. It was evident from the two other black police sedans parked by the sidewalk that a team of other security men had already arrived.

Led by her arms into the living room, she paled at the sight of several assistant detectives pulling books, pictures, and other items off their shelves to search the spaces behind them. But an even greater shock came when she spotted Elke standing by the couch, arms folded and staring at her with a disbelieving and furious expression on her face.

"What is the meaning of this, sister?" Elke demanded. "I get off work and walk in here, only to find these Kripo men tearing up our place.

When I ask the reason, they only tell me, 'You'll find out soon enough.' And now here you show up… *in handcuffs*? What have you done?"

Detective Wagner stepped forward, introduced himself, and flashed his badge. "Frau Schröder, my apologies. I regret the intrusion, but certain charges have been filed against your sister and this is the standard procedure we are required to follow."

"But what are the charges against her?" Elke persisted. "Klara, what on earth are they—"

"I am not at liberty to discuss the charges with you now, Frau. And I must insist that you refrain from communicating any further with your sister while we are here—unless you wish to be escorted off the premises." He turned to the Kripo man who'd been leading the search, and nodded. "Herr Cullmann, take Fräulein Neumann upstairs. I want her to observe your probe of her bedroom."

"Yes, sir." Cullmann, a short, weaselly looking character with a long nose and squinty, black eyes, grabbed Klara by the arm and walked her up the staircase with two other men on their heels.

Klara glanced over the banister at Elke, who gazed at her with mouth agape and head shaking in complete bewilderment. She was too numb with fear and disorientation to cry. She only knew her heart was about to melt with terror, knowing that with each step she took, she was that much closer to having the condemning evidence of her high treason exposed.

The little weasel, Cullman, seemed to detect her distress and leaned over to whisper in her ear. "Worried about something, Fräulein?"

Klara stared straight ahead, trying desperately not to reveal any obvious signs of guilt or fear. Mildred Harnack had once told her *that* was the only way for an innocent person to avoid pressure from Nazi police to make a false confession. Klara certainly knew she was not innocent as far as the leaflets were concerned. *But the police don't know that yet… and there's still a chance,* she thought. *I know I hid that lockbox extremely well. Please, God, don't let them find it.*

"Don't worry," the weasel continued. "Once we find whatever your hiding, you'll be able to confirm that it's really yours and that we didn't simply plant the evidence."

Klara was escorted to a corner, held in place by the arm by another assistant as Cullman directed the others to ransack her room. The men spared not a square inch, yanking drawers out and dumping her private clothes and papers on the floor, tapping on walls and lifting the rug, searching the mattress thoroughly for telltale slits.

Two of the men entered the closet. Klara closed her eyes, fearing the discovery of the evidence she knew the Nazi courts would view as her death-deserving treachery. *Please, Jesus, please.*

The men rummaged around for several minutes as Klara breathed only in short spurts, sweat beading on her forehead. Finally, the two emerged.

"Didn't find anything useful, Herr Cullman," one said, the disappointment in his voice apparent.

Klara nearly fainted with relief. Her prayer had been answered!

"*What?*" Cullman near screamed. "We didn't come all the way here to leave empty-handed. There *must* be something in there. Go back and check again."

"But Herr Cullman, we—"

"*I said go back and check again, dammit!*"

The men resumed their search. Less than a minute later came the cry that Klara had been dreading: "*Found something!*"

The men came out, one carrying the small, decorative lockbox containing the ten Circle leaflets that Klara had intended to destroy only yesterday.

"My, my. What do we have here?" the weasel chortled, rubbing his hands together. "Just an innocent, pretty little box, eh, Fräulein?" He pulled a stool in front of him. "Just set it down on this and let's see what's inside. Where is the key, Fräulein?"

Klara hesitated.

"*I said, where is the key, Fräulein Neumann?*" Cullman nearly screamed.

"It's inside that wooden top that was knocked over on the floor over there." *The top that Vati used for my first lesson on rocket gyroscopes when I was seven.* "It unscrews into two halves."

One of the assistants went over and picked up the toy. Unscrewing it, he found the key and handed it to Cullman, who motioned to the man holding Klara.

"Bring Fräulein Neumann over here and have her face me while I open this," the weasel said. "I'm dying to see her expression."

Klara stood rigidly behind the box, her arms clamped by two assistants. Cullman inserted the key and turned it. The lock clicked. He placed his hands on the ends of the lid to open it. Before doing so, he glanced at Klara, a sinister grin on his face. He lifted the lid and began to examine the contents.

The raised lid prevented Klara from seeing what he was discovering, but she already knew what he would find any second now. She braced herself, waiting for him to hold the leaflet up triumphantly and read the second line out loud for all to hear:

> "But no one can deny any longer that the catastrophe
> of National Socialist policy threatens us all."

She waited. Cullman kept rummaging, a frown forming on his face. *What is taking him so long. Get it over with!*

The weasel looked up and stared at her for what seemed an eternity. She gazed at him steadily, unflinching, though her body felt as though it would collapse at any moment.

Finally, he slammed the lid down. "Nothing here. Take her downstairs."

Klara descended the steps with her escorts, feeling that she was walking on air.

There could be only one explanation, she knew. An angel of God must have intervened. She barely heard anything that was being discussed between the men, other than that her next destination was the Alexanderplatz police station—no doubt to be booked for the serious crime of listening to foreign radio. *At least it won't be for high treason.*

As the men walked her out the door, Klara looked over her shoulder at her sister. A slight smile tugged at the corners of Elke's lips.

Immediately, Klara knew who her angel had been.

CHAPTER 33

Berlin, Germany
October 3, 1942
(Three days later)

L t. Colonel Bremmer glanced at his watch and grimaced. In ten minutes, he needed to walk from his office to the basement isolation cell for his first official interrogation of Klara Neumann. He was not looking forward to it.

This time, the gloves will be coming off, he thought resolutely.

This time, the girl would have to face the consequences for her rebellious behavior against the National Socialist state and its laws. Most importantly, this time, Klara Neumann would not be given a free pass to lie about her lack of recent contact with the Friedmann family or her knowledge of their whereabouts. Gerhard Bremmer's SS career was on the line, and Klara Neumann's misplaced, Jew-protecting impulses were no longer going to stand in the way of getting that final piece of information.

As he sat at his desk and stared blankly at the cover of Klara's arrest report, Gerhard's face burned over the memory of Senior Colonel Nebe's stern reprimand of three weeks ago.

"Bremmer! You have disappointed Reichsführer Himmler, and in doing so have delayed your promotion yet again. Do you wish for it to

finally come through? Then stop whining about the difficulties you've been experiencing. Finish your job here, and capture Jakob Friedmann! How long must we all wait? Don't you realize we're in the middle of busting that Red Orchestra cabal? And that Friedmann Jew could hold vital information on Arvid Harnack's radio transmission operations and on other Orchestra members still at large! The state prosecutors are going to need that Jew to testify once the trials for the Harnacks and the other leaders begin soon. So, if you want that promotion, Lt. Colonel Bremmer, no more excuses. *Get Jakob Friedmann!*"

When he'd left that demoralizing session with Nebe, Gerhard knew he had only one more card to play in the search for the elusive Jakob Friedmann.

He thought he'd come close to victory just two weeks ago with the capture of Jakob's friend, Aaron Bierwagen. Bierwagen had worn his expected disguise, and he was apprehended while resting from a morning run at the Beethoven monument in Tiergarten Park—the exact location where Erich Neumann had suggested he might be found.

Unfortunately, on the way to his third interrogation session, Bierwagen had hurled himself from an open corridor window. If he hadn't committed suicide, Gerhard was certain he would have cracked and revealed Jakob's location. Still, Bierwagen *had* confessed to a couple of interesting things during his *second* torture session. First, that he indeed knew Jakob Friedmann, and had talked with him several times in connection with their mutual support of Herbert Baum. Second, that Jakob once mentioned that his parents and sister were in hiding somewhere, and that he and a longtime Aryan family friend named Klara would occasionally visit them all there.

With that revelation, the report of Klara's foreign radio listening could not have come at a more fortuitous time. It had been filed with the Kripo by Herr Freitag's landlord only a few days after Bierwagen's suicide. Immediately, Gerhard set to work arranging the sting operation that would catch Klara in the act of committing a consequential crime—one that would give him the excuse he needed to arrest and interrogate her thoroughly on any and all related matters.

Everything had worked as planned. Gerhard finally had Klara exactly where he wanted her: in a desperate situation where he could show her that refusal to cooperate fully would definitely lead to dire consequences, not only for herself but for her own family.

Still, this last card is not going to be an easy one to play. Gerhard reached in his drawer, pulled out his brandy bottle, uncapped it, and took a long swig.

Strange, he thought, how his perspective on Klara had shifted so rapidly over just the past two weeks. Up until then he'd always taken pains to go soft on her out of his desire to maintain his friendly, even affectionate, relationships with her sister and father. The change had started with Senior Colonel Nebe's reprimand and warning. Gerhard realized immediately that his future SS career hinged entirely on doing whatever it took to get Klara to talk, including the application of physical and psychological pressures. If that meant sacrificing her father's friendship and his potential support for Gerhard's dream position of overseeing von Braun and the Peenemünde rocket team, so be it. At this point, he knew he stood no chance of being promoted to that or any other job unless Himmler was satisfied that he'd finished the policing job in Berlin.

Gerhard took another pull of brandy and returned the bottle to its drawer. Just before exiting his office for the interrogation session, a thought occurred to him. *She needs to understand that the rules have changed.*

He returned to his desk and picked up the envelope containing the photographs he'd specially requested from the Gestapo. *These should help.* Tucking the envelope along with the arrest report under his arm, Lt. Colonel Gerhard Bremmer whirled and strode resolutely toward the door.

As soon as he sat down and took in Klara's face and posture across the narrow interrogation table, Bremmer could tell that the past two days and nights in her cell had produced the intended effect. Her eyes bleary and her cheeks pale from lack of sleep and a few measly morsels of bread for food, she slumped in her chair, barely able to keep her head from sagging. The single light bulb dangling only a foot or so above her head cast a garish, white cone of light that further exaggerated the dark shadows under her eyes.

Bremmer turned to look over his shoulder at his assistant who stood at the cell entrance, awaiting instructions. "Leave us," he said gruffly. The man saluted and walked out, slamming the iron door shut behind him.

After a few moments of silence and staring at her coldly, Bremmer broke the ice.

"Hello, Klara," he said softly.

Klara's eyes gradually focused. She flashed a tiny, tired smile of recognition. "Hello, Colonel."

She's probably thinking this interview with me will be as cordial as our previous ones. He needed to disillusion her. Fast.

"For your family's sake and for yours, I deeply regret that it had to come to this, Klara, but you've left me no choice. I have a tape machine that will record every question I pose, and every answer that you give. And you need to know that from now on, should you refuse to answer my questions fully and truthfully, things will get worse for you. Much, much worse. Do you understand what I'm saying, Klara?

Klara nodded wearily.

After turning on the recorder, Bremmer opened the arrest report file and perused the first page. "Do you admit that you were in the Freitags' living room on the afternoon of September 30, listening for at least ten minutes to the German-language BBC news broadcast on Herr Freitag's radio?"

"Yes, I admit to that."

"And do you admit to listening to that same BBC news station for extended periods in the afternoons over the past seven weeks?

Klara hesitated briefly. "I don't deny it."

"Were you aware during the times you were listening that your actions constituted a very serious crime against the National Socialist state?"

"Yes, I was aware."

Bremmer reached under the table and switched off the tape machine. He already had everything he wanted for the official record. No surprises so far, just as he'd intended. The rest of this first session would be devoted to the things he *really* wanted to hear from the girl— things that required some off-the-record exchanges.

"And what was your reason for doing so, Klara?"

Her shoulders lifted in the barest shrug, her eyes seemingly fixed on the center of the table. "I-I suppose it was just out of my own stupid curiosity."

"Curiosity? How so?"

"At the hospital, I heard things from some of our wounded soldiers. They told a different story about the war from what I'd heard on the Nazi news channel. Herr Freitag once bragged to me that his radio could pick up the BBC, so out of curiosity, I decided to tune it in one day to see if their version of the war lined up with the version I was hearing from the soldiers."

"And did it?"

"Much more so than the Party channel's. I found it all very interesting, so to keep myself from boredom during the afternoon while Herr Freitag's little boy slept, I started to get in the habit of listening to both channels. Really just to entertain myself and satisfy my curiosity by comparing them."

"I see. And who would you talk to about the different version of war news offered by the BBC station?"

Klara's quizzical expression projected innocence. "Talk to? I talked to no one, sir."

A bald-faced lie. She's hiding something. Time to start pressing.

"Is that so? Tell me, Klara, who do you know in the Neukölln district?"

Again, that blank look. "Sir, I'm not sure I know anyone in—"

"Yes, you do, Klara. One of my agents spotted you leaving the U-Bahn station there a while back and returning several hours later.

She paled for a split second but recovered quickly. "Oh, of course, Colonel. Now I remember… I was invited by one of my fellow nurses to attend a meeting of a literary club she was just starting up."

"Literary club? And what kinds of things were you discussing there?"

"Basically, just people's views on a book they were all supposed to read… *Don Quixote*, as I recall. I personally found the discussions boring and never went back."

Another lie, even though it sounds plausible and innocent enough, Bremmer thought. He'd heard that even the Führer was a devoted fan of the author Cervantes.

"And what were you doing in Stettin last month, Klara—at the apartment of Ruth von Kleist-Retzow, a friend of that banned Confessing Church pastor, Dietrich Bonhoeffer? Where do you know her from?"

Bremmer noticed Klara's face tense, but once again she offered a seemingly plausible answer: "I met Ruth several years ago when my boyfriend from the American Embassy—Joshua Peters, whom I sure you remember—invited me to attend a retreat that Dietrich was hosting in the countryside. At the time, I wasn't aware of any government decree against attending his religious events outside Berlin, and so I accepted Joshua's invitation. At Dietrich's suggestion, we made an overnight rest-stop at his friend Ruth's, where the three of us got to know each other and became friends before Joshua and I drove to the retreat the next day."

"I see. And your *second* trip to Stettin last month?" Bremmer pressed.

"A few weeks earlier Ruth had called me to say hello and catch up. She knew how much I'd enjoyed the Stettin countryside, and so she invited me out to visit her and her granddaughter for a day of hiking and horseback riding. I took up her offer."

"Yes, yes. That does makes sense," Bremmer smiled and nodded. "But tell me, Klara… during either of your visits with Ruth, were any of Dietrich Bonhoeffer's relatives there as well?"

"His *relatives*, sir?"

"Yes. I'm thinking, for example, of Dietrich's cousin, Arvid Harnack and his wife, Mildred... ever happen to encounter them at Ruth's, or perhaps hear their names?"

Klara frowned and shook her head. "Those names don't sound familiar to me, Colonel."

No doubt lying about that as well, Bremmer thought. *She's had time these last couple of days to think through her excuses.* He knew he could seriously press her further on this Bonhoeffer-Harnack connection, but he would circle back to that later. It was now time to strike to the heart of the matter.

He folded his arms on the desk and leaned forward, his face only inches from hers. "Why did you lie to me, Klara?"

She jerked her head back slightly, her startled expression confirming the shock effect he'd hoped to achieve. "Colonel, I am not lying. I have told you the truth, I—"

"I am not talking about what you've told me so far, which I'll suspend judgment on for now. What I'm referring to is that night of the riots in November '38, when you lied to me about your lack of familiarity with that old Jew you attempted to rescue."

"But sir, as I told you then, he was someone random who we—"

Bremmer smacked his hand down on the desk. "*Stop right there!* Do you take me and my Kripo organization for *complete* buffoons, Klara? Did you think we would never check out the name of the man you tried to help, and never discover that it was *Hermann Friedmann, the father of Jakob*? Given your long-time relationship with Jakob and his sister, there is no way you could not have known who the man was. And yet you insisted over and over—as you are still doing in my very presence—that you had no connection with him!

"But that wasn't all . . ." Bremmer continued. Based on Klara's flustered expression, he knew he was finally hitting the right notes.

"Sir?"

"You lied to me on another occasion, assuring me after that asylum incident with Leah Friedmann that you had faithfully heeded my warning to avoid any contact with the Friedmann family or any other

Jews. So why was it that my agent spotted you several months later in Tiergarten Park, conversing with Jakob's sister, Sophie?

Klara tried to avert her eyes. *Got her. Keep going.*

"Why did you lie to me about them, Klara?" he asked softly.

"B-Because Sophie and her family have always been very dear to me, and I didn't want to get them in trouble."

"Yes, yes, I understand, Klara," Bremmer said soothingly. "You have been a good, loyal friend to them for many years. Always trying to protect them from the troubles of the times. I've long known your Christian heart on the matter, and that's why I decided not to confront you previously on your lies about the Friedmanns.

"But now, Klara, things have changed. You see, we now strongly suspect that the Friedmanns—Jakob in particular—are not the poor, innocent victims you've always imagined them to be. In fact, Jakob has been identified as the perpetrator of some major national crimes, and he needs to be apprehended and brought to justice without further delay. And that is why I need some specific information from you."

Klara stared at him. He could tell from her trembling lips that the panic was starting to set in. "W-what is that, sir?"

His eyes bored into hers. "I need you to tell me—*right now*—where Jakob Friedmann and his family are hiding."

She blinked her eyes, hesitating. "B-but Colonel, I haven't seen any of them in over two years. I—"

That's it! Bremmer leaped up from his chair and slapped Klara across the face, knocking her partially out her chair. "*I said—where is the hiding place of Jakob Friedmann and his family? Answer me, Klara!*"

Her hands cuffed behind her back, Klara struggled to right herself in the chair. Her tears flowed freely. "Sir, I want to help you, but—"

Bremmer sat down. He placed his hand on the back of her head and pulled it toward his face. "There you go, lying once again. I know you're lying, Klara, because one of Jakob's friends just confirmed to us that Jakob and his family have met you several times at this hideout in recent weeks. Now, you just need to tell us where that hideout is."

Klara looked down at her lap.

Bremmer sighed. "Still won't divulge, eh?" He picked up the envelope he'd brought from his office and pulled out the two photographs he'd specially ordered from the Gestapo. He stood and walked around the table and stopped beside Klara, holding one of the photographs directly in front of her face. "Take a look at this."

She kept her chin bowed and her eyes closed, shaking her head slowly.

He grabbed her hair and yanked her head up. "*Look at this, dammit!*"

She opened her eyes and gasped at the sight of Mildred Harnack lying on a stretcher. Her face was beaten and swollen, her lips mangled and her eyes sunken in their sockets, glassy with agony.

"Do you know what you're seeing here, Klara? This is the tragic result befalling a stubborn Aryan woman accused of serious crimes. A woman who persisted in her lies and refusal to cooperate with us by truthfully answering the questions posed to her. You must not think that our enhanced interrogation methods are reserved for male suspects or Jews only. Would you like to see another example in the second photograph?"

She shook her head, her breathing coming in short gasps. Bremmer debated showing her the other photo of Mildred's husband, Arvid, tied between two bedframes, being tortured with thumbscrews and whips, but decided she'd already gotten the point and threw the first photo back on the table.

He knelt beside her and spoke softly. "God knows I don't want that to happen to you, Klara. But you *must* help me, and here's how. If you will tell me where Jakob and his family are hiding, and we are able to confirm that you are telling the truth, I will personally see to it that all charges against you for the offense of listening to foreign radio will be completely dropped. You will be free to resume your life as you see fit. But if you don't cooperate here and now, the charges will stand, and you will face further, far harsher interrogation by the Gestapo. Not only on the whereabouts of the Friedmanns, but also on all the other matters we discussed earlier concerning your supposedly innocent interactions with Dietrich Bonhoeffer and his friend Ruth. I guarantee, your future interrogation sessions will not be as mild as this one. Do you understand?"

Klara nodded.

"Good. Now, where is Jakob Friedmann?"

He waited. And waited. Klara gazed at her lap.

Finally, she spoke. Her voice was amazingly calm. "I truly don't know where Jakob and his family are hiding, sir. I haven't seen them in years."

Verdammt! Bremmer glared at the ground and shook his head angrily. "Stupid, stupid girl. You will regret this."

He stood slowly. After gathering his files from the table, he walked toward the cell door, despondent over his bleak prospects. Unfortunately, Klara Neumann had ruined his plan, and quite possibly his career along with it. Now it appeared that both of them would have to pay a heavy price.

He knocked on the door and called for his assistant.

The man looked at him expectantly, his face twisted with that familiar, sadistic grin. "Next level for the girl, sir?"

Bremmer stared at him for several seconds, debating with himself. Suddenly, an idea occurred:

The rocket man will help for the sake of his daughter.

He nodded to his assistant. "Tomorrow, 7 p.m."

CHAPTER 34

Berlin, Germany
October 4, 1942
(The next morning, 6 a.m.)

Klara sat on the cold, concrete floor of her isolation cell and leaned back against the wall, pulling the thin woolen blanket she'd been allotted closer under her chin. She listened to the silence, strangely unconcerned as to what the new day might bring.

After the terrifying experience in Bremmer's interrogation room yesterday, last night had been a relatively peaceful affair. Even though her anxious thoughts and self-recriminations had permitted only short periods of nightmare-plagued sleep, at least she'd been able to meditate and pray with an intensity she'd never experienced before.

Additional comfort came from the memory of her bold decision to refuse Bremmer's tempting offer. It would have spared her from further torture, and granted her freedom, but it would also require her betrayal of the Friedmann family. She knew that decision had not come out of her own strength or willpower. Something inside her had taken over, preventing her from eagerly accepting Bremmer's easy way out, assuring her with a clear sense that her refusal would be God's desire. That he would carry her through whatever might come.

She wondered, was the strange calm she was experiencing now the special peace that Dietrich Bonhoeffer had once described to her at the pastors' retreat—the peace beyond understanding that God promised to those he'd called to walk through the "Valley of the Shadow of Death"?

Klara was on the verge of dozing off when the cell door opened.

A highly agitated woman with dark, disheveled hair and wearing a revealing party dress was shoved into the already cramped space. The door slammed behind her.

She introduced herself as Monika Krause. She turned out to be an inebriated chatterbox who would not stop screeching about her unfair arrest on charges of leading an organized prostitution ring with the goal of political subversion.

After two hours of listening to Monika's nonsensical squawking, Klara came to the conclusion that the woman was either seriously demented, or an intentional plant by Colonel Bremmer to further weaken Klara's already fragile constitution. Mercifully, the woman finally ran out of breath and silently sat on the floor, staring morosely at the ceiling.

Thank you, God.

The silence did not last. Monika lowered her head and looked at Klara with a devilish grin. "You ready to face that beast, Habecker?"

"Habecker? Who's he?" Klara asked cautiously.

Monika threw her head back and let out a long, hideous laugh. "Walter Habecker is the Gestapo's chief torturer. I heard about him from one of my SS boyfriends. He's short, fat, has a gray, bald head with sinister, sharpshooter eyes, and a toothbrush mustache even tinier than Hitler's. Shows no mercy with the screws and clamps, laughs at the screams. I hear there was one woman who he—"

"*Fräulein Krause!*" Klara glared at her angrily. "Please don't burden me with stories about this man. It's hard enough as it is without having to envision the worst possible scenarios."

The chatterbox fell silent. Her eyes flashed indignation as she drew her knees up to her chest and wrapped her arms around them, obviously sulking over Klara's lack of appreciation. It wasn't more than a half a minute, though, before she was at it again.

"They'll probably break me for treason just like my friend Cora," she muttered, half to herself. "If so, it's curtains." She drew a finger slowly across her neck. "Plötzensee Prison guillotine." She looked toward Klara again, the same evil glint in her eye. "Did you know, Fräulein, what the prison attendants say about death by guillotine?"

Before Klara could stop her, the chatterbox pressed on, her voice rising. "May not be as quick and painless as you'd think. A prison guard I know witnessed one. He said the eyes of the severed head fluttered and twitched in the basket for nearly *five minutes* after the blade struck. And the headless body was still gushing blood, even after—"

"*Will you just shut up?*" Klara screamed. "*I don't want to hear this. I...*". She broke down in sobs and huddled herself in a corner, arms covering her head.

Neither woman spoke for a long period, their breathing the only sounds in the stuffy cell.

Klara's mind drifted into a fog of memories, both pleasant and painful. Occasionally, the photograph Bremmer showed her of Mildred Harnack would flash before her eyes and she would feel like retching. Poor beautiful, intelligent Mildred—the American literature teacher and PhD student who was willing to come join her German husband, devoting their lives to resisting Hitler and the evils of Nazism. She had always spoken to Klara with a special affection, inspiring and exhorting her to never lose hope for the ultimate victory of their difficult cause. How devastating it had been to see this kind, vivacious woman stretched out and displayed like a bloated, bloodied corpse—a *barely living* corpse that would most likely face its own execution by guillotine at some point soon.

Her reverie was jolted by a banging on the door and the sound of keys rattling in the slot. The door opened.

"Fräulein Neumann, you have two minutes to get yourself ready."

Klara squeezed her eyes shut. Her thoughts and prayers ran wild.

Please God, help me. Don't let me fail you or the Friedmanns. Oh God, if I break, will you ever forgive me? No! No! I can't think like that, God. Please forgive me for thinking that way. But what if they… No! Oh, God, please, save me from this…

"It's time, Fräulein. Up we go." An SS guard's hand lifted her by the arm. She stared into his face. He was younger than the other guards who'd been handling her previously, and somehow seemed gentler. He led her out into the corridor and shut the door behind them.

A few steps down the passageway he leaned over and whispered in her ear. "You have a visitor, Fräulein."

Klara looked at him with a startled expression. "*Visitor?*"

At the first sight of her father's face gazing at her through the metal grating covering the visitor booth's window, Klara lost all sense of caution. She thrust her fingers through the lattice to grasp his hands.

"Oh, Vati… Vati . . ." Klara murmured.

"It's all right, Liebchen," Erich crooned, his voice choking. "I'm here now."

"You have ten minutes," the guard barked before closing the door of the booth.

Erich motioned for Klara to draw her face as close as possible to the grating to avoid having their voices picked up by hidden microphones. She was shocked at how thin and pale he'd become, the worry lines marring his face. He seemed to have aged twenty years since the last time she'd seen him.

"Klara, there's very little time, so you need to listen to me carefully."

She nodded, incredibly relieved just to hear his voice and desperate for whatever comforting words and advice he could offer her.

"I know about the BBC-listening charges against you, and that you confessed to them, but I'm not going to waste time asking you why or chastising you about that. There's only one thing that matters to me now. And that is to do whatever it takes to help you come to your senses."

Klara felt a strange tension in her throat. Did he think she'd lost her mind? Was he on her side, or . . .?

"W-What do you mean, Vati?"

He peered at her intensely. "Elke called and told me what happened. Your mother and I rushed home from Peenemünde, and I spoke with Colonel Bremmer late last night. All I can say is we're extremely fortunate to have him as a family friend. He told me about the offer he'd made to spare you from enhanced interrogation and a long prison sentence, and that you'd turned him down. Klara, is this true?"

She lowered her eyes. "Yes, Vati."

"Klara, look at me."

She raised her eyes and saw the pain and fear in his. Already, she could sense her resolve crumbling under the weight of her father's loving concern.

"I know what the Friedmanns have meant to you, Klara. Although he didn't have to, Colonel Bremmer told me everything, including your lying to him about your attempt to rescue Herr Friedmann and your meeting with Sophie. He's convinced that you know where they're hiding, but that you're unwilling to divulge it.

"Klara, for God's sake, I beg you, do not place your tender heart for the Friedmanns above love for your own family. Especially your mother, who's . . ." It was Erich who looked away this time, his lips trembling.

Alarm shot through Klara's body. Something had obviously happened. "Vati, what is it? What's wrong with Mama?"

"We just received the message three days ago. Walther has been reported as missing in action around Stalingrad. His unit was decimated with very few survivors, and most of those were taken prisoner. Your mother was already sick with worry over your brother when Elke called us about you. Last night, Mama had a fainting spell and she's still resting in bed, praying that I'll have some good news to bring her about you."

Klara's covered her face with her hands, shaking her head back and forth as she thought of the emotional agony that Mama must be experiencing.

Erich gripped the window grating with both hands. "Klara, it's in your power to make that happen. I know it is excruciatingly hard for you, but please tell me where the Friedmanns are hiding. You've been friends with Sophie for so long, and I am convinced that you know their location. *Please, Klara!* If not for yourself, then for the sake of the mother and father who love you and can't bear the thought of what will happen if you don't."

Klara stared at him, her lips trembling. *Just tell him and be done with it. Vati is begging me to take the easier way, not for myself but out of my love for him and Mama. There's no shame in that. Take it, before it's too late.*

She grasped her father's hands once again through the grating, on the verge of yielding up the information he sought.

"Vati, I . . ." she began, but her voice trailed off. It was the same speech-arresting spirit that had prevented her from revealing the final puzzle piece to Colonel Bremmer yesterday. A spirit that caused her to envision Jakob Friedmann and his parents as they were dragged out of their hiding place and hauled away to certain death—all while their betrayer, Klara Neumann, stood next to Bremmer, watching each of them pass by with her arm outstretched in the Nazi salute.

"Yes, Klara… go on," Erich urged.

This time, her voice did not give out. "Vati, I haven't seen any of them in years, and I truly don't know where they might be hiding."

Erich sat speechless.

The door of the booth opened. "I'm afraid your time is up," the guard said. "Let's go." He pulled her hands away from her father's and forced her to rise from her stool.

As he led her out the door, she glanced over her shoulder. Her father was crying, his hands locked to the grating. "*Klara!*"

Seeing the depth of his concern for her tore at her heart, nearly causing her to break. If the Gestapo succeeded in forcing her not only to betray the Friedmanns, but to confess to *all* her crimes in support of the Circle and Sophie's escape, she knew this could well be the last time she'd see Vati and her family again before her execution.

Still, the spirit would not allow her to retract her decision. Come what may, she would *not* cut a deal to betray *anyone* she had sworn to protect.

"*Vati*," she cried back, *"I love you and Mama and Elke. Please pray for me!"*

Upon returning to her cell, Klara discovered that she had been granted one small grace: once again, she was blessedly alone. The chatterbox, Monika, had been taken elsewhere. Silence prevailed. Several pieces of bread and a bowl of watery soup with a bit of cabbage had been shoved through the food slot on a small tray. Despite her hunger, she was still too wound up to eat anything, and left the food where it was on the floor.

They could come at any time now, she realized before leaning against the wall, completely exhausted and too drained to worry or think. Within moments, she had drifted off.

CHAPTER 35

Berlin, Germany
October 4, 1942
(7:00 p.m.)

"*Fräulein Neuman. It is time for your next appointment.*"

Klara awoke with a start as the same male SS guard entered and helped her stand. As he led her out into the corridor, the words formed with clarity in her mind and heart.

God, I trust you. Prepare me for whatever lies ahead. If I endure, it will be you who sustains me. If I break, it will be you who forgives me. My life is in your hands, Lord. Help me, Jesus.

Once in the corridor, a stern-faced female guard stood waiting.

"I'll take her from here, sir," she said to the SS man.

He nodded and handed Klara over. She braced herself, knowing her supreme trial was about to begin.

The guard grabbed her upper arm. "Come with me, Fräulein Neumann."

After they'd taken several steps down the corridor, the guard glanced at her with a slight smile. "One more stop, and you'll be on your way home.'"

By the time the Kripo police sedan dropped Klara off at her house in Charlottenburg around nine-thirty, her head was still spinning from her incredible, lightning-fast transition from abject terror to complete and utter relief.

"You will sign this document, Fräulein Neumann," Colonel Bremmer's assistant administrative officer had directed her only an hour ago. "Once you do, all your troubles will be over."

Klara had read the paper, in which it was stated that she had confessed to her crime of foreign radio listening. It had also stated that the examining officer had determined that her intentions, while knowingly wrong and contrary to National Socialist law, had centered exclusively on self-entertainment. There was no evidence of treasonous intent or action to discuss or to spread what she had heard. The final paragraph had concluded that no prison sentence, but rather a one-year probation period, had been recommended by Lt. Colonel Gerhard Bremmer and approved by an authorized representative of the People's Court. Klara was free to resume her daily activities with the understanding that any violation of her probationary terms would constitute a major crime against the state and would result in the harshest possible consequences.

To her amazement, there had been nothing in the document requiring her to accept any type of plea deal involving the Friedmanns. All things considered, she was being let off scot-free with seemingly no strings attached. She had signed immediately.

But what could possibly have led Colonel Bremmer to avoid following through on his threat? She asked herself once again as she walked toward the front door. *After all, I did clearly reject his plea deal, and I confirmed my refusal later with Vati, as hard as that was. The colonel could have chosen to hammer me.*

Whatever the reason for Bremmer's decision, Klara knew that God was behind it. He had seen her through many valleys over the past years, and he was now, finally, raising her to the heights. Sophie had been set free, and the rest of her family was out of immediate danger.

There is someone else I need to thank, she thought as she put her hand on the doorknob. *My angel. I don't know how she possibly did it, but without her help, there is no doubt—a heavy guillotine blade would soon be dropping on my delicate neck.*

When she opened the door, the sight of Elke standing alone in the hallway with arms crossed caused her to draw up short. The sisters stared at each other for a long moment before they broke and rushed to embrace each other.

"Elke," Klara said softly in her ear as she continued to hug her. "How did you do it?" She broke away and stepped back slightly, looking at her suspiciously. "You *were* the one who removed those items from my lockbox before the Kripo arrived, weren't you?"

Elke smiled faintly. "Yes, it was me. That was a bit stupid of you, wasn't it, sister? I mean… trying to stash away ten of the most hateful, damning tracts against the Führer and the Third Reich that I can possibly imagine. Where on earth did you come across those? Never mind. Don't even try to answer, since I know I won't want to hear it."

"But you were at work all day—you left before me, and you arrived home after the Kripo were already here searching the place. So how did you . . .?"

"It pays to have my favorite BDM student working at Kripo Headquarters," Elke said.

"*What?* You mean… *Trudi Schuster?* But she's just a low-level clerk. How could *she* have possibly done anything to help?"

"Trudi often overhears some of those conceited, big-mouthed Kripo detectives gabbing about some of their upcoming arrests. The morning of *your* arrest, she heard Detective Wagner talking to his assistant about their plan to carry it out, and the location as well. She knew I'd be concerned, so she called me at my training class and warned me about what was going to happen. I went home immediately to make sure you didn't have anything that the Kripo might discover in your room."

"But what made you think I'd have any incriminating things? And what would lead you to check inside my lockbox?"

Elke cocked her head. "Klara, have you forgotten what I've always told you? You are not good at hiding your secrets from me. Did you think I was *totally* oblivious to your negative feelings about the Führer and National Socialism? So, when I got word that you were to be arrested for listening to foreign radio, why *wouldn't* I consider that you might have reading materials or other things that supported your anti-Nazi thinking? And why *wouldn't* I think to look where I *knew* you would keep your most private writings, just like me? In your lockbox, of course! My only problem was finding out where you'd hid it."

"So... how *did* you find it, and then open it without my key?"

Elke grimaced. "I must have spent a half hour thrashing through your closet before I made a lucky guess and looked behind those old medical books. Vati gave me his master key when I lost mine several years ago, and I used it to open the box once I finally located it. And once I saw those leaflets and read one, I knew that if I wanted my sister to have any chance of avoiding a treason charge, I had to burn them before the Kripo arrived."

Klara's eyes filled with tears. "Elke, you've always looked out for me despite our differences. I am so thankful you were never like those other BDM girls who turned in their family members for the slightest remark against Hitler."

Elke's face was softened by a tender smile for several moments before her familiar, stern expression returned.

"That is true, Klara. But you need to know that things can no longer be the same between us."

"W-what do you mean?"

"I mean that we can't live in the same house anymore. From now on, we shouldn't even be seen with each other in public places. You've made yourself too dangerous, Klara. And though I will always care about you, I personally abhor the choice you've made to despise the Führer and work against everything he's trying to do to protect our country."

Klara's jaw dropped. "*Elke!* After seeing the effect of Hitler's SS and men like Colonel Bremmer on your own husband's sanity, how can you possibly still believe—"

Before she could fully voice her objection, an upstairs door closed. Klara looked up just as her father appeared at the top of the staircase.

"*Vati!*"

Erich ran down to greet and embrace his daughter at the foot of the stairs.

"Vati… is Mama . . .?"

He nodded. "She's all right. She's still in bed recovering from the stress. When I told her you were being released and were coming home, she perked up considerably. She's anxious to see you."

"Oh, Vati… can't we go up together right now, I—"

Erich placed his hands gently on her upper arms. "We will, Liebchen, in just a few minutes. But . . ." He lowered his head as if troubled. "She agreed I should talk with you first."

Klara sensed something was wrong—very wrong. *What is going on?*

"What is it, Vati?

He led her by the arm and motioned for her to sit next to him on the couch. Elke remained standing with arms folded.

"Klara, I might as well say this straight out. All of us are ecstatic that you are home safely. But your release and freedom were obtained at a price."

Klara stared at him blankly. A chill of foreboding coursed through her body.

"What kind of price?" she asked hesitantly.

He sighed heavily. "I had to reveal the Friedmanns' hiding location to Colonel Bremmer."

Stunned to the core, Klara glanced wildly between her father and sister. Surely, she must not have heard him right. "But… Vati… how could you possibly reveal it if you don't even know where it is. *I* don't even know!"

He grasped her firmly by her forearms and looked her directly in the eyes. "Klara, you've known where it was all along."

"*What?* What would make you say that, Vati?"

"After you refused to tell me anything during my visit yesterday, I went to Bremmer and pleaded for one more opportunity to get him the information he wanted on the Friedmanns. I knew it was a long shot, but I told him I wanted to search your room one more time to see if any clues might have been missed by the Kripo. He agreed, giving me three hours to conduct the search and get back to him by phone.

"I nearly turned your room upside down before I finally found something in one of your old school notebooks that the Kripo had cast aside. It had a page near the back with several addresses listed, but no names attached to them. One of them, though, seemed more freshly written and was flagged on the side with a small letter "S" enclosed in a circle. I truly had no idea if this was connected with Sophie and her parents, but I was desperate, so I called Bremmer who said he'd have it checked out. Two hours later he called back and said we'd indeed located the Friedmanns' hideout. Jakob was there visiting when the Kripo arrived. He and his parents were taken into custody along with the woman who was sheltering them. And based on that outcome, Bremmer told me he was willing to have you released and home by tonight."

Klara buried her face in her hands, her chest heaving with the sobs.

Erich placed his hand on her shoulder. "Klara, this was entirely my own decision. I know you were ready and willing to submit yourself to torture or worse in order to keep protecting Jakob and his family. But, Liebchen, I knew that if that came to pass it would literally destroy your mother, especially coming on top of Walther's situation. And so, I had to act, even though I knew it would go against your wishes. Klara, can you forgive me, knowing that your mother and I could not bear the thought of you . . ." His voice trailed off; the horrid thought left unstated.

Finally gathering herself, Klara took his hand off her shoulder and placed it between her own. "Yes, Vati, I forgive you. But that doesn't change the facts. I can only believe that Jakob and his parents are going to be sent to their deaths, while here I sit in my comfortable house with my loving family, enjoying my glorious life as a loyal follower of the same evil man who's going to exterminate my friends."

After a long moment of awkward silence, Erich broke the ice. "Well, at least we clearly know where you stand, Klara. I think it's time we go upstairs and bring your mother a little comfort."

As they rose from the couch and started toward the staircase, Elke finally begged the obvious question, "Vati, did Colonel Bremmer ever say why Sophie Friedmann wasn't caught in the roundup, and where they thought she might be?"

"He said the parents claimed she'd left recently to join an escape attempt by some Jews to Denmark. He said the Gestapo would keep looking for her, though."

Klara barely managed to conceal a small, ironic smile, confident that Sophie was now safely in New York. *They'll be looking for a very, very long time—unsuccessfully.*

Ascending the stairs, she imagined herself seated once again across the interrogation table from Colonel Bremmer.

"Did you get what you wanted?" she would ask him.

"I now have everything I really need," Bremmer would answer smugly.

"Except for one thing," she would say.

"And what's that?"

"A beating, human heart."

CHAPTER 36

Rocket Test Facility: Peenemünde, Germany
June 29, 1943
(Nine months later)

Gerhard Bremmer settled in the lounge chair with his legs crossed, looking on proudly as Reichsführer-SS Heinrich Himmler called for a toast from the late-night, informal gathering of leading Peenemünde rocket men.

"Gentlemen!" declared the bespectacled, owl-faced, former chicken farmer who had risen to become the second most powerful man in the Third Reich. "To the promotions of two men who will no doubt ensure the continued success and development of our Fatherland's arsenal of Vengeance Weapons[*]."

He raised a full glass of vintage wine in the air. "First, to Dr. Werner von Braun, promoted last month to the rank of SS Major. Dr. von Braun, you and your team should be very proud. As of today, there have been twenty-four firings of that magnificent A4 rocket since the first test launch last October."

---

[*] V-weapons: The collective term referring to the Nazis' new "flying bomb" and ballistic missile weapons.

"*Zum Wohl!*" shouted the audience of more than a dozen men. They sat in a semicircle facing Himmler and his two promotees. Each raised their glass in deference to von Braun, the undisputed hero of modern German rocket development.

"And second," Himmler continued. "Please offer congratulations to the Peenemünde team's good friend and enthusiastic supporter, *Gerhard Bremmer*, who has been newly elevated to the distinguished rank of full SS Colonel."

"*Zum Wohl!*"

This time, the response was more tepid. General Dornberger, who'd himself been recently promoted and was now the Wehrmacht's overall coordinator for *all* V-weapons development projects including the A4 rocket, seemed particularly unenthusiastic.

He didn't even raise his glass, Gerhard noticed. *But why am I surprised?*

Gerhard knew from various sources that Dornberger had long distrusted the SS organization. He especially feared the possibility that the SS (Himmler) was actively trying to displace the Wehrmacht (Dornberger) as Hitler's designated overlord for V-weapons development.

No doubt, our SS presence here as guest visitors is making him uncomfortable.

Gerhard also noticed that his erstwhile friend and favorite rocket man, Erich Neumann, had barely raised his glass for the second congratulatory toast. *I haven't seen him since all that unpleasant business with his daughter Klara months ago. Wonder if he's still simmering over that? Too bad. He'd been such a loyal friend.*

Himmler went on to explain Gerhard's new job. "Colonel Bremmer will initially be assigned to act as the unofficial liaison between the SS and the Peenemünde test facility. Assuming that Dr. von Braun and General Dornberger persuade the Führer at their next meeting to give the go-ahead for full-scale A4 production, Colonel Bremmer's role will become *official*. His duties will be expanded to support the required greater involvement of my SS organization in the oversight of A4 affairs.

At this last suggestion, some of the rocket men glanced at each other. *Obviously,* Gerhard mused, *most here haven't yet been fully apprised of Himmler's scheme to bring all A4 production and operational elements under SS control. But they'll learn soon enough.*

Himmler quickly switched topics to introduce the main entertainment of the evening. "Dr. von Braun! I believe it is high time we all sit back and enjoy a pre-showing of the spectacular film you and General Dornberger have created to impress the Führer at your upcoming meeting. Please, take over from here."

Von Braun stood and saluted, a mile-wide grin on his face. "Of course, Reichsführer. It would be my honor." For the next twenty minutes, von Braun provided commentary as the audience relived the sequence of events associated with the historic test launch of the first full-scale A4.

Gerhard, having already viewed an earlier cut of the film, found his mind returning to the concern that had been keeping him awake at night.

Himmler gave me a promotion in title, but will he ever follow through on his pledge to reward me with the job I'm truly after? Overseeing the A4 production priorities and performance of the vaunted Peenemünde rocket men—*that* was the only job he had sought and waited so patiently for. But was it possible that Himmler might assign him to some lesser role, and give the desirable oversight job to someone else?

The basic problem, Gerhard knew, was that despite the good words that von Braun and Erich had previously offered on his behalf, Himmler still seemed to appreciate Gerhard more for his reputation as a ruthless interrogator of city criminals than for his abilities in managing the development of advanced rocket weaponry. Admittedly, given Gerhard's lack of real experience in the latter area, maybe he shouldn't be so surprised that the administratively astute Reichsführer-SS would naturally tend to pigeonhole him into his more familiar role.

In *that* regard, Gerhard had certainly proven his mettle to Himmler with his brilliant scheme last October to exploit Neumann family connections, leading directly to the capture of Jakob Friedmann. And while Jakob, even under torture prior to his execution last February, had not yielded any useful information regarding other still-at-large Red Orchestra or Harnack Circle members, Himmler had been satisfied. *Finally*, Gerhard had fully met the Reichsführer's demand to remove the last of those Herbert Baum-supporting vermin from the streets of Berlin.

Great job of policing, Gerhard! Nebe and Himmler had commended him. *Just a few more weeks to clean up the paperwork and your promotion will certainly come through!*

Yes, it certainly had. *At long last!* And how satisfying it was to know that, in Himmler's eyes, he had made an important contribution to crush the domestic anti-Nazi resistance. In that regard, the list of achievements had been impressive. First, the Herbert Baum group had been completely extinguished. Second, the Circle and other parts of the notorious Red Orchestra had been demolished—with Arvid and Mildred Harnack brutally tortured and executed along with many others associated with them. Third, that silly but troublesome leaflet-producing group of students at Munich University known as the *White Rose* had been caught in the act, its leaders sent to the guillotine three days later. Really, what other organized resistance was left in the country?

But still, Gerhard thought, receiving Himmler's accolades and an impressive new rank in the SS were one thing; having the position he really wanted was quite another. *I need to stop grousing. At least the Berlin quagmire is behind me and the beginning of a new career at Peenemünde beckons. Just be patient.*

"And now, gentlemen," Wernher von Braun exclaimed. "The moment we've all been waiting for! Let's all join the launch controller's countdown . . ."

Rising from their seats, the assembly stared wide-eyed at the movie screen and bellowed out the last seconds of the countdown prior to the A4 engine's ignition:

"Five... four... three... two... one . . .!"

Smoke billowed from the tail of the forty-six-foot rocket. It lifted from its platform, spurring the men in the room to shout exuberantly. After about thirty seconds, the thrilling, live shots of the missile switched to animated cartoons of the trajectory, indicating speeds, heights, and range achieved on the A4's maiden test voyage that fateful day. At the end of the film, inspiring words filled the screen:

October 3, 1942
"We Made It After All!"

Gerhard's chest swelled with pride for his country and its committed defenders like the men in this room. Patriotic men like himself who were willing to persist in the face of adversity and setbacks to achieve that final victory.

Yes, he had to concede, *it is undeniable that our Wehrmacht suffered terrible defeats at Stalingrad last February and in North Africa last month. But with weapons like the A4 about to rain thousands of their one-ton warheads on Allied cities and armies, who can doubt that Germany will regain the upper hand and emerge victorious in the end?* What an honor it would be to personally lead the SS's oversight of this glorious A4 enterprise! Hopefully, that honor would soon be his.

He gazed around the room. Every man was overcome with emotion. Their right hands either covered their heart or stretched toward the screen in the Nazi salute.

After the lights went up, several of the rocket men walked over to shake Gerhard's hand and offer their congratulations. Erich Neumann waited patiently for the others, then stepped forward. A hesitant smile was on his face, and he seemed unable to look Gerhard directly in the eyes as he extended his hand.

"Congratulations, Colonel. Well deserved."

"Thank you, Erich. Your support over the years certainly has played a part."

Erich laughed nervously. "I'd say the support has been mutual. I fully realize you could have come down harder on Klara than you did, and I'm grateful for your forbearance. I love my daughter, but I'm rather ashamed of what she did to put you in that position."

Gerhard smiled and nodded. "Very appropriate feelings. I understand how hard it's been for you." *Considering how lenient I've been with his daughter, Erich Neumann is still very much in my debt,* he mused. *That could prove very useful once I formally become his SS boss.*

For years Erich and his family had been a source of friendship and an important connection for Gerhard's evolving SS career aspirations. Sadly, after his unpleasant interrogation of Klara and Elke's rejection of his romantic interest, the friendship bonds had frayed. On the other hand, now that his promotion to full colonel had finally come through, a whole new dimension to his relationship with Erich Neumann was starting to form.

Gerhard aimed to exploit it.

(Berlin: One week later)

The mournful wail of the air raid sirens began around 1:30 a.m. Klara rolled over and pulled the pillow over her head. She desperately wanted to remain asleep and avoid the tormenting memory of last night's phone call from Elke.

She knew there would be ten minutes at most to get dressed and go down to the basement shelter of the Mitte apartment building where she was now living alone. That was, if she chose to do so. Some residents, weary of yet another false alarm and encouraged by the city's improving air defense performance against the frequent nighttime RAF raids, had been willing to take their chances and remain in bed.

Tonight, I think I'll join them, she decided, pulling the pillow over her head. The way she was feeling now, even the remote possibility of a direct bomb hit on her bedroom did not seem such a terrible thing.

When Elke had called with the news of Heinz's unexpected death from what the staff claimed to be acute pneumonia in the psychiatric ward of the SS military hospital, Klara had tried her best to recover from the shock and be as supportive as she could. It wasn't easy.

After expressing her grief over the loss of her husband, Elke had exploded with a ten-minute rant against the "Russian sniper-bitch" who'd mercilessly shot him while he was lying helpless on the ground. She swore she would one day track her down and cut her heart out. She'd also railed against the lack of respect the SS medical people had shown Heinz over the past few weeks. Despite her frequent objections, they'd insisted on continually treating him like a raving lunatic rather than the war hero that he was. Some of her sharpest words were reserved for Colonel Bremmer, who had callously refused to take any more calls from her. He'd even gone so far as to request that his name be removed from the list of attendees for Heinz's bedside medal ceremony.

"I can't believe what a snake the colonel is underneath all that friendly, caring exterior," Elke complained bitterly. "He certainly had Heinz and me fooled all these years. But now, when the chips are down for us, I see who he truly is. He is *not* an honorable soldier in the Führer's service like Heinz was... he's a two-faced, career-hungry manipulator!"

Klara had suppressed the urge to throw in a few more adjectives of her own. Recalling Bremmer's hurtful joke about Heinz being a useless eater, she couldn't help but wonder: given his apparent romantic interest in Elke, had Bremmer himself played a role in Heinz's sudden demise?

Once Klara had hung up the phone, the full realization of what she'd heard unleashed the same flood of emotion that she'd experienced over news of the executions of Jakob, Arvid, and Mildred. Heinz's suspicious death was the latest reminder of the oppressive darkness of Nazism that continued to squeeze her family, her friends, and her country in its unrelenting grip. And with the domestic German resistance effort now virtually crushed, what hope remained for individual citizens like herself to continue the fight?

Listening to the droning of the approaching RAF planes, Klara kept her eyes open as she awaited the familiar thump of exploding bombs. Strangely, they never came.

Something's different... what's going on?

Voices in the corridor. She jumped out of bed, donned the clothes she always kept handy for such occasions, and opened the front door. Several people from the floor above were descending the stairs, chattering away.

"They're dropping *paper*, not bombs!" someone shouted from the first-floor landing.

Klara followed the others down the stairs and out into the street. She looked up to see the bright rays of searchlights waving back and forth, stabbing the cloudy night sky as tracers from the antiaircraft flak guns streaked upwards. The droning sound of the planes became deafening as the bulk of the fleet passed directly overhead. As the searchlight rays swept the bomber-laden sky, Klara saw what appeared to be a snowstorm of pieces of paper, illuminated by the beams of light. It wasn't long before several pieces fluttered to the ground nearby and people raced for them. One piece landed no more than ten feet from where Klara stood. She rushed to pick it up. To her surprise, it appeared to be some kind of propaganda sheet. She tucked it into her pocket and walked to the side alley where she could examine it in privacy. She began reading, and her heart nearly stopped.

Manifesto of the Munich Students

(This is the text of a German leaflet, of which a copy has reached England. A group of students from the University of Munich, known as The White Rose wrote and distributed it last February)

"The German people stand aghast at the catastrophic defeat of the Wehrmacht at Stalingrad. 330,000 German men have been irresponsibly and uselessly hounded to their death by the brilliant strategy of the former army corporal,

Adolf Hitler. Führer, we have you to thank for this tragic outcome.

"Freedom and Honor! Hitler and his confederates have for the past ten years used, abused and twisted these two beautiful German words until they have become loathsome. They have thrown the highest ideals of a nation into the gutter! What they mean by freedom and honor, they have shown only too well in the ten years of destruction of all personal freedom, all freedom of thought and all moral principles of the German people. The eyes of even the most stupid German have been opened by the terrible blood bath in which they endeavor to drown all Europe in the name of freedom and honor of the German nation."

"The day of reckoning has come, the reckoning of our German youth with the most detestable tyranny our people have ever had to suffer. In the name of the whole German nation, we demand from the State of Adolf Hitler the restitution of personal freedom, that most precious possession of Germans, out of which we have been cheated."

"The German name will remain forever dishonored if German youth does not at last arise, revenge and atone, destroy its tormentors and help build up a new spiritual concept of Europe."

Klara reread the document twice, one hand covering her mouth to stifle the sobs. After all the pain and heartache of contributing to the Circle's resistance effort over the past few years, rarely if ever seeing any fruits from her labors, tonight she had been rewarded mightily. Klara had struggled to discreetly plant even one of her leaflets. It did not matter that *this* leaflet had originated with the White Rose group, and not with the Circle. The groups were each a part of one collective undertaking to stir up the population to defeat National Socialism.

She recalled Arvid Harnack once saying that her efforts with the Circle would seem like David attempting to fight Goliath without his slingshot. Well, tonight, as in the days of old, David appeared to have his slingshot fully engaged in the battle. To see tens of thousands of these leaflets drop from the sky and into the hands of the German citizens, it seemed like a miracle.

She ran back to the street, eager to see the reactions of her fellow citizens. Surely, they would be reading the same thing she had. Surely, they would be speaking to each other with a whole new and emboldened commitment to rise up and defend freedom and honor in Germany!

Many people had exited the shelters and were indeed showing great interest in the leaflets. However, it was not the kind of interest that Klara had anticipated or hoped for.

"Would someone help me start picking up these worthless pieces of trash and throwing them in the garbage can?" One man called.

Another man held up one of the leaflets. *"What a crock! The English actually think they're going to win the war. Well, here's what we think of that, limeys!"* He set the paper on fire with a lighter.

A massive explosion above caught everyone's attention. The gathering crowd cheered wildly as a flame-enveloped RAF plane spun out of control, falling toward the ground. Several people shook their fist at the sky. *"That'll teach you Brits to think your Mosquito bombers can match up to our Luftwaffe's Messerschmitts!"*

A short, elderly man near Klara looked up from his leaflet and shook his head sadly. "I don't know what the British were thinking. Stalingrad was six months ago. We've already taken the hit and are recovering. They'd better watch out... silly stunts like this are only going to stiffen our backs."

Thoroughly disheartened by the bravado and defiance, Klara ran back to the alley where she could be alone once again. She leaned back against a wall and reread the leaflet, her hands and lips trembling. She reached the end and shut her eyes. *All we managed to do was strike*

Goliath on his bicep with a pebble, and now he's alerted and eager for revenge. We failed, and there's nothing now that I can do about it.

She began to weep inconsolably. Out of nowhere, a strong, voice-like thought broke through her own. The words were vaguely reminiscent of something Dietrich Bonhoeffer had once suggested to her. *"You haven't failed, Klara. I will show you the way and what is next. Just keep taking one step at a time and trust me."*

Klara's eyes flew open and she searched the shadows, but there was no one nearby. She leaned back against the wall once again and sighed deeply. *Thank you, God.*

PART V

GOLIATH'S REVENGE

CHAPTER 37

Mittlebau-Dora Concentration Camp Complex: Nordhausen, Germany
October 25, 1944
(Sixteen months later)

Colonel Gerhard Bremmer stood at the podium behind his new boss, SS Major General Hans Kammler, peering down at the ragged rows of wretched, rain-drenched prisoners arrayed before them on the roll call square of Mittelbau-Dora's main subcamp.

Situated just outside the rural town of Nordhausen at the southern base of the Harz Mountain range, the Dora complex had been constructed by the SS over a year ago. Its purpose was to house thousands of slave laborers next to the *Mittelwerk** company's new underground assembly plant for mass production of the A4 rocket (now redesignated as the V-2).

General Kammler, recently appointed by Reichsführer Himmler to the coveted position of "Special Commissioner for the V-2 Program," had clearly decided that marked improvements in prisoner accommo-

---

* *Mittelwerk*: "Central Works" — a private German company dedicated to operating facilities for the large-scale production and quality control of Nazi buzz-bomb and rocket weapons

dations had not resulted in the desired effect on their rocket-building productivity. It was time to set things straight.

"*So… this is how you repay us?*" Kammler's voice blasted from the loudspeakers on each side of the speaker's platform. "Last year we built you nice new wooden barracks, well-supplied with sanitary and heating devices, with modern equipment for kitchen and laundry. You always have running water and can take showers. You have a hospital, a cinema, and a canteen. God in Heaven, we even built you a sports ground with a swimming pool! All of this and more was generously provided by the Reich! We hoped that Dora's more pleasant living conditions would inspire you laborers to help achieve our ever-increasing rocket production goals. *And what do we receive from you ungrateful slugs in response to our generosity?*"

Kammler paused and surveyed his audience of malnourished and exhausted Russian, Polish, French, and Dutch prisoners of war, captured resistance fighters, and political prisoners. These were the men whom the SS had imported to Nordhausen from the occupied territories and were now forcing to slave away for up to sixteen hours a day, seven days a week in the damp, dust-saturated network of tunnels at the nearby Mittelwerk assembly factory. He seemed to take no special notice of the dozen or more dead workers who'd been brought in on stretchers and placed into formation. Alive or newly deceased, every worker was obligated to have their presence recorded at evening roll call before being permitted to retire for a scant few hours of sleep in their barracks or be carried off to the Dora camp's crematorium.

"I will tell you what we receive, especially from the more skilled laborers among you," Kammler continued as the chilling rain pelted the miserable souls who'd been standing at attention for over two hours. "We receive your sloppy work, your inattention to detail, your deliberate slowness in completing your assigned tasks. Because of your carelessness and laziness, some rockets produced here are not performing as expected.

"Perhaps you have forgotten, but allow me to remind you. You are being kept alive *only* to help us build these rockets according to the specifications and schedule dictated by your overseers. Should you continue to fail, you will be deemed utterly useless to the Reich, and I need not explain what *that* would portend."

Once again, Kammler paused, this time nodding emphatically to reinforce the gravity of his implied threat. After several seconds, his dour face broke out in a gratuitous smile as he stretched his arms wide. "However, my friends, there is still hope. Should you decide to finally stop your slacking and put in the effort required, your longevity and continued enjoyment of your improved accommodations will be ensured. To do this, you must take responsibility not only for the quality of your own work, but also for the work of your comrades, reporting anyone who you feel is failing to meet expectations."

Kammler turned and pointed to Gerhard and the other two men who stood at attention behind him, their hands folded behind their backs. "And to help encourage you along those lines, as of tomorrow morning I will be directing my assistants here to devise and implement a set of new, more rigorous inspection procedures that should help root out any bumblers and sluggards. Once these are in place, you will do well to pay greater attention to your assigned tasks."

Gerhard knew all too well that the ultimate responsibility for carrying out Kammler's directive to root out the problem people would fall on *his* shoulders.

He was not at all happy with the situation. *It should be* me—*not Kammler—standing at that podium as V-2 Special Commissioner, giving directions to everybody else.*

Obviously, things had not turned out as he'd expected—not due to any fault of his own, of course. In fact, in hindsight, Colonel Gerhard Bremmer was convinced he had unfairly been shunted off to yet another dead-end career post...

Gerhard's problems started fifteen months ago—after Wernher von Braun and General Dornberger received the enthusiastic approval from the Führer to proceed with full-scale V-2 production. Following their successful meeting, Gerhard had entertained high hopes for his transition from merely being Himmler's unofficial SS liaison to the Peenemünde facility to something far more impressive in scope and authority.

Unfortunately, the evolving war situation soon caused a major upheaval in Himmler's plans for Gerhard's next job...

After a massive and highly damaging British bomber raid on Peenemünde in late August, Hitler deemed the testing site there to be unsuitable for mass production of the V-2. He ordered Himmler and his SS to construct the bomb-resistant, underground Mittlewerk factory at Nordhausen. Himmler decided to turn the job over to General Kammler, who had already developed quite an impressive reputation as a leader of major SS construction projects—including the gas chambers at Auschwitz.

Several months later, following the Allied invasion of France, Hitler decided to put the SS in charge of *all* V-2 production, testing, and operational functions—demoting the Wehrmacht (General Dornberger) to a subordinate role. Himmler, pleased with Kammler's performance in leading the Mittelwerk construction effort, promoted him to become the V-2 Special Commissioner, to whom Dornberger and the Peenemünde rocket men now reported directly.

Gerhard soon learned that his name was never even seriously considered by Himmler for the prestigious position. Just as he'd feared, his dream of becoming the SS overseer of V-2 production and performance had been impeded by Himmler's jaded view of Gerhard's talents as being better suited for policing responsibilities. Instead of directing the efforts of the esteemed Peenemünde rocket men, Himmler had limited Gerhard's role with the V-2 production effort to the unpleasant task of enforcing order, discipline, and punishment among the V-2 slave labor force—under the direction of General Kammler.

No doubt as a consolation prize of sorts, Himmler had granted Gerhard a salary increase and job redesignation as "Chief Assistant to the V-2 Special Commissioner." While preserving his primary role as the Mittelwerk slave-labor whipmaster, Gerhard's new title ensured that he would also be privy to all of General Kammler's consultations and decisions regarding the performance of the V-2 and the rocket men supporting it. Unfortunately, it also ensured that he would be a primary recipient of Kammler's wrath if ever V-2 production volume or battlefield performance failed to meet expectations.

That hadn't taken long. By the middle of October, less than two months after the first operational V-2s were launched against London from sites in Northern France, Belgium, and Holland, significant performance issues were being observed. Though the massive rocket explosions were clearly terrifying the English population, far too many V-2s were failing to make it anywhere close to their target. Many were barely making it off the launch pad before crashing into the English Channel.

"This is a disgrace! I will not have my Vengeance rockets wasted like this. I put your SS in charge, and they must fix the problem now!" the Führer raged at SS Reichsführer Himmler. As a result, Himmler was furious with SS Major General Kammler, who in turn, sought his own culprits to blame. SS Colonel Gerhard Bremmer had become one of Kammler's favorite targets.

It all seemed so unfair, so beneath his true capabilities. Little wonder that, despite his impressive new title and expanded job responsibilities, Gerhard Bremmer's spirits were at an all-time low…

The morning after General Kammler's harangue against the prisoners, Gerhard sat wedged between General Dornberger and Arthur Rudolph (the civilian, chief technical engineer for V-2 rocket production) at the Dora camp's SS conference table. He closed his eyes and took deep, even breaths, trying his best to mentally prepare himself for what he knew was coming.

Seconds later, General Kammler entered the room in his usual pompous manner, bringing all three assistants to their feet, saluting in their usual obsequious fashion. Part of the challenge for Gerhard from this point forward would be disguising the jealousy he'd been harboring toward his boss, Kammler, ever since the latter's appointment as the rocket program's special commissioner.

Kammler took his seat and removed his cap. Despite his own antipathy, Gerhard could not help but marvel once again at the man's undeniably impressive physical appearance. Broad-shouldered with a high forehead under gray-streaked, dark hair, Kammler had brown, piercing and restless eyes. His mouth, with its underlip thrust forward as though in defiance, indicated brutality, derision, and overweening pride. Possessing a doctorate in civil engineering, he always seemed concerned with showing others what a splendid and intelligent fellow he was. But he was simply incapable of listening, he had no time for discussion or reflection, and getting him to change his mind was quite out of the question.

Kammler glared alternately at the three rigid men facing him across the table. He directed his first acerbic observations to the man on Gerhard's left.

"So, General Dornberger. It appears that, despite the 65,000 modifications that you and your Peenemünde rocket men insisted we incorporate into our original V-2 production design, we are *still* encountering major operational performance issues. Our agents in England report that the rockets are often missing their targets by miles. The explosive effect has been less than desired due to problems with the warhead proximity fuses. And some rockets are still blowing up before they reach the end of their trajectory—and we don't know why. I ask you, General, how long will it take for von Braun and his people to figure out what the problems are and how to fix them?"

"If we are serious about really getting to the bottom of these issues," Dornberger said calmly, "we will need to have five to seven more rockets per day allocated to Peenemünde and other sites for testing purposes."

"Five to seven *more* rockets... for testing purposes only?" Kammler nearly screamed. "Is enough ever enough for you people? With Mittelwerk's current production output, that would leave us only twenty-eight to thirty rockets per day for war operations. That is totally unacceptable. Surely, General Dornberger, with all your brilliant rocket scientists, you must already have *some* idea of what is causing these problems, don't you?"

Dornberger cleared his throat. "There's a good possibility that the accuracy of the rockets that make it through the atmosphere will be markedly improved once we install the new radio guide equipment at launch sites. But those rockets that are landing ridiculously short of their targets, or mysteriously exploding soon after launch, present another problem—one that technological improvements alone won't solve."

"And why not?" Kammler demanded.

"Because the problem likely lies not in the design, but in the manufacturing process here at Mittelwerk. Something is not being made correctly."

Kammler turned to Arthur Rudolph, the V-2 chief production engineer, seated on Gerhard's right. "Rudolph, what do you think? Do you agree with that, and if so, why are we not making things correctly here?"

Rudolph shifted in his seat. "It could be some flaw in the assembly procedures that we haven't yet detected. But far more likely, in my opinion, it's due either to random cases of inattentive, lazy workmanship that you mentioned in your speech to the prisoners yesterday, or possibly even to deliberate acts of sabotage."

Kammler nodded. "Now we are finally talking sense. Recall that's why we're all here today—to agree on some new, tighter inspection procedures to catch the *real* culprits and, if they turn out to be some of the prisoners themselves, to punish them accordingly. This will set the right example for the others."

His accusing eyes now bored straight into Gerhard's. "And that is where *your* services come into play, Colonel Bremmer. As we've discussed before, I believe you have allowed far too many prisoners to get away with shoddy work. No longer. Once we've finished here today with defining the new procedures, I'll expect you to enforce them consistently with an unforgiving, iron rod. In particular, there must be no mercy for saboteurs. Clear?"

Gerhard swallowed hard. "Perfectly clear, sir." *Once again,* he thought bitterly, *my grand new title of Chief Assistant to the V-2 Commissioner has been exposed for what it really means.* Rocket weapon science had nothing to do with it. It seemed that his only real purpose here was to be the designated instrument for carrying out General Kammler's brutal impulses against the prisoners. *Well, if that is what I'm being ordered to do, then as a high-level SS officer, what real choice do I have but to obey?*

"General, if I may?" Rudolph asked meekly.

"Yes?"

"I don't believe that our typical inspection procedures will be sufficient to root out saboteurs, if that's what we're dealing with. That will, in my opinion, require having someone technically knowledgeable who can not only spot subtle flaws in workmanship, but also distinguish sabotage from careless error."

"Brilliant idea!" Kammler exclaimed. "And do we have anyone in mind for such a distinguished task?" He looked from man to man.

A light flashed on in Gerhard's head. "I believe I have the perfect man in mind, sir."

Indeed, the man owed him a debt, and it was high time to collect on it.

CHAPTER 38

Mittlebau-Dora Concentration Camp Complex: Nordhausen, Germany
November 2, 1944
(One week later)

The moment Erich Neumann stepped off the small passenger plane at a private airstrip on the outskirts of Nordhausen, he noticed a faint but distinct odor in the foggy, early morning air. *The smell of burning flesh*. Wernher von Braun, who'd previously inspected Mittlewerk's underground V-2 factory, had warned Erich to expect it. A new crematorium had been erected nearby due to the increasing rate of prisoner deaths, which far exceeded the original plan to ship all the bodies a hundred miles south for disposal at the larger crematorium at the Buchenwald concentration camp. As a result, Nordhausen-area residents were subjected to daily doses of the nauseating odors.

I wonder if this is a harbinger of what's to come on this trip, Erich fretted.

After reading Colonel Bremmer's telegram requesting him to report to the Mittlebau-Dora facility, Erich realized that there was no possibility of refusing what was bound to be an unpleasant task. SS General Kammler now had the final say over the activities of the Peenemünde rocket men, and to ignore a direct request from Kammler's chief assistant would be tantamount to disobeying a strict order. Besides that, Erich's personal debt to Bremmer was stacked so high that it smothered even the thought of refusal. In fact, if it had not been for Bremmer's timely personal intervention recently, Erich might still be languishing in an SS prison along with von Braun and several others.

The triggering incident for Bremmer's rescue effort had been a casual dinner at a Peenemünde engineer's house one evening last March. Von Braun and Erich had both attended, along with some junior assistants and local civilians. A female dentist who was an SS spy later reported that von Braun and his colleagues had expressed deep regret that their rocketry expertise was being devoted to a military weapon like the V-2 and not to developing a vehicle for interplanetary space travel. They'd said they felt the war was not going well and, according to the spy, had generally displayed an attitude of defeat.

Reichsführer Himmler, who had long harbored suspicions about von Braun's loyalties to Nazism and the V-2 program, ordered their arrests by the Gestapo. They'd all spent the next two weeks locked in separate cells in Stettin without knowing the charges against them. It was only after General Dornberger and Colonel Bremmer pleaded desperately to Himmler that von Braun, Erich, and the others were indispensable to the V-2 program's success that they were finally granted a probationary release from prison and reinstated with the program.

"They could easily have decided just to free Wernher alone and sent me and the others on to a concentration camp," Erich admitted to his wife when he returned home. "Without Bremmer's testimony on my behalf, I wouldn't be here today."

Gertrude had reluctantly agreed. "Even with the difficulties that Klara and Elke have experienced with him over the past couple of years, I have to admit that Gerhard has continued to be a good friend to our family, despite my original doubts about him."

Let's just hope that friendship will continue through this next assignment... whatever it turns out to be, Erich thought warily as he contemplated his upcoming meeting with Bremmer to discuss the particulars of the colonel's concerns and expectations.

At some point, Erich knew, his friendly SS "piper" might demand to be paid.

When Erich arrived at the Dora subcamp, Colonel Bremmer's directions seemed reasonable. "Professor, what I need you to do each day for the next week is to conduct a thorough inspection of the guidance stabilization platforms. They're assembled in the Mittelwerk facility's Cross Tunnel 28. With all your design knowledge and testing experience at Peenemünde, there is no one more capable than you of recognizing something amiss with those complex beasts. At the end of each day, we'll discuss your findings and see if we can spot any alarming trends."

Erich realized that he had no choice in the matter. He was thankful that at least the assignment seemed to make sense.

Chief Production Engineer Arthur Rudolph then led him on a two-hour tour of the spacious Mittelwerk facility, which was even more awe-inspiring than he'd anticipated. Bored into the hillside were two large parallel tunnels, each over a mile in length and separated by six hundred feet. A series of more than forty smaller cross-tunnels connected them. The layout supported a highly efficient production system that was based on a railway track in one of the main tunnels along which a V-2 missile frame would slowly move. New components would be added as these were individually assembled in and delivered from shops in the various cross-tunnels.

Once the tour was done, Rudolph escorted Erich to the entrance of Cross-Tunnel 28 and wished him well on his first day on the job. This would consist primarily of observing the team of five prisoners assembling the V-2 guidance and control instrument platforms and inspecting their final products.

Erich took a seat beside the foreman in the observation window that overlooked the team's worktable. "Do you really expect to detect problems in detailed workmanship from this distance? We're at least ten feet away from the nearest worker."

"Oh, of course not, sir," the man replied in a rather patronizing tone. "The foreman's purpose here is simply to keep an eye on prisoner behavior. See if anyone seems to be lagging or tries to communicate with their fellows. During their shift, each of the five men here are responsible for turning out three assembled platforms. This requires positioning the gyros, accelerometers, and onboard analog computer, then making all the necessary wiring connections and tightening screws. Product quality is inspected after each shift. Every prisoner is required to place slips of paper bearing their identification number alongside the platforms they produced."

Erich looked at him. "For punishment purposes in case problems are discovered in the inspection, I assume?"

"Exactly, sir."

"How often has the inspector here discovered anything amiss?"

"Only a few times, sir, and those were all fairly obvious mistakes that turned out to be due to prisoner fatigue and lack of focus. They were beaten and whipped severely and warned never to repeat the offense if they wanted to live. And so far, that seems to have cured those problems. But that's not to say that our local inspector has been able to spot every subtle defect that a determined prisoner might be able to inflict upon the product. I suppose that's why you're here, sir, is it not? To lend us your more discerning, expert eye for a week?"

Erich nodded grimly. "So it seems."

Six hours later, following his exhaustive inspection of the fifteen V-2 guidance platforms produced by the day's first shift, Erich once again found himself facing Colonel Bremmer in the SS executive conference room. He had some news, but he couldn't help but feel reluctant to share it so soon with Bremmer, who seemed anxious to grab at any straw presented to him.

"Discover anything interesting today, Erich?" Bremmer asked eagerly.

"Well, Colonel, I did spot a couple of anomalies in one of the assembled platforms, though I can't say for sure if it was due to deliberate action or just a mistake due to prisoner fatigue."

"Oh? What was the problem?"

"There appear to be two separate wiring connections that were only partially soldered, and which *could possibly* come apart during flight stresses. These can be hard to spot, but I was looking very closely and managed to discover them."

"And what would be the effect if they *did* come apart in flight?"

"It would result in failure of the analog computer to receive information from the gyros. The computer would then not be able to create and transmit the required corrective signals to the rocket's tail fins. The missile would veer out of control and crash soon after launch or, at best, land far away from its targeted destination."

Bremmer's eyes widened. "A catastrophic failure of the kind we've seen far too many times lately! And doubtless due to sabotage. Congratulations, Professor. It's only your first day here, and already you've made an important contribution."

Erich, not wishing to place undeserved blame that could result in a death sentence, hurried to qualify his finding. "Oh, sir, I agree it could *possibly* be a case of attempted sabotage, but I think that judgment at this point would be very premature. I would need to observe the same prisoner's output over the next several days to see if there is any repeated pattern."

Bremmer's benign smile belied his obvious annoyance. "Just continue to carry out your daily inspections, Professor. And please permit *me* to make the final determination for characterizing this particular incident. After all, dealing with the suspected offender is the job I was entrusted with. And I am obligated to faithfully carry it out."

"As you wish, Colonel," Erich said meekly.

The two men stood and saluted. Erich turned to walk out the door, relieved to have the first day's work behind him and desperate for a good night's sleep at the Mittelwerk company's local hotel.

Bremmer stopped him in his tracks. "Professor, before you leave, I will need, by 8 p.m., a copy of your summary report—signed by yourself and Herr Rudolph—of what you discovered today, including the names of all five men on the shift you were monitoring. Be sure to denote the name of the prisoner suspected of sabotage."

"Colonel, I happen to have a copy right here." Erich pulled the copy of the report from his pocket, marked an "X" next to the prisoner in question and handed the piece of paper to Bremmer.

He was two steps out the door when the thought struck like a thunderbolt:

My God... what is he planning to do with that?

CHAPTER 39

Mittlebau-Dora Concentration Camp Complex: Nordhausen, Germany
November 2, 1944

L ater that night, Gerhard Bremmer sat in his private quarters. After two hours with a young Nordhausen prostitute followed by another solid hour drinking straight whiskey, the burning rage in his heart still hadn't let up. This was *not* how his job was supposed to turn out.

The arrogant son-of-a-bitch!

No matter how much he tried, Gerhard could not stop obsessing over the devious order that General Kammler had laid on him regarding the suspected saboteur. When Gerhard objected, he'd been met with a biting reprimand and warning to never question Kammler's authority again. He'd walked away with a sick feeling in his stomach, knowing that tomorrow he would be expected to publicly promote an outright falsehood to satisfy Kammler's craving for immediate results.

It did not trouble Gerhard so much that Kammler's directive went beyond the scope of necessary measures to discourage sabotage. Or that Erich Neumann would not be happy with the part that *he* would unwittingly end up playing. No. Erich Neumann's approval and feelings, just like the Dora prisoners, were expendable. The only thing that *really* bothered Gerhard was the disdainful way that Kammler spoke to him. He'd left little doubt that he considered Gerhard's policing role to be the only one for which he would ever be suited. But it had not stopped there. Kammler had also taken it upon himself to dictate *how* Gerhard should do his job—even to the point of writing out the specific lies Gerhard must use in rationalizing his actions to the prison population. Basically, Kammler had made it perfectly clear that Gerhard was nothing more than Kammler's lackey, and that his long-time career hopes had truly reached a dead-end.

Could the man have been any more degrading? Gerhard thought bitterly as he drained his glass and poured himself another round.

He had another concern—one that could soon drown out all his others.

The war was not going well at all. Rumors were circulating among some of Gerhard's higher-level army contacts that Germany stood little chance of weathering the storms converging rapidly from both western and eastern fronts. Yes, there was also some talk of a secret, massive counteroffensive that Hitler had in the works. But if that and the V-2 campaign against England and western Europe failed to achieve their objectives soon, the Third Reich could be doomed. And if *that* occurred, who would be at the top of the Allies' lists for capture and reprisal? They would be Hitler, his chief officers, and any leaders in the SS organization. Especially any SS men associated with running or policing the concentration and slave-labor camps.

Men exactly like himself.

At some point soon, Gerhard might need to prepare for the worst.

For a blessed moment, his troubled thoughts faded as he stared into the fireplace where the embers continued to glow. He imagined his deceased wife and children standing on their favorite lakeside beach, waving for him to join them in the water. He was starting to run toward them when the fantasy morphed into the real image hanging above the fireplace. It was a large photograph of Adolf Hitler and Heinrich Himmler standing on either side of a beaming General Hans Kammler, who was holding a model V-2 rocket in his hands. It was the day that

Kammler had received his promotion to V-2 Commissioner, and he was insistent that every single SS officer above the rank of lieutenant at the Mittlebau-Dora facility must have the wonderful event prominently displayed somewhere in their office or private quarters.

Gerhard glared with disgust at the scene. *An unholy trinity if ever I've seen one.* His eyes focused in on Kammler. *The son of a bitch. The grinning, supercilious, son of a bitch.*

He picked up the half-full whiskey bottle and heaved it against the wall, laughing hysterically as it crashed into pieces against the image of the boss he had come to hate.

⁂

The next morning at nine o'clock, the strident voice blared over the loudspeaker in the Dora camp's mess hall for SS officers.

"All prisoners, civilians, and SS personnel will report immediately to Tunnel B, Hall 41 for a special address by the Chief Assistant to the V-2 Commissioner."

Erich Neumann looked up from his plate of barely touched bratwurst and eggs and stared at Arthur Rudolph who had joined him for breakfast.

Rudolph shrugged. "Probably just another one of Bremmer's verbal thrashings to vent his frustrations over poor performance. But who knows?"

The men rose and strode out of the dining room toward the tunnel. Hall 41, just inside the entrance, had been excavated well below the regular level of the tunnel. It was over fifty feet high and contained a crane that was normally used to erect a finished rocket for final calibration and testing. Today, however, as Erich and Rudolph pushed their way through the crowd of workers, Erich noticed something strange. Instead of a V-2 rocket, the crane suspended a horizontal steel crossbeam from which dangled five short lengths of rope spaced at regular intervals. The end of each rope was tied in a noose.

Stomach twisting with his sudden realization of what this special address might be about, Erich glanced at the speaker's platform that was occupied by Colonel Bremmer, flanked by several of his junior SS assistants.

Before he could react, an SS officer approached Rudolph and saluted. "Herr Rudolph, Colonel Bremmer requests that you and Professor Neumann join him on the platform." Without waiting for the two men's assent, the man whirled and led the way to the steps. Bremmer spotted them there and motioned impatiently for them to join the group on the stage. Erich and Rudolph had no sooner ascended the stairs and positioned themselves next to Bremmer when the latter raised his hand for quiet and launched into his prepared tirade.

"One week ago, General Kammler informed all of you of some coming changes to our inspection procedures. I am here to report that these have already had a positive impact. Yesterday, an act of attempted sabotage was detected and reported by one of Dr. von Braun's leading guidance and control experts who has joined me on this stage."

Erich's face went white as the eyes of the five hundred or more prisoners crammed into the hall turned to observe him. He stared in disbelief at Bremmer. *What is this? Rudolph and I simply signed off on the bare facts of the problem I observed. I never confirmed that it was—*

"As I warned you, sloppy work or inattentiveness that result in product defects will be punished severely. But deliberate sabotage, my friends, is another matter altogether. General Kammler has made it clear that such acts cannot be tolerated and deserve the ultimate penalty. To show you what we mean . . ."

Bremmer turned and nodded to one of his junior assistants standing by a door beside the stage leading to a small anteroom. The assistant saluted. He disappeared for a few seconds, then returned at the head of a small parade of five stumbling, bloodied, and barely coherent prisoners. Each had his hands tied behind his back and a piece of timber secured in his mouth. The prisoners were yanked along by their accompanying SS guards and forced to take up positions in a line underneath the crane-suspended steel beam facing the crowd. The guards placed the nooses around their necks and tightened them, then stepped back.

Erich recognized the prisoner in the middle as the one who had made the faulty wiring connection, and the others on either side as his co-workers in Tunnel 28. *Why are all five being executed?*

Bremmer clarified things using a brutal, twisted logic. "It is true that only one of the men you see before you is technically guilty of the crime. However, the others—his co-workers on the same shift—are held responsible for not keeping a close eye on their comrade's actions, and so will suffer the same punishment. This, my friends, is our new order of prisoner mutual accountability and discipline at the Mittelwerk V-2 factory. Each man here should observe the example we are about to set today and think hard about its implications for his own work effort in the future."

Without further delay, Bremmer stepped back from the microphone and nodded at the leader of the SS prisoner escort, who in turn signaled to the crane operator. The loud, electrical hum from the crane's suspension engine failed to drown out the gasps, groans, and cries of horror that emanated from the crowd as the prisoners were slowly hoisted into the air and strangled to death.

Five minutes later, the last twitches of the bodies had stilled. Each dangled limply, five feet above the floor. "Take a good look, my friends," Bremmer intoned. "And in case you are tempted to forget, we will leave the men hanging just as you see them now for the next several days. When you travel through this hall, the sight will motivate you to perform quality work and hold your comrades accountable for doing the same. That is all. You are dismissed to your daily tasks."

Sickened to the core, Erich watched as Bremmer and his assistants trooped off the stage. He looked at Rudolph, who stood frozen beside him with a dazed, troubled expression on his face as he continued to stare at the execution scene.

"*This is a travesty!*" Erich muttered vehemently. "My report never claimed the prisoner's action was deliberate sabotage, and I told Bremmer that to his face."

Rudolph shrugged helplessly.

Erich turned and hurried after Bremmer and his entourage. He caught up just before the tunnel exit. "Forgive me, Colonel, but may I have a word… in private?"

Bremmer stopped and glared. "All right, but make it fast, Professor. General Kammler is awaiting my report on today's event."

"Colonel Bremmer, I must protest the use of my report to justify the extreme action taken today."

To Erich's great surprise, Bremmer closed his eyes, sighed, and nodded sympathetically. "Erich, between you and me… I admit that what was done today was extremely harsh. But you shouldn't take things so personally. It was not your doing. It was *Kammler's* decision to force this early example to make sure we get our point across so that future sabotage acts will be discouraged.

"Think, Erich, of the German civilian lives that will be saved as a result of more of our V-2 rockets reaching their targets, intimidating and convincing the Allies to sue for peace. You and I were merely obeying our orders and doing our part to save more German lives in the long run, were we not?"

"But, Colonel," Erich persisted. "To imply that it was *I* who identified the crime as an act of sabotage as opposed to an innocent mistake? That was not what I told you and it wasn't what I said in the report, and still you—"

Bremmer held up his hand. His face was set in stone, and his eyes flashed angrily. "I advise you to stop right there, Professor. You are in no position—either officially or personally—to cast aspersions on the actions I was required to take under orders from General Kammler, nor on my use of your report as I saw fit to support these actions."

His face red with indignation, Bremmer stared in cold silence for several long seconds. "Professor Neumann, under normal circumstances, you know your unauthorized complaint against me would be grounds for a severe official response. But since I recognize and honor our friendship, I will forgo your offense this one time. However, allow me to remind you, Professor, that both your rocketry career and the probability of a long prison sentence, or worse, for both you and your daughter, Klara, are held by very thin threads over a *very* hot fire." He shook his forefinger in front of Erich's face. "And whether you like it or not, *I* am the one holding the ends of those threads. Should you insist on further challenging my authority or official decisions in any way, be prepared for the consequences. Do you understand me?"

The mention of Klara's name struck more terror in Erich's heart than anything else Bremmer had just threatened. He lowered his eyes, completely cowed. "Yes, Colonel, I do understand."

Bremmer looked at his watch. "*Verdammt*, I must be going. And you to Tunnel 28 with your new batch of prisoners, correct? Hopefully they will have learned their lesson, and future actions like this won't be necessary."

"Thank you for your time, Colonel." Erich stepped back, saluted, then walked away to resume the most terrible week of his life. He now understood clearly why both of his daughters had come to despise the man whom he had long considered to be a good family friend.

CHAPTER 40

Berlin, Germany
November 23, 1944
(Three weeks later)

Klara settled herself in the rear seat of the taxi, wondering if the short journey from her Mitte apartment to the family house in Charlottenburg would be interrupted by yet another Allied bombing raid. She hadn't been home in over a month, and she did not want to miss tonight's casual get-together with Elke and her former student, Trudi Schuster.

The letter she'd received from her father yesterday morning added extra urgency to her visit. Pulling it out of her purse, she reread his words:

Dear Klara:

It pains me greatly to write you about this. I would have preferred to call, but the phone connections to Berlin have become seriously impaired due to all the bombing and heightened security. The sad truth is that Mama's health and emotional state have been declining rapidly over the past few weeks. Her stomach pains have become more frequent and severe, and she's now experiencing long moments of mental disorientation. The doctors here at Peenemünde haven't pinpointed any definite cause, but they believe it may be related to her depression over the lack of news about Walther since his apparent capture by the Russians. She frets constantly over you and Elke, with the terrible bombing attacks you're being subjected to in Berlin. The medications the doctors have prescribed are helping a little, but I worry that she seems to be generally on a downward slide.

No doubt making things worse for her is the news we received a few days ago: some of our Peenemünde people, including myself, have been directed to relocate to a new facility in the Nordhausen area. That will mean a significant disruption in your mother's routine, and I'm not sure how easily she'll be able to adjust.

If it is at all possible, Klara, would you be able to take some time off from your Charité duties and come visit us for a couple of weeks? We should be settled at our new location within a month or two. It's in the countryside, and I'm sure you would find it to be a welcome, if temporary, respite from those air raids you've had to endure over the past months. Also, though I know things have been strained between you and Elke for quite a while, could you possibly speak to her and urge her to join you? Your mother misses both of you terribly, and given her grief over Walther and Heinz, I believe it would do her heart so much good to see and talk with you and your sister again as a family, despite your differences. I've written Elke separately requesting this, and I'm hoping that the two of you will see fit to come visit Mama and me at the countryside home. It would be a great blessing for both of us, I assure you!

Please write back soon to let me know what you've decided and when you might be able to come. I miss you terribly, Liebchen.

— Your loving Vati

PS: I will be leaving tomorrow for a short working vacation in western Europe. As always, your prayers for me and your mother would be greatly appreciated, just as you know we are praying for you, Elke, and Walther.

Klara refolded the letter and returned it to her purse. She well knew from past conversations with Mama that the term "working vacation" was Vati's code word for an important special assignment. This one, she strongly suspected, was connected with the V-2 rocket that Joseph Goebbels had recently announced on public radio as Germany's newest miracle weapon.

She also knew from Vati's description that something was seriously wrong with Mama, and she began to consider the possibilities and best time for travelling to Nordhausen for a visit. Could she convince Elke to join her, or would her sister's impossible schedule and constant pre-occupation with her leadership role in the *Wehrmachthelferin's*[*] Berlin air defense organization preclude any time away from the city?

At least the two of us are finally back on speaking terms with occasional visits. Hopefully, Elke wouldn't become too distracted by the presence of Trudi Schuster at the three girls' monthly Skat card game tonight, thereby preventing any chance for Klara to probe her concerning her willingness and availability to accompany Klara to Nordhausen.

An evening of Skat, drinks, and an important family matter—all with Trudi Schuster in the mix. What could possibly go wrong? Klara thought wryly as her train pulled into the Charlottenburg U-Bahn station.

Elke stared bleary-eyed at the fan of Skat cards in her hand. "Trudi, why does my sister keep looking at me like I'm some kind of odd duck?"

Trudi Schuster peered over her own cards at Klara, who was seated directly across from her at the dining room table. Both were trying

---

[*] *Wehrmachthelferin*: German Armed Forces' Female Auxiliary Corps

desperately to control their laughter over Elke's strange appearance tonight. "I think it might be best if Klara answers that for herself, Elke."

It was interesting, Klara thought, to see Elke and Trudi finally breaking through the formalities of their five-year relationship as BDM trainer and her favorite student, addressing each other on a first-name basis. *Must be the four rounds of Jägermeister we've each downed.*

"Well, Klara?" Elke pressed. "What about me is arousing your curiosity tonight?"

"I guess I'm just rather shocked to see my National Socialist, poster-girl sister out of uniform for a change, with a cigarette dangling from her mouth and her hair unbound and mussed like one of those Hollywood starlets." Klara pushed her hair behind one shoulder, batted her eyes and flashed a mock, seductive smile. "Playing cards, no less! Somehow, it disturbs the pristine image I've always had of you. You know? I think I may even like what I'm seeing!"

"Well." Elke sniffed as she placed her cigarette on the ash tray and picked up her newly filled shot glass. "Thank goodness that at least you've found *something* to like about me. After that huge mess you got yourself into with the Kripo last year because of your rebellion against everything I've stood for, I thought the only thing you really *liked* about me and Trudi was the fact that we bailed you out and refused to betray you to that two-faced rat, Colonel Bremmer."

Klara winced. It was apparent her sister was slipping into another one of her typical doldrums fueled by alcohol and her memories of losing Heinz. With Trudi here, she knew she had to be very careful how she responded. The last thing she wanted was for Trudi to witness one of Elke's explosive, half-drunken rants against Klara's anti-Nazi views. While she was confident that neither Elke nor Trudi would intentionally turn her in to the authorities, the whole subject was extremely touchy, and Klara didn't want Trudi to get drawn into what could easily turn into a sister-to-sister screaming match.

"Elke, you know good and well there are a lot of things I like and respect about you, even if I never embraced the Führer and National Socialism like you," she said gently.

Elke peered over her cards with a cocked eyebrow. "Oh, yes? Name one."

"Well, for one, I admire what you and Trudi are both doing with the Wehrmachthelferin to help defend our city from these monstrous air attacks. While I'm usually cowering in our local bomb shelter, you two are putting yourselves in harm's way out there in the Tiergarten flak tower, helping keep the anti-aircraft crews supplied with food, water, and first-aid. I personally find that to be quite admirable, and I'm proud of you for having the courage to do it. There. Will that do? Now will you please just shut up, stop badgering me, and play your hand for Heaven's sake?"

All three women burst out laughing, obviously relieved to have the delicate issue of Klara's admitted disdain for Nazism put aside with a timely bit of humor.

"Unfortunately," Elke said. "That's why I can't promise to join you in visiting Mama and Vati for the foreseeable future. I never know from day-to-day when our women's unit will be called to duty, and I've got to be there to lead them."

Klara decided to turn the tables. "Trudi, is my sister's leadership so brilliant and indispensable to your unit that there's absolutely no one who could fill in for her for a few days so she can visit our parents with me?"

Trudi glanced uncomfortably between Elke and Klara, who both stared expectantly at her as if she were a municipal judge on the verge of rendering her final decision in a civil court case. "Well, I can understand your parents' desire to see you together again after all everyone's been through. I know mine would want the same. But it's true, Klara. There's really no one else in our unit with Elke's boldness and presence of mind... someone who can keep all the girls from panicking when the bombs are dropping so close around us. I suppose on balance, I agree with your sister that we really can't do without her, even for a short period." She looked at Elke shyly, as if seeking her approval. Elke's glistening eyes, slight smile and nod confirmed her own reaction. The bonds of devoted, mutual loyalty and affection between the former student and her admired teacher were never more clearly on display.

"I can't imagine how frightful that must be, especially the night raids where you can't see the bombers, and the searchlights and explosions are flashing all around," Klara ventured softly.

Elke downed the rest of her fifth shot of Jägermeister. "Actually, from a sheer terror standpoint for us and the gun crews, the nighttime raids by forty or so British Mosquito bombers pale in comparison to the daylight raids by those American Flying Fortresses. Thankfully, those have been far less frequent, but when they come in their waves of hundreds of planes that seem to blanket the sky, it looks and feels like Armageddon has arrived."

"The noise must be incredible too," Klara prompted.

"That's putting it mildly. Before we started mandating plugs for everyone, several of our girls had their eardrums blown out by the constant blasts. A few others simply curled into little balls, unable to take the dreadful noise of the bombs and the constant pounding of our flak tower guns. The girls have toughened up, and the earplugs have helped. But still, we occasionally have to dismiss someone who simply can't take the pressures anymore."

"I can't believe our tower's been so lucky as to avoid a direct hit so far," Trudi observed. "Sometimes I can't help but think we're living on borrowed time."

Elke shook her head angrily. "It's probably because the Allies are so busy targeting the more vulnerable areas of the city. Oh, I get so mad every time I think of that new carpet-bombing technique they're now using—like that one in Darmstadt a couple of months ago that killed more than 8,000 innocent residents. They're intentionally going after our helpless civilians, trying to break our morale."

"Isn't that what Germany did against Rotterdam and the English cities earlier in the war?" Klara asked.

Reminded of the unavoidable facts, Elke merely scowled and rolled her eyes. After a couple of card rounds played in mutual silence, she eyed Klara discretely. "Do you ever think of your old diplomat-boyfriend, Joshua, and wonder what he's doing now? Do you imagine it's possible he might be in the cockpit of one of those American bombers come to obliterate Berlin?"

Klara cocked her head. "Elke! Why would you ask such a thing? I have no idea what Joshua is doing now. Yes, I do think about him now and then, but certainly not in the role you're suggesting. You keep bringing him up. Why is that?"

Elke looked back down at her cards. "Oh, I don't know. For some reason he keeps popping into my mind. I thought he was a very nice and attractive man when I met him, and likely a good match for you if it weren't for the fact that he's no doubt now fighting on the American side."

Klara was about to respond when the first wail of the air-raid sirens sounded.

"*Oh, no!*" Elke cried. "Our peaceful night of cards ruined. Well, Trudi, at least our unit's off tonight so we won't have to endure another round of that head-splitting bomb-bashing in the flak tower."

"Time to head for our shelter?" Klara asked.

"Oh, I suppose," Elke replied wearily. "Although it's been quite a while since we've had any real damage here in Charlottenburg. Nothing like that raid last year that killed hundreds in our area. I'm so tired tonight. Just the thought of dragging myself into that cramped shelter in our backyard is enough to make me want to just sit this one out in the dining room and take my chances. But if the rest of you insist . . ."

Trudi hesitated. "I think I'm going to run home to my house and urge my parents and little sister to take shelter in the basement They've been pretty cavalier about these raids lately, choosing to stay put in their living room and assume they won't be harmed."

"Trudi," Klara objected. "Your house is two blocks away... will you have time?"

"We usually have at least ten minutes from siren start until we hear the first bombs dropping. If I start now, I can—"

Trudi froze at the unexpected sound of a series of multiple, rapidly approaching explosions. "What is *that?* They couldn't possibly be here already! How did they get through our—"

The huge blast coursed through the house, shattering the front window, extinguishing the lights and knocking all three women out of their chairs and onto the floor.

Elke was the first to gather her senses. "Is everyone all right?"

Dazed but unhurt, Klara and Trudi slowly picked themselves up and together with Elke entered the living room to assess the damage. In the darkness, Elke was finally able to locate a flashlight in a drawer and beamed it around the room. Aside from some fallen pieces of plaster mixed with shattered window glass, there appeared to be no significant structural damage. Pointing the light beam through the window, Elke illuminated a smoking, fifteen-foot-wide crater in the middle of the street.

"A few feet closer and we'd all be singing with the angels," Elke muttered.

The women stepped outside and looked down the street. Crushed, flame-enveloped houses across the street marked the bomber's path for several blocks. "Looks like he flew right up the pipe," Klara said.

Trudi suddenly let out a horrified scream. *"My family's house is down there!"* She took off running with Elke and Klara in pursuit.

By the time they arrived at what was once the home of Trudi Schuster and her family, firemen and air raid wardens were already digging frantically through the piles of debris, searching for any sign of life. The scene was practically identical to the ones playing out in the demolished neighboring homes. Klara and Elke stood on either side of Trudi, struggling to keep her from breaking away and making a pointless dash into the still-smoldering rubble.

"Found three!" shouted a fireman wielding a shovel atop one of the piles. "Bring stretchers and blankets."

Trudi shrieked and collapsed to her knees. *"No, God. No!"*

It took several minutes for the bodies to be completely extricated, placed on the stretchers and covered from head to foot. One by one, each stretcher was picked up by two wardens and carried reverently past Trudi and the others. The last covered body appeared to be no more than four feet in length.

"Please, may I just see my little sister's face... one last time?" Trudi pleaded with one the bearers, her hands folded as if in prayer.

He shook his head sadly. "Best not, Fräulein, trust me. Far better to remember her the way she was. I am so sorry."

The bearers moved on, leaving Trudi clutching her stomach and convulsing violently.

Elke took her into her arms and hugged her closely as Klara stroked her back and shoulders.

"I'm here for you, Trudi," Elke whispered. "You know I'm here. You won't be alone." Her eyes glistened with a mixture of tears and the reflection of some small flames that had reignited in the rubble of the neighbor's house.

"Do you see now, Klara," she whispered over Trudi's shoulder, "why I can never leave this city... even for a day?"

In her familiar bed in the slightly damaged Charlottenburg residence the next morning around 3 a.m., Klara awoke with a start from her strange dream.

She sat up, listening carefully for any sounds of Elke consoling Trudi in the next room. The total silence confirmed that exhausted sleep must have finally overtaken both girls.

Klara lay back down, trying to make sense of things. No doubt prompted by the memories and events of last night, the short dream had seemed so real... and disturbing.

In it, she had been running frantically toward the head of a military airstrip where a single, large American Flying Fortress with its propellers whirling prepared to take off. A man—presumably the pilot—was just starting to climb the ladder toward the cockpit. She had no idea *who* the man was. All she knew was that she had to grab his attention and warn him not to enter, or he would end up taking the plane on a mission that would shatter the lives of many innocent civilians.

"Sir," she called out as she came close. "Are you the pilot? Please don't enter that plane. Too many people are going to die, yourself included."

The man stopped just before stepping inside. He turned and grinned at her.

The man was none other than Dietrich Bonhoeffer.

But how can that be? I heard from his fiancée that he's still in Tegel Prison in Berlin, awaiting trial for his supposed involvement in that assassination attempt on Hitler last July.*

"Oh, don't worry, Fräulein Klara," Bonhoeffer assured her. "I'm just the co-pilot. The pilot will make sure we get to where we need to go. Our plane's navigator is coming right behind you with his wife. They're about to say their last goodbyes."

Klara whirled. To her utter shock, Joshua Peters and Sophie Friedmann stood locked together in a deep kiss. After several interminable seconds, the two broke away from each other and turned to face Klara. Their faces broke out in delighted smiles as they rushed toward her, arms outstretched.

She was torn between screaming with the joy of mutual reunification and collapsing with heartbreak from seeing the love of her life stolen by her best friend.

It was then that she woke up.

What is going on with those two?

---

* Bonhoeffer was accused of colluding with his brother-in-law and others in the Abwehr and Wehrmacht to plan the failed July 20th, 1944 "Valkyrie" assassination attempt on Adolph Hitler's life. He was finally tried and found guilty by a drumhead Nazi court on April 8, 1945, and he was executed by hanging the next day at the Flossenbürg concentration camp.

CHAPTER 41

London, England
November 24, 1944

First Lieutenant Joshua Peters, US Office of Strategic Services (OSS), had noticed the two single women trying to catch his eye ever since they'd taken seats at the opposite end of the 400 Club's crowded bar nearly a half hour ago.

After downing numerous refills of whatever they were drinking, the women put their money down and got up to leave. As they passed by Joshua on their way to the coatroom, one girl stopped, gave her friend a sly look, and strolled to where he was seated at the bar. She put her hand on his shoulder, leaned down, and whispered seductively in his ear.

"Hey, handsome. You look like you could use some cheering up. Come on home with me and my girlfriend… we'll take good care of you, I promise."

Joshua was in no mood for a wild fling, especially considering his critical meeting first thing in the morning with the head of the SHAEF[*] London office intelligence section. He looked at her and flashed a

---

* SHAEF: Supreme Headquarters, Allied Expeditionary Force

weary, apologetic smile. "Thanks for the offer, but this isn't a good night for me."

She smiled at him quizzically. A medium-height brunette with an attractive, narrow face and shapely figure accented by her tight-fitting, lowcut party dress, the girl appeared to be in her early twenties. She didn't have the hardened look of a hooker. More likely, she was just an exceptionally aggressive specimen of the hordes of young English girls eager to date and possibly marry one of the friendly, money-padded American GIs now stationed on their soil. In this case, an undisguised desire for physical gratification appeared to be the girl's main motivator.

"Oh, come on soldier-boy," she prodded. "I guarantee we'll make it much better for you."

"Thanks, honey, but this just isn't the right night for me."

The girl cocked her head back and her eyes flashed indignantly. "Well, when *is* the right night for you, Yank? I'd heard you lusty American soldier-boys were *always* ready and looking for a good time with us poor, shy, little Brit girls. Are you the exception to the rule?"

Joshua simply shrugged, turned back in his seat and lifted the half-empty glass of bourbon to his lips.

"Suit yourself, cowboy," the girl huffed and stalked off with her friend.

Good decision, he congratulated himself. The last thing he needed was a lascivious, sleep-deprived night resulting in a guilt-plagued conscience and a muddled mind during the meeting with Colonel Hawthorne, the SHAEF intel section head. Especially since it was at that meeting where he anticipated receiving details of his most important assignment to date in his burgeoning career in military intelligence.

It was amazing, Joshua reflected, how closely that assignment—as it had been initially described to him back in the States—was aligned with his dream of returning to Germany to retrieve and marry his first and only true love: Klara Neumann.

When he'd left Klara at the Stettin train station nearly six years ago, Joshua had promised that he'd come back for her, despite his concern that he might not see her again for years to come, if ever. Once back in America, he'd worked hard to honor his commitment to get Herbert Friedmann's personal account of what had become known since 1938 as *Kristallnacht* (Night of the Broken Glass) published in a major US news outlet. Sadly, its authenticity had been questioned by every editor he'd interviewed, and he'd been unsuccessful. He had mailed a letter to Klara via the ghost staff managing the affairs of the evacuated US Embassy in Berlin, apologizing for his failed efforts so far, but he hadn't been sure if the letter had ever reached her.

With the start of the war in Europe and constant cajoling by his father (now retired from his deputy ambassador role), Joshua's attentions had been drawn to completing his college degree in linguistics at NYU and preparing to enter the US foreign service. The following two years of hard study and coed chasing had dimmed, but by no means erased, his memory of Klara or his longing to be with her again. But still, with Germany enmeshed in total war on two fronts and contact in any form between its ordinary citizens and foreigners virtually impossible, the idea of a physical reunification had seemed so remote that he'd nearly given up all hope that it would ever happen.

The Pearl Harbor attack on December 7, 1941 had changed everything. Within days, Hitler supported the Japanese by declaring war on the US, pulling America at last into the European fray it had long sought to avoid. Joshua had been eager to rush to join the huge surge of patriotic American men crashing the local Army, Navy, and Marine Corps recruiting stations. His father, however, urged him to wait for a service opportunity more compatible with his German language skills and diplomatic experience.

It had proven to be wise counsel. In mid-1942, Joshua was personally visited by two friends of his father's. Both men were senior officers in the newly established OSS, which President Roosevelt had chartered to collect and assess strategic intelligence information required by the Joint Chiefs of Staff.

"We understand that you had several occasions while in Germany to converse with Wernher von Braun concerning your mutual interest in rocketry," one of the officers observed. "Given your familiarity with the German language and passion for the subject, how would you like to become part of a small OSS team that's working with the British to gather and analyze intel on a powerful new rocket the Nazis are rumored to be developing?"

Joshua had jumped at the opportunity and quickly proved his aptitude for the job. Two months ago, he received an OSS distinguished service award for his superb translation and analysis of several Nazi-authored research reports on rockets and guided missiles that he'd discovered while accompanying the allied armies advancing through Rome, Italy. His achievement soon came to the attention of some senior Allied intelligence experts. They recommended that Joshua be included on a new team of operatives being readied for insertion behind British and American combat units poised to advance over the French border into Germany. The purpose of the team was described in general terms as an effort to track and capture high-profile German scientists involved with Nazi secret weapons programs.

"You'll be given more detailed information on the specific goals and tasks of this team once you arrive in London," he was told last month. It hadn't been much to go on, but the very thought of returning to Germany had reignited a vague hope of somehow eventually making his way to Berlin and discovering Klara Neumann alive and well.

Then, only two days before his departure for London, he'd received a totally unexpected phone call. It was from Sophie Friedmann. Sophie had just arrived in New York after a long and harrowing journey from Switzerland, and she was staying at her uncle's home in Brooklyn. She said she had quite a story to tell him, including some news about Klara. The two met for dinner that evening in the city, and after relating the story of her escape from Berlin and Klara's role in helping her, Sophie handed Joshua the note that Klara had written. When he read that she was still waiting for him, he'd broken down in tears.

If he ever needed a clear sign as to the ultimate goal he would pursue once in Germany, he now had it. As he and Sophie parted, he'd hugged and thanked her, promising that upon his return from his next mission he would work tirelessly to get her father's account published by a reputable outlet.

⁂

Joshua finished his drink and placed the money for his tab on the bar. As he waited for the bartender to arrive, he turned in his seat and looked toward the stage where the band was performing a snappy swing number. How fortunate the 400 Club had been, he thought. Many London pubs and entertainment venues had been decimated during the Blitz of 1940–41. Now though, in late November 1944, fear of sudden death by bomb was no longer the primary topic of conversation for London's late-night revelers. Instead, exuberant dancing and talk of the impending Allied victory had become the norm, as exemplified on the dance floor of the 400 Club tonight.

Some day before long, Klara Neumann and Joshua Peters will jitterbug together on that very floor, he vowed to himself.

Chapter 42

London, England
November 25, 1944

At 8:30 a.m. on the fourth floor of the London War Office, Joshua stood ramrod straight in front of the massive stainless steel desk, hands at his sides. Out of the corner of his eye, he took note of his good friend and designated mission partner, Lieutenant Alec Benjamin of the British Army Intelligence Corps. Alec was clearly fidgeting as the two men waited for the sallow faced SHAEF officer to look up from his papers.

If this guy takes any longer to acknowledge our presence, Joshua thought irritably, *we might as well forget about our lunch with the ladies.* He could only imagine the string of curses in Alec's mind, awaiting the slightest excuse to be unleashed. Alec had never been one to tolerate the obvious disdain that so many mid-level, desk-bound SHAEF coordinators like this one seemed to enjoy displaying toward their junior field partners.

Finally, Colonel Nathan Hawthorne, a former British army quartermaster now serving as SHAEF's London G2 (Joint Intelligence) section head, sat back in his chair. He removed his horn-rimmed glasses and rubbed his eyes. "At ease, gentlemen," he muttered as he replaced the glasses and reached for a black folder on the side of the desk.

Joshua relaxed his shoulders, clasping his hands behind his back. He shot a quick glance at Alec, who rolled his eyes and shook his head at the sight of Hawthorne studying the folder's first page. Would the man *ever* get around to the business at hand?

Hawthorne peered over the top of the folder. "So according to this, it appears our project has been blessed with the services of two of our respective nations' hottest new intelligence-gathering and analysis stars." He proceeded to enumerate in a monotone voice the highlights of each man's background and career. These included Alec's German-Jewish upbringing in Leipzig, his vital contributions to the British-Canadian capture of a Nazi *Enigma* encoding machine, and the two men's collaboration during the recent Rome mission for which Joshua had earned his award.

Finally closing the folder and placing it back on his desk, Hawthorne reached into his jacket pocket for a pipe which he proceeded to refill and light. He stared at Joshua and Alec for a long moment before blowing out a thick cloud of smoke. "Well, gentlemen, if you two are supposedly the best your organizations can lend me, then I suppose I should count myself lucky. Only time will tell. But one thing I can assure you both—your next mission will be a lot more demanding than anything you've experienced before. Are you ready to see what we have in mind?"

"We're ready, sir," Joshua and Alec said in near unison.

Hawthorne rose from his chair. "Good. Then follow me into our projection room, and I'll show you the layout."

As the men followed him down the corridor, Alec leaned over and whispered to Joshua behind his cupped hand. "Not sure we're going to make lunch in time. My fiancée's mother will probably tell her to break off our engagement."

Joshua chuckled. "Relax, lovebird. They'll wait for us."

Seated in wooden armchairs on either side of the 35mm projector near the center of the darkened room, Joshua and Alec sipped from cups of tea provided by Colonel Hawthorne's assistant.

"Please excuse these obligatory shots of Hitler in his heyday," Hawthorne apologized as he clicked through the first ten slides of early Nazi rallies and military triumphs. "Top brass wants every presentation to open with a reminder of the devil driving our business here. Hitler is still out there, and he still holds sway over Germany's determination to keep on fighting against all odds. That's why everything we do must ultimately lead to the eradication of his nation's capacity to continue making war."

The eleventh slide caused Joshua to sit up straight and focus. A huge map of the European war theater filled the entirety of the wall-to-wall screen. Color-shaded regions indicated the amazing progress the Allied armies had made since June, shrinking the periphery of the Third Reich closer to Germany's original borders. Within those borders, the map was marked with small triangular symbols colored either blue, yellow, red, or green.

"And *this* is *our* part of the job, gentlemen," Hawthorne said. "Each of those triangles represents a likely location of a major Nazi secret weapon research and development or production facility. Our task is to put an end to their operation and to exploit them for our own benefit.

"SHAEF Headquarters in Versailles—where you'll both be heading next—has pulled together over three thousand scientific and technical experts from the US and Britain. They've been organized into a number of teams who'll be following closely behind our soldiers as they advance into German territory. As the targets become located and positively identified, special SHAEF T-1 military units will swoop in to disarm and secure them. They'll soon be followed by the scientific teams, who'll immediately start their work of translating and interpreting the treasure trove of documents they're bound to find. Not to mention trying to locate and apprehend the German scientists who the documents will identify."

Alec spoke up. "What if the Russian army arrives at some of these places before the US or the Brits, sir?"

"The answer's simple, Benjamin. It means we lose them, and the Russians gain them. And from everything we know about the Soviets, they're certainly not going to share anything they stumble across with their western allies. Just like us, they see the capture and exploitation of German science and scientists as a huge benefit to their own country's plans for enhancing its world power."

"What do those green triangles represent, Colonel?"

"Glad you asked, Lieutenant Peters. Those are the sites identified in connection with the Nazis' V-1 buzz-bomb and V-2 ballistic missile— Hitler's Vengeance weapons. As you're obviously aware, they've been wreaking substantial havoc and terror on our British cities over the past few months—especially the V-2. Let's take a closer look at those on the next slide. There we are. What do you notice?"

"The big triangle next to the island just off Germany's northeast Baltic coast," Joshua ventured. "That's Peenemünde, right?"

"Correct. The original site for V-2 rocket development, assembly and live-fire testing starting back in 1942. Over five hundred of our British bombers made a concerted raid on it a year later and did a lot of damage, forcing much of the production capability to be transferred to an underground site near Nordhausen in central Germany." Hawthorne pointed to the exact spot on the map with his pencil and tapped it firmly. "That's where you see the other large green triangle displayed here."

"What about those smaller green triangles scattered all over the Dutch coast and northwestern Germany?" Alec asked.

"Those are identified launch sites—ones that our armies have yet to capture. Many of them are mobile and it's almost impossible to identify a precise location. The V-2s lift off from these sites and fly at five times the speed of sound. Takes less than seven minutes for one to reach London with its two-thousand-pound warhead and cause an explosion that can be felt up to twenty miles in all directions. You've already seen the panic these have been creating the past couple of months with conventional warheads, but can you imagine if Hitler decides to replace those with biological or chemical warheads? Many people are wondering what's been preventing him from doing just that.

"At any rate, hopefully these sites, just like the ones in northern France and Belgium, will soon be overrun and neutralized by our advancing troops. That would still leave the big production facilities to be captured and secured. It's doubtful we'll beat the Russians to Peenemünde, but the other location near Nordhausen seems well within our reach. *And it is that location, gentlemen, that will be the focus of your next mission.*"

A long silence ensued as Hawthorne allowed his last statement to sink in. "What're our main objectives, sir?" Joshua asked finally.

"You'll be receiving more specifics on those once you arrive in Versailles next Tuesday. But in general terms, your first objective will be to pave the way for one of the Anglo-American CIOS[*] scientific teams that SHAEF has organized specifically for the capture of the V-2 missile and the technology secrets behind it."

"Excuse me, Colonel, but what do you mean by 'pave the way'?"

"Means you'll be the first to check out and verify initial reports from frontline soldiers that a V-2 production-related facility has been discovered. You'll work together to make a preliminary assessment and confirm whether the site is legitimate enough to warrant one of the T-1 military units going in and securing it followed by a CIOS V-2 technology team coming in and going to work."

"And the second objective, sir?" Alec pressed.

"The second is a bit more complicated, Benjamin."

Hawthorne clicked to the next slide. A scratched-up photograph revealed a team of over ten German men. One man in the center of the front row was bedecked in a black Nazi SS uniform and flanked by a high-ranking regular army officer. The rest were either civilians or lower ranking army men. All stood grinning in front of a V-2 missile perched on a launch platform.

"Take a good look, gentlemen. Right there you see the brain trust behind the success of the V-2 miracle weapon. I know you're already familiar with him, Lieutenant Peters. That's Dr. Wernher von Braun, the architect and chief designer, in the center. Major General Walter Dornberger, the original director of V-2 development and operations projects for the Wehrmacht, is on his left."

---

* Combined Intelligence Operations Subcommittee

"I'd heard of von Braun, but I had no idea he was SS," said Alec. "Thought he was just a great scientist, doing his level best to serve his country."

"It's a strange situation," Hawthorne agreed. "And something that will have to be addressed by our allied judicial units. They will be in charge of deciding the fate of any accused Nazi war criminals. "Be that as it may . . ."

The colonel proceeded to click through individual, close-up photos of each man on the V-2 team. "Your second objective is to liaison between SHAEF and the independent British and US teams that are being formed to track down, interrogate, and attempt to recruit the future services of these men and their closest associates. Hopefully *before* the Russians can get to them."

"*Independent* British and US teams? Why aren't we all working together?" Joshua asked.

Colonel Hawthorne paused to take a long sip from his teacup.

"Each country wants to be the first to apprehend and speak to the V-2 men so they can recruit their services for their own national interests and purposes. One of your main challenges will be to always keep your SHAEF-hats on, and not let these independent national teams interfere with, or push around, our own T-1 and CIOS teams with some wild-eyed requests for cooperation on their terms. But don't worry, you'll hear much more about this once you arrive in France."

Hawthorne clicked through the remaining slides, none of which raised any significant issues. "Well, this is all I have for your mission introduction, gentlemen. If there are no further questions, we'll call it a day and you should prepare to depart for Versailles on Monday evening."

"Sir," Joshua said. "I was wondering if you could click back to that second to last closeup photo of the individual rocket team members?"

"Certainly."

Joshua stared at the photo. The man looked extraordinarily familiar. "Who did you say that was?"

"That's a civilian university consultant named Erich Neumann. Not too much known about him, other than he appears to be one of von Braun's chief technical advisors. Not clear what his specialty expertise is. Any reason for your interest?"

Erich Neumann... Klara's father! I knew it!

"I'm not sure, Colonel," Joshua said. This didn't seem like the right time to be revealing his personal connection to the man. "Something intriguing about him, but I can't quite put my finger on it."

Actually, of course he could. As he stared at Erich Neumann's photo, Joshua Peters imagined himself one day asking the Nazi rocket man for his daughter's hand.

CHAPTER 43

London, England
November 25, 1944

Emerging with Alec from the building after the briefing, Joshua squinted to make out a squadron of twenty Spitfires traversing the sun-drenched, mid-morning sky. Several passersby on the sidewalk had already paused to take in the sight. One little boy, towed by his mother, jumped up and down, alternately pointing and clapping his hands. An elderly man behind them looked up, raised his fist in the air and shook it in an expression of solidarity and long-repressed pride.

Londoners had good reason for such display, Joshua thought. After years of sacrifice and suffering, the smell of victory was in the air.

"Wonder where they're headed," Joshua mused.

Alec raised his hand to hail a taxi. "Probably going to link up over the channel with some of our Typhoon and Mosquito fighter-bombers. Then they'll go together to pound hell out of a couple of those portable V-2 launch sites in Holland… that is, if they can find one that the Krauts didn't manage to dismantle and camouflage in the woods behind some innocent-looking Dutch windmill."

Joshua laughed. "Never underestimate Nazi efficiency, right?"

A taxi pulled to the side of the road.

"Where to, sirs?" the cabbie asked.

"Marquis of Granby Inn on New Cross Road in Deptford," Joshua replied.

"Deptford?"

"Yes, that's right."

The cabbie hesitated. "A lot of road repair going on between here and there, sir. Bomb damage, you know. Probably best if you catch the tram from Victoria Station."

"Thanks, good point," Joshua said. "Will two pounds get us to the station?"

The cabbie nodded, then stepped out to open the rear door. Joshua and Alec climbed into the back seat and rested their briefcases on their laps.

Returning to his own seat, the cabbie checked his rearview mirror and eased the vehicle into the light traffic on Horse Guards Avenue. After turning onto Whitehall Road and settling into the flow, he spoke again, as if desiring to strike some common ground with his important-looking passengers. "I hear the Marquis serves up some of the best bangers and mash in the entire southeast London area, and the brew's not bad, either."

"Not only that," Alec said. "They're right down the street from the big Woolworth's store. After lunch with my fiancée and her mother, we'll encourage them to go shopping while my friend and I enjoy a few more rounds in peace and quiet."

"Now *that* sounds like a jolly pleasant afternoon! All things considered, sir."

Joshua reclined back in the seat and closed his eyes, contemplating the prospect of two more relaxing days and nights in London preceding the start of the mission. No doubt, Alec's future mother-in-law would go all out to make sure her two favorite soldier-boys were treated to a fabulous display of Jewish cuisine and hospitality at the family residence in the Lewisham suburb tonight. It would all be designed to send them off to France with lasting memories and cravings to spur them home as soon as possible, safe and sound.

Indeed, if Joshua's first celebratory meal shared with Alec, his eighteen-year-old fiancée Laura Ziegler, and her widowed mother Hannah on the Saturday evening following the men's return from their Rome mission was any indication, then he could count on being pampered and catered to like an Old Testament king. Of course, just like that time, the expectation would be for Alec and Joshua to *first* accompany Laura and Hannah to the 5:30 p.m. Sabbath service at the Zieglers' synagogue.

An elbow in the side interrupted Joshua's dozing reverie. "Hey, Peters, wake up. Is that what I think it is?"

Joshua blinked to reorient himself, noticing that the taxi had pulled into the departure lane at Victoria Station. He looked over to see Alec with his head half out his open window, pointing over some bomb-demolished buildings at something in the sky.

"*Driver,*" Alec shouted. "*Pull over now!*" The cabbie obliged. All three men quickly exited the vehicle and stood on the sidewalk, observing the incredible sight. About a mile away and a couple of thousand or so feet up, a small, dark object raced through the sky. The object resembled a miniature airplane with short, stubby wings and a large, cylindrical pod attached to the top of the fuselage, just in front of the tail. It seemed to be emitting a strange, rapid pulsating sound—like an old car that had lost its exhaust muffler and was trying to make it up a steep hill.

"*Doodlebug!*" the cabbie cried out the popular nickname as soon as he recognized the object for what it was: a pilotless, Nazi V-1 buzz-bomb. "By Jove, we haven't been seeing many of those lately."

"There's *part* of your reason," Alec observed, pointing at two elliptical-winged Spitfires that were converging from behind and to either side of the V-1's tail.

"Must be the newer model Spit. Older ones couldn't keep up like that," Joshua said.

Just then, both fighters let loose a volley of tracers that quickly found their way onto the body of the V-1. Flames shot from the tail area. Within seconds, the black bug exploded into myriad pieces that rained onto the rooftops below.

Joshua, Alec, and the cabbie joined the cheer that erupted from the crowd of excited bystanders.

"Another one of Adolf's Vengeance weapons bites the dust!" someone shouted triumphantly.

"Don't get too cocky. His second round's just getting started, and we all know now what those can do," someone else retorted.

All too true, Joshua realized. While the thousands of V-1 strikes launched against Britain since last June were indeed tapering off thanks to improved air defense measures, Hitler's second V-weapon flew far too high and too fast to be tracked by radar and shot down by anti-aircraft guns or planes. In sufficient numbers, the V-2 rocket could overwhelm British defenses, delivering death and destruction from the skies without warning. *What more motivation do I need for our V-2 hunting mission?*

Alec clapped him on the shoulder. "Enough for one morning, old boy? Ready for lunch with some enjoyable company? Come on, let's go catch the tram."

"Ah, there they are." Alec pointed to a corner table in the dining room of the Marquis of Granby Inn, where Laura Ziegler and her mother Hannah were waving to catch the men's attention. When they arrived, Laura stood to hug and kiss Alec with unabashed fervor as Hannah beamed her obvious approval.

She patted the seat next to her. "You sit here next to me, Joshua. You can keep me company while the children indulge in their love-whispers," she said, casting a mock, stern glance at Alec.

Alec took up the challenge. "I promise Laura and I will behave ourselves, Ima!"

"Hmmm, we shall see. So, tell me, Joshua," Hannah pressed. "What have you and Lt. Benjamin been up to this morning that would make you fifteen minutes late for your lunch appointment?"

Joshua winced. "Well, besides receiving instructions regarding our upcoming mission in France, we encountered a small incident on the way here." He went on to describe the V-1 scene.

"Oh!" Laura exclaimed. "Thank God no one was hurt. Do you think we'll be seeing the last of those horrible things soon?"

"We can always hope," Alec said. "But with Hitler's regime starting to collapse, he may well resort to some extreme measures. Even beyond what we've already seen."

"Of course he will," Hannah agreed. "If I had as much blatant evil to hide from the world's discovery as that man apparently does, I'd probably do the same thing."

Alec's face tightened. Rumors of Nazi extermination camps and atrocities against Jews and other ethnic groups were circulating more and more among the British populace. Only time would tell whether they were true or not, but Joshua couldn't help but notice the barely suppressed rage and anger that mere mention of the rumors alone seemed to provoke in his friend. Alec had once confessed to Joshua that the memory of anti-Jewish sentiment he'd experienced during his college days at Oxford University still stung. But even worse was the thought of Hitler exploiting and stoking such sentiment throughout Germany for the purpose of justifying the mass murder of Alec's fellow Jews. *That* was enough to arouse a beast-like fury on an entirely differ-ent scale within his soul.

Before Alec could comment, the waiter appeared and took the orders, after which the foursome engaged in lighter conversation until the meals arrived.

"Well," Hannah said after the server had departed, "I think it would be nice if Lt. Peters here gives thanks for all of us, especially in view of how God saved the two of you and others from yet another fatal Doodlebug strike this morning."

"Ima, Joshua's not Jewish," Alec said. "Should we be putting him on the spot?"

"Well, his first name is certainly Jewish," Hannah countered. "And anyway, I'm not asking him to recite the *Hamotzi*, for Heaven's sake. So, what difference does it make if he's a Jew, or a Christian, or anything else when it comes to thanking God for his deliverance?"

Alec grinned. "You've got me there, Ima. What do you think, Joshua?"

"Never thought I'd get such an invite in this elite company. I'm honored!"

As the meal and conversation progressed over the next half hour, Joshua couldn't stop himself from stealing occasional glances at Alec and Laura. The girl had large, dark brown eyes, shoulder-length jet black hair, and an intelligent, fun-loving personality that seemed the perfect complement to Alec's. Who could fault Alec for proposing marriage less than three months after their first date? Why not jump before some other handsome, well-heeled suitor attempted to steal her away while Alec was off fighting for his country?

The man certainly seems to have found his soulmate, Joshua thought with a certain amount of envy. He wished that his own soulmate, Klara Neumann, could be here with him now to enjoy the company.

Alec poured a final round of tea for everyone. Winking discreetly at Joshua, he proceeded to initiate the planned diversion tactic.

"I suppose you ladies are aware of the big sale going on at Woolworth's?"

Laura's eyes lit up. "Oh, that's right! Ima, I heard they've got a big new stock of cookware to sell. You know we've been wanting some good-quality replacements for the past three years, what with all the war shortages. And with tonight's dinner to prepare for the boys, maybe this is our perfect opportunity?"

Hannah thought for a moment. "Well, given your plans to hold the wedding soon after Lt. Benjamin returns from his mission, I suppose I could pick up some new tablecloths and decorations for the reception while we're at it." She cocked her head and frowned at Alec. "I presume you boys will be happy to accompany us there?"

Alec cleared his throat. "Actually, Ima, this might be a good time for Joshua and me to stay and discuss a few matters concerning our upcoming mission. You know we only have a couple of days before—"

"*Ha!*" Hannah cried triumphantly. "I knew it. Laura, they're just like your dear father... God rest his soul. They're going to stay here to smoke and drink while we women do the hard work of standing in line, looking for defects in the merchandise, and haggling over prices. Well, if they're expecting decent treatment tonight, they'd better be sober when we come back here, ready to take us to the synagogue at 5 p.m.!"

Alec sat back and crossed his arms in mock indignation. "*Ima*, how could you even *think* your boys couldn't stay sober for an hour!" After the laughter died down, Alec paid the check, then rose to escort Laura and Hannah to the exit.

Watching Alec walk out the dining room door with his arm wrapped around his fiancée's waist, Joshua felt a strange queasiness in the pit of his stomach.

Something did not seem right.

Chapter 44

Twelve Miles Southwest of The Hague (Holland)
November 25, 1944

The last thing Professor Erich Neumann would have wished for his fiftieth birthday was to be ordered by Colonel Bremmer to deliver a speech on behalf of the V-2 rocket men at today's celebratory launch event in Holland. After the atrocity he'd been manipulated to participate in at the Nordhausen production facility, Erich's heart simply was not into this ostensibly joyous occasion. Still, orders were orders, and for the sake of his career and his family, he would do his best to follow them.

"Think of what you are about to accomplish!" Erich exhorted the mixed group of technicians, scientists, German soldiers, SS officers, and local Dutch Nazi party officials who had assembled in front of the sandbagged launch control bunker. Standing beside Erich, Bremmer nodded his approval.

"In twenty minutes," Erich continued. "Training and Experimental Battery 444 of the Waffen SS Division for Retribution will have the distinct honor of conducting *the 250th launch* of a V-2 ballistic missile against enemies of the Reich. Gentlemen, you have all worked incredibly hard under the constant aerial threats to erect this mobile launch platform in such a short time. And even though they can't be here with us today, on their behalf, I can state that Dr. Wernher von Braun and the other rocket men could not be prouder of you. And neither could I!"

The crowd erupted in cheers and wild applause.

"Just as we're proud of you and von Braun's entire V-2 design and development team, Professor!" someone shouted.

"Here's to the V-2 rocket men!" yelled another.

Immediately, the entire crowd went silent, as if a vile curse had just been uttered instead of a mock toast of celebration.

Erich blushed, aware that he had just made a serious error, one that could result in him being led away to a concentration camp. In Third Reich official celebration protocol, it was always one's Nazi military superiors who must be acknowledged as the *first* wishing to convey their pride and thanks. Erich should have known better than to start his speech by calling attention to the heroic, god-like status which many of those gathered attached to von Braun, Dornberger, and their key assistants like Erich who had long worked closely with them. This was especially true in light of Himmler's recent suspicions about the rocket men's commitment to Nazi military priorities.

Erich looked uncertainly at Colonel Bremmer, who stared at the ground. Out of the corner of his eye, Erich noticed Brigadier General Hartmann, the ranking SS officer, approaching from the side. His expression indicated he was not at all pleased by what had just taken place.

Hartmann stood beside Erich, draping his arm over the latter's shoulders. He smiled and nodded arrogantly at the silent assembly for a few seconds before speaking.

"What Professor Neumann neglected to mention in his enthusiasm, is that there are *other* men of note who are also very proud of you. May I personally convey the admiration and thanks of SS Major General Kammler who, as you know, was appointed by Reichsführer Heinrich Himmler as V-2 Commissioner and Director of Operations last August. And most importantly, may I express the thanks and best wishes from the one man to whom all assembled here today owe their never-ending gratitude, allegiance, and devotion: our beloved Führer himself, *Adolf Hitler!*"

Dropping his arm from Erich's shoulders, Hartmann stood at attention, clicked his heels, and raised his right arm in the fascist salute, prompting everyone in the assembly to do the same.

"*Sieg Heil!*" Hartmann shouted.

"*Sieg Heil!*" all responded in unison.

General Hartmann glanced at his watch. "We launch in less than fifteen minutes. Everyone to their stations. Remember that just prior to liftoff, you'll each be handed a glass of the best French champagne to toast what we hope will be the full success of this momentous event."

As the men filed into or behind the bunker to assume their roles as either operators or spectators, Hartmann pulled Erich aside.

"Professor," he said quietly. "You know I could have you arrested for your failure to pay proper homage to our *true* national leaders in front of all these men here. Trust me, the SS is very aware that von Braun and Dornberger still begrudge our takeover of the V-2 program from the Wehrmacht last March, and that they both still desire all the personal honors and limelight for themselves. It would also seem from that little speech you just gave that, after serving so long as one of von Braun's chief consultants, your own sympathies may have become a bit misplaced."

He turned to Bremmer. "Colonel, did you not instruct this man on the proper etiquette for addressing an assembly such as this?"

Bremmer clicked his heels. "My deepest apologies, General. I had assumed that Professor Neumann would already be acquainted with the expectation that he would never fail to *first* demonstrate the respect and acknowledgements due his SS superiors. I was quite obviously mistaken."

Sweat beads formed on Erich's brow. He had come to hate the SS, but he realized well how they controlled the careers and even the lives of civilians working under them. "Please forgive me, General. I am indeed an admirer of Dr. von Braun and proud of what our team has accomplished. But I was sadly mistaken in neglecting to express my loyalty first and foremost to the Führer and our SS superiors for making it all possible."

Hartmann stared at him coldly for several long seconds before his face relaxed and broke into a congenial smile. He clapped Erich on the shoulder. "Well, Professor, no irreparable harm done. Anyway, why should we cast a cloud over the beautiful event about to take place? And besides that, Colonel Bremmer here told me that it's your *birthday*! Could you have timed it for a better day in V-2 history? Come on, let's all go into the bunker and celebrate it all together!"

Erich took a step back and saluted. "I am most grateful for your understanding and kindness, General. With your permission, before joining you I'd like to spend a few moments here alone to admire our bird before she takes off."

Hartmann smiled. "I can certainly understand that sentiment, Neumann. We'll have your champagne glass filled and ready for you when you come inside. You, of all people, deserve it!"

Letting out a deep sigh of relief as General Hartmann walked away with Bremmer, Erich turned to face the launching platform that had been constructed at the end of the railway spur two hundred feet away. Perched on top, the fourteen-ton, forty-seven-foot-long, black-and-white-painted behemoth stood majestically against the backdrop of today's clear blue sky.

Minutes from now, an inferno of burning liquid rocket fuel would blast out the bottom of the V-2, powering the massive vehicle into its flight toward London. Seconds after liftoff, the rocket's automatic guidance system—which Erich had worked hard with von Braun, Dornberger, and others to develop and test at Peenemünde—would take over from the ground control operators. With its destination programmed into the onboard computer, the rocket's gyroscopes would continuously track the craft's position in three dimensions. If the gyros detected any deviations in course due to air turbulence, engine thrust irregularities or the like, then rudders fitted to fins attached to the side of the rocket near the tail would automatically correct its heading and trajectory. If all went well, the rocket would travel along a roughly parabolic arc, reaching its highest point more than fifty miles above the Earth's surface before descending at supersonic speed toward its ground target up to 130 miles away from the launch point. The total transit time would be less than six minutes.

No wonder our V-2 technology is the envy of the world, Erich thought, pride billowing in his chest. The capabilities of *German ballistic missiles are at least twenty years ahead of any other nation.*

Unfortunately, as he well knew, V-2 accuracy was an issue. Even in the best of cases there could be no certainty until days later (*if and when* intel was ever received from the few trustworthy German agents operating in London) as to where exactly a V-2 might have landed, and what level of damage, injuries, and fatalities it may have caused.

For that reason and more, Erich Neumann had always been able to maintain a certain degree of emotional detachment from the numerous V-2 launches he'd observed. After all, with so many German cities being decimated by random, indiscriminate, Allied carpet-bombing attacks, why should Germans experience attacks of conscience for delivering a barrage of imprecise V-2 revenge strikes against English cities?

And besides all that, Erich reasoned, he had another good excuse for his lack of personal guilt over the effects of V-2 strikes. It was this: he knew in his heart that he had *never desired* the development of the V-2 as a weapon of war, but rather as the means to achieve a more noble vision for humanity. That vision, which von Braun had articulated so eloquently in private to his close associates, was for the V-2 to become the prototype for future mammoth rockets that would transport men into space, the Moon, the planets, and beyond.

Like von Braun, Dornberger, and most of the rest of the original V-2 design team, Erich considered himself, above all else, a *scientist.* All other career affiliations and political or military goals were distractions, things that a serious scientist sometimes had to take on if he had any hopes of seeing his vision and goals realized for the ultimate benefit of mankind. And so, if developing the V-2 required him to accept certain unsavory roles and to participate in the *temporary misuse* of the missile's awesome capabilities for unsavory war purposes, wasn't it all justified by the V-2's tremendous long-term potential for space exploration and colonization?

"Professor Neumann!" cried a technician from the bunker's entrance. "We're ten minutes away. Everyone needs to take their stations now, sir."

Erich took one last look at the object of his professional pride, then turned and walked toward the bunker.

Upon entering, an unexpected scene greeted him. Instead of the typical crew of three operators seated at the table of launch monitoring instruments, only two were in their places. In between them, an empty chair had been pulled back, awaiting its occupant. Behind the chair stood General Hartmann and Colonel Bremmer flanked by a contingent of junior SS officers and at least a dozen of the civilian technicians, scientists, and Nazi party officials. All held filled champagne glasses in the air, raising them in Erich's direction with delighted grins. In front of the table and just off to the side, a military photographer prepared his apparatus for what was certain to be a memorable photo in only a few minutes.

"Happy Birthday, Professor Neumann!"

General Hartmann patted the top of the empty chair. "Come, Professor, take your proper place. On this special day, who besides you should have the honor of pushing the button that will send our fearsome beast into the lair of the English dragon?"

Erich gulped in astonishment. A strange, sick feeling in the pit of his stomach took hold as he stood frozen, staring at the empty chair. Hartmann's grin faded. "Is something wrong, Professor? Why do you hesitate? No second thoughts about doing your duty, I hope?"

Erich smiled awkwardly and made his way around the table to the chair. He sat down, immediately rewarded with applause and a full glass of champagne from Bremmer. As the final two minutes ticked down and the surrounding conversation tapered off, he stared out the bunker's single window at the vehicle awaiting his final signal that would send it off on its lethal journey. For the first time, Erich imagined his own precious family being on the receiving end of the strike, not knowing that they had but six minutes to live. Suddenly, the advancement of science had ceased to sound like an adequate alibi for his role in V-2 design, development, and—as of now, for the first time—operation.

He looked over at the clock on the sidewall of the bunker. 1:19 p.m. One minute to go. A tense silence had taken over the entire room. Ten seconds...

"Prepare to launch," the lead operator on Erich's right said quietly.

"Prepare to celebrate," shouted General Hartmann.

Erich held the champagne glass in his left hand, his right index finger poised on top of the circular red launch button.

"Countdown—begin now!"

All in the room shouted out in unison: *"Five... Four... Three... Two... One . . ."*

Erich pressed the button. Smoke and flame shot from the V-2's tail, followed by a deafening rumble that caused the bunker to shake as if it were about to explode. The bird began to rise slowly off the pad. Everything looked good...

"Vengeance is ours! Raise your glass and smile at the camera, gentlemen!" Hartmann yelled.

As he complied, a strange thought flashed through Erich's mind that was part of a simple little English ditty he'd once heard as a child:

"Up, up, up it goes. And where it lands, nobody knows . . ."

(Marquis of Granby Inn, Deptford, England)

Joshua watched as Alec purchased two more drinks at the bar and headed back to the table.

So far, their time alone together had been well-spent, discussing the challenges they were likely to encounter on their upcoming mission and how they should deal with them. Certainly, it was a topic that Laura and her mother should be thankful they didn't have to engage in.

Joshua glanced at his watch: 12:26 p.m., London time. He assumed by now the women had found the cookware at Woolworth's they were hoping to find, and they would soon be showing up at the Inn's entrance.

"Joshua," Alec said as he placed the drinks on the table and started to sit down once again. "You know, I was just thinking—"

Suddenly, an odd, *c-rrr-umph* noise—something felt in the gut more than heard—whooshed from the floor. He looked at Joshua in wide-eyed astonishment. "What the—?" The men stared at each other, frozen.

Moments later, a tremendous blast originating from somewhere outside shattered the large dining room windows facing the street. Customers, including Joshua and Alec, who had not been injured or incapacitated by the glass sought cover under the tables or crawled behind the bar. It was a full minute before anyone could get their bearings as pieces of ceiling and masonry rained to the floor, dust rising throughout the room.

Alec coughed violently for at least a minute. He looked up at Joshua, kneeling next to him. "Are you all right?" Joshua asked softly. "Was *that* what I think it—"

"*Laura and Hannah!*" Alec cried out. He jumped to his feet and raced toward the exit, Joshua immediately behind. They rushed out of the building and stared down New Cross Road. A couple of hundred yards away, a massive cloud of billowing smoke mushroomed up from the rubble of what used to be an imposing four-story building across the street from the railway station. The mesmerizing sight confirmed Joshua's worst fear: Woolworth's had been obliterated by a V-2 strike.

Making their way down the street, the horrors were too much for Joshua's mind to fully take in. Bodies lay everywhere, some with their clothes singed off and their flesh charred. Cars were mangled wrecks, on their sides or upside down. Telephone poles lay across rooftops. A tram had stopped in the middle of the road; from what he could see through the windows, all the passengers were still in their seats and motionless—most likely killed by the shock waves. The street looked like it had been literally hosed down in a shower of blood, with body parts strewn across the road.

As he and Alec drew nearer to the V-2's impact site, Joshua was appalled to see men placing sheets of corrugated steel along the gutters to cover what was left of people and the blood that seeped from beneath. Several of the aid-givers called for their help in extricating victims from the debris, but the two had time only to pause briefly and offer their sympathies before continuing on to enter the shattered, caved-in, smoking remains of the former department store.

Ten minutes of frantic searching in the rubble yielded no sign of Laura or Hannah.

"Do you think they could have made it out?" Alec asked, his voice betraying the hopelessness of the situation.

Joshua looked around. "There's one section over there toward the rear corner where we haven't checked yet."

The men moved toward the area that Joshua had spotted where some other people were already searching. Splitting up to more quickly cover the area, each began the arduous process of sifting through rubble to detect signs of life.

Joshua had almost given up hope of finding anything in his vicinity when he saw a ghostly hand extended from under a pile of bricks and stone near the rear wall. Working as fast as he could, he finally succeeded in partially uncovering the victim. The sight of poor Hannah Ziegler, her chest crushed and her face mangled to an almost unrecognizable state, caused him to turn away and gag. Recovering after several seconds, he turned toward Alec to call him over, then thought better of it. Alec did not need to see this. Not yet. He removed his jacket and covered Hannah's partially exposed body as best he could.

He'd just closed his eyes and begun a quick prayer for Hannah when a howl of dismay arose from the area Alec was searching. He rushed over to find Alec and another man bending over what looked like a fallen wooden beam covered with mortar and other debris.

Pinned under the beam which lay across her chest, Laura Ziegler lay staring wide-eyed at the ceiling. Blood trickled from her mouth. She appeared to be alive and gasping for air, but just barely. Together, the three men strained to remove the beam, only succeeding when two others joined their effort.

Alec knelt beside his fiancée and held her hand in both of his. It was obvious she was not going to survive. Tears streamed down his face as he bent to whisper something in her ear and kiss her on the cheek. She managed to smile and nod slightly, looking at him lovingly before her eyes rolled back and she slipped away.

Joshua put his arm around his friend's shoulders as Alec wept violently, never releasing Laura's hand. Finally, Alec managed to gather himself. After placing Laura's hand on her chest, he stood and looked at Joshua. His whole demeanor had changed. No more tears. His face was set like stone, the fire in his eyes portending an internal volcano of long repressed, revenge-craving fury about to erupt.

PART VI

RED TRAP CLOSING

CHAPTER 45

Countryside southeast of Nordhausen, Germany
April 2, 1945
(Four months later)

In the backyard of her parents' new, SS-provided country cottage thirty miles from the underground V-2 factory, Klara leaned on her hoe, staring at her mother on the far side of the vegetable garden. Mama had dropped her own hoe on the ground and was leaning forward with her hands on her knees. She seemed to be trying to catch her breath.

"Mama, are you all right?"

Gertrude Neumann straightened slowly and waved. "I'm fine, dear. Just my sore back acting up again. After I dig up a few more of these puny spuds, I'll be through. Are you almost finished?"

"Almost. Why don't you just stop now, Mama? We already have more than enough potatoes to last two weeks, and you're not looking well."

"Don't worry, Liebchen. I'm really feeling much better today, and I need to make sure we'll have enough for Herr Keller and his wife as well as ourselves. Come on, let's get this over with before the sun sets and go warm ourselves by the fire."

Klara shook her head and sighed as she watched Mama resume her spading. When she'd arrived from Berlin last week on her second solo visit to Nordhausen following Vati's disturbing letter last November, Klara couldn't help but notice the marked deterioration in her mother's appearance. Standing next to Vati on the train station platform as they awaited Klara's arrival, Mama looked sad, her face drawn and pale. She'd clung to Vati's arm as Klara approached them. What a change from her previous visit when Mama had rushed to embrace her.

Klara was certain her mother was suffering from yet another flareup of her stomach ailment. This one had no doubt been triggered by her stress over Vati's sudden and unexpected departure for southern Germany last night along with five hundred other V-2 rocket scientists and supporting technicians. The men had been ordered by General Kammler to immediately evacuate the Nordhausen area *without* their families to prevent their vital technical knowledge and skills from falling into the hands of the rapidly approaching American, British, and Russian armies. Vati had tried to assure his wife and Klara that the separation was only temporary, but his words rang hollow during their last conversation in the cottage's living room yesterday afternoon...

"Gertrude, we've been promised by General Kammler that another special train will be ready by next week to bring all the families down to reunite with us in Bavaria. We'll all be protected there in the Führer's Alpine Fortress, where his best troops are being stationed with many months of food and supplies."

Mama was having none of it. "*Protected?*" she scoffed. "What does *that* mean? Protected like our fellow German citizens living near the ever-collapsing eastern and western fronts? Protected like our major cities that are being devastated by those Allied bombing raids? If *that's* the kind of protection we can expect in the Führer's magnificent fortress, then we may as well simply remain here and take our chances."

Vati sighed and his head sagged. What could he say? From what he'd admitted to her in private yesterday, Klara knew her father had given up hope that Germany could avoid a catastrophic defeat. The massive Ardennes Counteroffensive—which Hitler had launched mid-December in a desperate attempt to slice through the American and British lines to the Belgian coast—had been crushed by January. Over the next two months, the western Allied armies swept across the Rhine River into Germany while the Russians continued to roll up German-occupied territory in Poland and the Baltic countries. All Allied forces were now pushing relentlessly toward the heart of the country, with Berlin as the ultimate goal. The V-2 campaign had failed in the end to stem the tide. The last rocket had been fired last week, and advance US armored reconnaissance units had been spotted two days ago only thirty miles west of Nordhausen.

"We really have no choice in the matter, Gertrude. If I disobey Kammler's order and refuse to evacuate with von Braun and the others, the SS will certainly track me down. And if I'm faced with a desertion of duty charge, you know the consequences for all of us could be unimaginable."

"But Erich," Gertrude protested, her voice breaking. "With Klara having to return to Berlin to work at her hospital in two days, I'll be here alone. What if that second train that General Kammler has promised for the families never comes?"

Klara threw her arms around her mother's shoulders. "Mama, there is no way I am going to leave you here by yourself. Vati has already explained the situation to me, and I've decided to call the Charité tomorrow and tell them I'm resigning my position so I can stay with you here."

"Oh, daughter, no! You can't do that! You'll—"

"Hush now, Mama. Of course I can. And I will."

After a long moment of stunned silence, Vati reached over and grasped Klara's arm. "Thank you, Liebchen," he mouthed. His eyes were filled with tears.

"So, what do we do after you leave tonight, Erich?" Mama asked. "Simply wait here for a phone call from someone that our rescue train is here and ready to leave on a moment's notice, then race thirty miles to the Nordhausen station with all our luggage? Who will come to pick us up?"

Vati nodded. "I've already arranged for you and Klara to be picked up the day after tomorrow by my technical assistant and good friend, Johann Keller. He was not on the evacuation list, and he and his wife have a three-bedroom house in the town. They've graciously offered to shelter the two of you in their home, so you'll have some company and be able to make it to the station far more easily with their help whenever the time comes."

"If *ever* the time comes," Mama muttered. "And what if it doesn't? I trust Kammler to follow through on his promises even less than I trust the Führer, which is not saying much. How are Klara and I supposed to reunite with you *then*?"

Vati focused on the table for several moments. His face wore a pained expression, as if he were still debating with himself what the right answer should be.

"In that case, Gertrude," he said finally. "You should both follow the instructions of Herr Keller, who has my complete confidence. Depending on the way the battle lines progress as the Americans advance, he will know if it's better to remain in the town or perhaps move to a more remote, secure location that he's been preparing for both of our families. He'll tell you more about that when the time is right, and I have the directions. As soon as I can free myself from our SS overseers down south, rest assured, I will come looking for all of you. You're bound to be in one of those two places."

Mama asked the unavoidable questions. "And how are you going to 'free' yourself from the SS, Erich? What if you can't? What if they decide to . . ." Her voice trailed off and tears rolled down her cheeks once again.

Unable or unwilling to even attempt providing coherent answers, Vati simply rose from his seat and walked around the table to take his wife into his arms...

No sooner had Klara turned away to resume her own potato-harvesting than she heard what sounded like a soft moan behind her.

"*Mama!*"

Gertrude was kneeling on the ground, her hands keeping her from pitching forward onto her face. She appeared to be gasping for air.

Klara dropped her spade and ran over to help. She placed one arm around her mother's back and grasped her shoulder with the other. "Mama, what's wrong? Is it your stomach?"

Gertrude stared at the ground as her breathing slowly returned to normal. Finally, she sat back on her heels and looked at her daughter. Her face was ghostly white, and her lips were trembling.

"Mama, please... just tell me where you are hurting," Klara pleaded.

"I just became dizzy for a moment and lost my balance. I... I . . ." Her voice began to quaver. "Please... j-just help me to the house now, Liebchen."

Klara took her mother inside and helped her recline on the living room couch, then pulled up a stool beside her. Mama appeared to have recovered from her dizziness, and she studied Klara's face intently as she clutched her daughter's hand in both of hers against her chest.

"Mama, I know something's bothering you terribly," Klara said softly. "Please stop being stubborn and just tell me what it is."

Gertrude closed her eyes and sighed. "All this chaos has come on too suddenly. It's making me so confused. I didn't even *think* to include Elke in the plans for reuniting that we discussed yesterday with your father. And neither did either of you, for that matter. Once I realized it out there in the garden, it made me sick to think how callous and hopeless we've become about her situation."

"But Mama, you know the reason for that. It's only because Elke has made it clear she's staying in Berlin to the end, no matter what."

"I know, I know. But the truth is, I cannot bear the thought of losing either of you girls. I already lost Walther... and possibly even now your father."

A helpless silence ensued as Klara, for the first time, truly sensed the weight of her mother's burden. With Vati gone, with Walther still designated as missing in action, and Elke's survival of the Allied onslaught from air and ground on Berlin in grave doubt, how could Mama be experiencing anything but total depression and confusion?

Suddenly, Gertrude's eyes opened wide. "Klara, I know this may sound crazy after you already called today to resign from your nursing job. But is there any way you might consider returning to Berlin for a couple of days and making one more attempt to convince Elke to come join us? Explain to her our desperate circumstances and plead with her to—"

"Mama, believe me, I've asked her about this several times. I pleaded with her for hours the night before I left last week to come out here. But Elke simply won't listen. She wants to be with us, but she says her higher calling is to stay and die for the Führer in defense of Berlin if it comes to that."

"*It's the devil's calling that she's obeying!*" Mama nearly shrieked. She pushed Klara's hands aside and sat up. "Yes, the devil himself, masquerading all these years as an angel of light in the person of Adolf Hitler—the new Messiah to all those German Christians willing to blind themselves to his evil lies. I expressed my concerns to your father about the man for over a decade. But he kept telling me I was being overly sensitive. That harsh tactics and measures like Hitler's were sometimes required to eventually bring about a much greater good for the greater number of people . . ."

She shook her head. "Up until a few months ago, your father kept making excuses for every horrible rumor we would hear about Nazi atrocities. Just as Elke continues to do. To the point where she now considers it her calling to die for that devil in disguise who authorizes them. And unless God changes her mind, I've lost her, too." She bent forward and covered her face with her hands.

Klara was about to agree with her mother that only God could change Elke's mind and that there was nothing more she herself could do or say that would make a difference. But then, a vivid memory flashed in her mind: Elke, her protective mother tigress at the 1936 Nuremberg rally. Had not Elke gone out of her way to search for her disobedient little sister in the middle of the night, like Jesus leaving the flock of ninety-nine to search for his one lost sheep? Had not Elke put her own life on the line more than once to save Klara from physical harm, if not death?

After all she did for me, how can I be so self-centered and ungrateful as to throw up my hands and say, "I've done all I can… it's time to give up on her?"

Going back to Berlin at this point would certainly entail risks—not the least of which was the possibility of more ferocious Allied bombing attacks that could pulverize the railway system and prevent a return to Nordhausen. In that case, Mama would truly be on her own without any support beyond what the Kellers' might be willing to provide. The more likely outcome was that Klara would return empty-handed, with Elke refusing once again to listen to reason and to the raw appeal of her mother's concern. The prospects of success seemed bleak. And yet, despite it all…

"Mama, I haven't canceled my train ticket yet. I'll go to Berlin and try one more time to bring Elke here."

At 3:50 p.m. the following afternoon, Klara settled back in her seat in a four-passenger compartment at the rear of the train to Berlin and counted her blessings.

At least, she told herself, *Mama will be in kind, capable hands.*

Vati's technical assistant, Herr Keller, had shown up right on schedule early this morning with his open-bed truck and two helpers. They'd loaded the multitude of suitcases and other household belongings that Klara and her mother had boxed up the day before, then they'd journeyed the thirty miles to Herr Keller's townhome. On the way, Klara had told Herr Keller of her change in plans.

Though he'd expressed some concern over the possibility of the Americans overwhelming Nordhausen's defenses before Klara could return from Berlin, Herr Keller had assured her that in any case she could count on him and his wife to do all in their power to protect her mother. Should General Kammler's promised rescue train to Bavaria arrive before Klara's return, they would make sure that Mama was on it. Otherwise, should Kammler's promise prove empty and Nordhausen be on the verge of capitulation to the Americans, the Kellers would reassess the situation and make the decision whether to stay put or take Mama with them to their hideout in the southern Harz foothills.

Just before dropping her off at the station following lunch and a final, heart-wrenching conversation with Mama, Herr Keller handed Klara a map to the hideout. "Hopefully, we'll still be here in Nordhausen when you return, Klara. You should look for us here first, just as your father will be doing if he can get free. But if we're not here, *this* is where we'll be. Your father also has a copy."

No more than ten minutes into the journey, Klara peeked over the top of the magazine she was reading and smiled at the little girl sitting next to her mother in the seats opposite. The girl smiled back uncertainly before returning her attentions to her doll.

Reminds me of the time Mama took me to—

She had no time to complete her thought before the squeal of brakes sounded and the train began to decelerate.

"What's going on?" asked the woman next to Klara.

Within seconds, they had lurched to a complete stop. The frantic voice of the conductor came over the loudspeaker. "We are in danger of an air raid. All passengers are required to exit their cars immediately and head for the woods on the south side of the track. Leave your luggage behind."

Klara lined up behind the other terrified passengers, awaiting their turn to exit. Immediately upon stepping out, she heard the heavy droning in the sky and looked back in the direction from which they'd come.

She gasped in horror.

At this distance, the town of Nordhausen resembled a bubbling cauldron of explosions, smoke, and flames.

CHAPTER 46

Bad Sachsa: Spa-Town Northwest of Nordhausen, Germany
April 8, 1945
(A week later)

I should be in the Bavarian Alps now with the other scientists, hoping that Gertrude will join me soon.

Erich Neumann sat on the top step of the makeshift porch of the hideout cabin a mile from town, smoking a cigarette as he stared morosely at the large oak tree on the edge of the thick woods just beyond the clearing. Every couple of minutes, it seemed, a wave of emotion would engulf him as he thought of Gertrude and their early years together. Each time, despite his best efforts to hold onto it, the pleasant image would transition to the memory of the heavy knocking on the cabin door that had pulled him from his fitful slumber late last night.

It was Herr Keller. His face was marred by cuts and burns, and his voice was barely above a whisper. "Erich, I have terrible news. Our house took a near-direct hit in the bombing. My wife and I made it, but Gertrude was killed instantly."

The gut-wrenching news had doubled Erich over in agony. To suddenly lose his faithful, loving partner of nearly thirty years without even having a chance to hold her hand and tell her goodbye? How could he ever forgive himself for leaving her behind like that? His severe shock and grief had been tempered only by his relief at the news that Klara had made a decision to return to Berlin and had safely departed Nordhausen. She'd left right before the heavy American bombing attacks killed nearly 9000 residents and Dora camp prisoners.

Herr Keller had stayed only an hour, saying that he had to return to his wife in the hospital. Erich's first impulse had been to travel back to Nordhausen with Herr Keller, but the latter had convinced him that the devastation had been great and there was nothing left that Erich would wish to see. He'd promised instead to return the day after tomorrow to look in on Erich and discuss memorial arrangements. Erich had reluctantly agreed. Herr Keller then left him alone in the isolated old cabin. It had been refurbished recently, stocked with food and supplies from the nearby spa town by Herr Keller himself. It was the spot to which both men had agreed to have their families retreat to shelter themselves from possible maltreatment of surrendering Nordhausen-area citizens by revenge-seeking American soldiers.

Erich shook his head and groaned. *So here I am, all alone at our family hideout, with my wife dead, my son probably dead, and both my daughters in Berlin preparing to face the Russian onslaught. If I'd been evacuated as planned last week along with the other rocket men to that SS stronghold in southern Germany, at least I'd now be in the company of my fellow scientists, at merciful peace in the mistaken belief that I'd left Gertrude and Klara in safe hands with Herr Keller.*

For the thousandth time, Erich replayed the completely unexpected turn of events that had led to his present, desolate circumstances…

Eight nights ago, after leaving Gertrude and Klara and arriving at the Nordhausen train station two hours before his scheduled departure with the other scientists for Bavaria, Erich had been greeted by General Dornberger at the entrance.

Dornberger, dressed in civilian clothes, had grabbed his arm and escorted him inside to a corner table in a quiet coffee shop. He wasted no time in revealing the strange reason for their meeting.

"Professor, Wernher von Braun and I are facing a major dilemma, and we desire your help. As you'll recall from our meeting with Wernher at Peenemünde late in January, almost all of us V-2 men voted that if we were ever forced to surrender and had a choice in the matter, it would be the Americans to whom we should attempt to give ourselves up. As a group, if possible."

Erich nodded. At the time, he'd wholeheartedly supported the decision. Surrendering to the Russians who were closing in on Peenemünde had seemed out of the question. The Soviet Union was another police state, and a hated enemy that had suffered deeply at Nazi Germany's hands. They could never expect good treatment there. Britain, which had been targeted and battered by V-2 strikes, would hardly welcome the rocket men with affection, nor could it afford to finance the group's future space travel dreams. Neither could France, Germany's detested, longtime enemy.

The United States had seemed to be the rocket men's only logical choice, and General Kammler's later evacuation orders from Peenemünde and Nordhausen to southern Germany where the Americans were also strongly advancing seemed to have unwittingly validated their decision. The only remaining question was how the rocket men were to escape from their SS guards and make contact with US army intelligence units in Bavaria.

Dornberger went on. "Once we arrive at whatever mountain retreat General Kammler has set up for us there, we'll be under constant surveillance from the SS. Wernher and I fear Kammler might use us as bargaining chips with the Americans to secure his own freedom or, failing that, to have us all murdered to keep us from falling into enemy hands. But in any case, we're going to need some bargaining chips of our own if we have any hope of convincing the Americans to embrace us."

"So, what do we have that would be persuasive?" Erich asked.

Dornberger glanced around the room to ensure no one was watching, then stared at Erich intently.

"Classified V-2 Documents," he said. "Blueprints, plans, procedures. Troves of them. All the important ones that any country wishing to reconstruct the design and adapt it to their own military or civilian purposes would absolutely require along with the scientists like us, who alone would know how to interpret and employ them properly. Just before he evacuated Peenemünde, Wernher had the documents loaded onto railcars with critical V-2 parts and other materials and then transported to a remote area just outside Nordhausen. I did the same for a separate, smaller stash of records. And that's where *you* come into the picture, Professor Neumann."

"Sir?"

"If we rocket men are going to use them to bargain for our own freedom and eventual employment in America, we need to *hide* those vital records from the Americans until they've agreed to our terms. Assuming you are willing, we should be able to do just that."

"But... why *me*? And how, sir? Am I not accompanying you and Wernher and the others on the train to Bavaria in less than two hours? Am I not on Kammler's list and therefore, required to go?"

Dornberger smiled. "Wernher and I agreed that you were the only one of us rocket men who knew this area well enough to find a good hiding place and whom we trusted enough to supervise the transfer activity. As to how... well, I personally convinced General Kammler to write up evacuation exemption certificates for yourself and two other lower-level assistants on the original list. I told him the technical expertise of the three of you was urgently needed over the next few days to help sort out the logjam of vital V-2 documents and missile parts that are still sitting in those railcars outside Nordhausen."

"Are Kammler's SS people guarding them?" Erich asked.

"No. Only a few low-level civilian workers. But they're too preoccupied with their daily tasks to notice what you'll *really* be doing during that time, which is crating up the most important documents in the railcars and transferring them to the hiding location you specify. Von

Braun's assistants already have an idea of where that should be. Your first job will be to check the place out. Confirm its viability or find a better one in the vicinity, then make sure that the right documents get crated up and transferred and that the process goes smoothly. The assistants have been instructed on how to get the manual help needed, so you won't have to worry about that."

Erich cocked his eyebrow. "First job? Do I have a second?"

"Yes. And I must admit, it amounts to a personal favor. As I said, I have a second, smaller stash of important V-2 documents in one of the railcars that I would like you to hide in a *separate* location of your choosing. One that only *you* will know about, and which you'll reveal to me alone once you join von Braun's assistants at the end of your exemption and travel south to join the rest of us in Bavaria. I have my own two trusted assistants living in the area whom I've sworn to secrecy and who can get the manual work done for you."

Erich wondered briefly why Dornberger would want to maintain a set of hidden documents separate from von Braun's, but it didn't take long for the reason to dawn on him. Dornberger desired his own insurance policy in case von Braun should unexpectedly double-cross him and leave him out of any private deal with the Americans. *No need to press the man further about this.*

"And so, Professor Neumann, before I reveal any more details and names for you, I must ask, will you accept this challenge? If not on the basis of our mutual hopes for the preservation of our vital V-2 records for the benefit of future generations, then simply on the basis of your longtime friendship and loyalty to Wernher and myself? You have my word of honor. Should you accept and follow through on this mission, Wernher and I will make sure that you and your family members are granted top priority among the scientists and their families who we plan to recommend to the Americans for preferential treatment in any negotiations."

Erich didn't take long to answer. Considering the dire alternative of post-war life as a POW and even the potential for prosecution as a war-*criminal*, Dornberger's promise sounded like the most advantageous, long-term outcome possible for Erich and his family. He would be a fool not to accept the offer. "It would be an honor, sir, and I am most appreciative that you and Wernher considered me for this."

Dornberger reached out and shook Erich's hand. "Excellent. Wernher will be relieved to know. Ever since his automobile accident, he's been unable to attend to these matters himself, and their lack of resolution has been driving him crazy."

After Dornberger passed on a note containing the names and addresses of the assistants Erich was supposed to contact, Erich suggested a potential location for hiding the second stash of documents. "There's a woodsy area outside the spa town of Bad Sachsa where I've had my own assistant set up a hideout of sorts for our two families. I think it might be a perfect spot for burying some treasure."

Erich went on to describe the location, and Dornberger seemed to agree that it could work. Erich promised to draw a map of the precise location to give to Dornberger once he and the other assistants arrived in Bavaria.

The men finished their coffee and prepared to leave.

"Erich, one thing . . ." Dornberger said as they were about to stand up. "I know you and your wife live in this area and that you'd probably love to let her know you'll be here a few more days, maybe even try to go see her. But I'd strongly advise against that. The SS is likely to be keeping an eye on things, and any deviation from your special assigned duties while on temporary exempt status would likely be viewed with great suspicion. In fact, the less your wife knows about this whole affair, the better for her own sake in the event that someone unexpectedly betrays your true purpose."

"I understand completely, General. Thank you for the wise admonition. I think I'll rely on the memory of our last kiss to tide me over these next few days while I get the job done. I'd hate to get her all stirred up and then have to leave her yet again."

Erich devoted the entire following week to his special task. After selecting an abandoned mine shaft near the rural village of Dörnten on the northern edge of the Harz for the primary stash of V-2 documents, he'd used his temporary SS credentials to persuade the Nazi caretaker to sell him a space in a large antechamber in the back of the mine. With the help of von Braun's assistants and some other helpers, he'd managed to get dozens of crates filled with selected documents from von Braun's railcars and then trucked by night to Dörnten and deposited in the well-hidden storage space.

Burying Dornberger's records two days later proved much easier. Working again under the cover of nightfall with lanterns, shovels, and pickaxes, Erich and the second set of assistants dug a twelve-foot pit in a large field not far from Erich's cabin. In it, they placed five large, document-filled wooden boxes lined with metal and covered them with dirt. With that, Erich's special mission was complete.

It was on that same night—the night of April 5—that Erich and the others had seen the flames lighting up the sky over Nordhausen. Though they'd heard ominous rumbling sounds coming from the same direction over the previous two afternoons, this was the first time that Erich became certain the town had been directly targeted and was in deep trouble.

After dismissing his helpers, he'd driven back to his cabin, dreading what Gertrude and Klara might be experiencing but having no way to contact them…

Erich took a drag on his cigarette, allowing the smoke to settle deep in his lungs before he finally exhaled. He knew that when Herr Keller came to visit tomorrow, he would be forced to make a decision.

His job here was finished, his exempt status terminated. Tomorrow, the SS would expect him to report to the Nordhausen station promptly at 4:30 p.m. Assuming the trains were still running, he would catch the last one to Nuremberg, then head on to Bavaria where the other rocket men and their SS guards would no doubt be expecting him early the next morning. If for any reason he failed to show up at Kammler's alpine retreat for the rocket men on time, there would be hell to pay.

But there was another, far more important consideration: honoring Gertrude's memory. That would certainly require him to stay in town for a few more days to complete arrangements and conduct a fitting memorial with Herr Keller's help. There was no way Erich was going to rush through the process of grieving for his beloved wife of over twenty-five years.

No. When Herr Keller showed up tomorrow, Erich would tell him he planned to take a room in town for a few days and would appreciate his continued support. While there, he would try to contact Klara in Berlin to tell her the news about her mother and urge her to make it back to Nordhausen and then on to the Bad Sachsa hideout.

The V-2 rocket men and their SS protectors could wait. And if General Kammler didn't like it, he could go to hell.

CHAPTER 47

Somewhere Northeast of Nordhausen, Germany
April 11, 1945
(Three days later)

An exhausted SS Colonel Gerhard Bremmer lifted his head from his folded arms and stared groggily around the living room of the house he'd commandeered for official use several miles outside town. Yet again, the field telephone rang on the corner of the desk where he'd fallen asleep.

What now? Can't those incompetent junior staff idiots figure any-thing out on their own? Why are they always asking me *to do their thinking for them?*

The entire past week had been a grueling slog, fraught with con-stantly shifting orders from General Kammler for the burning of files and the evacuation of prisoners from Mittlebau-Dora and its subcamps to a confusing variety of destinations. Some prisoners were driven on foot toward the southern part of Germany or Austria to continue working in weapons production. Many others were sent by rail to the Bergen-Belsen concentration camp where they would be starved to death. Still others were marched off to the northeast, where the Nazis hoped to develop a final front against the Soviet army and throw the prisoners into the fray as cannon fodder.

This latest call was probably some nervous young lieutenant like the last one, who'd wanted to know if Kammler's command to shoot any stragglers included those who were being helped along by their fellow prisoners.

Of course, dummkopf! Gerhard would reply as before. *And shoot the helpers as well if they put up the slightest squawk. You know as well as I that General Kammler has no tolerance for delays of any sort.*

The infernal ringing persisted. Gerhard finally picked up the receiver. It was General Kammler, and he was not happy.

"Bremmer! Are you sleeping on the job, or what?" Kammler's tone was even more frantic and obnoxious than two days ago, when he'd chewed Gerhard out for what Kammler had termed his 'lackadaisical organization' of the Nordhausen area defense effort. It was a bogus accusation; Kammler himself—*not* Gerhard, his subordinate—was the one to whom Reichsführer Himmler had delegated the thankless town defense task. Gerhard was busy enough with the prisoner evacuation effort, and Kammler knew it.

"Excuse me, sir. Has something happened that I was—"

Kammler cut him off. "Are you aware, Colonel Bremmer, that earlier this morning American infantry units entered Nordhausen unopposed, and they are now plowing through the outer Dora camps where you failed to clear out all those rotting corpses?"

"But sir, did you not order me to concentrate on getting as many of the still-living prisoners out as we possibly could, and to leave the dead ones behind?"

A short pause ensued. "Well, regardless, it's too late now. Nordhausen and the V-2 factory are lost. We all have to start thinking differently. Which leads me to the most pressing issue of the moment, Colonel Bremmer."

"And what is that, sir?"

"Where is Erich Neumann? His special assignment ended, and he was supposed to show up at the Bavarian retreat early yesterday morning. But they tell me he never arrived! So, where is he? Did I not order you to monitor his progress and make sure he got on that train, Colonel?"

"Yes sir, you did, and I must confess to have failed in my duty on that score."

"Bremmer," his superior exploded. "I should have you *court-martialed* for dereliction. And if it weren't for our present dilemma and the fact that I know you've had other things to worry about, I certainly would. But for now, I need you to personally concentrate on only one thing: *find our missing Professor Neumann.*"

Gerhard breathed a sigh of relief. Kammler could have made things far more difficult. "Of course, sir. I look forward to redressing my oversight."

"Good. This has become a matter of extreme urgency," Kammler said. "Two days ago, one of my SS aides was standing outside the Bavarian mountain inn where we have all the V-2 men locked up in embarrassingly luxurious circumstances. He overheard von Braun and Dornberger who were sunbathing nearby. They were talking and mentioning some kind of 'buried treasure' near Nordhausen that their friend—who they laughingly referred to as 'Blackbeard Erich the Pirate'—had hopefully secured by now. I personally called and pressed them directly about this, but they denied it was anything other than a casual joke about Neumann's delayed appearance.

"I don't like the sound of this, Bremmer. Something's fishy. Neumann had access to some important V-2 records as part of the task I assigned him. You know those documents could be a vital part of any negotiations we may have to make soon. I need you to find Neumann *immediately.* Do whatever's required to squeeze out of him what he's *really* been up to this past week and whether there's any truth to these buried document rumors. And Colonel... make no mistake. If you value your future, you will not shirk your orders this time. There is simply too much at stake here for too many people."

Gerhard nodded. As much as he would have preferred an assignment away from the spreading American army presence, he knew there was no deflecting the bullheaded Kammler from a decision that could easily result in a fruitless wild goose chase.

So how to begin?

It had been five months since Gerhard had last dealt with Erich Neumann. Their interaction then had been poisoned by the sabotage incident that Gerhard had tricked Erich into manufacturing in order to satisfy Kammler. No doubt, Erich would still have those prisoner executions on his conscience, and his anger at Gerhard's betrayal would always simmer in his mind. He would probably not cooperate easily with any attempt by Gerhard to ascertain the truth about what he'd been up to lately.

But it doesn't matter what Erich Neumann's state of mind is. He is going to cooperate with me... so long as I can locate him, that is.

Gerhard already knew where he planned to start looking.

On the rural highway five miles from Bad Sachsa, Gerhard sat in the backseat of his speeding, open-roofed staff car, mentally rehearsing the argument he would employ to try and convince Erich Neumann to peacefully cough up his treasure.

He glanced to his left and recoiled at the sight of Johann Keller slumped in the seat beside him. Keller seemed barely conscious, his face bloodied and his right arm lying limp and twisted at an odd angle on top of his leg.

My hunches were correct on both counts, Gerhard congratulated himself. First, that Erich Neumann's abandoned countryside cottage might hold some useful clues as to his current whereabouts. And second, that Johann Keller's allegiance to Erich could not withstand the pain of physical torture.

When Gerhard and his two SS aides went to the cottage this morning and encountered Keller rummaging around in the attic, they'd dragged the slight man downstairs and forced him to sit on a stool with his arms pinioned high up on his back. In no uncertain terms, Gerhard demanded he tell them what he was doing there and everything he knew about Erich. When he'd hesitated, the aides had beat him mercilessly. It had taken less than two minutes for them to wring a full confession.

"What were you doing here, Herr Keller?"

"When Professor Neumann and I learned that American troops were about to enter Nordhausen, he dropped his plans for his wife's memorial ceremony and fled town to the hideout we'd established. I decided to remain behind and take my chances with the Americans, but I also promised the professor that I would check out the cottage here to make sure that no incriminating papers had been left behind in the attic when his wife and daughter had fled the place."

"Hideout, you say? And where exactly is *that*?"

Two more vicious punches to the kidneys and an excruciating hammerlock had done the trick. Not only had Keller revealed the hideout location in Bad Sachsa, but he'd also admitted that Erich had supervised the burying of some important V-2 documents in a nearby field.

"You will come along with us to that hideout now, won't you, Herr Keller? Time is of the essence, and we can't be taking the chance you've been lying to us."

The men had crammed Keller into one of the back seats and now, after a two-hour drive, they were approaching the turnoff to the winding, rustic lane on the outskirts of the little spa town which would take them up the hill to Erich's cabin.

Gerhard could only hope Erich would be as compliant as Johann Keller in revealing what Gerhard needed to know: where they had hidden those documents.

What a shame it's all come down to this, he thought. *After all the good times we shared together over family meals at Erich's home with Gertrude and the girls.* He thought of Elke, and of the romantic feelings he'd developed for her before she abruptly cut him off due to her supposed love for her crippled husband, Heinz. What a wild and delightful relationship they could have enjoyed together, if only she'd cooperated. He also thought of Klara, and all the lies she'd spun to protect her Jew friends that had resulted in no end of troubles and delays for Gerhard's

Berlin Kripo investigations. *Well, if not the girls, at least Erich deserves better than what I'll be forced to offer him.*

The SS aide who was driving looked back over his shoulder. "I believe this is the turnoff, sir."

Gerhard popped three amphetamine pills into his mouth, chewed, and swallowed them quickly. He'd been relying more and more on these to keep himself going, and he needed to be as alert as possible for this next phase of the treasure hunt.

"Yes. Take it, Lieutenant."

⚒

Colonel Gerhard Bremmer and Professor Erich Neumann faced each other across the cabin's tiny kitchen table as Bremmer's two aides passed the time smoking and offering their mock apologies to the slowly recovering Johann Keller in the next room.

Bremmer lowered his eyes and shook his head sadly. "First Erich, allow me to express my deepest condolences for your loss of Gertrude. Such a kind and generous woman, who did so much to help you raise your three beautiful children."

Expecting at least a modicum of acknowledgement from Erich, Bremmer was disappointed to be met with nothing more than a cold, harsh stare. Clearly, Erich was still enmeshed in his bitterness over their previous encounter. *Just as well*, Bremmer thought. *I abhor being hypocritical about these things, anyway. Let's get on with it.*

"Erich, let me come straight to the point. I know *you* know where those V-2 documents are hidden. Please. Just tell me where they are."

Erich continued to stare. "I'm not sure what you're talking about, Colonel. I completed my mission of sorting out documents in the railcars as General Kammler ordered, and that was it. As for hidden documents... I have no knowledge."

Bremmer took a deep breath, trying to project an outward calm despite the amphetamines beginning to take their effect.

"Look, Erich. Let's just face the truth, shall we? When it comes time to surrender, neither you nor I are going to be well-received by our captors. Granted, my situation as an SS officer would seem to be far more perilous than yours. But that doesn't mean they'll be willing to let *you* off scot-free and welcome you with open arms as a rocket scientist for their cause—even if you end up revealing your treasure to them. Don't make the mistake of thinking the Americans will be any less judgmental of our alleged crimes against innocent civilians than the other Allies would be."

Erich's eyes narrowed. "*Our* alleged crimes? What are you implying, Colonel?"

Bremmer pulled from his tunic's inner pocket the original document signed by Erich that had consigned the five Dora camp slave laborers to death for their acts of sabotage.

"How do you think your war crime will be viewed by your prospective future American employers if I were to reveal this clear evidence to them, Erich?"

Erich gulped and looked aside. "Not very well, I suppose."

Bremmer nodded. "On the other hand, if you'll promise to take me to where the V-2 records are, I will hand this incriminating piece of paper over to you right here and now. You can rip it up in my presence. Of course, I must warn you. If we get there and the documents are not where you say, your life is immediately forfeit. As is your friend's here. I can't have you reneging on a deal this important to both of us, Erich."

Erich glared at him. "Colonel, I am not so dull-witted as to imagine you won't kill me and Herr Keller as soon as I show you where the documents are. Why would you need or want us around anymore if it's *you* who would be able to negotiate alone with the Americans for your *own* freedom?"

Bremmer smiled. "You underestimate your value to me, Erich. You always have. You see, by offering to the Americans not only my knowledge of where the treasure is hidden, but also where *you*—an extremely important future scientific asset for their country—are being kept hidden by my aide under lock and key, I will only increase my own currency with them when I try to negotiate. In exchange for my freedom, they will have not only the buried treasure, but also yourself…

one of the most highly regarded scientists on the renowned team of Peenemünde rocket men. Think of the glorious, unencumbered future you can have in America… and myself, well, wherever I choose to live out the rest of my life in peace and anonymity. We will both emerge as winners!"

Erich thought for several moments. "Will you promise to spare Herr Keller as well?"

"Of course. Why would I want to have his murder on my conscience?"

Erich nodded. "All right. I'll show you where things are buried. Hand me the document." As soon as it was in his hands, Erich ripped it up into small pieces, which he then gathered up and stuffed in the pocket of his trousers.

The men stood. Bremmer smiled and extended his hand toward the adjoining room where the others were. "Show us the way, Professor."

Erich went over to check on Johann Keller's condition. He was slouched in a chair, appearing dazed and confused. He smiled weakly as Erich knelt beside him and lightly caressed his uninjured shoulder.

Erich stood and motioned toward the corner of the room. "We'll need the lanterns and shovels there. It'll take at least an hour to dig down to where the boxes are, and it's getting dark." After he and the two aides gathered the equipment and loaded it into the storage compartment of the staff car, Erich walked back toward the cabin.

"Where are you going now, Erich?" Bremmer demanded.

"It's chilly out here. I want my coat."

Bremmer motioned for one of his aides to follow and keep an eye on Erich's movements. Moments later, the two returned and all the men—including the still woozy Johann Keller—got into the car. After driving the bumpy dirt road on up the hillside behind the cabin, they arrived near the middle of a wide, open field overlooking the spa town.

Erich pointed to the spot. "That's it."

Bremmer nodded at his aides. "All right, set up the lanterns and start digging. Would you mind helping them, Professor, while I keep Herr Keller entertained in my staff car? I have a few more questions I need to ask him."

After digging away for over an hour, the three men finally reached the top of one of the boxes.

"We've hit something, Colonel!" one of the aides shouted. They dug around the box just enough to expose the lid. As soon as it was free, the aide pulled out his pistol and shot the lock off. Lifting the lid, he let out a triumphant cry. "They're here!" He pulled out one of the bound sheaves of papers and motioned for Erich and the other aide to precede him out of the pit. After they'd all climbed out, the aide handed the sheaf to Bremmer for review.

Bremmer took it over to examine under one of the lamp lights. The papers looked legitimate, with all the proper markings and expected scientific jargon.

"Good. That's it." He walked back over toward the others. He looked at Erich and Herr Keller, who stood beside the car, scrutinizing his every move.

"Thank you, gentlemen, your work is done."

Bremmer nodded at one of his aides, who pulled out his Luger pistol and pointed it at Erich and Johann. He motioned toward a thicket of trees at the edge of the field.

"Please come with me."

Erich realized immediately what was happening. "What are you... *Colonel! You said you would . . .*" his choking voice trailed off.

Bremmer shook his head. "I'm very sorry, Erich, but there comes a point where even one's old friend can become essentially useless and too much of a burden for others to have to carry along on their shoulders."

The SS aide cocked the pistol's trigger. "*Move, you two!*"

Bremmer, standing between his aides a mere three feet from the two men he had just betrayed, looked into Erich's eyes. "I truly am very sorry, Erich."

Erich stuck his hands in his coat pockets, closed his eyes and nodded. "I truly do understand, Colonel. There's just one thing."

"Oh, and what's that?"

With a blindingly fast motion, Erich gripped the small pistol in his right pocket, pulled his hand out and fired at close range, striking the aide with the gun in the middle of his stomach. He turned to the other aide and fired off a second round, striking the man in the face. As Gerhard Bremmer struggled to pull his own Luger from its holster, Erich fired yet again, this time hitting him in the upper left side of his chest and dropping him to his knees.

Erich dragged the mortally wounded Bremmer by his collar to the edge of the pit and forced him to kneel in front of it.

Bremmer looked at him with eyes that had clearly given up any expectation or even hope for mercy. The man was now coughing and spitting up blood.

"Colonel Gerhard Bremmer," Erich muttered, his voice choked with emotion. "For everything you did over the years to worm your way into the lives and hearts of my precious family for your own selfish purposes, and then manipulate and finally toss us all aside like dirty rags… I have only one last thing to say—*Enjoy your buried treasure.*"

Erich lifted his booted foot, placed the muddy sole against Bremmer's face, then kicked him into the twelve-foot pit.

CHAPTER 48

Berlin, Germany
April 19, 1945
(Eight days later)

Klara dumped the last of the weekly ration of withered potatoes into the pot of boiling water. Once cooked, she knew the little spuds would have the consistency of mush and taste like cardboard. She could only hope that when accompanied by stale slices of bread spread with blackberry preserves, they would at least prove edible for Elke, Trudi, and the three younger BDM members who were meeting tonight at the Neumanns' Charlottenburg residence. As for Irma Brubeck, the meddlesome local BDM political officer who'd insisted on calling the meeting, Klara could care less whether she enjoyed the sparse meal or choked to death on it.

This will certainly be no worse than the girls would get from their parents at home, Klara consoled herself as she drummed her fingers on the stove, waiting for the water to boil. *And a week from now, it'll probably be remembered as a lavish feast.*

Arriving back in Berlin from Nordhausen two weeks ago, Klara had noticed a lack of even the most basic food products on the store shelves. Everyone she knew was complaining of a persistent, gnawing hunger compounded by a strong sense of impending catastrophe from every direction.

The near-daily US and British bombing raids were terrible enough. Many homes had been destroyed, tens of thousands of residents killed, and much of the city's infrastructure demolished. Klara was hearing that Berliners should expect their gas, electricity, and running water to be cut off any day now.

But it was the threat of the coming Red Wave, more than anything else, that was striking the average citizen's heart with fear. Elke said that the Wehrmacht was rapidly crumbling after the Soviets captured the Seelow Heights only sixty miles from Berlin's eastern edge three days ago. Complete encirclement of the city by Russian forces appeared to be only a few days away. Many BDM girls and their leaders, like Elke, were receiving hastily arranged weapons training to prepare them to support the defense of the city suburbs, should things come to that. As a result, any faint hope that Klara might have entertained of convincing Elke to flee to Nordhausen and reunite with their mother had been dashed. Since telephone lines there were cut, she could only pray that Mama had survived the bombing attack—the one she herself had narrowly escaped.

Klara jumped at the sound of Elke's voice in the kitchen entryway. "How is our elegant dinner coming, Klara? Should I have Irma the Dragoness show us her film now, or wait until afterward? She's chafing at the bit."

"Should be ready in about ten minutes. Let's eat first." Klara glanced over her shoulder and flashed her sister a wicked smile. "Maybe Irma will get sick from these awful potatoes, and we won't have to listen to her screech at us for over an hour."

Elke winced and put her finger to her lips. "That's wishful thinking if I've ever heard it! Klara, I know it's hard for you, but you really *must* keep your words and expressions in check around Irma tonight. You know how that woman can take a seemingly innocent comment and twist it into treason. And you thought *I* was bad. Anyway, I should get back to the living room. Goebbels is about to make his big speech on the radio, and Irma's insisting we turn up the volume to reinspire any girl here who might secretly be harboring a faint heart. Let us know when things are ready."

As Klara continued to prepare the meal, Joseph Goebbels's oddly reverential voice blared from the radio. Irma had been sure to turn it up to near full volume in the other room.

"German citizens! On the eve of our Führer's fifty-sixth Birthday, at a moment of the war when things stand on such a knife's edge... I stand beside the Führer today as fate challenges him and his people with its last, most severe test. I am confident that fate will give him and his people the laurel wreath of victory... if the Führer's people accept his task and fight for it as if it were the word of God. If they do not, then they do not deserve to live any longer..."

Klara stirred the potatoes absent-mindedly as Goebbels rambled on. *So, all Germans deserve to die if they fail to fight for Hitler as if he were God?* she thought bitterly. Had not Dietrich Bonhoeffer warned the German Christians years ago that their idolatrous substitution of the Führer for the true Messiah would lead to Germany's downfall?

Dietrich had certainly paid a heavy price for his refusal to embrace such sacrilege. In fact, Klara had heard rumors of his execution in a concentration camp for his involvement in the Hitler assassination plot on July 20. *The cost of discipleship.*

Other, more ordinary citizens were also finally learning what it meant to be accused of failing to do their duty to the Führer. Like the poor man Klara had spotted two days ago on her way back from the market. He was hanging from a lamppost with a placard suspended from his neck, and something had impelled her to cross the street and join the small crowd of onlookers.

"Allow me to read this as a warning to all of you here who may be entertaining similar inclinations," one of the Gestapo men overseeing the scene had intoned. "'I chose to spread lies of Germany's possible defeat, and so I deserve my fate.'"

What would they have done to me, Klara wondered, *if they'd caught me just yesterday, on my way back from the market, doing nothing more than staring at that leaflet I'd seen pasted on a wall?* When she'd read it, the words had thrilled her:

Berliners! Soldiers, men, and women!

You have heard the order of the lunatic Hitler and his bloodhound, Himmler, to defend every city to the utmost. Is Berlin to share the same fate as other German cities on our borders?

NO! Write your "no" everywhere! Form resistance cells in barracks, shops, shelters! Throw all the pictures of Hitler and his accomplices out into the gutter! Organize armed resistance!

Klara's heart had pounded with a mixture of exhilaration tinged with guilt over the knowledge that active resistance like this—once the driving force of her daily life—was no longer a personal consideration. Fear of the consequences if caught was one reason. But also, faced with the coming Soviet-led apocalypse, resistance against the Führer and Nazism would seem to be a futile, if not counter-productive, waste of one's remaining energy. Would Hitler's removal deflect the Soviet advance and thirst for revenge? Would life under Stalin and Communism be any better than life under Hitler? Either way, Klara believed her country and city were doomed. The only thing worth fighting for from here on was personal survival. If she and Elke somehow managed to make it through the hell about to erupt, then hopefully one day they could reunite with their parents—assuming they were still alive—and find a way to escape to America.

Joseph Goebbels was obviously viewing the same, desperate situation in an entirely different and more patriotic light.

"Listen, Germans! Millions of people look to Adolf Hitler from every land on the earth, still questioning whether he knows the way out of the great misfortune that has befallen the world. He will show the peoples that way, but we must look to him full of hope and with a deep,

unshakeable faith... We do not need to tell him, for he knows and must know—Führer command! We will follow! We feel him in us and around us. God give him strength and health and preserve him from every danger... May he remain what he is to us and has always been—Our Hitler!"

Klara could only close her eyes and grit her teeth at the chorus of "*Heil Hitler*" emanating from the living room at the conclusion of Goebbels's speech. Unsurprisingly, the loudest voice by far belonged to Irma Brubeck. Klara wondered how she would maintain her own composure during the upcoming meal and afterward, during the film. With Irma's obnoxious proclivity for pro-Nazi blather and for accusing other girls of disloyalty to the cause, it would be no easy task.

Just take a deep breath and press on.

Following the meal, Elke, Klara, and the other girls sat around the kitchen table, stifling their giggles at the sound of Irma Brubeck's vile curses as she attempted to get the film projector working in the living room.

"She's been at it for ten minutes now," said one of the younger girls. "Maybe she'll give up and we can all go home."

As if on cue, Irma Brubeck appeared in the kitchen entrance. Immediately, the others silenced their merriment and assumed serious expressions.

Irma cast a stern look at Elke as she addressed her by her latest rank in the Wehrmachtshelferin. "Captain Schröder, the projector's finally working. Would you please escort your team into the living room and get them settled so I can begin the presentation?"

Klara could tell that her sister was annoyed with Irma's pompous tone and wanted to say something to put her in her place. After an awkward silence, she answered mildly. "Of course, Lieutenant Brubeck."

Smart, Klara thought. Though Elke outranked Irma in terms of the formal hierarchy, the latter was known to have close personal and political connections with Artur Axmann, the overall national leader of the Hitler Youth. Given Irma's reputation for going right to the top with her complaints about her personal enemies, it would not be wise to needlessly irritate or provoke her. Especially in *these* dangerous times.

One by one, the girls trooped out of the kitchen and took their seats on the living room chairs and couch, preparing themselves to endure Irma Brubeck and her latest film from the Reich Propaganda Ministry.

They did not have to wait long for the Dragoness to live up to her reputation.

"As you can see, there is no point in hoping that Stalin's devils will show the slightest mercy to Berliner women, girls, or even babies. Just look what they've already done in Poland and East Prussia."

Irma's voice had a strangely triumphant timbre, her eyes an even stranger glow as she spoke to the series of grisly black-and-white images flashing by slowly on the screen. "Woman over seventy defiled, Polish nun gang raped forty-two times by vicious Russian horde," read the caption to which Irma pointed.

Klara shifted uncomfortably in her chair and glanced across the room at her sister, who stood stiffly with her arms folded. She wondered if Elke was having the same reaction. *The Dragoness almost seems to get a morbid arousal out of showing the rest of us this special, sexual brand of horror. Either that or maybe she's just gloating because it happened to someone else and not her.*

After the film mercifully ended fifteen minutes later, Irma turned the lights up. Two of the girls looked as if they were on the verge of being sick.

Irma gave them no chance to recover. "Hopefully now you can see why it was necessary for Reichsführer Himmler to draft even our elderly, World War I veterans into the Volkssturm[*], and to challenge all able-bodied, patriotic women like ourselves to actively support them and our Berlin-area Hitler Youth, SS, and Wehrmacht units in combatting these Soviet pigs. It's a matter of life or death. Any woman or girl captured by them can expect to be brutally raped, tortured, and killed."

---

* *Volkssturm* (People's Storm): A national militia set up by Heinrich Himmler at the end of WW II for the defense of German cities, drafting into its ranks all men between sixteen and sixty not already serving in some military unit.

Trudi Schuster tentatively raised her hand. "Lieutenant Brubeck, I understand the urgency. But when will we finally receive our weapons and be told what to do?"

Irma smiled archly and nodded toward Elke. "For that, I must defer to your captain."

"When I receive the message from our local Volkssturm commander," Elke said, "I will contact each of you and we'll gather at the high school near the Zoo Flak Tower where the weapons are being stored. There, we'll pick them up and also be given our specific assignments. I only know that there's a plan to erect some barricades in the streets not far from the Tower. We may be directed to support our men there in the fight, filling in for those who have fallen."

"Does that mean we'll be firing at Russians from our front lines, just like the men?" one of the girls asked nervously.

The Dragoness did not wait for Elke to respond. "*Of course,* it means that, Private. What kind of idiotic question is *that*? As a BDM member who just watched that film, did you expect you would be asked to do nothing more than pick some pretty flowers and hand a bouquet to our brave men putting their lives on the line for you?"

Completely cowed, the girl leaped to her feet and snapped the fascist salute. "Forgive me, Lieutenant. I should have known better than to ask such a cowardly question."

Irma nodded curtly. "We are at a time and place in history where feminine weakness and vacillation cannot be tolerated. Each of us here will be tested to see if our loyalty to the Führer involves more than mere words and sighs of adoration. I, for one, plan to pass that test. Can the rest of you say that as well? *Heil Hitler!*"

All the girls stood and shot their right arms out.

All except one.

After glaring at Klara for several moments, Irma did not even condescend to address her directly. "Captain Schröder, I do not understand why your sister is still sitting there stone-faced while the rest of us are confirming our willingness and intention to fight and die if necessary for the cause of our Führer."

Elke hesitated. "My sister is capable of answering for herself, Lieutenant," she said finally.

"All right then," Irma sneered at Klara. "Fräulein Neumann. Please explain to all of us your obvious lack of enthusiasm for the Führer, and why you are so different in that respect from your own sister. You know she has long been the epitome of loyalty and commitment to him."

Klara glanced at Elke, whose face had turned pale. Other than Elke and Trudi, up until now no one in the city had been privy to Klara's true feelings about the Führer and Nazism. If she expressed them now, the Dragoness would make sure that the next Berlin citizen to dangle from a lamppost with a placard around their neck would be Klara. The Neumann family's reputation and Elke's ability to lead her team would be destroyed. *Think of something... quick!*

She looked straight at Irma. "I assure you, Lieutenant Brubeck, it is not for lack of loyalty and commitment that I failed to stand and salute the Führer along with you and the others. Though I chose the nursing profession and did not continue my involvement with the BDM like my sister, I consider it my honor and my duty to take my place beside each one of you as we defend this city and the country we love—to our last breaths if required. I may not have the weapons training that the rest of you have received, but I guarantee you, I am at least capable of wearing a belt of stick grenades and can carry ammunition belts to anyone who needs it."

Klara's voice took on a highly indignant tone. "I did not feel it necessary to stand because I firmly believe the Führer—whose spirit we feel inside us and around us as we just heard Herr Goebbels tell us—can already sense the love I feel for him in my heart. And in any case, I am certain that at this critical stage he would be far more concerned with my concrete actions on his behalf than with mere gestures and words of affirmation. However, if it would make you and the others here feel more certain about me . . ." She stood and raised her right arm. "*Heil Hitler!*"

The Dragoness stood open-mouthed as all the other girls in the room smiled and clapped in appreciation. "Well," she finally managed.

"If that belated offering is a sincere expression of your beliefs, then I suppose I'll have to accept it like the others here. But just remember, Fräulein Neumann, as you yourself have said, it's your action in the streets that will prove or disprove your fidelity. I'm sure we'll all be watching."

"Lieutenant Brubeck!" Elke nearly shouted. "You need not badger my sister any longer. You've made your point, and she's made hers. No more of this! We will spend the rest of our time here tonight talking about some possible tactics we can employ against the invaders. We'll need to respond as a cohesive *team*."

After the meeting concluded, Irma and the other girls walked out the front door to the respective homes. Elke turned and grabbed Klara by the arms. Her face was set like flint.

"Don't think you had me fooled for a minute, Klara. I knew *exactly* what you were really thinking about the Führer when the Dragoness challenged you."

Klara looked down at the ground. "I'm sorry, sister... I know I shouldn't have—"

"Look at me, Klara."

Klara slowly raised her head. To her surprise, Elke's face had softened into an admiring, affectionate smile.

"Do you know how incredibly proud I am of you?"

CHAPTER 49

Mittlebau-Dora Concentration Camp Complex: Nordhausen, Germany
April 25, 1945
(Six days later)

T he baby-faced orderly drove the jeep over to the side of the gravel road and beckoned to the two men walking in the opposite direction.

"Lieutenants! Major Staver would like a word with both of you in the command post. He has something he wants you both to see. I'll turn around up ahead, then come back and give you gentlemen a lift."

Joshua Peters and his British colleague, Alec Benjamin, exchanged pained glances. The two SHAEF intelligence officers had been returning to their quarters following dinner at the abandoned SS main barracks in the recently liberated Mittlebau-Dora camp. They'd mistakenly thought their first full workday inspecting the captured V-2 assembly tunnels was finally over.

"Haven't we seen everything in this hellhole already?" Joshua muttered as they waited for the jeep to return. "What now?"

Alec grimaced. "If it's a photo taken from yet another angle of those hundreds of emaciated prisoner corpses lined up outside the sub-camp,

Major Staver can spare me the repeat performance. I've seen enough evidence of death and misery around this place to last three lifetimes."

"I know exactly what you mean. It's incredible. Staver said over three thousand bodies were found scattered helter-skelter when the US 104th Infantry arrived here nine days ago. All either starved to death, worked to death, or killed by mistake in those Allied bombing raids before liberation." He shook his head. "What a screwup. Sounds like those raids did hardly any damage to the V-2 assembly tunnels they were trying to target, but they ended up killing thousands of civilians in the town itself along with a lot of prisoners who were confined in the nearby sub-camps."

"The ultimate price paid by innocent people who were forced to build rockets to kill other civilians in London and Western Europe," Alec observed bitterly. "Seems it was the wrong people who had to pay."

"That's why we're here, right? To find the ones who designed and directed the rocket production. And when we do, let our governments decide whether to hang or hire 'em. Who knows? Maybe Staver will finally have something to tell us in that regard."

"Let's hope so."

The men jumped into the back seat of the jeep. A half-mile down the road, the orderly banged his palm on the steering wheel and let out a soft curse.

"What's wrong, Corporal?" asked Joshua.

The orderly pointed ahead to several military vehicles backed up at a railroad crossing, waiting for a long train of machinery-laden flatcars to pass by at a snail's pace. "Staver's stash," he said irritably. "Looks like we'll be here a few minutes, sirs."

"What's Staver's stash?" Alec inquired. "And what's the train got to do with it?"

After stopping the jeep behind the last vehicle in line, the orderly turned in his seat and explained. "Major Staver's doing everything in his power to have every single V-2 rocket part he can find in the assembly tunnels hauled out and delivered to Antwerp on the Belgian coast. From there, they'll be shipped directly to the States and studied for possible use in the continuing fight against Japan. I've heard the major's already gotten a hundred tons shipped, and he's hoping for several hundred more. Staver's stash, as the grunts helping him refer to it."

Alec cocked his head back. "Does SHAEF Headquarters know Staver is doing this? Why does the United States get the privilege and benefit of having all the critical V-2 parts from Nordhausen and not Great Britain? Weren't *we* the ones who suffered directly?"

The orderly hesitated. "I'm not sure, sir. That might be a question to put to the major when you see him."

"I may just do that," Alec huffed.

Joshua was tempted to caution his friend not to make a big fuss to Major Staver on a matter that was only peripherally related to their specific mission. But as he recalled the horrible deaths of Alec's fiancée and her mother in London in the Woolworth's store V-2 strike, he thought better of it. Alec was still hurting, and he had a hair-trigger temper. It would not be wise to provoke it.

Major Robert Staver, the energetic Stanford engineering graduate and assistant director of the US Army Ordnance Department's Special Mission V-2 project, sat up straight in his chair and narrowed his eyes at Joshua and Alec across the desk. It was clearly time to illuminate both men on their proper roles and his expectations.

"Gentlemen," he said gruffly. "You are *not* here to question my decisions about shipping V-2 parts exclusively to the US. Those are between me, my superior, and your own superiors at SHAEF. Allow me to remind both of you, your mission from now on is to be centered on one thing and one thing only—helping me and my project team find and interrogate the key rocket specialists responsible for designing and building the V-2—*before the Russians can get to them.*"

Alec pressed his case. "And what will happen to them after that, sir? Will they be turned over to US custody for US scientific benefit, just like the rocket parts? With no consideration for international war crimes charges against them?"

Staver's face turned red with indignation. "Lieutenant Benjamin, I know where you're trying to go with your insinuations, and I strongly advise you to cease and desist if you wish to remain a part of this effort. Let's stick to the essentials, Lieutenant."

Alec bristled, ready to defend himself, but thankfully chose to relent. "Of course, sir. Please forgive me for allowing my patriotic sentiments to override my better judgment. It won't happen again, sir."

"Do we have any information as to their possible whereabouts?" Joshua asked, eager to reset the discussion.

Staver sighed and shook his head as he took a drag on his cigarette.

"Only thing we know for sure is that General Kammler, who was the top SS overseer of the entire Nazi V-2 effort, ordered an evacuation from Nordhausen to Bavaria for about five hundred of their top scientists. Wernher Von Braun is very probably with that group. As of yet, we have no idea of their status down there. But that still leaves over 4,500 other V-2 connected scientists and technicians from Peenemünde and Nordhausen. We suspect many of them are scattered and in hiding somewhere out there in no-man's-land between our British-American front and the western fringe of the Russian army.

"We're just beginning to discover the names of these people from a telephone list left behind by the SS in a tunnel supervisor's office," Staver continued. "One of the men in particular seems to present an especially high-value target for us."

"Who is he, sir, if I may ask?" Joshua asked.

Major Staver held up a finger. He reached in one of his desk drawers and pulled out a red folder. From that, he extracted three eight-by-ten, black-and-white photographs.

"These were found yesterday."

He placed the first two photos side by side between Joshua and Alec.

"Is that what I think it is?" Alec gasped, pointing to one of the photos. "Five men hanging from a crane-supported beam? Looks like a mass execution just took place inside one of the tunnels!"

"You've got that right, Lieutenant. And in the second one, we see three officials standing on a platform. The one in the SS uniform is addressing a crowd of prisoners from a microphone. Notice he's point-ing at something off to his left. The other two are focused in the same direction. Those men are the ones who supposedly orchestrated the hanging, according to one of the surviving prisoners who claimed to have been present."

"Do we know who they are?"

"That's Kammler's right hand man, Colonel Gerhard Bremmer, in the middle. On his right is Arthur Rudolph—who we think is von Braun's chief V-2 production engineer."

"What about the man on the left?"

Joshua gulped, as he already knew the answer.

"That's Professor Erich Neumann, a renowned guidance and control consultant to von Braun. Used to teach at a Berlin university before he got roped into the V-2 effort."

Alec shot Joshua a quizzical look. "Didn't they mention that guy to us in the London office? Is he the same one?"

Joshua nodded. "Appears to be," he said grimly. He had not been ready then, and after seeing the photo, he was *definitely* not ready now, to reveal his personal connection with Erich Neumann and his daugh-ter Klara to Alec or Major Staver.

"Why in the world would a guy like that be overseeing a mass exe-cution?" Alec mused.

Staver smiled grimly. "That's not the only odd thing our good Pro-fessor Neumann seems to have involved himself with . . ."

He placed the third photo down on top of the first two. "We found this one framed and in a big pile of trash outside the SS officers' mess hall. Someone obviously forgot to destroy it completely, or maybe they just didn't care anymore.

"What's this?" Alec muttered as the men stared together at the image of a large group of German SS, Wehrmacht soldiers, and civil-ians gathered around what appeared to be some kind of launch console. All were grinning and raising their champagne glasses to a dark-haired man sitting on a chair in the middle with the index finger of his right hand poised above a button. It was Professor Erich Neumann, and he was the only one not smiling.

"A special occasion," Staver replied. "Read the translated caption underneath."

Joshua read the words out loud:

A Cause for Celebration!

250th Successful Launch of the Vengeance-2 Rocket

Training and Experimental Battery 444, Waffen SS Division for Retribution

Date: November 25, 1944
Time: 1:20 p.m.
Target: London, England

Guest Launch Master:
Professor Erich Neumann,
Peenemünde Rocket Team

On His 50th Birthday!

Heart in his throat, Joshua looked hesitantly at his British friend.

Alec's whole body had tensed, his jaw twitching with what could only be fury over the implications of what he was reading, but he said nothing.

Major Staver must have noticed the strong reaction. "Something wrong, Lt. Benjamin?"

Alec said nothing for several awkward seconds. He looked blankly at Staver. "It's nothing, sir. Just a reaction to seeing all those smirking Nazis celebrating such an event."

"Yes, well, hopefully we'll be able to capture their most important scientists like von Braun and this guy Neumann. See if they're interested in making amends for all their sins."

"*Amends*, sir?" Alec asked heatedly. "In Neumann's case at least, I'm hard-pressed to imagine any amends that would suffice. Unless it involved placing his own neck in a noose and shoving him off a cliff."

Staver stared at him coldly. "A lot of our top government people will likely feel the same way once they look more closely at this case, Lieutenant. But there are also a lot of officials who will strongly deny these photos constitute valid, definitive proof of Neumann's guilt for war crimes. After all, there's no direct evidence that he himself is specifically *ordering* the murder of civilians. Even if he does appear, in the one photo, to be observing an execution taking place and, in the other, he's presumably obeying an order to push a V-2 launch button. And if he can't be proven to be a war criminal, that certainly should leave him eligible to bring his talents to the US or Britain and start majorly contributing to our own rocketry programs. The same goes for von Braun and the other V-2 men. In any case, that'll be up to our governments to make the final decision on the V-2 rocket men's fate, not ours. Our job is simply to find them and bring them to heel.

"The problem is, we don't know for sure which of them went down to Bavaria and who's now just floating around in the countryside. That's where you two come into the picture. I need you to use your intel wizardry to concentrate on finding this man Neumann and call in one of your SHAEF T-1 teams to secure him before the Russians get to him. We'll handle things from there. I know it's a tall order. But that's why we brought you here. Are we clear now on your mission from this point forward?"

"Yes, sir," Joshua and Alec said in unison.

"Good. You'll start tomorrow. Corporal Benson will give you a ride back to your quarters.

"Major Staver?" Alec asked, his face set like stone.

"Yes?"

"Request permission to make a copy of these photos for my possession… they'll help me identify our target if we encounter him."

Staver shook his head. "Negative, Lieutenant. These images are far too sensitive and potentially damning to just be handing out like candy. I can't take the chance that they'd somehow find their way into the hands of overzealous war crimes investigators. That could greatly complicate our plans to put this guy to work on our respective countries' rocket science development projects. So, I suggest you simply imprint those images on your mind as best you can.

"I understand, sir."

On their way to the jeep, Joshua stopped and grasped Alec's arm. "What did you make of all that?"

Alec looked at him closely. "There's no question in my mind, Joshua. The timing was impeccable. *That* was the V-2 strike that killed Laura and her mother. And now I know who was responsible. Those photos are incriminating. If we ever catch the man, unlike Staver, I'd be hard-pressed *not* to take him directly to the war crimes investigators and present the evidence. There's no way he should be allowed to get away with mass murder simply on grounds of his scientific value. In my opinion, Staver's concerned with American interests only. If it were my call, I'd turn the photos over right *now* to our SHAEF superiors. Let them decide what to do with them."

Joshua shrugged noncommittally. He thought again about revealing his personal connection to Erich Neumann. Once again, he put it off, knowing it could stir up a hornet's nest of emotion and suspicion on Alec's part.

The men approached the jeep to find the orderly fiddling with the volume of a crackling portable radio on the vacant front seat. He looked up as they drew near.

"Big news on the Berlin front, sirs."

"What's that, Corporal?" Joshua asked.

"Russkies finally completed encircling the city today. They're launching massive artillery strikes on the suburbs and city center. Stalin's claiming the city will fall very soon."

Joshua drew a deep breath and turned to look toward the eastern horizon. Though Berlin was nearly 150 miles away, he thought he detected a strange, pulsating glow, low in the otherwise pitch-dark sky in the direction of the city. Its color was red.

He wondered if Klara was still there.

CHAPTER 50

Berlin, Germany
May 1, 1945
(Six days later)

Captain Elke Schröder pulled her head back inside the tall, glassless window frame on the third floor of the shell-damaged apartment building on Pestalozzi Strasse in the northern section of Charlottenburg. The floor and walls of the former living room shook noticeably from the closely spaced, deafening blasts of nearby Russian artillery and tanks.

"Street's all clear, so far," Elke said.

Leaning with her back against the frame of a second blown-out window several feet from Elke's, Irma Brubeck gripped the shaft of a stick grenade in one hand as she repeatedly tapped its cylindrical charge against the palm of the other.

"We'll blow the bastards to kingdom come, if they ever get here."

If the Dragoness doesn't blow us all there first by accidentally detonating that thing, Klara thought as she sat on the floor with the other girls along the opposite wall. *What a horrible ending after all our preparations.*

She tried her best to envision a more positive outcome to the dangerous mission that Elke and her small, all-female defense team had been assigned by the local Volkssturm commander. The team had participated in seven practice runs yesterday, under the close supervision of the deputy commander, a retired Wehrmacht weapons officer. Each girl knew exactly what was expected.

Collectively, their mission was to delay the progress of any Soviet mechanized column that might choose Pestalozzi Strasse as its preferred route. The girls had been instructed to hurl their team's allotment of two Molotov cocktails and six stick grenades through the windows onto the leading tank and any accompanying infantrymen. Their main purpose was to create a distraction, drawing the Russians' attention away from the building on the opposite side of the street. There, two heavy machine guns and a handheld Panzerfaust[*] had been placed in upper floor windows and a ground-floor entrance to be operated by Hitler Youths. Once the girls set things in motion, the youths would open fire on any exposed infantrymen and the flank and treads of the lead tank, hopefully destroying or at least disabling and blocking the ones behind.

After tossing their explosives, the girls were to immediately flee the building via its rear escape ladder. Racing five blocks down the street through courtyards and back alleyways, they would rejoin the motley assemblage of Hitler Youth boys and elderly Volkssturm soldiers manning the barricade. From there, the chivalrous, old-school Volkssturm commander had told them, they were each free to remain at the barricade with the men or to run another half mile to find protection with other civilians taking shelter in the base of the huge and supposedly impenetrable, SS-defended Zoo Tower.

"The other girls here may choose what they wish, but I will remain at the barricade," Elke had told the commander without hesitation in front of the others.

---

[*] *Panzerfaust*: A hand-held, disposable, bazooka-like antitank weapon with range of about thirty meters

"*As will I,*" Irma Brubeck had chimed in. "If you ask me," she'd huffed, "any girl here who chooses to desert the fight at the critical moment is a coward and deserves to be *shot,* just like the men." All the girls had stared at her with open-mouthed, horrified expressions reflecting either their intimidation or—as in Klara's and Elke's cases—disgust. Seeing the negative reactions, the Dragoness relented ever so slightly. "But each to their own, I suppose."

The mid-morning sun's rays streamed through the windows for a brief second before being obscured once again by the thick smoke that swirled outside. Klara snuck discrete glances at the girls sitting against the wall. She wondered if anyone else's entire body trembled like hers, wondered if their teeth chattered as relentlessly. Each girl seemed lost in her own world. Trudi Schuster held an empty wine bottle in her lap, gazing at it vacantly as she turned it around and around in her hands. One of the three younger BDM girls rested her head back against the wall, her eyes closed, possibly praying. The other two simply sat with their arms crossed and legs stretched out in front, staring down at their laps.

Klara looked across the floor and watched Elke pull a small flask from her inside tunic pocket, uncap it and take a substantial swig. As she was about to put the cap back on, she noticed Klara staring at her. She grinned and raised the flask as if making a toast. "Want some?" she mouthed. Klara smiled back and shook her head. Elke made a funny face and stuck her tongue out playfully, prompting Klara to do the same. *Just like old times in church*, Klara thought fondly. She greatly appreciated her sister's attempt at tension relief.

As she watched Elke turn and resume her observations out the window, Klara marveled at her sister's decision to do battle today wearing the SS tunic worn by her beloved husband Heinz on the day he'd been shot by the female sniper at Sevastapol.

"Are you *crazy*?" Klara had chided her. "It's bad enough thinking what the Russians might do to you if you're captured *without* that on. But can you imagine what they'll do if they see those two SS lightning bolts on your collar?"

"I don't plan on allowing myself to be captured, and neither should you," Elke had replied. "And besides, wearing this and remembering who wore it before me will give me the extra strength and desire to keep fighting when things get desperate, as I know they will."

Desperate. That was for sure, Klara thought. Despite Goebbels's passionate reassurance over the radio yesterday that General Wenck's massive relief force had already broken through the Soviet encirclement, and that help was—

"*They're coming!*" Elke yelled. "*Girls, get ready!*"

She slid down below the sill, motioning frantically for Klara, Trudi, Irma, and the other BDM girls to take their well-rehearsed positions underneath the two windows overlooking the street.

"What are you seeing, Captain?" Trudi whispered, her voice shaking.

"Two T-34's are already coming down the street and a third just turned the corner. No doubt there're more tanks behind that one. Foot soldiers flanking them on both sides. Lead tank looks like it'll pass by here in less than a minute. Remember, we'll have only ten seconds total to dump everything we have. No mistakes."

Elke peeked above the sill. "Five tanks now. Let's have our cocktails . . ."

Klara and Erika, the youngest of the BDM girls, each retrieved a gasoline-filled bottle plugged with a gas-soaked wick made of rags. They handed them to Trudi and Irma, who now crouched under separate windows. Upon Elke's signal, the plan was for Klara and Erika to each strike a match and light the wicks for Trudi and Irma, who would then have three seconds to hurl their welcoming gifts out the window and down onto the unsuspecting Russians. Elke and the other two BDM girls would then throw two stick grenades each in rapid succession out the windows.

"About thirty seconds now," Elke said. "Trudi, Irma... peek over the sill and take a quick look. Do you see what I see? Idiotic lead tank commander's standing in the open turret hatch, half his body exposed."

Both girls nodded.

"Aim directly for him. Rest of us, wait for all the cocktails to explode first, then throw one of your grenades just in front and the other at the side of the tank's treads. Got it?"

All the girls nodded. Trudi and Irma crouched, their bottles poised to have the wicks lit by Klara and Erika. Klara could hardly breathe as she held her match, ready to strike against the box when the command was given.

"Ten seconds! *Girls, this is it!* Trudi and Irma, stand up. Klara, Erika, strike your matches now."

Klara did so, holding her lit match with shaking hand a few inches from the wick of Trudi's bottle.

"Three... two... one . . ."

"*Light 'em and toss!*"

The wicks flamed brightly.

The two bottles sailed toward their target. Unable to see past Trudi, Klara held her breath, awaiting the result.

Two explosions occurred nearly simultaneously.

"*Got 'em!*" Trudi screamed. "He's on fire!"

"*Tank's slowing!*" Irma yelled.

Elke looked at the other two BDM girls with the stick grenades. "Our turn, ladies. Remember your aim points. *Now!*" One by one, each girl pulled the cords on their two M15 potato mashers and threw them. Seconds later, a series of six explosions rocked the walls of the building. Klara and Erika crowded around the windows with the others to observe the results of their effort.

Chaos had erupted below.

The lead tank's hatch had taken a direct hit from Trudi's cocktail. The commander, fire engulfing his upper body, had managed to extricate himself and was rolling on the ground screaming in agony. Two infantrymen rushed over and tried frantically to beat the flames out with their bare hands. The tank itself had come to a stop, blocking the ones following. Several infantrymen lay on the street or sidewalk with a limb or head missing—one man having been blown up on top of the tank's barrel by the grenade blasts. The commander in the following tank screamed orders and pointed in the girls' direction. Several of the infantrymen who'd taken cover behind the tank raised their submachine guns as the tank's barrel began to swing.

It was at that moment that the Hitler Youth boys on the opposite side of the street let loose with their own devastating barrage, confusing and splitting the Russians' defensive response. A Panzerfaust projectile streaked toward the lead tank and impacted it between the turret and the body with a loud clank. A flash was followed by a puff of smoke and small explosion. For a couple of seconds—nothing. Suddenly, the lid of the tank blew into the air, followed by a rush of bright red and yellow flame and sparks.

"Get out, now!" Elke bellowed as the first bullets from the infantrymen struck the exterior wall.

The girls raced toward the rear door leading to the fire escape. Elke held it open as the others filed out one by one, Klara being the last. She had just stepped onto the platform when she heard Elke scream. *"Irma, what are you doing? Come on!"*

Klara turned back and looked over her sister's shoulder. Irma was lying under one of the windows, curled up in a fetal position. Her arms covered her head as a fusillade of bullets zipped through the two window openings and slammed into the top of the wall opposite, ripping it to shreds.

"Irma!" Elke cried out. "You have to get away from there. Just crawl along the floor to me. The bullets are angled too high to hit you!"

Irma peeked out between her arms and stared at Elke briefly, then shook her head and curled up into an even tighter ball. The Dragoness—who'd earlier berated the other girls on the deserved consequences of their cowardice—had suddenly become too petrified to move.

Elke grabbed Klara's arm. "Sister, go on with the others. I'm going in to get her."

"No, Elke, don't. You'll—"

The blast from the exploding tank shell obliterated the entire front wall around the window under which Irma had sought refuge. Elke and Klara were hurled back against the fire escape's railing as plaster and small pieces of Irma Brubeck shot through the doorway, splattering on their faces and clothes.

In a state of shock, Klara was barely conscious of Elke grabbing her by the arm, lifting her and leading her down the steps. Her voice sounded like it was calling from far away through some long tunnel. "Klara, we can't stop. The soldiers will be coming up to finish off any survivors."

By the time they reached the bottom of the escape, Klara's head had cleared sufficiently to see Trudi and the three BDM girls beckoning to them from behind the rear gate of the courtyard. After reuniting briefly with tears and hugs, the girls ran for five blocks down a back alley, turning left at a side street that led them back to where the barricade had been erected.

As soon as the exhausted girls emerged from between the tall apartment buildings, the men saw them and spread the word. Klara and the others were astonished to find themselves greeted with a chorus of cheers and lifted helmets or caps from over thirty Hitler Youth and Volkssturm soldiers of all ages.

The Volkssturm commander motioned all six girls over to his position and, after receiving their salutes, removed his helmet and greeted them warmly. Shaking Elke's hand, he addressed her directly. "Captain, you and your team deserve medals." He pointed up the street to where the destroyed tank was still blocking the Soviet advance, though efforts were clearly underway to push it to the side of the street. "Thanks to you and those brave boys on the other side of the street, we've bought a little more time to set up that antitank gun," he said, nodding toward a group of men struggling to position and stabilize the wheeled, bulky cannon. "Just got here a couple of minutes ago. It's not much, given what we're facing, but at least it's something, and now we should have time to get it ready." He looked at her with probing eyes. "Tell me, Captain, did you lose anyone back there?"

"We lost one, Commander. My lieutenant, Irma Brubeck, was killed by a direct hit on our perch by a tank shell."

The commander bowed his head for a brief second then lifted it again. "Captain Schröder, you and your girls have already done more than anyone in their right mind could expect of you today. In my view, you are all heroes of the Reich. I urge you now... take your girls on back to the Zoo Flak Tower and leave the rest here to me and my men. We won't be able to hold out for long, and once we start to crumble, it'll become a bloodbath—nigh impossible for anyone to escape to the rear. You girls will have a much better chance of surviving inside the Tower with the SS defending it. Please, Captain, it's bad enough that I'm having to sacrifice our young boys on this line without adding our womenfolk to the mix."

"*Commander, they've cleared the blocking tank!*" yelled one of the men from the top of the nearest barricade rubble pile.

The commander gave Elke one last pleading look. "Go... take them on back now."

Elke saluted, and the commander rushed off.

She turned to face the rest of the girls. "You heard what he said. You all know the route to the Tower. I truly love and am so proud of each of you. Now, go on, before I lose myself in emotion."

The girls hesitated. "What about you, Captain?" Trudi asked.

"As I vowed before we took on our mission, I'm staying here to the end."

"*But why, Elke?*" Klara objected. "If you're fighting on for the sake of the Führer, at this point that's just—"

"I'm *not* fighting for the sake of the Führer any longer, Klara. I'm fighting on because... because . . ." She looked down at the ground in embarrassment. "In truth, I don't know why I'm fighting on. I only know that I must."

Each of the three BDM girls came forward and gave Elke a hug and final salute, then whirled and ran off.

Elke turned to face Trudi and Klara. "Time to get going, you two. Come on, don't make it harder on me than it already is. Give me your hugs."

Trudi shook her head firmly. "There's no way I'm leaving you now, Elke. You're the only friend I've ever really had, and you've taught me too well what it means to be loyal and brave."

Elke smiled at her through the tears streaming down her cheeks. She turned to Klara, her lips trembling. "What are you still doing here, sister? You, of all people, certainly don't need to stay here and fight on for the Führer like the rest of us hopeless fanatics."

Klara gripped Elke's arms and looked her in the eyes. "I'm not fighting for the Führer, Elke. I'm staying here and fighting on for *you*."

Maybe it was her adrenaline pumping from their earlier encounter with the Russians. Or perhaps, it was a case of foolish feminine bravado. Something most of the old men and teenaged boys observing from behind the barricade couldn't really understand but could all definitely admire.

Whatever it was, Trudi Schuster had just decided it was up to her to answer the Volkssturm commander's call for someone to come to the aid of the two Hitler Youths stationed in a rubble-protected shop doorway fifty yards in front of the barricade.

The boys had volunteered for what would almost certainly be a suicidal task: one providing submachine gun cover from the doorway while the other ran out into the middle of the street with his Panzerfaust, firing off a shot at the front of the next lead tank when it was less than thirty yards away. If all went well, the armor-piercing projectile would penetrate to the crew compartment and ignite it, stopping the vehicle cold and producing yet another major traffic jam.

Unfortunately, just as the destroyed tank five blocks up the street had been pushed out of the way and the column resumed its advance, the boys realized their Panzerfaust had jammed. They signaled frantically back to the men at the barricade, but with the lead tank closing, no one had seemed eager to step forward and make the run to their location with a replacement.

Trudi Schuster knew it was her time to act. Over the objections of Elke and the Volkssturm commander, who both thought the situation hopeless, Trudi had insisted on being handed two loaded Panzerfausts which she'd promptly slung over her shoulders. She then ran behind the barricade, to the sidewalk, and up the street to the boy's position.

"Thank God, looks like she made it," Elke muttered as she peered over the barricade rubble, her own Panzerfaust aimed toward the approaching tank. "But the Russians are sending their infantrymen a few yards ahead of the tank to check doorways. If one of those Hitler Youth boys has any hope of making it out to the middle of the street before they discover him, he'll need to do it soon."

Klara, lying beside her sister, prayed that Trudi had found herself a safe place to hide; or even better, an escape route from the back of the shop.

She looked around at the woefully undermanned firing positions on either side of them. Besides the Panzerfausts in the hands of Elke and the seven Hitler Youths spread out along the line, only the tripod-mounted MG-42 machine-gun emplacement and the antitank cannon had any real chance of doing anything to slow or stop the T-34's. The archaic World War I vintage rifles wielded by the other men would be virtually useless.

I know exactly how they feel, Klara thought, glancing at the box of ten stick grenades she'd been allotted. Given her limited throwing strength and lack of training, these would have no real effect except at very close range, and by then it would likely be too late.

"Come on, *come on…* get out there… you're losing your chance," Elke growled impatiently as the tank approached relentlessly, making horrendous grinding and creaking noises as it moved along on its metal tracks.

"*There he goes!*" Klara shouted.

As one of the Hitler Youths sprayed the advance guard of Russian infantrymen with submachine gun fire from the shelter of the shop, his partner emerged from the entryway. With his Panzerfaust shouldered, he ran toward the middle of the street. He made it only halfway before a bullet from one of the infantrymen struck him, crumpling his body and sending his weapon clattering to the ground. The covering fire from the shop ceased immediately, and a chorus of groans and curses erupted along the entire barricade.

The commander shouted the order to prepare to fire along the entire line at his signal.

Klara watched Elke look through the sight on her Panzerfaust and tighten her finger on the trigger. "They're still well out of effective range for these things—thirty yards is the maximum." Suddenly, she lifted her head and shouted.

"*Trudi!*"

The entire line of barricade defenders as well as the Soviet infantrymen seemed to freeze at the sight of Trudi Schuster racing onto the sidewalk with the second Panzerfaust. With no covering fire, she reached the curb, knelt on one knee no more than twenty yards from the front of the oncoming metal beast, and fired.

Nothing. The projectile, obviously a dud, bounced harmlessly off the tank's heavily armored plates.

Trudi dropped her weapon and stood slowly, seemingly resigned to her fate.

"*Trudi, no! Run!*" Klara jumped up and screamed.

Trudi turned toward the barricade as the tank approached, stood straight and extended her right hand out and up. A final fascist salute to those she'd sought to protect.

A hail of bullets from the infantrymen ripped through her body, knocking her on her face. Without mercy, the Russian tank driver veered toward the curb, causing the vehicle's tread to pass lengthwise over Trudi's entire body.

"*Oh, my God!*" Elke gasped, dropping her Panzerfaust and turning away from the horrendous sight of her favorite student's grisly demise. Klara fell to her knees, retching.

"*Fire everything we've got!*" The commander yelled as Elke yanked Klara by the arm down beside her.

It was too late. Fired from less than forty yards away, the lead T-34's first projectile scored a direct hit on the anti-tank cannon before it could even get off a round. Seconds later, the barricade's heavy machine-gun position was wiped out by a barrage of fire from the tank and Russian infantrymen with submachine guns surging around its sides.

Another tank projectile blasted a huge hole in the barricade near Klara and Elke just as a streak of tracer rounds exploded the head of the Hitler Youth boy beside them. A second tank had just steered up beside the first and was now repositioning its big gun to bear on the defenders. The Russian firepower was overwhelming, raking the entire barricade with a near constant fusillade of hot metal.

The defensive line disintegrated. Men and boys began dropping their weapons and running—at least those who hadn't already been blown apart.

Klara, looked up at her sister in utter disbelief. Elke had raised herself to a kneeling position on the barricade's makeshift parapet with her Panzerfaust over her shoulder in firing position. She swung it from side to side, seemingly uncertain of her target. Zipping bullets threatened to rip her exposed head off at any moment.

"Elke, what are you doing? What are we waiting for? Let's go!"

"*Run, Klara!*" Elke shouted over the din. "You know where the Tower is."

"Elke, you're not possibly going to—"

"*Yes, I am, dammit!* There's nothing more for me, but there is for you. Now get out of here."

Klara hesitated, unsure. Suddenly, something inside her snapped.

"*Elke, you're coming with me, or I'm staying here with you. You decide.*"

Elke looked over her shoulder at her sister, then back at the T-34, now only thirty yards in front of the barricade. She dropped her weapon and grabbed Klara's hand.

"You win. Let's go."

CHAPTER 51

Berlin, Germany
May 1, 1945

Just as the girls turned down the cross street that they assumed would provide the most direct route to the Zoo Flak Tower, another Russian tank with its surrounding cadre of infantrymen rounded the corner ahead and headed in their direction.

Elke yanked her sister into a recessed shop entrance.

"Forget the Tower. We're already cut off!"

"What'll do we do?" Klara asked frantically, knowing they had only moments to act before they were spotted and captured, shot, or worse.

Elke looked left and right, still breathing heavily from the run. Finally, she stopped panting and stood straight, her mind obviously made up. She grabbed Klara by the arm.

"Our house is only half a mile south of here. If we have to die together, at least let's do it *trying* to make it there."

Klara nodded, a strange sense of confidence and hope filling her chest as she peered into her sister's clear, blue eyes and saw the steady, unyielding resolve. She had always either admired or hated that determination, depending on the circumstances.

The girls made it two blocks before an artillery shell exploded in the middle of the street, knocking them both off their feet. Dazed, they stood slowly and looked around, uncertain where to proceed.

Suddenly, a male voice called out from somewhere just down the sidewalk.

"Girls! In here! Quick!"

A short, elderly man with a white beard motioned vigorously to them from the ground entrance of an apartment building. He held the door open for them as they drew near. "You're lucky I saw you. Hurry… I'm about to lock this place up and join my family in the basement. Everyone else in this building all fled for the Tower. They're choosing suicide, if you ask me. The Russians will shell that place to shreds."

"Thank you, sir. You are incredibly kind to take us in with you," Klara said as she passed him on the way inside.

"Hey!" the man shouted suddenly. Both girls drew up short.

He glared at Elke. "If you're planning to stay in *my* basement with *my* family, you're going to have to remove that SS jacket."

Elke looked at him hesitantly. "Oh, sir, this was my husband's tunic… he died fighting bravely at Sevastapol and I'd like to—"

"I don't care who the hell it may have belonged to, Fräulein! Haven't you heard the reports about what the SS did in Poland and Russia? If Russian soldiers should happen to discover us, and you're still proudly wearing that *thing* in our presence, they're sure to tear us all limb from limb. So, if you want to join us, take it off and give it to me… now!"

Elke complied quickly. The man rushed over and dropped it in a nearby dumpster before rejoining the girls and escorting them down the back stairwell to the apartment basement. They were greeted there with the surprised stares of the man's wife, daughter, and granddaughter.

"Who are these women, Oskar?" the wife asked suspiciously.

"Found them stranded on the sidewalk just outside as I was locking up."

Oskar looked plaintively at his wife, seeming to already know what she was thinking. "Frieda, we can't just turn them away. They'll be killed for sure if they're caught outside. Surely, we can make our food and water stretch—"

"Stretch for how long, Oskar?" Frieda interrupted angrily. "Two days, three?"

"As long as it takes for all this shooting and shelling to pass us by. It's not going to last forever."

"And then what? You know good and well the Russians will send more people. They'll be skulking around the street and upstairs like a bunch of cats, just waiting to pounce on any of us starving rats down here who dare stick our noses out of this cellar to beg them for a little food or drink."

Apparently realizing the implications of her own logic, Frieda threw her palms up in the air. "Oh, what's the point of it all? Might as well let them stay with us. Sooner or later, the little we have down here will run out, and we'll have to give ourselves up anyway."

"*Mama, please don't talk like that!*" Frieda's daughter scolded her, drawing her own trembling daughter close to her side. "Once it's calmer outside we'll find a way to sneak more food and water down here... won't we, Papa?"

Oskar hung his head, uncertain what to say. Clearly, he realized the prospects for long-term survival in the basement were nil.

Elke spoke up. "Frau, my sister and I do not wish to burden you any more than you obviously already are. Forgive us for accepting your husband's kind offer. We can see now it simply isn't going to work." She motioned to Klara. "Come on, sister, let's go. Maybe we can—"

"No, no!" Frieda exclaimed. "Please stay. And forgive *me* for letting my fears overwhelm my better Christian impulses. Somehow, as my daughter Fredericke suggested, we'll find a way to . . ." Her voice trailed off as her husband walked over and put his arm around her shoulders.

Suddenly, she shook her head as if to clear it and looked at her granddaughter, a thin girl with shoulder-length dark hair and an angelic face who appeared to be about sixteen. "Adele, please pull down those extra blankets from the shelf and help our guests get comfortable while your mother and I prepare the first meal in our new cave."

It wasn't long before everyone was seated on the bench or blankets, eating pieces of stale, black bread with small bowls of barley soup that had been warmed over a portable gas burner, and a half-cup of water each. After relating their own harrowing story of barely evading a massive bomb blast that had killed over a dozen people and wiped out the nearby home of some friends, Oskar and his family listened with rapt attention as Elke described the ordeal at the barricade.

"I can't believe it's come to this," Frieda lamented. "Our beautiful city in ruins, our boys and girls fighting and dying in the streets . . ."

"We have our all-wise Führer to thank for that," Oskar said bitterly.

"Papa, please don't start," Fredericke pleaded, glancing nervously at Klara and Elke with an apologetic expression. Klara half-expected her sister to raise some objection, but to her surprise and relief, Elke simply kept on eating, appearing not at all fazed by Oskar's comment.

Hours passed as the muffled explosions outside continued, rising to a crescendo around 6 p.m. before tapering off around ten. Klara and Elke spent most of the time alternately dozing off and conversing softly with Adele and her mother. Frieda busied herself darning a shirt, while Oskar fiddled with the flickering kerosene lamp and shuffled through several stacks of papers he'd brought down in a small suitcase from their apartment. Though no one spoke of their fears, the tension in everyone's face was evident in the harsh lines revealed by the lamplight.

Despite her best efforts to keep her mind focused on other things, Klara couldn't stop imagining what their first encounter with Russian soldiers would entail. How would they react to each person in the cellar?

It was nearly eleven when a sudden burst of submachine gun on the floor above was followed almost immediately by raucous yelling, laughter, and boots tromping in the hallway directly overhead.

The Reds had arrived.

Within seconds, the thumping of footsteps on the stairwell accompanied by gruff voices speaking in Russian caused six pairs of eyes in the cramped cellar to stare at each other in panicked alarm.

"*God help us!*" Frieda cried out softly.

"Shhh!" Oskar hissed, He muffled her mouth with his hand and pulled her in close by his side on the small wooden bench next to the furnace.

Sitting on the concrete floor against the wall opposite, Klara, Elke, Fredericke, and Adele squeezed closer together, holding each other's hands as they all held their breaths and peered warily toward the cellar door. *Any second now,* Klara knew. She closed her eyes and prayed, awaiting the inevitable.

A short burst of bullets shattered the door's lock, leaving a gaping hole in its place.

Klara gasped and grabbed Elke and Adele's hands as the door swung open.

Three Soviet soldiers, guns poised, entered the room and stopped to size up the terrified occupants by the dim light of the kerosene lamp. Everyone remained frozen, uncertain how to proceed.

Finally, Oskar stood slowly and offered one of the men a bowl of soup. He shook his head and smiled, still silent. Releasing one hand from his weapon, he pointed to the watch on Oskar's wrist then motioned for him to remove it and hand it over.

A second soldier, a short man with the ruddy cheeks of a peasant farmer, grinned and pulled a flask from his tunic pocket. It had no top and was apparently empty. He raised it in a mock toast. "Hitler dead. Stalin... long live!" he announced in thickly accented German.

Klara and Elke glanced uncertainly at each other. Could it be true?

The second soldier's voice turned surly. "Schnapps. Where schnapps?" he demanded, stepping forward and thrusting the empty flask in front of Oskar's face.

Oskar shrugged his shoulders helplessly.

The soldier—who appeared to be the de facto leader of the three— looked briefly at Frieda, then turned toward the younger women huddled together on the floor. Pocketing the flask, he picked up the kerosene lamp and stooped down beside them. One by one, he examined their faces, as if judging the finalists of a beauty contest. His gaze seemed to linger the longest on Adele, who clung to her mother. He stood and said something in Russian to the first soldier who moved over a few steps to examine the space on the other side of the furnace. Seeming to approve of whatever he was assessing, he looked back and nodded.

The leader looked once again at Oskar and his wife, then turned and pointed the gun at Fredericke. "Let go your girl."

"*No... please!*" Fredericke begged, clinging even tighter to her daughter.

"Want her die?" the leader growled, repositioning the muzzle of his submachine gun only inches from Adele's face. Grabbing the girl's arm, he wrestled her away from her mother's grasp and handed her over to his comrade.

After speaking a few words to the third soldier, he pointed in turn at Oskar, Frieda and Fredericke. "You three... go!" he ordered, motioning toward the cellar door beside which the third soldier stood, beckoning them to follow him outside.

"*Mama!*"

Klara and Elke could only watch with helpless, horrified anguish as the soldier who held Adele clamped his hand over the girl's mouth from behind as her mother and grandparents were forced one by one out of the room.

Where is he taking them? And why—

Klara's naïve question was answered when the leader kicked the door shut behind them and said something to his comrade, who immediately began wrestling the slightly built Adele back behind the furnace.

At the sound of Adele's muffled cries, Elke rose to her feet. "Don't do this. Please, sir, have him take me instead... I promise I'll be good to both of you."

The man gawked at her in astonishment. Slowly, his lips curled in a leering smile as he nodded appreciatively. "You next. Sit."

For Klara, the next two minutes seemed to pass like an eternity in hell. Even with her hands over her ears, she was unable to completely block the sounds of the ferocious, animal-like grunting punctuated by Adele's sharp screams of pain.

Finally, silence. Deathly silence. Klara uncovered her ears and glanced at her sister, whose crossed arms, tightly shut eyes, and twitching jaw gave hints of the raging fury burning inside.

The lead soldier leaned over to observe the scene on the other side of the furnace. Whatever he saw caused him to cock his head back, his face contorted in obvious dismay.

"Drisnya!"

A furious exchange in Russian ensued between the two men without the slightest sound from Adele. While arguing, the leader kept glancing over at Klara and Elke as if he was reconsidering what to do with them. At last, he walked over to the door, opened it and spoke to someone who had apparently been stationed just outside.

Conversation concluded, he walked over and picked up the blankets that Oskar and Frieda had left behind and tossed one each in Klara's and Elke's laps.

"Put over heads," he commanded. "If take off, you dead."

Hesitantly, the girls complied.

Klara trembled violently as she listened to what sounded like the two soldiers lifting Adele and carrying her out of the cellar. She could only assume that the first soldier had lost control of his lust and killed her, and that the men were now, for some reason, feeling a need to dispose of the evidence.

As soon as they left, she sensed someone else enter the room and close the door behind themselves.

A few seconds of silence, then whoever it was walked over and yanked the blankets from the girls' heads.

Directly in front of them, a female Russian soldier with blond hair tucked under her wedged, red-starred cap, stood with submachine gun pointed. Just as the male soldier had done earlier, the girl picked up the kerosene lamp, stooped down and held it before her, examining Elke's and Klara's faces. Klara saw that the girl had an almond-shaped face, high cheekbones, a wide mouth, and gray eyes that seemed to convey a cold hatred.

What is her purpose? Is she here to keep us guarded until the men come back to finish their business with us?

The girl shook her head slowly from side to side. "Nazi whores," she muttered softly in German as she placed the lamp back on the floor. She pointed her gun at Elke's chest. "You. Move over."

Elke stared at her blankly for several seconds, as if she didn't understand. The girl slapped her viciously across the face. "Said... *move over!*" She motioned with her gun to a point against the wall just a few feet away. Elke edged her way toward the spot, all the while keeping her gaze locked on the Russian.

The girl turned her attention and the point of the gun back to Klara alone. With a sneering smile, she used her free hand to reach into her tunic pocket. She pulled out a small, black-and-white photo—a head shot of Hitler—which she proceeded to wave slowly and tantalizingly in front of Klara's eyes.

"Ah... Führer, Führer," she purred. "Don't you wish he here with you now?" She wiped the photo slowly and teasingly down Klara's neck, across her chest and along her thigh. Eventually tiring of the game, she rammed her gun's muzzle through the center of the photo so that it remained affixed to the tip like a piece of speared trash.

Holding it up to Klara's face, she waved it in front of her lips. "Now eat your Führer, Nazi bitch."

Klara tried to turn her face away, but the Russian girl grabbed her chin and yanked it back as she thrust the photo-covered tip of the gun's barrel against Klara's clenched mouth.

"*Eat Führer!*" the girl shouted, pressing the barrel tip so hard that Klara was forced to open her mouth and receive it. She squeezed her eyes shut, expecting the fatal burst any second.

"*Oy!*"

The gun barrel tip slipped out of Klara's mouth. She opened her eyes and blinked, just in time to see Elke withdrawing her BDM dagger from the side of the Russian girl's neck.

Blood spurting from her jugular, the girl dropped her weapon and keeled over on her side. Elke sprang on top of her like a savage beast, stabbing her over and over in the chest and face—as if avenging the torture that Russian female sniper had inflicted upon her beloved husband Heinz.

"Elke, stop!" Klara screamed. She lunged and managed to grab her sister's arm from behind, just in time to prevent yet another needless strike as the girl's spasms of death continued for several more seconds.

Panting heavily, Elke dropped the knife, sat back on her heels and stared at Klara. Her eyes were glazed, her face and blouse splattered with blood. She looked back and forth between the dead girl and Klara several times, as though confused. Suddenly, her eyes filled with tears.

Klara reached out and took her sister into her arms, holding her head tenderly against her chest as she caressed her hair.

"Let's go home," she whispered.

After cautiously exiting the cellar and—to their surprise—detecting no sign of the Russian soldiers, Oskar, or his family on the floor above, the girls crept up the stairwell and down the entrance hallway, emerging from the building into the early morning darkness.

The street appeared devoid of humanity as they made their way south along Wilmersdorfer Strasse toward the Neumann family residence. Although heavy bombardment and gunfire could be heard in the direction of the *Reichstag* government building to the northeast, all seemed quiet in the immediate vicinity. Emboldened by the apparently clear path ahead, the girls raced down the center of the broad sidewalk.

The loud crack of a rifle from somewhere behind echoed down the street.

Klara took a few extra steps before she noticed Elke was no longer beside her. She stopped and turned, gasping at the sight of her sister lying face down, blood seeping through her blouse from the gunshot wound to her upper left back. She ran to help, praying that whoever had taken the shot would decide to move on to other ripe targets.

Elke was still conscious and able, with Klara's help, to crawl to a sheltered doorway. After ripping a swath of material from the bottom of her dress, Klara formed a makeshift bandage and wrapped it around her sister's shoulders and under her armpits, tying it behind her neck.

Realizing there was no possibility of making it to a medical facility, and fearful of abuse by passing Russian soldiers, Elke insisted on doing the best they could to make it home. With a supreme effort, Klara somehow managed to help Elke stand up and stumble along the four blocks past Kant Strasse to their home, finally making it up the stairs and into her bedroom.

The following afternoon, despite the nonstop efforts of Klara to make her sister comfortable, it was clear from her labored breathing and ghastly white pallor that internal bleeding was taking its toll. From Klara's nursing experience, she knew Elke was not going to survive the night. Her only consolation was knowing that she would draw her last breath in her own bed—in the familiar environs of her childhood.

Klara sat on the side of the bed, clutching her sister's hand as she watched her life ebb away.

She leaned over and whispered tearfully in her ear. "Stay with me, Elke. Don't leave me. I'll get help soon, and you'll... you'll . . ." Unable to finish, she simply buried her face against her sister's neck.

After several seconds, a gentle hand stroked the back of her hair. Elke's voice was still coherent.

"It's all right, Klara. You did everything you could, and you got me here. Will you just do one thing more for me?" Klara pulled her head back and looked at her.

Her sister's eyes were moist. "When you get to Heaven and see them, please tell Heinz and Walther and Vati and Mama that I loved them very much. And... while you're at it... please tell Jesus that I'm so very sorry."

"Sorry... for what, Elke?"

"For turning my back on him and making the *Führer* my life's obsession. For blinding myself to all of Hitler's lies and atrocities committed in his name... and . . ." Her voice fell off to a near whisper as a tear streamed down her cheek. "For teaching so many other young girls like Trudi to do the same."

Klara held Elke's hand to her lips and kissed it. "Why don't you just tell them all yourself when *you* see them?"

Elke's mouth trembled as she tried to smile. Her voice was now very weak. "You never were a good fibber, Klara. I know there's no chance of Heaven for me. I'm an idolizer and a murderer. After what I did to that Russian girl, there is no way God will—"

Klara placed her finger on her sister's lips. *"Elke, shhh!* I can't believe you've forgotten."

"For-forgotten?"

"Our favorite Bible story: The Thief on the Cross. Don't you remember?"

Elke labored to take a breath. Her eyes took on a glazed appearance. Klara knew she had only moments left.

"Elke, it's not too late... no matter what we've done. Just be like the thief. Ask Jesus *now* to be your Savior... I *know* he loves you, he'll forgive everything, and he's standing there waiting. Just reach out and take his hand to Heaven, Elke."

Klara watched as her sister's eyes closed, fearful that she hadn't comprehended her last plea. Suddenly, Elke's eyes fluttered open once again. She lifted her right hand and touched Klara's cheek.

"I have always loved you, Klara, and I always will. We will see you again."

With that, Elke slipped away.

CHAPTER 52

Berlin, Germany
May 3, 1945

The next morning, Klara awoke to a cacophony of Russian voices shouting to each other downstairs.

She lifted her arm from across her sister's blanket-covered body and got out of the bed. Hurrying to the window, she drew the curtains and looked out.

The sky was bright blue, and all sounds of battle had ceased. The street below was filled with Russian soldiers. Some were smoking and talking in small groups. Others were frolicking around like little children on bicycles they'd commandeered from somewhere or other.

Klara heard bootsteps ascending the stairs. In moments, the soldiers would discover her alone with her dead sister.

Maybe it was her sheer exhaustion, or perhaps it was simply her resignation now to accept the inevitable. Whatever the reason, she didn't feel especially afraid.

The bedroom doorknob clicked.

She took a deep breath, then turned to embrace her fate.

A Russian officer in full battle dress, his face covered with grime, entered and stood with his pistol drawn. He was flanked by two subordinates with submachine guns.

"Are you alone?" the officer asked Klara in German.

She gulped and nodded.

He motioned with his pistol toward Elke's covered body on the bed. "Who is that?"

"My sister, sir. She died just a few hours ago from a gunshot wound." Klara could hardly believe the calm, detached sound of her words, which masked the agony she was feeling over losing Elke.

The officer sent one of his men over to check. He lifted the covers, looked briefly, then quickly lowered them again and nodded at his superior.

Holstering his weapon, the officer approached Klara slowly. She stiffened, thinking he was about to assault her. To her surprise and relief, he stopped two feet in front of her, clasped his hands behind his back and bowed slightly.

"I am Captain Ivanov of the 19th Guards Mechanized Brigade. May I know your name, please?"

"M-my name is Klara Neumann," Klara stammered.

"Are you related to the man whose portrait my men discovered in the library downstairs... Professor Erich Neumann, I believe?"

Klara marveled at Ivanov's surprisingly cultured speech, which displayed only a small hint of an accent.

"Yes, Erich Neumann is my father, sir."

"From papers and photographs we found in his desk, it seems your father has some professional connection with Dr. Wernher von Braun, the famous German rocket scientist. Is that correct?"

"Y-yes, sir, my father is a technical consultant to him."

"Do you know where your father and Dr. von Braun are now?"

Klara hesitated. *How much should I reveal? Plead total ignorance, or . . .?*

"Sir, the last my sister and I heard from my father nearly a month ago, he was being transferred along with some fellow scientists from their workplace in the Nordhausen area to somewhere in Bavaria. I have no idea *where* in Bavaria they might be, or even if they ever made it there."

Captain Ivanov peered at her, as if trying to discern whether she was telling the truth.

After several tense seconds, he nodded curtly. "Fraulein Neuman, I am very sorry for the loss of your sister. We will assist you in seeing that she receives a proper burial. As for you, you are now under my personal care and protection and have nothing to fear." His severe expression gave way to a slight smile. "I am sure you are hungry. Would you like something to eat?"

Klara stared at him, relieved, but dumfounded. No doubt, Captain Ivanov viewed her father and his family as committed Nazis, deserving the worst of punishments from the victims of their evil philosophy and actions. So why the special treatment? Memories of SS Colonel Bremmer and his devious methods flashed through her mind. *Careful... there's a trap ready to close somewhere.*

Exhausted and famished, Klara put her reservations aside. "Yes, sir. I would most appreciate that."

PART VII

FINAL COUNTDOWN

CHAPTER 53

Berlin, Germany
June 18, 1945
(Six weeks later)

For Klara, the arrival of Captain Ivanov and his men at her house on May 3—the morning following the city of Berlin's official, unconditional surrender to Russian forces—had marked the end of imminent threats to her own physical survival and sexual integrity.

It had also marked the beginning of a multi-week period of cultural disorientation, seclusion, and daily life catering to the cooking and cleaning needs of her new household.

No doubt, Ivanov and his men had treated her with civility. They'd helped her bury Elke in a small, nearby church cemetery that had somehow managed to survive the bombing and shelling. There had been ample food provisions from the Russian army supply wagons in the form of bread, tinned meat, potatoes, pea soup and herring slices. She'd even been treated to bawdy, nightly entertainment provided by a steady stream of battle-weary, love-deprived Russian soldiers eager to unwind, dine together, and sing accordion-led songs of victory with their commander and Klara. They affectionately referred to her as their "beautiful German hostess."

But despite all that, the boring, daily housekeeping routine combined with the soldiers' ribald antics and unsanitary personal habits soon become insulting and oppressive.

"I keep telling you, Fräulein Neumann," Captain Ivanov had insisted impatiently whenever Klara complained to him about her continuing confinement when many of her neighbors seemed able to get out and about. "While your special situation as the daughter of one of the major V-2 scientists is being investigated by our intelligence people, you are under my personal care and protection. The streets are still dangerous, and I can't afford to take any chances with your safety."

It was only last week that Ivanov had finally permitted Klara to take short, chaperoned walks to the recently reopened local bakery, or to check on the survival and status of friends and acquaintances who lived in the vicinity. She had jumped at the chance, and this morning she'd convinced Ivanov to allow Heidi Schmidt—her former fellow student at the Berlin University medical school—to accompany her to the bakery.

After filling their bags there with items purchased using their new Soviet-issued ration cards, the two girls set off on their return trip home. Across the street, one of Ivanov's men pedaled along the sidewalk on a confiscated bicycle, keeping a watchful eye.

From what she was now hearing from Heidi, Klara had been relatively fortunate. For tens of thousands of other female Berliners of all ages, the physical and emotional hell they'd experienced at the hands of drunken, celebrating Russian soldiers had *not* mercifully ended on May 3. For many, the agony had only just begun.

"Honestly, Klara," Heidi sighed as the girls walked through the rubble-strewn Charlottenburg streets. "If you hadn't taken the initiative to come search me out at my apartment yesterday and talked me out of my despair, I would probably be lying dead on my bed right now from that tablet of cyanide I'd been storing away… just in case."

Klara moved closer and locked arms with her friend. She knew from their first conversation that Heidi had been accosted and violated on two separate occasions by a meandering soldier who'd broken into her apartment building a week after the city's surrender. "With what you've been through, it would be hard for me to blame you. Thank God, I found you before you decided to follow the example of our brave propaganda minister, Goebbels."

"I haven't heard. What did he do?"

"The day after Hitler shot himself and poisoned his new bride, Eva Braun, Goebbels and his wife took cyanide pills after forcing one down the throats of each of their young children."

Heidi recoiled in disgust. "And so ended the dream of the Thousand-Year Third Reich for our glorious Führer and his favorite little club-footed mouthpiece, Goebbels."

Klara nodded grimly as she looked across the street at two emaciated old women standing in front of a pile of rubble that towered above them. They were scratching away at the base with a coal shovel under the supervision of a Russian soldier, loading the refuse onto a little cart. *At this rate, it will take them weeks to move that entire mountain. I wonder if they'll live to finish the job.*

"Poor Hannah Richter," Heidi muttered, shaking her head in revulsion and pity as she recalled the fate of a fellow apartment dweller.

"The pretty redhead…about thirty years old? I remember her. What about her?"

Heidi grimaced. "When the apartment manager and I finally made it out of our basement and upstairs to her place, we found her lying back on a chaise lounge in her slip with an oversized blouse draped over her torso. She was groaning terribly, and her boyfriend and another woman were trying to tend to her. The woman pulled us aside and told us that, the night before, a bunch of completely soused Russian soldiers had broken into Hannah's apartment and discovered her trying to hide behind a wooden partition. They plied her with alcohol, then they lined up and each took their turn. Hannah said there were at least twenty, but she didn't know exactly. When I went over to offer my sympathy, her swollen mouth was sticking out of her face like a blue plum. The other woman asked her to lift her blouse and show us her breasts, which were all bruised and bitten. Oh, Klara, just saying this makes me want to gag all over again."

Klara put her arm around Heidi's waist. "I'm so sorry."

"Actually, I'm not sure she wants to survive. She just confirmed she's pregnant, and she's sickened by the thought of bearing a Russian bastard. I told her what *I* would do if I'd gotten pregnant, but she's not of the same mind."

Klara cringed at Heidi's implied solution. But knowing she was in no position to judge other girls' ways of dealing with their horrific experiences of rape, she said nothing. *Better to change the subject.*

"So where are you and the other apartment dwellers getting your food now?"

Heidi rolled her eyes. "We've all nearly run out of whatever scraps we'd managed to store up before the Russians came. Last week an official came by. He ordered us all to report to work the next morning to a heavy machinery factory that the Russians are intent on stripping so they can then ship the parts back to their own country.

"For the next four days, we all toiled away for ten hours under the hot sun, carrying heavy zinc bars from the factory warehouse to several railway cars lined up on a track that must have been at least fifty yards away. We were fed well, and we were told we'd be paid for our efforts whenever the new currency system starts to operate. They told us to come back again later this week, that the work would last until the factory gets emptied out in about a month or so. It's slave-work, but it's better than nothing. After that, we'll presumably be on our own again, scratching and clawing like rats for every morsel—just like before."

Klara felt a twinge of guilt over her own relatively lush circumstances under Captain Ivanov's protection. "Hopefully by then, the occupation authorities will have things sorted out and we'll all be able to find some reasonable work that suits our abilities. Don't you think?"

"If they don't decide to ship us all off to Siberian prison camps," Heidi snorted. "I know that's what they think we all deserve."

The girls walked on in silence, passing small, tired caravans of people surrounding pitiful handcarts piled high with sacks, crates, and trunks. Most seemed to be headed east toward... who knew where or why? In one case, a woman was harnessed to a rope, pulling the cart like a horse while her child sat on top of the pile and an old man did his best to push from behind.

Finally arriving at Heidi's apartment, the girls hugged and said their goodbyes.

"I hope you're treating your captain well, Klara," Heidi said enviously. "As attractive as you still look, I can't believe he hasn't demanded you pay the usual price."

"I suppose not every Russian soldier is cut from the same cloth," Klara said.

At least not in the officer ranks, she thought as she waved and walked away.

Hopefully, the intelligence officer whom Captain Ivanov had said would be waiting to meet her today when she returned would turn out to be just as chivalrous.

◦◦◦

Major Alexei Kuznetsov, Soviet Military Counter-Intelligence Agency (SMERSH), leaned back in Erich Neumann's favorite leather armchair and blew out a long cloud of cigar smoke. After the uniformed female aide entered the library and set two cups of rich Viennese coffee on the side of the desk, Kuznetsov picked one up and offered it to Klara.

"It's taking a while," he said. "But gradually, things seem to be returning to some civilized standards in this city. I hope you'll enjoy this more than the ersatz crud we've all had to endure the past few weeks."

Klara smiled uncertainly. "Thank you, sir." She wondered where the major planned to take this abruptly arranged conversation, though she was sure it would have something to do with her father.

"I trust that Captain Ivanov and the follow-on occupation troops who've been lodging here have been treating you well and are looking after your welfare?" the major continued in a solicitous tone.

"Oh, yes sir, I couldn't have expected more… under the circumstances." She couldn't resist adding: "Certainly better than the treatment I know many other German women have received from some of your soldiers."

The major's face hardened. "Yes. It does seem that some excesses occurred. But you must realize, Fräulein, that was certainly not the intent of Comrade Stalin. He expressly forbade such behavior. Unfortunately, some of our Russian men could not contain their anger over the memories of watching their own women raped, their children hung upside down and stabbed or burned, and their babies' heads bashed against walls by your Nazi SS beasts."

Klara blushed and looked down at her lap, realizing she was not going to win points with the major this way. She thought of Elke's husband Heinz and his story of SS atrocities. Major Kuznetsov had a point.

Kuznetsov's face relaxed a touch. "But regardless, Fräulein Neumann, we have another important matter to discuss today. Something more relevant to your own situation."

He placed a folder that he'd been concealing in his lap on the desk and opened it. He studied the first page intently for several seconds, then looked up.

"We have received information from an undercover agent that leads us to believe your father is alive and hiding somewhere in the Nordhausen area—which is currently in the US zone of occupation. Apparently, for reasons unknown, he did *not* accompany Wernher von Braun and his key V-2 men south to Bavaria, where they managed to escape the SS and turn themselves over to the Americans in early May. However, we also have confirmed that your father was a highly valued member of the famous Peenemünde rocket men, and that the Americans are eager to find him and have him join von Braun and the others in the US."

Vati? Still in Nordhausen? Klara stared in shocked surprise at Kuznetsov as she tried to process the news and its implications. *Is he with Mama? Are they—*

Kuznetsov wasted no time in coming to his point.

"Fräulein Neumann, as I'm sure you'll appreciate, the Soviet Union desires your father's unique rocket expertise in support of our country's future military and scientific goals. And so, we're hopeful to contact him before the Americans and present him with a highly attractive offer that would convince him to come join us.

"But we have a problem—we don't know exactly where your father is hiding. And that's why I am here today. We need your help in finding your father, as well as helping us to convince him to accept our offer."

So, there it is. Now, it all made perfect sense. The main reason she'd been so generously treated over the past few weeks while her case was being investigated was to curry her favor to lure her father to their side.

Klara knew her father didn't trust the Russians, and neither did she. Like von Braun, Vati had expressed a clear preference for surrendering to the Americans if it came to that. And if she had her own preference, it would be to go with him to the US. There, she'd have the chance to start a brand-new life, hopefully reconnecting with the only two people in life, besides her parents, with whom she still had any emotional ties: Sophie Friedmann and Joshua Peters.

Still, if she had any hope of reuniting with Mama and Vati, she realized the Russians were her only conduit. She would need to play the game by their rules.

"May I know what your offer to my father would be?"

Kuznetsov smiled. "Of course, Fräulein. If your father agrees to swear loyalty and devote his talents to our side, he and his family will not be required to live in Russia but will be able to remain in Germany—in the Russian occupation zone. He will be put in charge of his own rocket development company and granted a lucrative contract. He will also be guaranteed total immunity from any war crimes charges."

Klara bit her lip. Given her own desire to get to America with her parents, this clearly was not her own preferred scenario. But would Vati think differently?

The major sensed her uncertainty. "Oh, and one other thing, Fräulein Neumann."

"Sir?"

Kuznetsov pulled a single sheet of paper out of the file and handed it across the desk. "I am sure that you and your father will take a special interest in this."

As soon as she saw the handwriting, she recognized its source. Tears formed in her eyes as she silently read through the lines:

Dear Klara,

I pray that you are well. This is your brother, Walther. I am writing from my cell in a Soviet military prison camp somewhere in Siberia, where I have been confined since my capture in 1942. Sister, it devastates me to tell you this, but I must be blunt.

A month ago, three officers in my unit, including myself, were found guilty by a military tribunal of committing a horrific war crime against Russian soldiers in the Stalingrad area. Sadly, our honest and valid protestations of innocence were not accepted, and we were all sentenced to death by firing squad. However, in my case, I was told that my sentence had been temporarily put on hold, for reasons I did not understand at the time.

Yesterday (June 10), I learned the reason from the prison commandant and a visiting Soviet intelligence officer. They first told me that you had survived the assault on Berlin and were now residing under special military protection at our Charlottenburg residence. That information brought me immense relief, tempered by the tragic news that our dear sister Elke did not make it. I was then informed that the Soviets believe Father is hiding somewhere in Germany, and they have narrowed down the search area. They told me they will soon be contacting you to enlist your services in finding and convincing him to join the Soviet rocket development program. They also told me that, should you be successful in your efforts and Father agrees to their terms within the timeframe they require, the Soviet authorities will commute my death sentence to a ten-year period of hard labor, minus time already served.

Klara, I am so sorry to put you in this awkward and difficult position. God knows I now see the horrible mistake that so many of us (though not you, sister!) made in believing Hitler's lies and serving the National Socialist military effort, even if only out of a pure, patriotic fervor. I also know that I am innocent of the crime of which I am accused, but I will not evade execution unless Father is found and comes to agree with the generous terms that the Soviets plan to offer him. I can only say, Klara, that I wish to survive this ordeal and devote my life to the service of a better world for all of us. That possibility is now in the hands of God, you, and Father. I so hope I will one day soon be able to visit with and embrace you and our parents, and that you and I can share some of those delicious Bavarian chocolates you always tried to hide from me in your closet. Along with a bottle of our favorite Jägermeister, of course.

Your Loving Brother, Walther.

Klara's hands shook as her tears fell on the page. Even if coerced, the letter clearly had Walther's handwriting and style of expression. It left her with no doubts as to its authenticity, and no choice as to her own obligation.

She looked up at Major Kuznetsov.

"All right, I'll do whatever I can to help you."

"Excellent." Kuznetsov took the letter back and returned it to his file, which he then closed and moved to the side. He stamped out his cigarette and leaned back in his chair. "Do you have *any* idea where your father might be?"

Klara recalled the last instructions she'd received from Herr Keller. If she were ever able to return from Berlin, she was to check Herr Keller's house in Nordhausen first to see if her parents were there. Failing that, she was to check the isolated hiding place that Herr Keller had constructed in the Harz Mountains for which he'd given her a map.

She conveyed what she knew to Kuznetsov.

"That certainly helps," the major said. "But we have another problem, Fräulein Neumann. Time is running extremely short. Under a new agreement reached by the Allied forces, in two days Nordhausen and the surrounding area will be transferred from American control to our Soviet zone of occupation."

Klara cocked her head. "But shouldn't that make it easier for us to find my father?"

"It would, except we know the Americans will be making every effort to find and convince him to join the US side before the transfer happens. If they're successful in getting to him before we can make our own offer, we could lose him... and sadly, your brother Walther as well."

Klara realized that if Walther was going to have a chance of avoiding the firing squad, she would have to help the Russians find Vati—quickly.

"So, what can we do if he's in the US zone?"

Kuznetsov lit another cigarette. "It will certainly be difficult, but I have already organized and will be leading a special team to escort you through the lines to the two likely locations you've mentioned. Since we don't have the resources to search both places at once, we will start first at Nordhausen as you suggested. There is absolutely no time for delay. We must leave tonight."

CHAPTER 54

Nordhausen, Germany
June 19, 1945

Passing by the heaps of ruins along the fire-bombed residential street where Johann Keller had lived, Klara could only shake her head.

There's no way anyone could have survived this, she thought gloomily. She stared out the backseat side-window of the black sedan that Major Kuznetsov had commissioned for last night's risky journey from Berlin through the heavily patrolled US occupation zone to Nordhausen. She could only assume the three men in the car were all thinking the same thing: *we're wasting our time here.*

Kuznetsov pointed at something out the front window and made a comment in Russian. The burly driver and the thin, dark-haired man in the rear seat beside Klara—whom she understood to be the designated negotiator for this delicate mission—both nodded grimly.

Kuznetsov turned his head toward Klara. "This does not look promising. Are we close to Keller's place?"

"Yes," Klara replied. "I think I recognize that wrecked house on the corner. His place should be right up the next block." And seconds later:

"*There!*" she cried. Her excitement collapsed into a groan at the sight of the decimated structure.

The car slowed and pulled to a halt next to the curb.

"If that was it," Kuznetsov muttered, shaking his head. "We can forget about finding your father in this town unless you can think of some other place he'd be."

"Major!" Klara blurted. "There's a man plowing through the rubble next door. I think he might be Herr Keller's neighbor. May I get out and speak with him? Maybe he knows something."

"Sir, I don't think we have time for this," the negotiator complained. "Shouldn't we head immediately for that hideout in Bad Sachsa? If the Americans get to Neumann first, we'll lose out on—"

Kuznetsov interrupted impatiently. "We'll leave for Bad Sachsa early tomorrow morning. *After* we've done our due diligence in scrubbing this area first. I can't afford to tell my superiors we missed our target because of an incomplete search.

"All right, Fräulein Neumann, go talk with him. But be brief."

Klara approached the man cautiously, dreading the possibility that he would have bad tidings to bear regarding her mother's fate. "Hello, sir," she called. The man stopped shoveling and looked up suspiciously as Klara approached. Once Klara explained her connection to the ruined house next door, the man relaxed and opened up.

Klara learned from him that Herr Keller had survived the bombing and was now temporarily staying in a small boarding house two streets over. Unfortunately, the man didn't know what had become of Keller's wife or Klara's mother. Armed with the information, she returned to the car and the group set off for Keller's new location.

After directing the driver to park across and down the street at a discrete distance, Kuznetsov gave Klara his strict instructions. "Remember your story line. Ask only for your father's current whereabouts and say nothing of our mission."

Klara entered the building and spoke to the manager who gave her Herr Keller's room number. She walked up the stairs and knocked politely on the third door on the left. She held her breath, hoping for the best, but preparing herself for the worst.

The door opened.

"Klara! Mein Gott!" Herr Keller stood with mouth agape. He appeared to have lost a substantial amount of weight and had several burn marks on his face. He reached out to embrace her, then pulled her inside and closed the door behind them.

Klara drew a deep breath as she looked him straight in the eye. "Herr Keller… are they . . .?"

Keller's head sagged. "Klara, I am so sorry to tell you that your mother was killed instantly when the bomb struck our house. My own wife succumbed to her injuries several days later in the hospital."

"*Oh, God, no!*" Klara sunk to her knees, clutching her stomach. Herr Keller knelt beside her and took her in his arms as she wept bitterly.

It made no sense. Of all the good and faithful mothers in Germany, Mama was the least deserving of such a violent, ignominious ending to her life.

Her mother had always provided the comforting arms and tender shoulder for Klara to cry on whenever her frequent childhood illnesses or vitriolic quarrels with other children overwhelmed her. Mama's had been the moderating, gentle voice that kept Klara and Elke from hating each other through all those adolescent years when the girls' different responses to Nazism had threatened to undo the family. Most importantly, it was Mama with her devout Lutheran beliefs who'd provided the earthly model and encouragement for Klara's compassion toward others less fortunate, for her strong faith in God and her trust in Christ—spiritual gifts for which she would always be grateful.

Oh, Mama… if only I'd told you before I left for Berlin how much you've meant to me… please, Jesus, tell her for me now and hold her tight…

Finally gathering herself, Klara told Keller about Elke's death in Berlin and that she herself had only recently managed to get back to Nordhausen to search for her parents. She then asked if there were any news on her father.

Keller pulled his head back and smiled slightly. "That's a better story."

"Please tell me. I swear I can't take any more bad news."

"Your father never left with the other scientists for Bavaria." Keller said, confirming what Klara had already heard from Major Kuznetsov.

Keller went on to explain her father's involvement with the V-2 document burial effort and his fatal shooting of Colonel Bremmer and his aides at the Bad Sachsa site. After disposing of the bodies, Erich and Keller talked and decided it would be safest for Erich to remain there at the Bad Sachsa cabin for the time being. His hope had been that his daughters would eventually join him there.

"So, is that where he is now?" Klara asked, still reeling from Keller's graphic description of her father's deadly encounter with Bremmer.

"Yes... though very likely not for long."

"Why is that?"

"He's on the verge of making a deal to surrender to the Americans just before this whole area transitions to Russian control in two days. In exchange for asylum in America along with assurances that he won't be subject to war crimes prosecution, your father would reveal the location of the V-2 document stashes and offer his own services in translating and explaining how to put them to best use for American interests.

"Last week, when I went up to visit him in Bad Sachsa, he asked me to make initial contact with US intelligence officers here in Nordhausen to propose the idea. They seemed very enthusiastic about it, and the plan is for me to escort a couple of their people to Bad Sachsa tomorrow to negotiate and confirm the terms of the deal and accept your father's surrender to American authorities."

Klara immediately recognized the huge conflict. *Tomorrow?* If the Americans succeeded in contacting her father first, he would very likely surrender to them and be gone by the time the Russians arrived to make their own offer. It was *that* offer on which the life of her brother Walther depended.

"What time tomorrow will you be leaving for Bad Sachsa?"

"They will be picking me up about noon. It's about a two-hour trip." He looked at her and grinned. "I assume you will want to go with us? I'm sure we can find an extra seat in their car. I can only imagine the joy your father will experience when he sees you!"

Klara was relieved, knowing she and the Russian team planned to arrive early tomorrow morning and would beat the Americans there. She would play along with the plan she would have preferred herself, if only Walther's life wasn't at stake.

"That sounds wonderful, Herr Keller. I can't wait to see Vati and hug him again. If I'm back here by eleven-thirty tomorrow, would that suffice?"

Keller waved his hand. "Why don't we save you the trouble and just plan to pick you up? Where are you staying?"

Klara hesitated, realizing she didn't even know where in the town she and the Russian team would be lodging tonight. She only knew it would be at the house owned by the Russians' Nordhausen agent.

"Oh, p-please don't worry about that, sir," she answered evasively. "You can trust me; I will be here by eleven-thirty tomorrow."

Keller cocked his head. "Klara, is something wrong? Are you in a safe situation?"

Should I let him in on the truth?

Klara smiled and touched his arm. "I am fine, Herr Keller. I'm staying with a nursing friend of mine from Berlin. Her parents have a small home just outside the town. I'm afraid I couldn't even give you the directions. Trust me, it'll be much easier for her and her father to drive me here like they did today."

Keller scratched his head as he looked at her worriedly. "Well, if you're sure . . ."

"I'm sure, sir. I will meet you here tomorrow morning, right on time."

Klara awoke from her restless slumber, certain that she'd just heard a soft knocking on her bedroom door. She sat up and listened closely.

Nothing.

Leaning over, she turned on the lamp beside her bed and checked the time on the wall clock. Just after 2:30 a.m. *Must have been a dream.* She turned the light off again and lay back on the bed, sighing wearily and wishing that dawn would arrive quickly so they could all just get on with things...

Earlier yesterday afternoon, after driving the surprisingly short distance to the Russian agent's house following Klara's meeting with Herr Keller, Major Kuznetsov had announced to the team that they should be prepared to leave at six in the morning. That would put them at Bad Sachsa around eight and, with the aid of Klara's map, would easily have them face-to-face with Erich Neumann in his cabin well before the Americans arrived in the early afternoon. After a shared light supper, Kuznetsov had dismissed everyone to their rooms, telling them to relax and get a good night's sleep.

All had seemed set until the telephone downstairs had jingled about 8 p.m. What followed shortly thereafter was an absolute torrent of vile Russian cursing and shouting. Klara could tell it was Major Kuznetsov, and he was clearly not happy about something he'd heard. Over the next hour, Klara listened to the muffled, agitated voices of Kuznetsov and the other men downstairs. *What in the world are they discussing,* she'd wondered. Eventually, they'd trailed off.

She was just about to doze off again when she clearly heard the soft knock once again. Turning on the light one more time, she walked cautiously to the door and cracked it open. "Yes?"

In the low light, she could barely make out the man's face but recognized him as the Russians' local agent who owned the house.

The man held up a folded piece of paper.

"Please read this and destroy it immediately afterward," he whispered. That was it. After handing the note through the crack to Klara, he turned and crept off down the darkened hallway.

Baffled and alarmed, Klara shut the door. She hurried to her bed, sat down, and began to read.

Major K. has received word that your brother, Walther, was executed two days ago following a new general decree by Stalin against convicted war criminals. It is not clear why your brother's vital role in our mission was ignored. We have been ordered to proceed with the mission, but we will no longer be negotiating terms with your father. The plan now is to forcibly abduct and bring him into the Russian zone. From there, he will be deported to Moscow where he will be treated as a former enemy combatant and required to work with other captured Nazi scientists on Soviet military projects. Because of these developments, you will not be accompanying our team this morning to Bad Sachsa, and you will be left here to your own devices.

My conscience detests this treacherous action against your family on the part of my government and compels me to alert you to it. The bigger question is how to alert and protect your father before our team arrives there. I see but one solution: you must get back to Herr Keller within the next hour and have him contact the American intelligence people. They will know what to do. There is a bicycle leaning against the right side of the house. Keller's place is only a mile down the road, and you know the way. Viel Glück.

Klara reread the note twice, her heart pounding and her mind spinning as she struggled to believe and accept its implications. *Walther executed?* Was this simply a nightmare from which she would soon wake? Why would the Russian government be so *stupid* as to foil their own best-laid plans for gaining her father's voluntary cooperation? Was this some kind of trick? Or was it actually possible for a paid agent of the Soviet Union to show compassion for the plight of a Nazi rocket man and his daughter—to the point of betraying his country's cause and putting his own life at risk?

And yet, Klara thought as she recalled the team's subdued conversation over their supper a few hours ago, *there* was *something about the way that man looked at me when I talked about my concern for my brother, and how I was so thankful that the Soviet Union would even consider offering to spare his life.* It seemed to be a look of sorrow and empathy, as if he knew what would be coming because he'd seen it happen before.

She looked at the clock. Nearing three. Her heart was sick over Walther, but she had no time to mourn. If she had any hope of rescuing Vati from a Russian abduction, she had to act now.

Dressing quickly, she threw on a sweater, turned out the light, and exited the room. The reassuring sounds of heavy snoring accompanied her stealthy footsteps along the hallway, down the stairs, out the front door, and into the warm June early morning air. Just around the corner of the house, she spotted the bicycle leaning against the side. Exactly where the agent had said it would be.

Johann Keller was doing his best to calm her nerves, but Klara couldn't stop her feet from rapidly tapping the polished wooden floor like a snare drummer as she sat on Keller's living room couch. "He should be here any minute now, Klara. Don't worry."

It had taken twenty minutes to navigate the one-mile, straight-shot distance to Keller's apartment on the bicycle. The building manager woke to her frantic pounding and let her in the front door with nothing more than an irritated, curious look. Racing up the stairs, she'd banged on Keller's door, calling his name and announcing herself. He'd opened it quickly and she'd burst in, gesticulating wildly as she explained her father's desperate situation. Keller had immediately understood what needed to happen. Rushing down to the telephone at the front desk, he'd put in a call to his American contacts, who'd told him they would send someone over pronto to confirm things with Klara and put a rescue plan in motion for her father.

Klara sighed and checked her watch. It was almost three thirty.

Finally came the expected knock on the door. Herr Keller leaped from the couch to answer as Klara held her breath.

Keller stepped aside to let in a man garbed in a dark brown tunic with tan pants, shirt, and necktie.

The man removed his cap and smiled at Klara, whose hands flew to her mouth.

First Lieutenant Joshua Peters rushed to embrace her.

CHAPTER 55

Bad Sachsa, Germany
June 20, 1945

If the imminent danger of her father's circumstances had not overwhelmed all other considerations, Klara knew exactly how she would have insisted on spending the rest of the day and coming night: *in our own private room at some quiet little inn, locked in each other's arms as Joshua smothers me with kisses and tells me how his love for me never wavered these past six years—how he's come back for me, just like he promised.*

But there had been no time to pursue such romantic fantasies.

After listening to Klara's frantic account of the Russians' abduction plan, Joshua sprang into action. Putting in an emergency call to his colleague Alec Benjamin at local OSS headquarters, he'd explained the situation and—knowing he wouldn't be able to hide it any longer—apprised Alec of his previous relationship with Klara and her father. He'd requested Alec to order an armed T-1 support team to be sent to the Bad Sachsa hideout location as soon as possible. Joshua, Klara, and Herr Keller had then gotten into Joshua's staff car and, after picking up Alec, made the two-hour drive there together.

As the four now walked cautiously onto the front porch of Professor Erich Neumann's cabin at the end of the steep dirt road above the small spa town, Klara's heart raced with anxiety. Already burdened by Mama's recent death, how would Vati respond to the tragic news about Elke and Walther? Klara dreaded having to tell him and witness the wrenching pain she knew it would bring. And yet, she couldn't deny her own growing sense of excitement over the prospects of asylum and new life in America for her father and herself. She desperately hoped that Vati would accept the terms from Joshua.

Joshua rapped firmly three times on the cabin door.

Erich Neumann sat in his armchair in stunned silence, smoking one cigarette after another as he struggled to absorb the shocking, tragic news that Klara and the man he recalled as her pre-war American diplomat-boyfriend were delivering him.

When Klara finished her emotional accounts of Elke's death in Berlin and how she'd just been informed by her Russian protectors of Walther's betrayal and execution, Erich simply nodded, turned his face away, and stared vacantly at the floor, his lips quivering.

Apologizing for his abruptness, Joshua launched immediately into an urgent appeal on behalf of the US Government. "Professor, the Russians could be here in less than two hours with the intent of abducting you to the Soviet zone. We don't have time to fully negotiate and confirm with my superiors the final terms of your surrender to us as we'd originally planned. But is there anything we can say or do now that would help you to understand and trust our good intentions? At least enough to come with us to Nordhausen to finalize the terms?"

Erich slowly lifted his head. He looked into the eyes of Joshua, Klara, Alec, and Herr Keller, one by one. All of them stood respectfully in front of him as they anxiously awaited his decision. He focused his gaze on Joshua.

"Well, Lieutenant, I suppose you could start by reminding me. If I do go with you, what will happen to me? Will the Americans *really* treat a despised Nazi rocket man better than the Russians would?"

Joshua exchanged awkward glances with Alec, then smiled. "You can ask your friends, Wernher Von Braun and General Dornberger that question, Professor."

Erich's eyes widened. "*Von Braun and Dornberger?* What happened to them?"

Joshua nodded. "They and the scientists who were with them surrendered themselves to American forces nearly two months ago in Bavaria. I'd say they're all faring quite well now under our protective care. In fact, von Braun and Dornberger are both now in Nordhausen. They're extremely anxious to help us locate you and any other V-2 scientists and technicians who may be in hiding nearby. They want to reunite you all in town and have you evacuated with them before the Russians take over this area. The eventual plan is to have all the top V-2 scientists like von Braun, you, and your families brought to America to help the US rocket development effort. In fact, they have *you* near the top of their list of over eighty key individuals. If you agree to come, you'll be living a far better life than you could ever hope for as a slave of the Soviet Union."

Erich looked at him suspiciously. "But will the Americans try to levy any war crimes charges against me? Or will they recognize that everything I did was an obedient response to the commands my SS superiors gave me, and exonerate me on that basis?"

Joshua glanced at Alec once again and shifted awkwardly. "Professor, we know from von Braun and General Dornberger about the critical part you played in the V-2 program and what your specific role was as a guidance and control expert.

"We also know about your V-2 document-hiding activity. We've already found the big stash in that Dörnten mine shaft. But General Dornberger told us there's a second stash you hid for him somewhere around here. Those documents are extremely valuable to us. If you show us where they are hidden and agree to come to our side, those actions will clearly demonstrate your interest in making future contributions to American scientific progress. They would also show your willingness to make amends for any belligerent wartime actions as our enemy. In fact, I can say with all confidence, that your decision to come join us would be viewed very positively and—in the absence of any *provable* evidence of war crimes—rewarded with preferential future treatment as a scientist in America."

Erich cocked his head. "But how am I to be assured of that, Lieutenant? Your word of honor? While I do have a high regard for you personally based on my recollections from those pre-war days when you were courting Klara, I still—"

Alec Benjamin, who had been virtually silent up to that point, exploded with surprising vehemence.

"The time for vacillation and negotiations is over, Professor! Either you take our word and come with us now, or you are free to remain here and take your chances with the Russians. But keep this in mind— if you refuse our offer and allow yourself to be taken by them, you will have only yourself to blame. Especially when you hear about your former V-2 colleagues' contributions to interplanetary space travel, while you yourself rot away in professional obscurity or worse under Stalin's iron-fisted rule."

Klara recoiled at Alec's harsh tone, but she knew her father needed to understand the full consequences of his decision. "And besides that, Vati," she said. "If you refuse the offer... you'll lose me. One way or another, I'm going to America." She edged closer to Joshua and grasped his hand.

Erich stared at the two in amazement for several seconds before his face finally broke out in a concessionary smile. "Seeing you two together again, I should've known. Seems I now have no choice."

"It's the last train from Nordhausen before the Russians take over the area tomorrow," Joshua explained to Erich and Klara as the two hastened to pack a large suitcase with Erich's clothes and belongings.

"It'll leave at six-fifty tonight, heading for Witzenhausen, which is just inside the newly defined US occupation zone, and hopefully the first stop on your way to America. Von Braun and Dornberger will be on it, along with any other rocket men and their families that Major Staver's people have managed to round up. Alec and I aim to make sure that the two of you are on that train."

"What about Herr Keller?" Klara asked. "Isn't he coming with us?"

Keller looked at her apologetically. "I'm afraid not, Klara. I still have some close relatives in southern Germany who'll be needing my help and have asked me to stay behind. I can't deny them my support. I'll be accompanying you all to Nordhausen, but from there we'll be parting ways."

"But first we've got to get all of you out of harm's way *here*," Alec said. "It's already nearly six-thirty. And based on what they told Klara yesterday, that Russian team could show up here by eight... right?"

"What about our armed T-1 support unit?" Joshua asked. "Didn't you put in an emergency request?"

"I did... and they said they'd do their best, but they couldn't promise they'd be able to assemble the right people and have them out here before nine. Said there were too many emergency operations happening right now for them to respond to every request."

Joshua grimaced and shook his head. "You're right. We need to get out of here and get the professor and Klara to the Nordhausen train station. But before we go . . ." He stared hard at Erich. "Professor, if we're going to put that V-2 document stash you've been hiding for General Dornberger into play for future American benefit as well as your own, *now* is the time to tell me exactly where you buried it. The reason being that as soon as we get off this hill and into Bad Sachsa, I'm going to make a call to Major Staver in Nordhausen. I'll ask him to send some people up here fast to dig up the crates, with a truck big enough to handle all of them. If all goes well, they should have them back at Nordhausen and loaded on your train by the time it leaves."

Erich waved a hand toward the rear wall. "They're twelve feet deep in a field, about a mile and a half up the dirt lane behind the cabin. But trust me, the place is hard to find. There are a lot of switchbacks and forks along the way. It's easy to get lost, even with a map."

Joshua looked at his watch and thought for a moment. "Before they commit to sending anyone out here, Staver will want to know that I have personally verified and visibly marked the site. Professor, how long would it take us to get up to that field and back again?"

"No more than a half hour, I'd guess."

Joshua nodded. "It's only six-thirty. The Russians likely won't be here for another hour and a half, so here's what we'll do. Professor, while Lt. Benjamin waits here with Klara, I'd like you and Herr Keller to accompany me in the car to that field and show me *precisely* where the stash is buried. There's no room for error. I'll take careful notes on directions while the two of you confirm and mark off the site. When we return, we'll pick up Alec and Klara and head down to Bad Sachsa where I can make my call to Staver. Then we're all off to Nordhausen. If the Russians ever get here, they'll find either an empty house or an armed T-1 team in jeeps waiting to greet them. Any objections?"

Hearing none, Joshua made the call. "All right, let's go."

Before exiting with Erich and Keller, Joshua drew Klara aside.

He leaned over and kissed her lightly on the cheek. "You'll be safe here with Alec, and I'll be back before you know it."

She smiled hesitantly. "All right, but please hurry."

Chapter 56

Bad Sachsa, Germany
June 20, 1945

"Lieutenant Benjamin, I see a pot on the stove. Can I make some tea for you?" Klara offered, attempting to break the long, icy silence that had descended the moment Joshua and the others had closed the door behind them.

"No thank you, Fräulein."

Klara sat down awkwardly across the small dining table from Alec, wondering if she should try to make conversation.

Why is he so intent on ignoring me? In fact, from the very moment Joshua introduced her earlier this morning and mentioned their pre-war relationship, Lieutenant Benjamin had seemed cold, almost hostile toward her. Of course, he *was* a British Jew, and she was the daughter of a German V-2 scientist. Some natural antipathy was to be expected.

This is getting too awkward. Make the first gesture. "Lieutenant, I can't thank you enough for what you and Joshua are doing to rescue my father."

Alec barely raised his eyes. "Well, I won't try to speak for Joshua since—as I've *now* learned—my good friend and partner already had close, cordial relations before the war with you and your father. But in my own view, your father certainly doesn't *deserve* rescue."

Klara swallowed hard, not expecting the ungracious retort. She struggled to think of an appropriate response.

"I definitely understand why you and many others would feel that way, Lieutenant."

Alec looked up and slammed his hand down on the table.

"Fräulein Neumann, please don't pretend to know how 'I and many others' feel about what your father did! You have no idea, I assure you."

Klara glared at him as indignant anger welled up in her chest. "Why would you say that, Lieutenant? Of course, I'm aware that my father was a V-2 scientist, and that the weapon he worked on caused a lot of death and destruction, especially in England. Just like your British bombs took the lives of a lot of German civilians. But why would my father be any *less deserving* of forgiveness and a chance to restart his life than the British and American warlords who ordered the torching of our cities?" *And the death of my own dear mother,* she wanted to add, but for some reason held in check.

Alec folded his arms across his chest, closed his eyes and shook his head. "*That* has to be the single most idiotic, self-righteous denial of accountability for Nazi sins that I have ever heard. Did you ever stop to think, Fräulein, about who it was that started this war? Who was ultimately responsible for every bomb, for every family torn apart, for every atrocity committed over the past dozen years?

"Well, Hitler, of course."

"*Wrong.* The ultimately responsibility lies with each and every German citizen who helped bring Hitler to power by allowing themselves to be seduced by his fantasies of racial superiority and world domination. It lies with every German man and woman who closed their eyes and ears to the evidence of Hitler's murderous actions, or anyone who simply dared to disagree.

"And I'm sorry to say this, Fräulein, but the responsibility also lies with brilliant but cowardly little men like your father, men who knowingly and enthusiastically threw themselves into becoming the sharpened tools of Hitler's war machine and the perpetrators of his war crimes."

Klara cocked her head. "War crimes? You're claiming my father committed *war crimes*? What evidence do you have? Is helping design a German rocket to explode in England any more of a war crime than designing a British bomb to explode in Germany?"

"There was no crime in designing the rocket. His crimes, if that's what they are ultimately proven to be, lie in his actions taken during V-2 production and operation."

Klara shook her head emphatically. "I'm sorry, sir, but I don't understand. This is not making any sense."

Alec sighed. "Perhaps these will help." He reached into his inside tunic pocket for a brown envelope from which he pulled several black-and-white photos. Klara blanched as she recalled the last time she'd been subjected to the same tactic—by SS Colonel Gerhard Bremmer in the Berlin Kripo interrogation cell.

Alec laid one of the photos on the table and pushed it gently toward Klara. "Here's one of the first sights encountered by American troops entering the underground V-2 factory where your father worked so faithfully. This was the final resting place for some of the factory employees, who apparently failed to fully please their SS bosses."

Klara gasped and turned her face away from the grisly image of hundreds of corpses stretched out across the tunnel floors. A few poor souls appeared to be still alive, though bruised and emaciated beyond belief. She already had heard much about the horrors of the Nazi concentration camps and crematoria, but this was the first time she'd actually seen photographic evidence of the mass carnage that had taken place.

"It's horrible," she muttered finally. "But I still fail to see what this has to do with my father. I *know* him, and I know he would never deliberately associate himself with something like this."

She stopped speaking momentarily as Alec laid down the next two photographs side by side in front of her.

"What is this?" she asked. "Is this Colonel Bremmer and... *oh!*"

She stared at the photo on the left, recognizing Bremmer standing at a microphone on a platform with her father beside him, appearing somewhat dazed. Bremmer was pointing at something off to the side. When she looked over at the second photo, it was easy to surmise what Bremmer had been pointing at: the bodies of five dead laborers, dangling from nooses suspended by a huge crane.

Klara sat in frozen silence, horror gripping her body from top to bottom. Still, she struggled mightily to fight the worst-case implications. "I have no doubts a man like Bremmer could have ordered something like that. But why would my father be guilty of anything other than observing this terrible spectacle? Maybe he was simply following orders."

Alec cocked an eyebrow. "*Simply following orders?* Yes. You may be right, Klara. I can't say these photos constitute definitive proof that your father bears direct responsibility for the atrocity. But they certainly are suggestive of *something* seriously amiss in his pursuit of scientific progress in support of the Nazi cause. And if you add these two photos to the verbal testimony of several of the prisoners who were present at that hanging, well, there could be some questions about the exact nature of your father's involvement."

Klara nodded, unable to look Alec in the eyes.

"But even without this, there *is* one war crime for which your father is *unquestionably* guilty. At least in my mind."

Tears welled up in Klara's throat. What else did this angry, British intelligence officer have in his possession to torture her with?

Alec pushed the other three photos aside and placed down the image of the 250th V-2 Launch Celebration depicting Vati on his fiftieth birthday, sitting in the launcher's chair, surrounded by grinning Nazi SS and party leaders raising their champagne glasses.

Klara noticed how unhappy her father appeared in the photo. He was the only one not smiling. "W-why is this a war crime?" she stammered.

Up until now, Lieutenant Alec Benjamin's face had displayed the hardened, angry look of a prosecuting attorney, his voice the cruel, disciplined edge of a Kripo investigator.

With Klara's question, Alec's entire demeanor changed. His chest heaved and his lips trembled as he struggled to get the words out.

"It's a war crime to *me*, Klara, because six minutes from the time your father's finger touched that button on his console, my beloved fiancée, Laura, and her mother Hannah were dead in a London shopping store. Laura died in my arms, her chest crushed by the weight of a heavy beam that fell across her. If they'd only known, your father and the other men at the console would have further cause to smile and celebrate: two more worthless British Jews, wiped off the face of the earth along with 166 other innocent Londoners."

Klara stared at Alec in open-mouthed, utter shock. With a trembling hand, he reached into the envelope again and pulled out a folded press clipping which he offered to Klara, but she shook her head. She knew Alec was telling the truth, and she had no need to read the detailed account of the tragedy.

She pushed her chair back, stood, and walked over to the kitchen sink. She looked out the small window toward the wooded area behind the cabin, blinded to everything except an imagined scene of her father sitting alone at his launch console, surrounded by piles of mangled, open-mouthed corpses.

She shook her head to clear it, wanting desperately to put things in perspective.

Lieutenant Benjamin had every right to express his pain after witnessing his fiancée's horrible death. But in her heart, and despite the photographic implications, she knew her father. She was certain that Vati would never *intentionally* order, or even approve, of the targeted killing of innocent civilians or POWs.

Yes, given that his work was now being directed by the SS, he *may* have been obligated to stand next to Colonel Bremmer and watch that crane-hanging atrocity. And yes, there was no sense denying that Vati had willingly pushed that launch button, knowing it could very likely result in the deaths of dozens of innocents 150 miles away. But how would those actions make him any more of a war criminal than the countless British and American bombardiers who had released tons of incendiary bombs on heavily-populated German cities like Hamburg and Dresden? Hadn't they done that knowing the primary intent of their missions was to kill huge numbers of civilians and thereby force Hitler to seek peace terms?"

Klara peered at Alec, who was now standing by the front window looking for signs of Joshua and the other men's return. It would be pointless to try to apologize on behalf of her father. Alec was too emotionally distraught, and he would never believe her sincerity. Better to simply ask him the question that weighed most heavily on her heart.

"Lieutenant, may I ask what you will be doing with those photographs?"

He did not even turn to look at her, but merely spoke over his shoulder. "When we get to Witzenhausen, I'll be obligated to turn them over to the American and British intelligence people who will be interrogating von Braun, your father, and the other rocket men. Standard procedure for anyone seeking asylum who's had a German military or Nazi Party affiliation."

"These will hurt his case badly, won't they?"

Alec nodded. "As I said, they aren't definitive proof of anything. But they certainly won't help."

"Lieutenant, what was your purpose in showing those pictures to *me*?"

Alec hesitated, shifting awkwardly. Finally, he turned to face her. "In truth, Fräulein Neumann, I should not have done that. I admit, your obstinate demand for evidence got the better of me. But now that you're aware, I certainly can't stop you from alerting your father so he'll be better prepared to answer for whatever he was truly doing and thinking when those photos were taken. Maybe his interrogators will interpret things differently than I, but somehow, I don't think so."

The sound of gravel in the front driveway caused Alec to whirl. "They're back. Are you ready to go?"

On the narrow dirt road from the cabin into Bad Sachsa, Klara sat squeezed between Herr Keller and her father in the rear seat of Joshua's staff car.

She tried not to let her fears show. She would apprise him about the photos after they got to the train station and had some time alone. For now, she simply wanted to enjoy seeing his obvious relief over surrendering and being in safe, familiar hands.

Their car had just rounded a sharp bend when Alec cried out from the front passenger seat. "*Who is that?*"

A black sedan had pulled over by the side of the road a hundred feet ahead. Two men in ordinary, civilian dress stood in the middle of the road, waving their arms for Joshua to slow down and stop.

Klara recognized them both immediately: Major Kuznetsov and his negotiator.

She leaned forward and pointed, nearly shouting in Joshua's ear. "That's the Russians! They got here early!"

"*Don't stop!*" Alec yelled.

"*I don't plan to!*" Joshua pressed his foot to the accelerator.

Kuznetsov pulled a pistol from his jacket pocket and let off a round from about twenty feet away.

The bullet penetrated through the windshield, narrowly missing Joshua's head before embedding itself with a thud in the cushion between Herr Keller and Klara.

The two men jumped aside as the car sped by, slightly clipping Kuznetsov in the process and knocking him down. By the time he was able to stand, it was too late.

Joshua peered in the rearview mirror. "He just threw his gun down on the ground in disgust. Time for them to hightail it back to their own zone and console themselves over a few shots of vodka."

After reaching the bottom of the hill and entering the town, Joshua pulled the car over to a small inn and parked. While the others waited in the car, he went to the inn's office to request the use of a private phone line to contact Major Staver and confirm the precise location of the buried V-2 documents. Once that was done, it would be on to Nordhausen to catch the train.

Still overwhelmed by their close call with the Russians, Klara and the others said little to each other. Klara was content to hold the hands of her father and Herr Keller beside her, as Alec sat silently in the front seat, seemingly absorbed in his own thoughts.

Ten minutes later, Joshua emerged from the office and walked up to the car. He opened the driver's door, a wide grin on his face.

"Nordhausen, anyone?"

CHAPTER 57

Nordhausen, Germany
June 20, 1945

"*What's going on?*" Lt. Alec Benjamin shouted out the window of the staff car at the harried train station policeman. He was one of several who were frantically trying to direct the massive throngs of pedestrians converging on the train station's entrance.

The man hurried over and tried to explain. "Seems that word spread to a couple of the nearby refugee centers that the Russians are arriving in force at midnight and that all the V-2 scientists are being evacuated on the last train. The refugees have heard the horror stories of Russian units arriving in town, drunk and looking for revenge, and now they also want to get out. Problem is, there's no more room for anyone on that train."

"There *has* to be room for four more, officer," Alec said. "We have one of the rocket men and his daughter in our back seat. My comrade and I have been ordered by the commanding US officer here to escort them on that train to Witzenhausen. They're expecting us."

The policeman studied him for a second then nodded. "Well, if that's the case, sir, I suggest you park your car right up ahead and walk the rest of the way to the entrance. You'll never get the car any closer with this mob crushing you from all sides."

After threading, pushing, and at times, shoving their way through the panicked crowd and into the station, the foursome finally reached the platform where their train was scheduled to depart later that evening.

Klara stared incredulously at the scene. There must have been at least a thousand people—V-2 scientists and their families—standing along the platforms, waiting to fit themselves into the boxcars and passenger cars. In front of them, several squads of US soldiers stood with weapons prominently displayed, forming a barrier between the V-2 families and the pressing lines of refugees.

Joshua approached one of the soldiers who appeared to be an officer. He nodded and signaled to another uniformed man down the line who came running over.

"This is Professor Erich Neumann and his daughter?" he asked, looking them both up and down as if to confirm their identities.

"That's right, Corporal," Joshua said impatiently.

The man broke out in a wide grin. "I'm one of Major Staver's assistants. Dr. von Braun and General Dornberger have been anxiously awaiting your arrival. Everyone else on their list has now been accounted for. Given all this unexpected mayhem, our commander wants the train to depart as soon as they can finalize some repairs on the locomotive. If you'll please come with me, I'll take you to your seats in the VIP car."

"Before we board... has Major Staver sent anyone out to Bad Sachsa to retrieve those V-2 documents?" Joshua inquired.

"He led a small team out there himself sir, right after you called to inform us of the situation. They won't make it back here in time to board the train, but they're planning to drive separately to Witzenhausen and join everyone there tonight."

Joshua breathed a sigh of relief. "Excellent. All right, Corporal. Then by all means, please take us to our car."

As they approached the second passenger car behind the locomotive, Klara recognized a familiar face standing alone on the step, waving vigorously at them.

Dr. Wernher von Braun looked as dapper and handsome as when she'd last seen him, seven years ago at the US Embassy diplomatic ball in Berlin.

"*About time you joined us!*" Wernher cried as he rushed up to shake Erich's hand and clap him on the shoulder. After a few words with him, he turned to embrace Klara.

"Somehow I knew we'd never get him here without you!"

At the conductor's announcement of yet another half-hour delay, a collective groan erupted from the anxious V-2 family members occupying the seats of the passenger car.

Klara looked up at Joshua in the seat beside her, sighed wearily, and laid her head back on his shoulder. Everyone was exhausted. They'd already been sitting in the stuffy cabin air for over an hour as repairmen continued to work on the locomotive. Many of the younger children were becoming cranky and rambunctious.

Only a few minutes after boarding—before Klara had any real chance to speak with him—her father and some of the other key scientists had been called forward to the adjoining car. Vati had said it was some kind of special, private meeting with von Braun and Dornberger. Seeing Klara alone, Joshua moved from his seat beside Alec Benjamin and taken her father's place beside her. At long last, the two had been able to speak candidly and affectionately to each other.

Any awkwardness from the six years of separation dissipated in an instant. Klara listened intently as Joshua briefly described his times in college and later the OSS, hoping all the while that he wouldn't suddenly confess to having a girlfriend who was waiting for him back in the States. "I'm convinced it was God's plan for us all along," he'd said when describing his choice of an OSS career and his latest assignment that had led to their eventual reunion. She'd been overjoyed to hear of

Joshua's dinner with Sophie Friedmann, especially how it had reenergized his determination to find Klara again. Klara made him promise to arrange a magnificent celebration for the three of them as soon as she was permitted to enter America. That celebration would be topped, she'd made clear, only by the special little private reunion that she anticipated between herself and Joshua tonight in Witzenhausen.

After Klara filled Joshua in on some details of her own experiences, she lapsed into an awkward silence as she considered whether to bring the sensitive subject up with him.

"What do you think my father and the other scientists are talking about?" Klara asked abruptly as she stroked Joshua's forearm.

"They're probably strategizing on how to respond to the interrogators," Joshua said. "Making sure everyone has their story straight and is consistent with the others." He peered at her. "Klara, you seem worried about something."

Klara glanced nervously up the aisle at Alec Benjamin who was sitting by himself five rows up.

I can't hold this in any longer.

"Joshua, were you aware of the photographs of my father that Alec has in his possession?"

He cocked his head and looked at her uncertainly. "Photos?"

She went on to tell him about her disturbing interaction with Lt. Benjamin back at the Bad Sachsa cabin.

Joshua stared at her with clenched jaw for several seconds after she finished. "I can't believe he did that. Somewhere along the line, Alec must have convinced someone to provide him unauthorized copies of the photos Major Staver showed us. But he certainly never told *me* about it."

"So, is he truly obligated to turn them over to the interrogators in Witzenhausen, as he claimed?"

"In his own mind, I suppose." Joshua shook his head. "But his decision would be based on the loss of his fiancée and her mother more than anything else. I'm almost certain that *Staver* was not planning to turn the original photos over. That man is absolutely committed to bringing all the key rocket men to America and putting them to work for us. He's going to resist anything that gets in the way of that, such as unproven war crimes accusations. And as Alec himself admitted, those photos by themselves don't *prove* your father committed a war crime."

"But if Alec does turn them over, they *could* affect the US government decision about granting both him and me asylum, couldn't they?"

Joshua bit his lip and sighed. "Yes, it's true they could greatly complicate things." He slapped his hand on his thigh. "*Damn!*"

She looked at him pleadingly. "Joshua, isn't there *something* you can do before we get to Witzenhausen. Can you go talk with Lt. Benjamin, and beg him to hold off on turning the photos over? At least until my father has had a chance to see them and prepare some kind of legitimate defense."

Joshua thought for a moment. "All right, but I can't promise anything. Alec will no doubt accuse me of personal bias, which is true. *That* was the reason I never mentioned my connections to you and your father to him or my superiors before today. I was afraid they'd remove me from the case. But at this point, we've nothing to lose. I'll see what I can do. Wait here. This may take a little while."

When the train finally lurched and began to roll forward, a round of wild cheering broke out among many of the V-2 families in the second passenger car.

For Klara, the moment was an uncomfortable reminder that in less than a half hour, the train would be reaching its destination of Witzenhausen only forty miles away. That was all the time Joshua had remaining to convince Alec not to turn the photos over. Once they exited the train, the intelligence people would be waiting to take all the rocket men and their escorts to a separate facility for processing.

Her glances up the aisle gave no clue as to whether Joshua was making any progress. All she could see were the backs of their heads. For some reason, Alec's head seemed to be bent forward, as if were either reading or writing something. *God, what is happening up that aisle?*

She leaned her face against the window and shut her eyes. The thought—almost like a voice—came out of nowhere. *Stop fretting. You've done all you can do. Let go. It's in his hands now.*

She smiled as she imagined herself sitting with Joshua by the bank of that quiet stream at the Stettin pastors' retreat, listening to Dietrich Bonhoeffer's advice for dealing with her upcoming trials. He'd urged her not to worry, since God would make his peace beyond understanding available to her at just the right time.

God, I ask your peace for myself right now. You know my great fears for Vati, and you know the hopes I have for both of us. I entrust them all to you, Lord. May your will be done…

As she so often did when she prayed, she must have dozed off. The next thing she knew, someone was gently squeezing her forearm. She opened her eyes and looked over at the uniformed man standing in the aisle. It was Lt. Benjamin.

Alec handed her a brown envelope. "Fräulein Neumann, I wanted you to have these." That was it. With a slight nod, he turned and walked back up the aisle to his seat.

In disbelief, Klara opened the flap of the envelope and peered inside. The four photos were all there. Also, inside was a handwritten note. She pulled it out and began to read:

Sometimes, it takes an honest rebuke from a good friend to set a man straight. From the moment I met you, I must confess that I allowed my anger over my fiancée's death to overwhelm any desire to hear of the pain and hardships that you might have experienced under the Nazi regime.

Joshua just told me about the tragic death of your mother from an American bomb. He also told me about your history as a staunch anti-Hitler resister who more than once put your life on the line for the sake of your Jewish friend and her family. What you did was in the spirit of your Christian friend, Pastor Bonhoeffer. I will always have great respect and gratitude for his efforts on behalf of the German Jews.

And because of that, Klara, I have decided to turn these photos over to you, as I'm certain you will know what to do with them.

No matter what you choose, I only ask one thing of you and your father...

Please, never forget.

Klara lifted her head and looked up the aisle, where Alec was peering back at her over his shoulder. Tears flowed down her cheeks as she mouthed the words, "thank you."

Alec nodded and smiled. It was the first time she'd seen him do so.

A sudden stir at the front of the cabin caught everyone's attention. One by one, led by Wernher von Braun, the seven rocket men who had been conferring in the next car reentered and stood together in the aisle. Professor Erich Neumann stood in the middle between von Braun and General Dornberger.

As the V-2 families in the car all cheered at the sight of their husbands and fathers, Klara noticed something strange: each of the rocket men held a half-filled glass of what appeared to be champagne.

Von Braun stepped forward with a huge grin on his face and held up his free hand.

"Ladies and gentlemen, young and old. The conductor has just informed me that three minutes from now, our train will cross the border into the newly defined US Zone of Occupation for Germany. My friends, this a momentous occasion. Once we cross that point, we can be sure that no Soviet forces will be able to threaten us with physical harm or force us into accepting their false promises of prosperity and security in the Russian zone. Even more importantly, once we cross that point, we will have taken the first giant leap into our grand new future as valued, contributing citizens of the United States of America."

Another sustained round of cheering exploded in the cabin, requiring von Braun to raise his hand once more for quiet.

"My friends, I cannot lie to you. Our path ahead will face some significant hurdles. We have much to prove to both the American government and public before they can fully trust us. We must prove that we are no longer associated in any way with the National Socialist organization or philosophy. We must prove that we are not guilty of any war crimes, and that we fully and emphatically renounce any former statements of loyalty to Adolf Hitler and the Nazi Party. Most of all, we must prove that we are absolutely committed to the future success of American military and space programs, and that as former V-2 scientists and engineers we are uniquely qualified to ensure that success. Are we all ready to do that?"

More raucous cheering and shouting.

The train began to slow noticeably as the conductor squeezed through the line of rocket men to whisper something to von Braun, who nodded and once again addressed the passengers.

"I'm told we are less than thirty seconds away from the formal point of crossing. I had hesitated to put forth the suggestion I'm about to make because of our tragic history of shooting rockets off for the wrong national cause… but all my fellow rocket men up here have convinced me it is now absolutely the right thing to do.

"And so, my friends, as we prepare to take this first step in our new life together, will you all please join hands in your rows and across the aisle, and prepare to join me and the V-2 rocket men for one last countdown?"

"We won't just sit for you, Wernher. We'll stand! You deserve it!" a man shouted from somewhere.

Klara stood with the others and moved over to grab the hand of a child across the aisle. She looked around. There was not a dry eye anywhere.

She looked up the aisle and saw Joshua standing pinioned between Alec and the bulkhead. He was looking at her, grinning and giving a thumbs-up. She wanted to run to him to share the moment, but there were too many people crowding the aisle.

Klara glanced at her father who was standing next to von Braun. Vati held the champagne glass in his hand, smiling broadly and looking for all the world like a man who had finally found his way out of hell and was about to set foot in paradise. Wernher placed his arm across Vati's shoulders and said something with which he appeared to agree. She caught his eye, and he lifted his glass to her. Even from a distance, she could tell that he was tearing up.

"Hey!" Wernher shouted. "Professor Erich Neumann has just volunteered to be our launch director! He'll be leading us all in the final countdown."

The conductor, who had been looking out the exit to spot the crossing point, turned and nodded to Wernher, who in turn looked at Vati and squeezed his shoulder.

Klara held her breath. She could only imagine what her father must be feeling. The last time he had performed in the role of launch director, he had pushed a button that had resulted in the deaths of dozens. This time, the performance was in celebration of new life.

Erich Neumann held his free hand up, the fingers spread wide. Everyone in the car followed suit. "Ready?"

"*Ready!*" the rocket men and their families shouted.

"All right, here we go . . ."

"*FIVE!*"

"*FOUR!*"

"*THREE!*"

"*TWO!*"

"*ONE!*"

EPILOGUE

CHAPTER 58

El Paso, Texas, USA
December 4, 1946

Mrs. Klara Peters (née Neumann) poured two cups of steaming hot coffee and brought them out to the living room of the tiny apartment on the third floor of the former US Army hospital annex at Fort Bliss.

She smiled at the sight of Joshua sitting on the couch with his legs outstretched, reading the morning newspaper. "I think you're becoming a bit too comfortable around here, Captain Peters," she teased. "Seems like once the US Army enticed you away from the OSS by offering that promotion as assistant military overseer for the famous V-2 rocket men, it's all gone to your head. Are you expecting this kind of personal delivery service from your wife all the time now?"

Joshua peeked over the top of the page and grinned slyly. "Only on my days off."

"I wouldn't get too used to it," Klara retorted.

"Hey, you won't believe what's on the front page today," Joshua said, gratefully taking one of the cups from Klara as he sat up and patted the couch seat beside him.

"Let me guess," she said as she nestled up close. "They're announcing this morning's launch, thus ensuring it will be a failure. I can't believe the lengths to which our famous *El Paso Times* will go, just to stir up a bit of excitement around here!"

Joshua chuckled. "Not even the US Army would be stupid enough to risk putting something like *that* in print prematurely. No, this is much more interesting. Here, take a look." He handed the folded paper to her and settled back to watch her reaction.

"*Oh, my!*" she gasped as she looked at the top half of the front page, where the second headline read:

118 Top German V-2 Experts
Builders of Nazi Secret Weapons Working for US

The half page article underneath briefly reminded *Times* readers of the terrible destruction wrought by the V-2 on England. It stressed the vital role played by the German rocket men, who were now in the employ of the US government, requesting US citizenship. Next to the article appeared a full-size photograph of Wernher von Braun and Joshua's boss, Major James Hamill of the US Army Ordnance Department. The men sat together at a desk covered with documents, grinning at the camera.

Wernher still looks like a famous Hollywood movie star, Klara thought admiringly. *What a far cry from those ugly images of Hitler, Goebbels, and Göring that most Americans have come to associate with the typical German male.*

"So, the secret's finally out?" she asked.

Joshua nodded. "In terms of being reported in the official press. But most locals around here have known of the rocket men's presence for at least several months."

"I'm surprised we haven't had any riots yet," Klara muttered.

She turned to page eight, where the article continued down half of one column. At one point near the bottom, she cried out in dismay. "Joshua, can you believe *this*? One of our rocket men, after complimenting America on its natural beauty and hospitality, has the nerve to gripe about the quality of the army food here at Ft. Bliss! My goodness, don't we Germans have enough cultural obstacles to deal with around here already?"

Joshua shot her a teasing look. "Well, Klara, after all, this *is* a free country. People can say pretty much whatever's on their mind. But don't worry, you'll have the perfect opportunity to help change the rocket men's tune once that first contingent of their wives and children arrive here from Germany next week. You know they'll be looking to you to teach them to adapt, learn the language, and make the right impressions on their new countrymen."

"I just hope the wives will provide their husbands with some of their favorite German dishes once in a while," Klara added. "Maybe that'll stop them from complaining so much."

She returned the newspaper to Joshua, stood, and stretched. She walked over to the bay window, which faced toward the White Sands Proving Ground's new V-2 launching site. In less than a half-hour, yet another one of the hundred or so missiles assembled from all those vital parts that Major Staver had managed to salvage from the Nordhausen factory would be put to the test. There had been five test launches at White Sands since last May. Three had failed. She wondered, would all the work that her father and the other rocket men had been putting into advising the Americans on V-2 operational improvements after the most recent failure pay off today?

She tried to imagine Vati with von Braun and the other German and American scientists and technicians taking their places in the concrete blockhouse near the launching pit. What would he be thinking? Would he be so absorbed with his technical responsibilities as to block out any concerns over the highly publicized war crimes trials now taking place in Germany? She hoped he would at least find a moment to offer a quick prayer of thanks to God for the good fortune that had so far allowed all the V-2 rocket men to evade any charges and make the slow transition from Witzenhausen to America.

What a whirlwind the past year and half has been for all of us…

For the rocket men, the interrogation process at Witzenhausen had been lengthy and arduous. Only a hundred of them had finally been cleared for temporary work assignments in America and transported across the Atlantic eleven months ago. Major Hamill had been assigned responsibility for their administrative and technical oversight. Given Joshua's personal familiarity with von Braun and Erich Neumann, Hamill recruited him to be his chief assistant. The men had eventually been taken to Fort Bliss and put to work there, helping to prepare for the first V-2 test launches on American soil.

For the rocket men's families, meanwhile, the journey to the US had taken a more circuitous route. After Witzenhausen, the families had been bussed to a former schoolhouse in Bavaria and housed there for nearly ten months until the US government finally granted them permission to join their men at Fort Bliss starting this month.

Klara's case had been an early exception to the general rule.

After Joshua had proposed to her two weeks after their arrival at Witzenhausen, the two had wed there a month later in a small, civic ceremony attended by her father. Joshua had then departed for the US to prepare for the rocket men's arrival. With several weeks of effort and his new boss Major Hamill's help, he'd finally convinced the State Department that Klara's exceptional skill with the English language would be useful in helping the German V-2 families make a smoother transition. She would need to arrive earlier to prepare things for them.

Eight months later, Joshua met Klara at La Guardia Airport in New York City in early October. The promised grand reunion with Sophie Friedmann had at last taken place. After touring the city together with Sophie's new boyfriend—a handsome Jewish lawyer from Boston—the foursome dined together at a Manhattan restaurant. There, Sophie shared the great news that she'd finally found a publishing house willing to print her father's account of his Kristallnacht experience.

The only sad note had occurred when Sophie and Klara said their final, goodbyes. Sophie confessed how, despite her deep love and appreciation for Klara, she was still struggling terribly to forgive Klara's father for betraying her family to SS Colonel Bremmer. The unexpected action had directly resulted in her brother Jacob's execution and her parents' deaths in a concentration camp. She understood that Erich had done it only to save his own daughter from the agony of Bremmer's Kripo torture cell and life imprisonment, but her devastation and anger were still there.

Klara tried her best to offer consolation and convey her own distress, saying she well knew her father had made compromises and done some things in his Nazi-connected past that would no doubt plague his conscience for the rest of his life. Things that not even gunning down Colonel Bremmer at Bad Sachsa, or the tragic losses of his own wife, son, and eldest daughter could completely atone for.

The two had parted with a tearful hug and mutual resolution to visit each other again one day soon, and Klara and Joshua had departed for Fort Bliss the next morning.

❧

Joshua interrupted her reverie. "Klara, have you decided yet?"

Klara whirled and faced him, a pained expression on her face. She had been contemplating taking the step ever since the first announced hangings of major Nazi war criminals in Germany at Nuremberg in mid-October. She'd promised Joshua last night that she would make her decision this morning. Time to put an end to the emotional turmoil that had produced severe headaches and nightmares for far too long.

"Joshua, do you think I'm doing the right thing?"

He looked at her sympathetically and shrugged. "There may be some people who'd disagree. Some who might say you're a typical post-war German, deliberately trying to bury your head in the sand. But you won't find any objections from me. Whatever you decide, Klara, I know it's coming from a pure heart."

Klara walked into their bedroom and pulled the brown envelope out of the drawer.

Returning to the living room fireplace behind the couch, she gripped the envelope in two hands and held it suspended above the low flame for several seconds.

She hesitated, knowing what her impending act would mean. It would erase all photographic evidence of potential war crimes against Professor Erich Neumann. She must have looked at the photos a thousand times since she'd received them from Lt. Benjamin, debating with herself whether to directly confront her father with them and plead with him to explain the motives for his actions. To either confess his sin, or to reassure her of his innocence despite the evidence. As his daughter who loved him, did she not have a right to know?

She closed her eyes for a moment. Clarity came at last.

I am not my father's accuser or his interrogator. Let God be the judge of his heart.

She reached into the envelope, removed Alec's note, and reread the last line:

"Klara, no matter what you choose to do with these, I only ask one thing of you and your father: *Please, never forget.*"

Pocketing the note, she dropped the envelope into the flames.

AUTHOR'S NOTE

Motivation For
The Rocket Man's Daughter

July 20, 1969
"That's one small step for man . . . one giant leap for mankind."

I'll never forget watching Neil Armstrong, the Apollo 11 astronaut, step off that lunar module ladder and utter the iconic words that thrilled the souls of over half a billion people around the world who'd tuned in to TV or radio for the occasion.

The amazing scene was especially inspiring on a personal level, since I'd just recently made my final decision to enter the University of Maryland's undergraduate program in Aerospace Engineering. Over the ensuing five decades of graduate school and a long career as a "rocket scientist" specializing in the guidance and control sub-discipline, I would frequently recall this famous scene and the plethora of historical commentary that accompanied it.

One typical example (my own paraphrase) of that commentary came as a surprise and was a bit disturbing at the time:

> *"Behind the success of what we are all witnessing today are the pure brilliance, bold vision, and unflinching commitment to scientific excellence of <u>Dr. Wernher von Braun, the "Father of Modern Space Flight," and his elite team of former Nazi V-2 rocket scientists</u>. It was only by their genius and leadership that Apollo 11's massive Saturn-V launch vehicle could have been successfully designed and built."*

Nazi? V-2? How, I rather naively asked myself at the time, was it possible that an admired, "virtue-loving" country like the United States of America could endorse such a travesty? Placing former Nazi rocket men—killers of thousands of civilians and slave-laborers in England and Western Europe—in charge of developing and fielding the American Saturn V moon rocket? Shouldn't people like these have been condemned to death or at least long prison sentences like other Nazi war criminals at the Nuremberg Trials immediately after the war? What was the US government's (and the American public's) moral calculus that could ever have justified the V-2 rocket men's employment and glorification as national heroes?

Three decades later, another related, troubling issue was being surfaced—this time in Germany itself. A 2003 university survey revealed that 70% of German citizens were "annoyed" that they were still being held collectively responsible for the Holocaust. A later survey showed that only 6% of Germans felt even "slight" personal remorse over Nazi war crimes or their own country's actions during WW2. This attitude, which was quite different from the immediate post-war situation, was reinforced by several excellent German books and movies (e.g., "*A Woman in Berlin*" – 2008) that brought to light the terrible abuse suffered by tens of thousands of German women and girls at the hands of Russian soldiers during the final weeks of the war. But the question remains as to whether this newer trend of dismissing all sense of accountability for past Nazi sins is really justified by the excuses commonly given:

"I would never have done that";
"They were only following orders";
"Many innocent German civilians resisted and suffered, too"

It was a desire to research and shed some useful light on these perplexing issues of moral culpability and accountability for Nazi war crimes in a historical fiction framework that inspired my writing of "The Rocket Man's Daughter."

My hope is that, after reading this novel and considering the portrayals of its fictional and historical characters, the reader will come away (as I have) with a better appreciation of the immense pressures and temptations faced by individual German families as they were confronted with the cultish lures, demonic decrees, and horrific final death throes of one of the most evil regimes in all of human history: Adolf Hitler and his Nazi Party.

Perhaps, as a result, we will not be so quick to make a blanket judgment of their actions and motives.

Historical Versus Fictional

Locales, dates, timelines, major events, street names, organizational structures, names of all high-ranking political, military and civilian officials, and names of German domestic resistance leaders (e.g., Herbert Baum) appearing in this novel are consistent with historical records.

With the exception of paraphrased quotes from anti-fascist propaganda pamphlets and recorded radio speeches by Joseph Goebbels, the actions and dialogue of all real historical figures (see list in front matter) who appear in the novel are products of my own speculation. However, I have striven to keep all these generally consistent with the overall character, recorded quotes, demeanor, major decisions and actions of these figures to the extent they could be gleaned from available historical descriptions.

Note that Chapter 14's written account by the fictional character "Herr Friedmann" of his experience upon entering the Sachsenhausen concentration camp on the night of November 9, 1938 ("Kristallnacht") is actually an abbreviated, edited version of the true account provided by Karl Rosenthal, a Berlin rabbi... see Item 14 in Selected Bibliography, pp. 115–135.

Whatever Happened To . . .

For those interested, provided below are some interesting biographical facts related to the life trajectories and outcomes for high-ranking Nazi officials, the "real-life" V-2 Rocket Men, and other historical figures with speaking roles in "The Rocket Man's Daughter":

Adolf Hitler: Following his suicide by a gunshot to the head on April 30, 1945, the bodies of Hitler and his bride of one day (Eva Braun) were doused in petrol by his SS aides and burned in the Reich Chancellery garden in Berlin. The cremation location was immediately above the infamous "Führerbunker," where Hitler and some his closest henchmen had been holed up since January to escape the final Russian onslaught. Today, the garden and bunker are covered over by a deliberately ordinary parking lot. The site was not recognized as the place of Hitler's death until 2006, when a plaque including historical background and a schematic diagram of the bunker was quietly placed nearby.

Heinrich Himmler: Hunted by the Allies after Germany's formal surrender on May 7, 1945, Reichsführer-SS Himmler attempted to avoid capture by disguising himself as a low-level Wehrmacht sergeant and travelling with some companions by car around the countryside. He was discovered and arrested on May 21, and taken to the headquarters of the Second British Army. When a doctor attempted to examine his mouth, he jerked his head away and bit down on a hidden cyanide pill. Within 15 minutes, he was dead despite frantic efforts to resuscitate him. The exact location of his gravesite remains unknown.

Wernher von Braun: After the war in 1946, von Braun and other key German V-2 scientists and engineers were secretly brought to the United States as part of "Operation Paperclip" to work with the United States Army on developing the country's ballistic missile program. Over the next fifteen years, von Braun and his team tested and improved upon their original V-2 rocket design, first at the White Sands Proving Ground in New Mexico and later at the Redstone Arsenal in Huntsville, Alabama. In 1958, the team successfully launched the first American artificial satellite, "Explorer I," using one their newly developed Redstone rockets. Von Braun and his research team were then transferred to the newly established National Aeronautics and Space Administration (NASA) in 1960. With a mandate to create giant rockets, he became the director of the Marshall Space Flight Center of NASA, developing the Saturn V rocket that would take the Apollo 11 mission to the Moon in July 1969. In addition to being the brains behind the development of rockets which helped the Americans reach the Moon, von Braun was also the leading spokesman of the United States for all space exploration matters in the 1960s.

Six weeks before the historic 1968 Apollo 8 mission to orbit the moon, von Braun was asked to testify before a West German court concerning his knowledge and involvement with the use of slave labor at the Mittelbau-Dora concentration camp. However, although he had visited the camp on several occasions and knew of the despicable conditions there, the court did not judge this awareness as the same kind of complicity as actually controlling the situation like a factory boss would. Hence, he was able to escape prosecution. Von Braun spent his last years working for the aerospace company Fairchild Industries of Germantown, Maryland. In 1977 he died from kidney cancer at age 65 in Virginia.

Walter Dornberger: Immediately after the war's end in 1945, General Dornberger (Wehrmacht V-Weapon projects leader) was put to work by the British army on a special scientific operation to completely evaluate the entire V-2 rocket assembly and to help interrogate other captured German rocket scientists. Soon afterward, he was arrested and imprisoned for two years by Allied Forces on suspicion of war crimes in connection with the use and abuse of slave labor at some of the mobile V-2 launch sites in Holland. However, the charges could never be proven, and he was eventually freed. In 1947, he made his way to America via the Operation Paperclip program and worked for the United States Air Force developing guided missiles. He later worked for the Bell Aircraft Corporation, rising to the post of Vice-President. He played key roles in the creation of the X-15 aircraft and later the Space Shuttle. Following retirement, Dornberger returned to West Germany where he died in 1980.

Arthur Nebe: After serving as head of the National Criminal Police (Kripo) until 1941, Nebe took over command of Einsatzgruppen B, an SS death squad that operated behind the front lines as the Nazi invasion of Russia progressed. He was one of the first to experiment with the use of poison gas (already in use in Germany as part of the Aktion

T4 program) to exterminate Jews and others in captured Soviet territories. In 1944, worried that the war was going badly and that he would be punished for his war crimes by the Allies unless he did something to prove his change of heart, Nebe secretly joined the German military's resistance effort and became involved in the famous July 20th plot to assassinate Adolf Hitler. When that attempt failed, Nebe was betrayed by his former mistress and was sentenced to death. He was executed at Plötzensee Prison on March 21, 1945 by being hanged with piano wire from a meat hook, in accordance with Hitler's order that the assassination plotters were to be "strung up like cattle."

Dietrich Bonhoeffer: On April 5, 1943, Pastor Bonhoeffer and his brother-in-law Hans Dohnanyi were arrested and imprisoned after the SS finally uncovered evidence of their involvement in "Operation 7"— the name given to the successful effort to smuggle fourteen Jews from Germany into Switzerland using false Abwehr papers in September 1942. He spent the next year and a half in Berlin's Tegel Prison, where he was often visited by his new fiancée, Maria von Kleist-Retzow (Ruth's granddaughter, who was half his age). While in prison, he continued his work in religious outreach among his fellow prisoners and guards. Some of the guards helped him smuggle out uncensored letters which were posthumously published as the classic collection: "Letters and Papers from Prison." In early April 1945, the diaries of Admiral Canaris, head of the Abwehr, were discovered, and Bonhoeffer was implicated along with other former members of the Abwehr in being associated with the 1944 assassination plot against Hitler. In a rage, Hitler ordered that all the Abwehr people be executed, and Bonhoeffer was led away just as he concluded leading his final Sunday service for prisoners in Tegel prison. After a sham trial, Bonhoeffer was sentenced to death and led away to Flossenburg concentration camp. There, at dawn on April 9, 1945, he was stripped of his clothing and led naked into the execution yard where he was hanged with five others. It was said by an eyewitness (a doctor) that Bonhoeffer had been "brave and composed" throughout his final moments, and that the eyewitness had "hardly ever seen a man die so entirely submissive to the will of God."

Arvid and Mildred Harnack: On September 7, 1942, the Harnacks were arrested by the Gestapo while on a short holiday to Lithuania. Both were severely tortured and sentenced to death in December as punishment for their leading roles in The Red Orchestra spy ring. Four days after their trial, Arvid and several of his co-conspirators were hanged from meat hooks by piano wire, a method designed to prolong their suffering. In mid-February, by Hitler's personal order, Mildred was beheaded by guillotine in Berlin's Plötzensee Prison. Her body was released to an anatomy professor at Humboldt Univerity, to be dissected for research into the effects of stress caused by awaiting execution on the menstrual cycle. She was the only American in WW2 to be executed on the direct orders of Adolf Hitler. Probably due in part to the Harnacks' known sympathies with Communist causes, the US government refused to ever acknowledge their deaths as official war crimes. US investigators claimed later that, although the Harnacks' work in leading a large group secretly fighting the Nazi regime was "laudable," their executions could be considered legally justifiable since they were spies and had received a trial.

Herbert Pfannmüller: Between 1939 and 1944, Pfannmüller (Director of the Eglfing-Haar Sanatorium) ordered the murder of 332 disabled children through gradual starvation diets or by luminal or morphine injections. He also acted during that period as an Aktion T-4 "assessor," examining over 4000 disabled patient registration forms and making recommendations for killing in several thousand cases. Pfannmüller was arrested by the US Army and interned at Eglfing-Haar in May, 1945. In 1949, he was tried before the Munich jury court for his euthanasia crimes. He was sentenced to six years in prison for directly committing or aiding and abetting manslaughter. After serving his sentence, Pfannmüller was released and lived in Munich where he died in 1961 at the age of 75. Despite the evidence and testimonies of others, Pfannmüller insisted to the end of his life that he had not been involved in any euthanasia crimes.

Hans Kammler: In the final weeks of the war, the movements of Major General Kammler ("Special Commissioner for the V-2 Program") became sketchy and contradictory. According to one report, just before the American Army arrived at the Bavarian mountain resort where the V-2 rocket men were being sequestered by the SS, Kammler and his staff fled the scene. Travelling to Prague by aircraft on May 4, 1945, Kammler and 21 SS men defended a bunker against an attack by more than 500 Czech resistance fighters on May 9. During the attack, one of Kammler's aides shot him to prevent his capture. This version of Kammler's demise was reportedly traced to General Walter Dornberger, who claimed to have heard it from eyewitnesses.

Arthur Rudolph: Among the initial cadre of V-2 scientists and engineers who accompanied Wernher von Braun to America in 1946 under the auspices of the secret "Operation Paperclip" program, Rudolph (Technical Director of V-2 Production at Nordhausen) supported the initial testing of V-2 rockets on American soil. In 1950, Rudolph was transferred with von Braun and others to the Redstone Arsenal in Alabama, where he was appointed as the technical director for the Redstone missile project. He became a US citizen in 1956, and he continued to work with distinction as technical director or project manager on a variety of ballistic missile programs for the US Army and NASA. In 1982, Rudolph was interviewed by the US Office of Special Investigations (OSI) concerning allegations about Rudolph's actions at the Mittelbau-Dora Concentration Camp in 1944, including his purported involvement in the slave laborer "crane-hanging" incident. Under duress, Rudolph reached an agreement with the OSI to renounce his US citizenship. In 1984, Rudolph and his wife departed for West Germany. Subsequent efforts to prosecute him proved unsuccessful, and he was granted West German citizenship. He died in Hamburg on New Year's Day, 1996, from heart failure.

SELECT BIBLIOGRAPHY

Among the numerous nonfiction books, biographies, online articles, and primary sources employed to support the development of historical context/detail, as well as real and fictional character dialogue for The Rocket Man's Daughter, the following proved especially helpful and are listed as recommended reading for anyone interested in further exploration.

1. Grunberger, Richard, *A Social History of the Third Reich* (Orion House, 2005).

2. Gellately, Robert, *Backing Hitler: Consent & Coercion in Nazi Germany* (Oxford University Press, 2013).

3. Bergen, Doris L., *Twisted Cross: The German Christian Movement in the Third Reich*, (The University of North Carolina Press, 1996).

4. Frøland, Carl M., *Understanding Nazi Ideology: The Genesis and Impact of a Political Faith* (MacFarland and Co., Inc., 2020).

5. Siemens, Daniel, *Stormtroopers: A New History of Hitler's Brownshirts* (Yale University Press, 2017).

6. Graber, G.S.: *History of the SS* (Granada Publishing Ltd, 1982).

7. Heath, Tim, *Hitler's Girls: Doves Amongst Eagles* (Pen & Sword Military, 2017).

8. McFarland-Icke, Bronwyn R., *Nurses in Nazi Germany: Moral Choice in History* (Princeton University Press, 1999).

9. Longmate, Norman, *Hitler's Rockets: The Story of the V-2's* (Skyhorse Publishing, 2009).

10. Ward, Bob, *Dr. Space: The Life of Wernher von Braun* (First Naval Institute Press, 2005).

11. Evans, Suzanne, *Forgotten Crimes: The Holocaust and People with Disabilities* (Ivan R. Dee, 2004).

12. Burleigh, Michael, *Death and Deliverance: 'Euthanasia' in Germany 1900–1945* (Cambridge Press, 1994).

13. Bryant, Glenn, *A Quiet Genocide: The Untold Holocaust of Disabled Children in WW2 Germany* (Amsterdam Publishers, 2018).

14. Gerhardt, Uta, and Karlauf, Thomas, *The Night of Broken Glass: Eyewitness Accounts of Kristallnacht* (Polity Press, 2021).

15. Metaxas, Eric, *Bonhoeffer: Pastor, Martyr, Prophet, Spy*, Eric Metaxas (Thomas Nelson, 2011).

16. Haynes, Stephen R., *The Bonhoeffer Legacy: Post Holocaust Perspectives* (Fortress Press, 2006).

17. Tonder, Gerry V., *Einsatzgruppen: Nazi Death Squads, 1939–1945* (Pen & Sword History, 2018).

18. McDonough, Frank, The Gestapo: The Myth and Reality of Hitler's Secret Police (Skyhorse Publishing, 2015).

19. Cox, John M., *Circles of Resistance: Jewish, Leftist, and Youth Dissidence in Nazi Germany* (Peter Lang Publishing, 2009).

20. Brothers, Eric, *Berlin Ghetto: Herbert Baum and the Anti-Fascist Resistance* (The History Press, 2012).

21. Gross, Leonard, *The Last Jews in Berlin* (Basic Books, 1999).

22. Nelson Anne, *Red Orchestra: The Story of the Berlin Underground and the Circle of Friends Who Resisted Hitler* (Random House, 2009).

23. Donner, Rebecca, *All the Frequent Troubles of Our Days: The True Story of the American Woman at the Heart of the German Resistance to Hitler* (Little, Brown, and Co., 2021).

24. Brysac, Shareen, Resisting Hitler: Mildred Harnack and the Red Orchestra (Oxford University Press, 2000).

25. Schafft, Gretchen, and Ziedler, Gerhard, *Commemorating Hell: The Public Memory of Mittelbau-Dora* (Board of Trustees of the University of Illinois, 2011).

26. Read, Anthony, and Fisher, David, *The Fall of Berlin* (W.W. Norton and Co., 1992).

27. Hamilton, Aaron S., *Bloody Streets: The Soviet Assault on Berlin* (Helion & Company Ltd., 2020).

28. Fallada, Hans, *Alone in Berlin* (Random House, 1947).

29. Anonymous, *A Woman in Berlin: Eight Weeks in the Conquered City* (Henry Holt and Co., 2000).

30. Vassiltchikov, Marie, *Berlin Diaries 1940–1945* (Random House, 1988).

31. Jacobsen, Annie, *Operation Paperclip, The Secret Intelligence Program That Brought Nazi Scientists to America* (Little, Brown & Co., 2014).

Acknowledgments

My thanks to Pat Ricucci, Tina Dow, Jan MacBeth and Janet Gardner for their helpful and illuminating reviews of the novel's draft manuscript, especially their comments regarding the story's character portrayals and historical accuracy. A special note of gratitude is offered to "Jan and Jan" for their detailed editorial observations, which helped improved the manuscript's readability.

I was fortunate to have the professional services of Natalie Griffin, who conducted a thorough and insightful manuscript critique and also performed detailed copyediting for the novel's final draft manuscript version. Natalie's numerous suggestions for text-styling, character portrayals, and historical fact-checking all proved invaluable in forming the finished product.

Many thanks are also due (as usual!) to my superbly talented and reliable publishing services consultant, Melinda Martin, for her meticulous work with the novel's interior print formatting, e-Book preparation, and artistic cover design.

And, as always, to my dear wife Nancy: Thank you for your many insightful, honest reviews and discussions of individual chapters, as well as your suggestions for story structuring and character development that had such a positive impact on the final form of *The Rocket Man's Daughter*.

About the Author

Driven by a lifelong passion for military and religious history, Bruce Gardner researches and writes creatively about the impact of major wars on the lives and faith experiences of everyday people. Retired from a thirty-year career in national aerospace and defense systems engineering, Bruce is actively involved in church and community volunteer work. He lives with his family in northern California. He is the author of the award-winning novels *Hope of Ages Past* and *Seeing Glory*. *The Rocket Man's Daughter* is his third novel.

Connect with the Author

Goodreads.com/AuthorBruceGardner

Leave a Review

If you enjoyed *The Rocket Man's Daughter*,
will you consider leaving a review
on your platform of choice?
Reviews help self-published authors
find more readers like you.